Taking the Shot

A.D. LYNN

Cover Concept and Design by Katie Golding, Goldnox Designs

Edited by Katie Golding, Goldnox Editing Service

Author headshot photo courtesy of Jen Moser Photography.

✺ Created with Vellum

For Kevin, who took me to my first hockey game, and everything else. Every love story I write belongs to you.

CHAPTER
One

COOPER

Gazing into Maddie's blue eyes, I reach for her, cupping her cheek. She's outlined by my dim lamp on the bedside table, casting a warm glow over my tiny, dark room. My gray bed sheets tangle around my legs, and her long, blonde hair tickles my arm. Smirking, she presses closer for another kiss, her bare chest brushing mine. Tingles rush down my spine.

"Round two?" she asks, tracing a pattern on my abs that has all my blood flowing south again.

"You betcha."

As her lips part for me, my phone buzzes on the nightstand for the third time. Maddie halts, raising an eyebrow at the interruption, and I sigh. I'd ignored it when we were in the middle of gettin' busy before, but it keeps ringing. I have a good idea who it is. Only one person in my life is this insistent, and now's not the right moment.

"You gonna get that?" Maddie asks, tugging the sheet up to her chin, a disappointing sign for my evening's aspirations. I picked her up in a campus bar and after a bit of flirting and my most charming smile, she said yes when I invited her back to my place. We had thoroughly enjoyed each other's company, and I had planned to enjoy it again. If my damn phone would stop interfering.

"I'm sure it's fine. This is more fun, anyway." I pepper kisses along her neck, and she wiggles against me. My phone stops buzzing, and I make good use of the silence. Maddie throws her leg over mine, and I'm just about to roll her on top of me when the ringing starts up again.

Shifting aside, I stare at the ceiling and take a deep breath. "Yeah, I should probably check that."

My mother is liable to send out a search party soon, despite living a thousand miles away. I love her, I do, but I need to breathe. And have a sex life.

Maddie tucks herself into my side, laying her head on my chest, and I reach for the phone. It's hard to focus with a hot, naked girl wrapped around me, but the picture of my mom on the display sobers me right up.

"Momma," I say into my phone, suppressing a groan. "This isn't a great time. Can I call you back?"

"Why isn't it a great time, pookie?" her southern voice drawls, defeating the purpose of my protest. I regret answering. Really, I regret even owning a phone right about now. "I was about to call Hunter to ask about you. I was worried."

"Having my best friend check up on me is a little extreme, no?" My mom huffs, but I'm distracted by my company. "There's nothing to worry about."

Maddie sits up, rustling the covers. Her bare chest bounces, and I lick my lips. Her naked body is beautiful, lush and curvy, and I want to savor it without my mom interrupting. Maybe I can still convince her to stay.

"What's that?" Momma asks, tone laced with suspicion. Ears like a bat. "Is someone with you?"

"Uh, yeah. Let me take care of this, and I'll call you back." Before she can argue, I hang up and toss the phone back on the nightstand.

"Don't go." I reach for Maddie, giving her my best seductive grin, but with a flash of toned thighs, she's already out of my bed. With a graceful scoop, she swipes her discarded clothes off the floor and I sigh.

"It's fine. I can't stay. I have other things to do tonight." Tossing me a smile over her shoulder, Maddie heads to my ensuite bathroom, as confident in her birthday suit as she was in her skinny jeans and crop top. God, her butt is cute.

"Hey, I don't want you to think—"

"Look, Cooper." She pops her head back around the doorframe, her cheeks still rosy from our activities. She holds her clothes in front of her chest, blocking my view. "I'm good. I get it. No strings, right? You made your expectations clear. And I had a *great* time."

She emphasizes the word and bobs her eyebrows at me, and my ego soars like the puck when Sidney Crosby sends a wrister into the net. Hell yeah, she did. Let no one say that Cooper Edwards doesn't give a woman the full-service experience.

Waving at my phone, she says, "It's kinda cute that your mom calls you, but I should go."

"Even if she's ruining the mood?" So much for round two. Or three.

Without answering, Maddie disappears into the bathroom, and I collapse against the pillows. Taking a few deep breaths, I pull the sheet up to my waist. Studying the Dallas Stars pennant on the wall, I try to calm my racing heart. I'm about to call Momma back when it rings in my hand again. Lord have mercy.

3

"Cooper? What's going on?" Her voice is shrill and panicky.

"Nothing, Momma." Rolling out of bed, I swipe my underwear off the floor. "What do you need?" I school my voice to hide my impatience. If she picks up on it, she's liable to talk longer on purpose.

I slide my boxers up my legs and toss the rest of my abandoned clothes in the hamper in the corner. Then I tug the navy comforter up on my bed and smooth it out, leaving my room neat and tidy. The way I like it. It's not big—the bed takes up most of the space, with barely enough left for a desk wedged under the window and a tall dresser by the hamper, but it's all mine. The drawn blinds keep out the evening darkness and the only things breaking up the stark, cream-colored walls are the poster of my favorite hockey team and a Harrison University pennant I bought from the bookstore my first week as a freshman.

"I just called to talk. Bless your heart. Is that a crime now?"

"No, no. I was..."

Crap, what to tell her? Not the truth. My mom thinks sex should be reserved for committed relationships and doesn't approve of casual hookups. "It's a big deal," she used to tell me, "reserved for people who are a big deal to you." She's sweet but old-fashioned. I know she grew up in a religious household, but that's not how it works for me. I like sex, and as long as I make it clear to my partner that it's a one-time thing, I don't see a problem with appreciating what the female population offers. Flopping back down on the bed, I wrack my brain for an explanation that will appease her.

"There's not a game today, right?" she asks. "I posted your schedule on the fridge, and I don't see a game."

"I was on my way to the rink for extra practice." That's a

4

lie. The shower is my next destination. I stink of sweat and girl and sex.

"Isn't it too late there? And what was that in the background?"

Why is she so involved in my business? I reckon it's a pitfall of being an only child. That, and her divorce from my father made it so I'm basically all she has. The guilt of that forces me to dig deep and inject a playful note into my voice.

"College life, Momma. You know we keep crazy hours."

I plump the pillow behind my head. My sheets still smell like Maddie's floral perfume. It's distracting. The water runs in the bathroom. Too bad I can't help her get clean.

Momma exhales. "I was hoping you had plans... with a girlfriend."

Not this again. Her inquiries into my love life have gotten increasingly frequent. And pointed.

Before I can say anything, she rushes on, "Or a boyfriend! We've never really talked about it, but that would be fine, too! I just wish you had someone special in your life."

I clear my throat. "Um, no. I'm not gay. But thanks for being open-minded about that, if I was."

"Are you sure? Because—"

"I'm sure." Flopping back down, I stare at the ceiling. There's no doubt about that. I love women. And as Maddie can attest, I'm good at it, too. What can I say? Hockey players get a lot of action. It's a benefit I've enjoyed for the past two and a half years of college. But my momma doesn't need to know that. She'd die if she knew I'd had a different girl in my bed every night this week. Or kill me.

"I have no problem with it if you are. The rest of Texas is more conservative than me. I love you no matter what, no matter who you love. I don't understand... you seem so uninterested in women! Why don't you have a girlfriend?"

I can't tell her the truth—her failed marriage, messy divorce from my dad, and utter heartbreak made me swear off relationships forever. She couldn't handle that.

Maddie appears in the doorway again, fully clothed. Her skinny jeans hug every perfect curve and her halter top shows off the cleavage that I was enjoying before my mom interrupted. Her blonde hair is back to sleek and smooth, no longer mused from my fingers. She smiles at me, stuck in bed on the phone, and mouths, "Bye," with a little finger wave. At least she handled it well.

Shooting her an apologetic expression, I wave back. It would be so much easier if I could just lie to my mom about the girlfriend thing and get her off my tail. Especially if it would keep her from calling constantly and interrupting my hookups. Or my post-coital bliss. If she thought there was a girl like Maddie in my life, maybe she'd leave me alone about it.

Although...

She lives a thousand miles away from Harrison University. And I won't be going home to Austin until the summer. That's almost five months from now. Sure, I might see her for hockey finals—knock on wood—but if I had a hypothetical girlfriend, we could simply break up by then....

"Cooper? Hello?" Momma asks, turning impatient. Her porch swing creaks in the background, and I picture her sitting on it and drinking her sweet tea. She makes it year 'round and adds about a gallon of sugar to every gallon of tea. "You still there? How are your Agriculture classes? And how's the team?"

Punching my pillow to get it into the right shape, I bite my lip and then blurt out the words before I can overthink them.

"Actually, Momma, I've been meaning to loop you in. I *do* have a girlfriend."

6

Her squeal pierces my eardrum, and I hold the phone away from me until the yelling subsides.

"Calm down," I say when she quiets. "It's not a big deal!"

"Oh, but it is! My boy finally has a woman! That's who I heard, wasn't it? Tell me everything. What's her name? Where's she from? Why haven't I seen a picture of her yet? When can I meet her? What about—"

"Mom." Dear Lord in Heaven. Make the words stop. "It's new. I don't want to scare her off. And actually, I'm seeing her tonight, so I gotta run!"

Pressing the red button before she can protest, I sigh and flop down on my bed. It's just me and the ceiling again.

I hope I don't live to regret that.

CHAPTER
Two

JASMINE

Hanging up my long, black winter parka, I shiver. January in Indiana is chilly, and they keep the lab at a cool sixty-eight degrees. Grabbing my white lab coat, I slip it over my colorful patchwork jeans and my "Han Shot First" T-shirt. Too bad it's not fleece-lined. The white canvas is built to protect, but the extra layer helps warm me up and my goosebumps fade. The first time I put on my very own lab coat, I felt like the biggest badass. I was sure all my dreams of making a difference in the world through chemistry were going to come true. I might cure cancer in this lab coat.

Tugging my safety goggles over my messy bun, I try not to get the strap caught in my long, wavy brown hair, but it pulls on a loose strand anyway. Ouch. I should be used to that feeling, but I still wince. As I head to my bench, I inhale the smell of astringent chemicals and lemon cleaning products. The mix of the two is probably not going to be the latest candle scent, but it's comforting and familiar to me. The predictable routine of the lab is soothing. Chemistry follows patterns and makes sense.

After putting on gloves, I check my samples and record my measurements in my lab notebook. Everything is right on track, as it should be. See? Predictable. Under control. I adjust the oxygen levels to keep things from reacting prematurely.

With its bright fluorescent lights and matte black counter-tops, the chemistry lab is one of my favorite places on Earth. A wide room, it becomes a maze of lab benches and equipment, but I could navigate it in my sleep. Shelves line the back wall from the floor to the soaring ceiling, filled with gleaming glass beakers.

The living room in the old Victorian house I share with my two roommates is another one of my favorite spots. We decorated it together and while the furniture is mismatched, it's warm and inviting. Homey. I also love this massive sycamore tree on campus with a low-hanging branch that's perfect for climbing and sitting on. It's great for studying or reading. The seventh-floor lab in the Dye Chem building is a weird addition to that list, but I'm comfortable here. Confident in my skin. It's hard-fought, so I treasure the places where I can really enjoy it.

A haggard grad student shuffles in. Her blue eyes are ringed with dark circles and she pushes her limp blonde bangs out of her eyes. She ignores me, but it's not personal. All grad students perpetually need a double espresso and at least eight more hours in the day. Plus, about three years of sleep. She doesn't have time to acknowledge me.

That will be me in a few years. While her fate doesn't look glamorous, the thought still sends a *zing* along my spine. I'll sit for the GRE in a few months, and then after I graduate in a year and a half, I'll be a zombie grad student myself. I hope.

Then I'll get a job at a pharmaceutical company and be able to spend every day in a lab like this, putting my skills to work and losing myself in the excitement of new experiments and possibilities. Of saving lives through science. Being in a place where I fit in and belong.

I straighten my shoulders. Positive vibes. Work hard, stay focused, no negative thoughts. I can do this. I'll think about my future and—

"Jasmine."

I flinch, and all my confidence evaporates at the sound of his voice. After dating for two years, I'd broken up with Chad at the beginning of my junior year. That was four months ago, and he hadn't taken it well. I'd avoided him all fall with only a few run-ins. This semester, it's a different story. He orchestrated things so we're in the same lab together and I see him often. Every time, I feel small and insecure. It's like I'm that naïve little freshman all over again who was so amazed that a smart older guy would be interested in her.

That girl was a sweetheart. She'd been so excited to have her first college boyfriend. Chad had appeared perfect on the outside—cute, smart, attentive. I was so flattered that he'd picked me. But then he'd become too attentive. He always needed to know where I was if we weren't together. He'd wanted to be with me twenty-four/seven. At first, I was flattered he wanted me all to himself, like it was a compliment. It seemed thoughtful how he'd order food or drinks for me. I convinced myself it was romantic when he always wanted to be the one to plan our activities. Until he stopped taking any of my preferences into account. He wanted to dictate what I should wear, watch, and eat. Even how I should spend my time and who I should hang out with. It took an intervention, but my friends helped me see it for what it really was. He wanted to control me, and now can't stand that I'm no longer under his thumb.

I take a slow breath to calm my nerves and turn around. Tall and thin with rounded shoulders and cheekbones that could cut glass, he adjusts the lab coat over his button-up and khakis. His sandy brown hair flops over his forehead and he tosses it out of his cold blue eyes. I can smell his expensive Armani cologne from here. He practically bathes in the stuff.

"Chad." It's a struggle to keep my tone even, but I manage.

Looking me up and down, he raises a judgmental eyebrow. "Interesting fashion choice."

He says "interesting" the way adults apply it to kindergarten paintings they can't decipher.

Glancing at my outfit, I shrug and bare my teeth, pretending it was a compliment. "Thanks. You know me. I hate boring clothes."

And Chad couldn't stand that about me. His wardrobe is straight out of a J. Crew commercial. Preppy twinsets and Lilly Pulitzer dresses are fine. Cute on the right person. They're just not my style. I like to wear thrift store gems and clothes that show off my nerdy love of sci-fi and fantasy. He prefers a more traditional look.

"There's a time and a place for conventional." He rolls his dark eyes with a huff. "You should really tone it down."

"And I don't need you to tell me when that is."

"I'm only trying to do you a favor." He shrugs. "With your grad school interviews coming up, how do you expect anyone to take you seriously when you dress so... flamboyantly?"

Yeah, jeans and a t-shirt. So wild of me. I grind my teeth together.

"I don't need your favors anymore. We're not together." I clench my hands into fists, my short nails tearing my gloves.

Chad narrows his eyes. "You should be thankful for my

help. You never would have made it through the weed-out classes without me."

Had he been this much of an asshole when I dated him? I take a deep breath. Yes. Yes, he had.

"I would have been fine in Organic Chem and Calc Two without you. I passed because I worked hard, not because of you."

"You wish." He snorts.

Oh, I have lots of wishes involving Chad. The most benign is that he would disappear. On vengeful days, it's more like I wish he'd die a fiery death. But the power of mental suggestion doesn't work—he's still here.

"Look, Chad, thanks to you swapping research advisors, we have to put up with each other. So I'd appreciate it if you'd keep your opinions to yourself." I clench my jaw until my molars ache. My temples throb.

He waves his hand around the lab space. "Another thing that's because of me. You wouldn't have even known to ask for a research position if I hadn't mentioned it."

I hate that he's right. But he can't take credit for my success. It turns out I was more competition than he expected. He couldn't handle that I excelled in class and got better grades than he did.

It was the final straw for me when Chad had tried to convince me to change my major. If my advisor, Dr. Michelson, hadn't stepped in and convinced me I was a gifted scientist, I might have fallen for it. It was what I needed to see the light and break things off, but it hadn't been an easy road since then. Slowly but surely, I'm putting myself back together and making choices for me, not others. Chad is not a fan, though.

"And yet." I clear my throat. "I'm here. So, could you try to be more professional?"

"Professional." He huffs. "As if I need any tips from you."

The grad student across the room takes notice of our interaction and moves in our direction, so I lower my voice and put some space between us.

"I'm serious, Chad." I turn away from our audience, blocking this confrontation. "Don't talk to me in the lab. Or anywhere."

Spinning on the heel of my bright yellow Doc Martens, I stride out of the room. The door slams behind me and I speed-walk, unseeing, until I've rounded multiple corners and there are thick cement walls between us.

I let myself lean against the cool cinder blocks, panting. My heart races, and I struggle to catch my breath. Every interaction with him leaves me shaken and off-balance. Why couldn't he have changed majors? Or transferred colleges? Or fallen into a Sarlacc pit?

After a series of calming inhalations, I push off the wall. I'd run out of the room still wearing my lab coat and goggles, but oh well. I'm not going back. Removing my torn gloves, I shove them into my pockets and brush off the powdery feeling they leave behind. Stripping off my gear, I bundle the coat under my arm and pace. I've left my parka there, but I'll take the tunnels under campus and get it later.

Right now, recovery is more important. Chad sucks away my soul, and chocolate is the only cure.

I wind my way through the chem building to the tunnel access. The underground tunnels were like a maze at first, confusing and disorienting, but after using them for three winters, they don't faze me anymore. They are well-lit and look like any other institutional windowless hallway. Plus, they connect to the Student Union, which is where I'm headed now.

Heading up the stairs, I wind through the dim wood-paneled halls and follow the delicious smell of coffee and pastries until I get to Starbucks. Tucked into a corner of the ancient building, the green mermaid beckons. Truth be told, I prefer Nancy Brew. It's my favorite coffee shop, located a block from my house downtown, and a quiet study spot with a cozy mystery theme. But I just need coffee in my veins. A mocha and a double chocolate croissant sound perfect.

Placing my order, I lean against the counter to wait. I still feel anxious after my encounter with Chad, but my pulse is slowing. Knowing that he's three buildings away helps.

I shouldn't let Chad bother me like that. But I hate how he controlled me when we dated. Seeing him in the lab is like a smack in the face, reminding me how dumb I was. His constant harassment takes the joy out of chemistry. I wish I could be calm and cool about it, like my roommate, Delaney. Or come up with sick burns on the spot like my best friend Staci. All I do is get flustered and run away.

"Jasmine!" I startle as the barista calls my name, banging my elbow into the counter. *Ouch.*

Grabbing my food and drink, I make myself comfortable in a leather wingback chair facing a window. The view of campus is pretty, even in January. The bare tree branches crisscross the pale sky in stark black lines. There's no snow on the ground to cover the brown, dead grass, but I focus on the beautiful, soaring old brick buildings. The tangible proof that students before me survived, and will continue long after me, too.

Taking a sip of the coffee, I inhale, then exhale. It anchors me and renews my confidence. I can do this. I'm not the same girl who fell for Chad. I'm stronger. Smarter.

And I've sworn off relationships. No man gets that kind of say in my life ever again. Hookups are fun, but me and boyfriends are like Frodo and the Millenium Falcon. They don't go together. I'm perfectly happy on my own, and that's how it's going to stay.

I finish my coffee and my snack, then toss my cup and square my shoulders. Staci had mentioned going out tonight. Drinking, dancing, letting go of this stress and forgetting about Chad—sounds like exactly what I need.

CHAPTER
Three

COOPER

No matter what's going on in my life, everything makes sense on the ice. Stress from classes and thoughts of the future fade away. I'm not consumed with worries about my momma and the big fat lie I told her yesterday. It's just me, and the guys, and the puck. Hockey has always been my favorite escape—that, or driving around aimlessly in my truck. No matter how much I missed my dad, I always had hockey.

The smell of the ice, the sound of the puck hitting the boards and the *swish* of my skates cutting a path through the frozen surface—my mind narrows to a single point, and I come alive.

I skate hard, working on our passing drills and taking shots on goal. Next week, we play third-ranked Notre Dame. It's our chance to prove that we deserve our number two ranking. Maybe we can even move up to number one and take out Michigan.

Coach blows his whistle, ending practice. I take off my

helmet and shake the sweat out of my hair. I'm tired, but in the best way. My muscles feel stretched out, used up. Almost as good as after sex. How in the world did I get a scholarship for this? Getting paid to play hockey is a dream come true. I'd love to play professionally, but I don't know if I have a shot at the NHL after college or not. So I'm getting my Agriculture degree and I'll be content to move home to Texas and work on a farm if hockey isn't in my future. At least I'll be outside with the sun on my face and my boots in the dirt if I'm not on the ice. Maybe I'll join a beer league or help coach pee-wee to stay connected to my favorite sport.

My teammates head to the locker room, and I follow. Wooden stalls line all four walls of the square room with an open space in the middle. Bright orange carpet with our navy Griffins logo in the center helps muffle the sound of twenty noisy hockey players, plus our coaches and trainers. Their offices are down a hallway off the main room, and the showers are around the corner in the other direction.

After stripping off my gear, I toss it into my assigned stall and line up to shower off the grime. The guys fill the air with genial conversation and general ribbing. The atmosphere is lighthearted and fun, as usual. Toweling dry, I throw on my clothes and check my phone. Turns out that my mom bugging me about my imaginary girlfriend is way worse than when she just wanted me to date someone. Three missed calls from her today alone.

As I stare at it, the screen lights up and buzzes in my hand. Momma. Again. I roll my eyes and shove it in my pocket, but not before my teammate and roommate Evan spies it over my shoulder.

"You ignoring your mom's calls?" He laughs and elbows me. "I'll talk to her."

"Leave my momma out of it."

Hunter and Jonas, our other two roommates and friends, shake their heads at his antics. The rest of the guys in the locker room go about their business, getting dressed and ignoring us. Everyone is used to Evan clowning around—no one notices it anymore. At six-three with shaggy blonde hair, he's like a big puppy off the ice. During a game, though, he's a force of nature. One of the best forwards on the team, he and Jonas lead the second line as an offensive powerhouse.

"Evan, you're an idiot." Jonas pulls his t-shirt over his curly brown hair, running his fingers through it. He's the most studious guy in our apartment, more likely to be found in the library than anywhere else. He's quiet and perceptive, and it makes him a damn good hockey player.

"All I'm saying is, you can give her my number." Evan bobs his brows suggestively, and I punch his bicep. Not too hard, because I don't want him injured. But hard enough that he'll think twice before talking about my mom again.

"Over my dead body," I growl.

"Mine, too." Hunter crosses his arms over his broad chest and glares at Evan. As my best friend, he's become as protective of my mom as I am. His own mom died when he was a baby and he soaks up the attention whenever mine comes to see us play. And I don't mind another guy watching out for her. With my dad gone, I figure she can use all the help she can get.

"Fine, fine." Evan holds his hands up in surrender. "I guess I'm the only one with a thing for MILFs."

"Ew, man." I scowl at him. "Never call my mom that again."

He laughs and turns back to his locker, leaving me to stare at my phone.

So far I've dodged my mom by teasing that she already

likes my girlfriend more than me, the relationship is new, and I don't want to come on too strong. Thank god I can make up details, and by the time I see her, be so devastated about our breakup that I don't want to talk about it.

But there's no way I could keep the guys off my back if they got wind of this. Creating a fake girlfriend seems desperate and pathetic. Honestly, I wish I'd never invented this stupid lie. It's more trouble than it's worth, and lying to Momma is bad enough. I don't want to lie to my teammates and friends, too.

"You ever wish you played closer to home?" Evan pulls his Harrison hockey shirt over his head, muffling his words.

I definitely debated. The University of Texas is right down the road, and I'd considered going there. But when Harrison offered me a full-ride, I'd jumped at the chance. I love my mom, but I needed to be on my own and see if I could survive. It was the right choice.

Guilt gnaws at my stomach, and I take a deep breath. I'll come clean to her tomorrow.

"You just wish my momma was closer so you could see her more often." I rub Evan's head, messing up his hair, and smirk.

"Ain't that the truth." Evan flips me off, then smiles.

"Hey Coop, we're going out tonight. You in?" Hunter's dark eyebrows raise in question as he applies deodorant.

"Where?" My phone vibrates in my pocket, but I ignore it.

"O'Bryan's."

"But The Cactus is within walking distance."

"It's also shitty." Jonas raises a pointed brow as he slips on his sneakers. His brown eyes gleam. "Dude, it's named The Ugly Cactus for a reason." He's not wrong. Filthy and too loud, I'm not sure why I like it. The Western theme reminds me of home, I guess.

"I don't know." I scratch my head. "Those bagpipes at O'Bryan's are so whiny. I'm not sure I can stand it."

"Says the guy who listens to country." Hunter laughs, shaking his dark hair out of his blue eyes. "Come on, it will be fun."

"I think it's my turn to pick. Let's go to The Cactus." Maybe my cell phone won't have any reception there and I can have a night off from Momma's pestering.

"You can drag us there in a few weeks for your birthday." Hunter pulls a shirt over his head, then buttons his jeans.

"Here." Jonas produces a quarter and lays it flat on his palm. "Call it."

"Heads!" Hunter and I both yell at once. Jonas rolls his eyes.

"You can't both be heads."

"Heads, it's O'Bryan's. Tails, it's The Ugly Cactus." Evan joins our circle around Jonas and stares at the quarter.

Flipping the coin, Jonas slaps it on the back of his hand. "Heads! O'Bryan's wins!"

I groan while the rest of the guys cheer. Even if it's not my first choice of location, I'll still show up tonight. O'Bryan's is always full of pretty girls. That's exactly what I need to get my mind off everything.

A handful of our teammates join Hunter, Evan, Jonas, and I at O'Bryan's. I don't enjoy the whiney bagpipes, but the beer is cold and they have a great selection on tap. It's a typical Irish bar—dark inside, decorated with Guinness signs and soccer pennants, but it's not as bad as I make it out to be. I just like to give the guys a hard time.

Scanning the dim interior of the pub, I look for anyone I

know. I'm not opposed to repeat hookups, but I've learned the hard way that coming back to the same well too many times can send the wrong message. I pride myself on my skills—I'm excellent in bed, and I always make sure my dates have a great time. I meet their needs first. But I'm clear with them up front. I'm not a relationship guy, and they won't change my mind. It's easier this way.

Love is just a concept created by Hallmark to sell cards. Anyone who thinks differently is fooling themselves—or someone else. So I don't promise something I can't give.

My eyes slide over a slew of girls until they land on a gorgeous bombshell. Petite and curvy. She stands out from the crowd in her blue TARDIS dress and matching combat boots. Her brown hair cascades in waves down her back, and I want to run my fingers through it. I'd love to go chat her up, but she's perched on a barstool next to some guy, and I don't poach. With his thick-framed glasses and floppy hair, he screams 'boyfriend material.' I can't compete with that, and I'm not gonna try. She looks bored enough for me to assume that they've been dating a while, but it's none of my business. I won't wreck a relationship for a hookup.

"Hey, Coop!" Evan claps me on the back, pulling my attention. "It's time for boilermakers."

I roll my eyes at his fascination with the drink, but I don't argue. I'd be happy to just sip on a Coors, but he likes the old-fashioned bomb shot. He has beer glasses, half-full, lined up on the bar, with the whiskey ready. Jonas and Hunter join us, and Evan counts down.

"Three, two, one, go!"

Laughing, we drop our whiskey shots into the beer and chug the drink as fast as we can. Tipping my glass back, the liquid slides down my throat. The beer is foamy and refreshing, but the whiskey leaves a burn. We slam our empty pints on the bar almost in union when we finish, and I wipe the sleeve of my flannel shirt across my mouth. Hell, yeah. It's definitely a rush. With a triumphant smile, Evan throws his arm around my shoulders and pulls me out to the dance floor, surrounded by a bunch of girls. It's great to be single. None of them are the TARDIS chick, but they'll do.

CHAPTER
Four

JASMINE

"Staci!" I hiss her name as my best friend primps in the restaurant bathroom mirror. Band posters cover the dark walls and the lights are so dim, I can barely see my reflection. I pop my hip against the black counter. "Are you kidding me? I can't believe this! I just wanted to drink and dance, not deal with a guy tonight."

She shrugs, unrepentant, and reapplies her bold red lipstick. It compliments her auburn hair perfectly. "I don't see what the big deal is."

"The big deal"—I grit my teeth and fluff my dark brown waves—"is that you set me up on a date. Without telling me."

"People go on blind dates all the time." Widening her blue eyes, she purses her lips and assesses me. My strapless TARDIS dress and matching blue combat boots earns a nod of approval. Staci's cream long-sleeved body con dress shows off all her assets, and she looks beautiful, but I don't tell her that. Best friends who trick me into blind dates don't get compliments. Besides, she's five-ten and has a figure like a Kardashian. She always looks beautiful, and she knows it.

"After they've agreed to them!" I take a deep breath and try to chill. She means well.

"Look, girl. We've been friends for twenty-one years. I know you. And you need this."

I put my hand on my hip and manage not to stomp my foot, but the urge is strong. "What part of 'I've sworn off dating' don't you understand?"

"All of it?" She doesn't bat an eye at my outburst—well, figuratively. Literally, she checks her mascara and fixes a smudge.

"Stace, it's not your life. It's mine." I keep my voice even, not whining, but frustration wells up inside me.

"I know, babe." Spinning away from the mirror, she faces me, putting her hands on my shoulders. I'm five-five, so she has to look down to pin me in her stare. Her gaze is a mix of compassion and worry. "I want the absolute best for you, and it feels like this 'not dating' thing has gone on long enough."

"This 'not dating thing'?" I use finger quotes to underscore my sarcastic tone. "You make it sound like I'm a toddler going through a phase where I won't eat vegetables."

She raises a pointed brow toward my foot. "Nearly throwing a tantrum in a restaurant bathroom—I don't know. You could have fooled me."

I stick out my tongue, further proving her point.

Sobering, she steps closer. "Chad messed you up." I flinch at his name, and she squeezes my shoulders. "He was a jerk. A really terrible human. But don't you think this choice is giving him too much power over you?"

Before I can answer, the bathroom door swings open, admitting a girl on teetering heels and the blaring sound of bagpipes. Live music night at the Irish pub almost always means either kilts or bagpipes. Tonight it's both.

The girl raises her brows at us and heads into a stall. Staci drops her hands from my shoulders with a sigh.

"Think about it, okay? If Chad still has control over you, then he wins. And you should give Kyle a chance."

I still can't believe she set me up without my permission. If she wasn't my best friend since birth, I'd probably bolt and never speak to her again.

"This is, what? The fifth guy you've tried to match me up with since September? Stace. It has to stop." And they've all been duds. I don't want the boyfriend material that she keeps throwing at me. One-night-of-fun types are more what I'm after.

"Why? He's cute and smart. Maybe you'll get lucky tonight and owe *me* instead." She smooths a wayward strand of my hair and I adjust her necklace, turning the clasp so it's no longer showing. Our primp game is strong. And our roles are about as familiar as this discussion.

"I don't need a date for that." I shrug. "I have sex when I want it."

I hope her massive eye-roll doesn't give her a headache. "Not this again."

"Sex is a biological urge. It doesn't have to be connected to a committed relationship if you don't want it to be." This argument is so well-tread between us, I think I have my responses memorized by now. And Staci's, too.

"We can disagree about this. I prefer my intimacy to be a little more... well, intimate. What can I say? Commitment is hot. But regardless, go check out Kyle. Take him home if you feel an urge. How long has it been, anyway?"

"None of your business." Long enough. Swallowing down my irritation at her question, I reach out and play with one of her curls. "Stace, I'm happy for you and Tate. He seems great for you. But that doesn't mean I need a guy, too."

Her eyes soften at the mention of her boyfriend's name, and she can't keep from smiling as she thinks about him. It's sappy but adorable. A senior in one of her finance classes, they met during a group project this fall and started dating. He's confident, her number-one turn on. It probably doesn't hurt that he's incredibly handsome, too. Mellow where Staci is intense, he seems to balance her out well. And I know from unwanted first-hand experience that they can't keep their hands off each other.

"He really is the best, isn't he?" She gives a dreamy sigh. "Is it so bad that I want this for you, too?"

"No." I pause, choosing my words with care. "But we're not the same. Different things can make us happy."

"I know." Staci stares at her reflection in the mirror, biting her lip. "I just thought—if you had a guy, too, we could double-date. It would be so fun! And I don't want you to feel left out."

"I don't mind being the third wheel. Or the fifth, when Delaney and Brian are around." Delaney shares our house, and she's been dating Brian since before they came to Harrison. They are inseparable, practically an old married couple, and committed to each other for the long haul. If I wanted a relationship, they'd be my goal. But I don't. I mean what I said—I'm not bothered being the only one in our group that's unattached.

"I know." She links her arm through mine. "But keep an open mind about Kyle. Maybe you'll like him."

With that, she pulls me out of the bathroom and back to the bar. It's a massive square in the middle of the dim restaurant, with circular wooden stools dotting the space. Soccer team adverts, Guinness signs, and Irish flags decorate the black walls. The band takes a break and the bagpipes quiet as Staci plops me down next to Kyle.

With shaggy light-brown hair and thick-framed glasses atop a crooked nose, he's cute, in a bookish way, with arresting gray eyes. He looks nice but isn't trying too hard in a plain black t-shirt and sneakers. That's a good start, at least.

"I'm out. Have a good night." Staci gives Kyle a wide, encouraging grin. To me, she mouths, "Be nice," as she scurries off.

I glare daggers at her before mustering a smile and holding out my palm. "Hi. Sorry, Staci didn't really give me a lot of background info. I'm Jasmine."

He shakes my hand limply and then takes a sip of his beer. "I'm Kyle. I'm in class with Staci."

"Oh, what's your major?"

Not a particularly inspired opening, but it's not like I signed up for this date. I don't want him pissed at Staci, though, so I try.

"Accounting."

"Sounds... interesting." It doesn't, but he doesn't need more encouragement than that before he's off and running. Monopolizing the conversation, he doesn't ask me about my studies or anything else. He prattles on for an hour about his impressive grades in all his business classes, his future career prospects—he's set to inherit the family real estate business— his most recent performance on a group project—he did all the work, and a fascinating story about the washing machine in his dorm—it malfunctioned. He only pauses when I order a beer.

Why did Staci set me up with this guy? Is it a punishment for the time I borrowed her pink cashmere sweater and accidentally spilled coffee on it? He's not as bad as Chad, but I'm done with guys who only think about themselves. The sex would definitely be unsatisfying. It's been a while, but I'm not that desperate.

"Uh, Kyle," I say, having to cut him off mid-flow... something about his cat. Kill me now. "I'm going to the ladies' room. I'll be right back."

I make my way back toward the restroom, then I pull out my phone and text Staci.

Jasmine: I hate you.

I tell her, in case she thinks I've gotten over the set-up. With my head down, I stare at my phone, shuffling through the crowd by the bar until I accidentally run into a muscular chest.

"Oh, shit." His full beer sloshes over the rim, spilling out and soaking us both. I meet his light brown eyes and my stomach does a somersault. He's tall with broad shoulders, a trim waist, and a rugged jawline that makes me drool. A cowboy hat covers his hair, but the hazel eyes that peek out at me under the brim are kind. "I'm sorry."

Lifting his feet, he shakes off one boot and then another, and then sets his empty cup on the bar and tips his hat in my direction, revealing short dark hair. "No problem, ma'am."

My belly does another dive at his southern accent. "I'm not nearly old enough to be called ma'am. And aren't you in the wrong get-up for an Irish bar?"

He shrugs, a charming smile tugging at the corners of his expressive mouth. "I suggested The Ugly Cactus to the rest of the hockey team, but I lost the coin toss."

I snort, trying to un-stick my wet dress from my stomach. I hope he doesn't notice the squelching noise. "You lucked out. This bar is far superior to The Cactus."

Smelling of vomit and cigarettes, that disgusting watering hole is in a strip mall right off campus. I've only been once, but it's the most typical college bar in Lafayette, Indiana.

They have themed drink specials every night and don't check IDs too closely. Even the name makes me want to roll my eyes.

Holding his tight orange Harrison Hockey shirt away from torso, he grimaces. "Yeah, but if I were there, I wouldn't be wearing beer."

"You'd be covered in way worse."

"True. Will it wash out of your dress?" He peers down at my blue police box dress. "I hope so, because it's awesome."

"Thanks! I made it myself." I smooth down the soggy fabric. It definitely looked better before I took a beer shower.

"Wow, that's cool. Which doctor is your favorite?"

My eyebrows hit my hairline and I blink. "Aren't you a jock?"

He mentioned the hockey team. Maybe he's a student manager or trainer, but he's built like an athlete. Muscular and yummy. He glances at his t-shirt, then back up at me, his hazel eyes darting left and right at my non sequitur. "Yes?"

"I've just never met a jock Whovian before." I toss my wavy hair over my shoulder.

"Then you haven't met the right jocks yet." He grins slow and suggestive, and wow. Despite being soaked, my body warms. Why couldn't Staci have a class with this guy? Because a forced date with him doesn't sound like a punishment. Spilling his beer was totally my fault—I was texting and not watching where I was going. He could have been angry, but he's polite and kind. And cute.

"You still haven't answered my question." Someone bumps into him, forcing him a step closer, and I notice the flecks of gold in his eyes. I wonder what the five o'clock shadow on his jaw would feel like on my skin. "Favorite doctor?"

"Thirteenth. You?" He smells like clean soap, and I want to stay in his personal space bubble as long as I can.

"Tenth."

"Do you ship him and Rose?"

"Hell, yeah. Who doesn't?" He hands me a wad of napkins from the bar. "Will these help?"

I dab at the fabric, but it doesn't make much of a difference. I smile up at him in thanks, though. He's considerably taller than me, and it makes me feel delicate. My chest flutters, and I clear my throat. "I actually needed an excuse to leave my terrible date, so this is perfect."

"Terrible date?" His eyes narrow, and he puts a hand on my arm. "Do you want some help? Because I can—"

"No, I can handle myself." Is there a way to prolong this conversation? Because I can see the outline of his pecs in his wet shirt, and damn. My mouth waters. "Nothing out of the ordinary. He was just self-centered and talked about himself the whole time. And trust me, he wasn't that interesting."

"Oh, that sucks. You deserve to be with a kick-ass guy."

He winks, like maybe he's that guy, and I wish I could make Kyle disappear.

"Thanks." My cheeks heat at the compliment. "You're saving me with the beer spill. It's my excuse to leave. But I feel bad about your shirt and your drink. I hope I didn't ruin your night."

"Nah, don't mention it." Touching the brim of his hat, his eyes twinkle. "It was truly my pleasure. Have a good night, ma'am."

"Jasmine," I shoot back as I walk away. "Anything's better than ma'am."

He smiles, slow and sweet, and it warms my insides. Whoever he is, that cowboy is way too hot for his own good.

Unfortunately, I still have to get rid of Kyle. Reluctant to leave Hot Cowboy, I turn away, affixing a frown on my face as I walk back to our spot at the bar.

"Look what happened," I moan as I approach Kyle. "Beer all over my dress."

Busy shooting off a text, he's slouched against the bar.

"Oh, that's too bad." Voice flat, he barely looks up from his phone. I don't believe him. At least there's no need to worry about one-sided feelings.

"Yeah. I'm gonna head home and change." I wave and move toward the exit. "It was nice meeting you."

It wasn't, but I can still be polite.

"Uh, yeah, you too. See ya 'round, I guess."

He doesn't ask for my number, and I certainly don't volunteer it. Waste of an evening. Staci's gonna hear about this.

I can't help but glance back at the spot where Hot Cowboy was standing, but he's not there. Too bad. I wouldn't have minded if he had invited me back to his place. Stupid Kyle, dragging me down.

For now, I'm going home by myself. Which is fine. Better than the alternative—being stuck with someone who wants more than I can give.

CHAPTER
Five

COOPER

Momma: So what's this special lady's name? Where's she from? What's she like?

Momma: What's her favorite food? What's she studying? How did you meet?

Momma: Good luck against the Irish! We'll talk later.

The bus ride home from Notre Dame is so loud our celebration reverberates in the confined space. That win felt good, though. We deserve to blast some music and let loose.

I check my phone, noting another missed call from my mom. There's no way she'd hear me if I call now, but maybe that can work to my advantage. If she can't hear me, she'll give up, right? And maybe she'll be distracted, recapping the game. Either way, I've ignored her texts and dodged her calls too long to put it off any further.

"Cooper!" she answers on the fourth ring, out of breath

like she had to run to get to the phone. "Congratulations on the assist! I watched it on the Big Ten channel tonight. How are you?"

"I'm good, Momma." And it's true. "The game was great. Notre Dame is a tough team—they're ranked high for a reason. We were really evenly matched, but we came out on top."

"The Irish played dirty. The refs should have called more penalties."

Bless her heart. My mom is a dyed-in-the-wool southern belle, but she's also a devoted hockey fan. I love that she's developed this passion for my sport.

"I agree."

"So, is your girlfriend a hockey fan?" Her voice turns coy, and I suppress a groan.

Standing up on the charter bus, I wave my hands and get Evan's attention. "Make some noise," I mouth, and he obliges.

"Mom," I hold the phone close to my mouth to be heard over the sudden whoops and hollers, "the guys are celebrating our win. It's too loud. I've gotta go."

I don't know what she says before I tap the end button and slink down into my seat. Of course she'd bring it up. I haven't even given her a girl's name. I need to up my fake dating game, but where do I start?

I sigh. The truth would probably be a good jumping off point. But it's too soon to stage my fake break up and abandon it now. And if I come up with a decent plan, I can still use this to my advantage. Right?

What would my fake girlfriend be like?

Hot, obviously. She doesn't have to look like a model, but there needs to be attraction and chemistry between us. Hypothetically speaking, of course.

An image flashes in my brain of the gorgeous girl I saw at

O'Bryan's a few days ago. I'm a sucker for long hair and sparkling eyes. But I need more than just appearance to satisfy Momma.

She'd like hockey, like my mom said, and enjoy cheering me on at my games. She'd have to be smart and funny. I'm not dumb, but I don't consider myself book smart, either. Like most ag majors, I prefer hands-on projects. Ag is a lot of plant biology so I've had to adapt, but I'd rather have my fingers in the dirt and the sun on my face than be stuck in the library. Regardless, I could never date a ditzy girl.

It's not like I plan on dating anyone, but for the sake of the exercise, it's important to consider everything.

Should I ask Shawn? A senior on the team, he's on my line, and a guy with a steady girlfriend. He and Isabella have been dating practically forever. So while he has some insight into the female mind, he probably doesn't remember what it's like to look at anyone else.

And I don't want the team to know about my imaginary girlfriend. I made it up to placate my mom, but in the wrong light, it could sound like a desperate move to be cool.

Regardless, I have to figure out what to tell my mom. What would this mythical girl study? What would she wear? A hot TARDIS dress? My mind fills in the blanks with Jasmine and her flirty smile. But it feels wrong to describe a real person to my mom, like a violation of privacy or something. This needs to stay in my imagination only. I know that I'd want a girl who is passionate but also kind. Someone who shares my interests. A girl who is witty and loves animals.

Damn it. Am I describing a Disney princess? I can't even decide what her name should be. I need to avoid my mom's calls, because I'm in way over my head.

"Hey, Coop." Hunter pokes his head over the seat in front

of me. "Great assist tonight. What did you think of the Notre Dame goalie?"

"Wicked glove. But we still snuck a few biscuits past him." I bump his fist. "You had a great goal."

"Thanks to your assist."

"You guys have an epic bromance, we get it." A few seats away, Reed, a senior defenseman, stands and glares. "Now sit down and shut up. I'm trying to sleep here."

Hunter gives him a smartass salute and sits down. I follow suit. With friends like this, I don't need a girlfriend. Hockey, and the guys on the team. I'm set.

But how do I explain that to my mom? Especially when I lied to her already? I should come clean. This isn't worth the stress. Next time I talk to her, I will.

And I probably can't put her off for too long. My birthday is this week, on Friday. Since we have a home game that night, the guys and I are going out to celebrate tonight. Not like we won't go out again on Friday after the game, but my teammates will use any excuse to party.

At least I get to pick the venue this time. I hope they're ready for line dancing at The Cactus.

"Happy birthday!" Evan and Jonas set a shot glass apiece on the tall table at the back of the bar. My teammates circle us, purple neon illuminating their wide smiles.

Gazing at my friends, I grin and toss back the shot. I've been working my ass off, and it's fun to have a night to relax.

"The Cactus, though, man?" Jonas shakes his head. "Another year older and your taste has not improved."

"You're lucky I didn't make y'all wear cowboy hats." I tip

mine in his direction. "You can take the guy out of Texas, but you can't take Texas out of the guy."

With that, I order another round of shots for everyone and check out the bar. It's a Monday night, not as busy as a weekend, but there are still lots of pretty girls to dance with.

"Hey ladies!" Eyes around us lock on Evan as he yells at the top of his lungs. "We have a birthday boy in the house tonight!"

That draws a crowd over to our table in the corner. Hunter pairs off with a gorgeous redhead. Evan and Jonas find a blonde and a brunette, respectively, and I talk to a girl with sparkling brown eyes and swinging black braids.

Leading her out to the dance floor, my phone buzzes in my pocket, and I check the display. My mom, again. Would it work if I told Momma I was out with the guys? She'd definitely notice the noise in the background and know it was legit. But she'd ask where my girlfriend is and if this girl hears that... no, it could get awkward. I'm going to tell Momma the truth. I really am. At the right moment, though, and this is definitely not it. With a twist of guilt in my belly, I let her roll to voicemail and try to focus on the girl in front of me.

She's pretty, but I'm off my game, I guess. I can't remember if I've already asked what she's studying. Usually a cute view is enough for me, but tonight my mind keeps wandering to Jasmine. Her outfit combination of clunky boots with a feminine dress caught my eye, for sure, and her witty banter kept me on my toes. If she were here tonight, could I get her to dance with me? Would she let me take her home?

The girl in my arms smiles at me. Shit, I'm being a dick—thinking about one girl while dancing with a different one. I'm better than this. Besides, I don't think about girls a second time, anyway. I've gotta get my head on straight.

The song ends, and one of my teammates, Mateo, pulls me off the floor for another shot. It burns, but in the best way. I should switch to beer after this. Or water. I wave to my dance partner as she heads to her friends. It's for the best.

Mateo throws back his shot, then slams down the glass. "Hey, man, what do you think our chances are against Michigan this week?"

A sophomore, and on the second line this year, Mateo takes his position on the team—and hockey in general—seriously. He rakes his hand through his black hair, dark eyes intense.

"Can you just relax and enjoy a night out?" I set my empty shot glass on the bar. "Go find a nice girl and flirt. Or guy. Whatever floats your boat."

"Hockey is life, dude. Next year, I want to move up to the first line with you and Hunter—win the Frozen Four. I don't have time for anything else. I'm committed."

I sigh. He is, and I can't fault him for it. I clap him on the shoulder, and we move over to a little high-top table. "Okay, I watched some tapes last week. Michigan is pretty physical, even if fighting isn't really allowed. So I think our best bet is to keep our game tight and clean."

He nods. "That makes sense. What about—"

"Nope." I cut him off. "I answered one hockey question. Now you have to go pick up one girl."

Shaking his head, he smiles and dimples appear in his cheeks. "I see how it is."

"Yep. It's my birthday! Consider it a present for me."

Scanning the dim interior, he points to a stacked blonde leaning against the bar. "That one."

"Good taste. Go see if she's interested."

I pat his shoulder as he wanders off, then I order a beer. Mateo's blonde target has a cute friend. I should go wingman for him and see if I can help. This time I will focus and give it my all.

CHAPTER

Six

JASMINE

One of the quirks of living in a house with a letter slot instead of a mailbox is that mail ends up littering the entryway. As I let myself into the mint green Victorian I share with my two best friends, I do my best not to leave footprints all over our letters. Quirky or not, I love the big old house we've rented. It's downtown and within walking distance of coffee shops and restaurants, plus it has an amazing patio and porch that we enjoy in the warmer months. It reminds me of a gingerbread house on the outside, and the inside feels cozy thanks to the personal touches we've all added. Delaney hung a print of Monet's *Water Lilies* in the living room because it's her favorite. Staci contributed a green couch that belonged to her grandmother. And I bestowed a colorful rag rug that I made from old t-shirts. The pipes may be noisy, and there's no dishwasher, but it's worth it for the worn, comfortable, and welcoming atmosphere.

I scoop the envelopes off the floor and drop my keys in the bowl on the bright yellow side table in the hallway. Flipping on the lights as I walk into the living room, I sort through the letters until I spot one with my name on it. I scan the printed return address—Eli Lilly, in their trademark red script.

My hands shake as I slide my woven bag off my shoulder and let it drop to the hardwood. Slipping a finger under the flap, I rip it open.

Where is everyone? I need company for this. But I can't wait until my roommates get home for the reveal. I have to know what it says now.

"Please, please, please," I pray, before unfolding the stationary and skimming the contents.

Ms. Turner, we are pleased to inform you that you have been accepted to our summer internship program.

"Yes!"

I'm jumping up and down too much to read the rest of the letter. Keys rattle in the door behind me, then it opens.

"Staci!" I grab her as she walks in and dance around the living room. "I got it!"

"Got what?" Amused, her auburn hair fans out behind her like a banner as she lets me twirl her in a spin around the space. Winter sunlight streams in through the tall windows, giving us a gorgeous sunset to complement my mood.

I wave the letter in her face. "I got the summer internship with Eli Lilly!"

Her heart-shaped face lights up in a wide smile. "Jaz, that's great! I'm so proud of you!"

Whipping her phone from her pocket, she taps the screen, and it plays "We Are the Champions" as we continue to celebrate. Maybe she set me up on a terrible blind date without my consent, but Staci has always been a supportive and encouraging friend. She only has my best interest in mind.

Delaney, our third housemate, walks in as we are dancing to "Celebrate Good Times." Curvy and short with clear gray eyes, her light brown hair is styled in a pixie cut that show-cases her delicate features. Outgoing and fun, she's always ready for action. Dropping her bag, she doesn't bat an eye at our antics, but throws her hands in the air. "Living room party! What's the occasion?"

"I got the Lilly internship!" Panting, I sink to the green, lumpy couch.

"Congratulations!" She tugs me to my feet, even though I'm out of breath. "This calls for a night out!"

I bite a fingernail. "But it's Monday."

"Who cares? I'm meeting Brian later, but let's celebrate in style!"

Delaney loves any excuse to get dressed up and party, and her enthusiasm is contagious.

"Why not?" Staci spins, grinning. "I've got a date with Tate, but we can pre-game."

"If we stick close to campus and go now, we can totally make it work. We'll squeeze in a quick celebratory drink first before we go out with the guys." Delaney grabs my palms and stares deep into my eyes, her gray ones sparkling. "You deserve it!"

She's right, I do. Lilly is one of the top pharmaceutical companies in the world and its headquarters are in Indi-anapolis, my hometown. I applied to internships all over the country, but this was my number one pick. And I got it! I can't wait to share my news with everyone.

I squeeze her hands in return. "Let's do it!"

∾

Jasmine: Guess who got a Lilly internship?!?

Mom: My baby?!? Congratulations! I can't wait to have you home for the summer!

Maya: Congrats, sis!

Maya: And I can see you this summer because I finally earned my way onto the day shift!

Mom: You can all come for weekly dinners

Mom: And we can have girls' nights when your dad is traveling! I'm so excited!

"Are you sure you're sober enough to drive?" Delaney asks, her gray eyes assessing me. Our impromptu celebration was the perfect break from my typical routine, but now I'm headed home. Staci and Delaney's guys are meeting them here at The Cactus. I wrinkle my nose at the smell of sour vomit and cigarette smoke that permeates the room. I might be sad to leave the company, but not the location.

Yes, they somehow talked me into going to my least favorite bar. But since this is where they already had plans, it made the most sense.

"Yep." I put my hand on my heart. "I had one glass of champagne an hour ago. I swear on Herbie."

Herbie is my beloved 1973 Volkswagen Beetle. I'm a little crazy about my car. Painted white with blue and red racing stripes and a number fifty-three on the hood, he looks just like the Love Bug. He fits my vintage style perfectly. Most of my friends haven't seen those movies—or tragically, only know the Lindsay Lohan version—but I remember watching the classics on lazy Sunday afternoons with my mom and sister. My car is my most prized possession.

Staci shakes her head, red hair catching the light of the bar. "I will never understand you and that car."

"You don't have to leave yet, you know, Jaz." Coming up behind her, Brian wraps his arm around Delaney's waist and she puts her head on his shoulder. "We could find you a nice guy—"

"Nope." I cut him off. "I can meet guys on my own, thank you very much."

Staci grabs Tate's hand and laces their fingers together. "But—"

"No more Kyles or Chads." I clear my throat and brace for the impact of my next words. Maybe they will back off a little. "I actually met a cute guy last time we were out."

My eardrums almost burst at the pitch of my friends as they scream.

"Tell us everything!" Delaney bounces on her heels and Brian laughs at her antics.

"There's not much to tell." I shrug. "He was hot. With a cowboy hat and an accent. But I had beer on my dress and I was on a date with Kyle—" I glare at Staci, who looks properly chagrined. "So I left. But my point is—I'm fine. I talk to cute boys. No set-ups or help needed. I'm good, and Chad didn't break me. You don't have to worry."

Staci pats my arm. "I'm glad to hear it, girl. I just want you to be happy."

"I know." I give them a little finger wave. "Thanks for taking me out to celebrate. See you tomorrow."

Nodding, she and Delaney each give me a hug and I head to the door.

My friends are the greatest. They took me out and made a big deal about my internship and even in The Cactus, I can't wipe the grin off my face. I'll have to call my mom tomorrow and give her a full report. Although she'll be excited solely because I'll be in Indianapolis, not because it's an excellent learning opportunity and great for my future prospects. She gave up her career years ago to support my dad and she doesn't really get why it's so important to me.

But I want to change the world, not merely stay home and support a guy.

Would Maya, my older sister, understand the significance? Married to her college boyfriend Joel last summer, she works as a nurse in a hospital maternity ward, and she seems happy. I don't talk to her as much as I used to, though. This is a good excuse to call.

The bitter January wind whips the door closed behind me as I cross the parking lot, blowing up my yellow sunflower-patterned skirt. I wrap my red peacoat tighter around me and wish I'd worn leggings. Herbie waits right where I left him. The contrast between my VW Bug and the jacked-up truck next to him is almost comical, and I stifle a laugh. Patting his hood, I unlock my door and slide behind the wheel.

I put the key in the ignition and turn, but nothing happens. Oh crap. The headlights don't turn on, nothing even clicks. Is it the battery? No automatic lights on this baby to save my ass if I forget to flip the switch, but I check and I shut them off like I was supposed to. That is a bad sign.

Having a classic car rocks, but it can be less than reliable. I try the key again, but no luck. Resting my head on the steering wheel, I beg Herbie to start. Nothing.

With a groan, I exit the car and try to remember which side of the backseat holds the battery.

That's the other thing about classic cars—they are quirky. The battery on a VW Bug is actually located under the rear seat bench. Normally I appreciate these eccentricities, but right now it's inconvenient. I think it's on the passenger side, so I slide the front seat forward.

"Jasmine?"

I spin at that voice. It's been a week since I've heard it, but it sends a thrill up my spine. I'd listen to him say my name forever. Well, preferably when my ride isn't dead, and when it's not freezing, but still. The way the syllables roll off his tongue makes my insides melt like butter.

Leaning against the red truck, Hot Cowboy spins his keys around his finger. "You need a hand?"

"Are you following me?" I say, injecting a teasing tone into my voice. "Trying to spill my beer this time so we're even?"

"No, ma'am." He tips his hat, crooked smile illuminated by the yellow glow of the streetlights. It's January, but I warm up under my wool pea coat. Damn, he's hot. "I told you, I love this terrible bar."

"Did you win the coin toss tonight?" I pry up the backseat bench and am victorious—there's the battery!

"Nah, it's my birthday, so the team had to go where I picked."

Straightening, I let my eyes linger on his broad shoulders. I don't have a type. Not fixated with the outer trappings, I'm much more concerned with what a person is like on the inside. But I have to admit, he's nice to look at. And those shoulders—something about them makes me want to grab on to them and climb him like a tree.

"Happy birthday to... I don't actually know your name."

"Cooper."

I was expecting something like Walker, Texas Ranger or Davy Crockett, but Cooper suits him. He holds out his hand to shake and as I take it, electricity zips up my palm and along my arm. Yes, please.

If only I could channel that to jump Herbie.

"To be fair, it's not actually until Friday." He sticks his hands in his jeans pockets, and that highlights his arm muscles. Isn't he cold in just a flannel shirt? Maybe his hotness keeps him warm. "But thanks."

Then he steps closer and peers over my shoulder. "I reckon that's the weirdest place for a battery I've ever seen."

"It's unique, for sure." I get a whiff of his aftershave, or maybe it's his cologne. It's woodsy, clean, and appealing.

"Do you have cables? Need a jump?"

Normally I'd rather gnaw off my arm than admit I need help, but I literally can't jump Herbie without another car.

After I grab the jumper cables from my trunk—which is in the front of my car, not the rear—Cooper re-parks his truck so his battery is closer. He watches as I set up the cables and doesn't try to mansplain how to do it. How refreshing. On my signal, he starts his truck, then wanders back over to me.

"So what brings you out to The Cactus? I, uh, didn't see you on the dance floor."

Was he looking for me? My stomach gives a little flip at the thought.

"Celebrating with some friends." I wave at the flannel shirt stretched across his impressive chest. "Stay dry tonight?"

"Yep, no spills." He rocks on the balls of his scuffed cowboy boots and smiles. When his crooked grin hits me, heat blossoms in my lower belly. "It was a fun time."

"Yet you're out here." And by himself.

"I am." He stares at me, his light brown eyes intense, and I want to step closer to him. But I can't tell if he's interested or just a Good Samaritan.

I glance at my watch to rein in my libido. It's probably been long enough to transfer a little juice, so I get in the driver's seat and give my key another twist. Still nothing. This will be expensive to fix. My stomach churns with anxiety. That means more shifts in the lab, and more chances to run into Chad. I huff, and Cooper comes over and stands by my driver's side door.

"Maybe it's the alternator. I'm not sure there's anything we can do about it tonight. Do you have friends inside who can give you a lift? You headed home?"

"Yeah, but..." If I get desperate, I can wait for my friends to give me a ride, but I don't want to interrupt their date night. And I refuse to enter that disgusting bar again. No, thank you.

"My momma would skin me alive if I left a lady in the lurch. I'm headed to campus. I don't mind. You can figure out your car tomorrow. I'd be happy to drop you off."

His accent is one of the cutest things I've ever heard. If I hadn't been on a date and covered in beer last week, I'd totally have propositioned Cooper. The thought sends another swarm of butterflies through my belly. Herbie's problem could have a silver lining.

"Your momma sounds formidable."

"You don't know the half of it." He gives a dry chuckle and that twist of his mouth slays me, gives me the courage to be bold.

"Will you be a perfect gentleman?" I remove my ignition key from the ring and tuck it under the floor mat for the tow I'm calling later.

"Absolutely." He touches the brim of his hat again and my pulse ratchets up a notch. I've never had a cowboy fetish before, never given it a second thought, but something about that hat and his biceps just do it for me. I'd like to see more.

I bob my brows. "That's disappointing. I like bad boys."

CHAPTER
Seven

COOPER

My mouth drops open as Jasmine saunters towards my passenger side. She smirks, and my brain struggles to catch up. Is this goddess flirting with me? She gives off a sexy librarian vibe, with her hot little body under her flouncy dress and her red pea coat. I'd love to peel it off her, but is she interested in a hookup? I don't want to take advantage of her or overstep like a creep if she just needs a ride home.

We're celebrating my birthday tonight, so I definitely didn't plan to go home alone. I'd danced with a lot of cute women, but none of the conversations I had with them piqued my interest like she did last week. My conversation with Jasmine had stayed with me until the moment I saw her again.

At first, when I spotted her long brown hair and her bright yellow dress on the outskirts of the dance floor, I thought I had conjured her out of thin air because I had been thinking about her so often. It didn't bother the girl I was with when I led her back to her group of friends and hightailed it over to Jasmine. I didn't want to come off like a stalker, following her to the parking lot, but I couldn't pass up the chance to talk to her again. Besides, my momma wouldn't hesitate to skin me alive if I left a girl in distress.

Hustling to her side now, I swing open the door and hold out my hand to help her into my mountain of a truck. When she puts her palm in mine, sparks zing up my spine and my pants get tight. At our contact, she steps closer, eyes wide. Her lips part. What would it be like to kiss her?

A car horn blares in the parking lot, making her jump, and the spell breaks. She climbs into my truck, smoothing her skirt underneath her, and I close the door and try to get a hold of myself.

Getting in, I take a deep breath and start the engine. "So, where do you live?"

She rattles off an address, but I watch her tuck a strand of brown hair behind her ear, only half-listening. My eyes flick to the long column of her throat. My lips want to taste her skin, but I swallow and focus on the road.

"I think I know where that is."

"Head downtown. I'll tell you where to turn."

The radio switches songs, and she frowns at it. "Country? Really?"

I tip my hat towards her, laughing. "What did you expect?"

Shaking her head, her long brown waves shift, and my fingers itch to touch her hair, to see if it feels as silky as it looks. "At least your bad taste is consistent. First The Cactus and now this."

"Bad taste?" I pretend to be offended. "Shouldn't you be nicer to me? I'm giving you a ride, after all. And what's wrong with country music?"

"I had to do a line dance to "Achy Breaky Heart" in the

fourth grade." She gives an exaggerated shiver. "I've never recovered."

"Well, that's fair." I tap the steering wheel and glance over at her lips again. Plump and full, they look soft and kissable. I'd like to find out. "Maybe you need a better introduction."

"And you're the person to teach me, yeah?" Shifting in the seat, she crosses her legs, angling herself towards me and revealing a peek of her thigh. When she catches me staring, she smiles. The coy look she sends me shoots straight to my groin. Do I have a chance with her? I need to remember how to drive, but she's so distracting.

"I could be." My voice comes out gravely, not nearly as smooth as I wanted. "Usually I have a 'driver picks' rule, but I like you. I'll let you change the channel."

Shit, I do like her. She's easy to talk to and the atmosphere in the truck is comfortable. An undercurrent of anticipation crackles down my spine.

Jasmine raises her brows at my confession but ignores it and fiddles with the radio knobs. "You're so kind."

"That's what I've been telling people! Try to spread the rumor, if you can." She giggles at my terrible joke and I don't analyze things any further. After she finds an Ed Sherran song playing, she relaxes back in her seat.

"Is this acceptable?" Waving a hand at the radio, she indicates the music and I nod my head.

"He's no Billy Ray Cyrus, but yeah."

"Thank god." She rolls her eyes but smiles, scooting closer to me. I can smell her perfume, something floral and alluring.

"Awfully high and mighty from the girl who's car died." Pulling up to a stoplight, I send her a flirty look across the console.

"So where do you live?" Jasmine twirls a curl around her finger. I get the vibe she's not asking for information or making conversation—innuendo laces her words. Or am I imagining it because it's what I want to hear? Right now, I want her to be interested in me more than I want a hat trick this weekend. God, don't let me blow this.

I'm not a "get her number" type of guy. I won't call her after we say goodbye the next morning. Cool or not, this has to be a one-time thing. But I want to see where this chemistry could go. Because it could be pretty amazing.

I clear my dry throat. "In the hockey condo near the rink."

"I've, uh, never been in Hockey Hall." That's the nickname of my condo because so many of my teammates live there. "I've always wanted to see it."

Meeting her eyes, the stare she gives me could set an ice rink on fire. I want her. Maybe it's her brightly colored dress, or the way she talks like she means everything she says. But something in me stood up and took notice when she came along with her witty remarks and homemade TARDIS dress. Or maybe it's just those clunky boots. I didn't know I had a combat boot fetish, but damn if they aren't sexier than stilettos.

"You're probably a nice girl—"

"I'm not," she cuts me off, fluffing her skirt and drawing my gaze to her hemline again. She's not tall, but her legs are smooth and lithe. They'd be amazing wrapped around my waist.

"I need to warn you. I'm not a relationship guy, and you—"

"I'm not, either. Well, I'm not a relationship *girl*," she stresses, words laced with scorn. "Boyfriends are the worst. I'm not looking for that. Besides, sex is biological. That it should only happen within the confines of a committed relationship is archaic."

Blinking, I stare for a minute, and my mouth drops open.

Maybe I got this girl all wrong. Wouldn't be the first time, but I'd expected to have to tell her not to expect anything from me other than a good time.

"So what you're saying is--"

"If you have an itch, scratch it." Her voice is matter-of-fact, like she can't understand why I'm confused.

I take a breath. Okay, this is new. But good. "I expected to have to have the talk first."

She shrugs. "Not with me, but thanks for the consideration. It's sweet."

Oh, that's sexy. She's sexy as hell.

"I don't deal in double standards," she says, giving me a closed-lip smile. "I hope you don't either."

She runs a finger up my arm and along my neck, making me shiver despite the heater running in the car. My body tightens in response.

"Nope," I choke out. "I think you broke my brain, that's all."

Jasmine laughs. A full, throaty sound full of genuine joy. "You're funny."

I smile because the compliment does something to my insides I don't really understand. But I like it.

"Alright." I keep my voice casual as I try to play it cool and not veer my truck off the road in my excitement at her words.

"We doing this?" She's quiet, staring at her fingers clasped in her lap and before I can think, I check traffic, and make a u-turn. Heading away from downtown, I drive toward my place instead, anticipation blooming into arousal in my veins.

"Oh yeah." I throw her a grin. Winning the Stanley Cup couldn't feel any better than this.

Waiting for the elevator up to my third-floor apartment, I grip Jasmine's hand. The doors open and we step in, and she turns to face me. Her gaze locks on mine like a challenge and a question. My answer is yes.

Cupping her cheeks, I brush my lips across hers, so slow it makes my chest ache. It's exploratory at first, testing the waters, but the water feels great. Her lips are soft and warm, and my blood rushes faster through my veins. Her floral perfume envelops me. Jasmine steps closer, flattening her palms on my back, and she opens her mouth, deepening the kiss.

God, she tastes delicious. Like the sugar cookies that my grandma used to bake for me when I missed my dad. I slide my tongue against hers and—

"Dude, get a room."

We spring apart and I flip off Charlie, one of our senior defensemen, waiting in the hallway. The elevator must have opened, and I didn't notice. I'm not embarrassed—I don't have room for that. All I can think about is scoring with this girl, and the goal line is less than a hundred feet away.

"We're trying. Get out of the way." Tucking Jasmine against my side, I hustle us down the hallway to my place. She giggles as I fumble for my keys.

"In a hurry?"

"To kiss you again? Yeah."

I finally get the knob to turn, opening the door and letting us in. The minute it swings shut behind us, I have her pressed against the wall, delving into that sweet mouth and kissing her senseless. Her hands are everywhere—in my hair, tugging up my shirt, roaming over my chest and abs. You betcha, that dog'll hunt.

Then she anchors those hands around my neck and jumps, locking her legs around my waist. God, I love a girl who knows what she wants and goes for it. I catch her like I'm returning an easy pass, holding her up with my palms on her perfect ass. This wall is good, but my bed would be even better. We should—

"Pookie! Surprise!"

We freeze. All the blood drains from my body. That voice. That pet name. What in the hell? Stiffening at the interruption, I set Jasmine down and peer around her.

Yep, this is my worst nightmare, sitting on my couch.

"Momma?"

CHAPTER
Eight

JASMINE

Momma?

This has to be the most terrible attempted hook up ever. Which is too bad, because I was really enjoying the way Cooper was kissing me. But the butterflies are gone and my body flashes hot with embarrassment. Getting caught making out by someone's mom—I thought I was past high school horrors. How fast can I get out of here?

"I tried to call," says the pretty blonde lady on the couch. She's in her late forties and despite the awkward situation, a wide smile lights up her face. "Surprise! I, um, didn't know you had company. But this is, um. Well, this must be your girlfriend!"

Girlfriend?

I jump away from him. Is Cooper cheating on someone with me? What a jerk.

Before I can do more than sputter, she's up off the couch and enveloping me in a tight hug. I'm hit with a wave of expensive, exotic perfume and I don't know why, but I hug her back.

"It's you!" She holds me by my shoulders to look at me, still smiling like she's found Baby Yoda. I try to edge away.

"Oh, no, I'm not—"

"Yep." Cooper grasps my hand, squeezing so tight it hurts. "This is my girlfriend, Jasmine. But Momma, what are you doing here?"

Girlfriend???

"I came for your birthday, of course! I just couldn't stand the thought of not seeing my baby." She throws her arms around him and this is my chance. He can make up whatever he wants after I'm gone. I step towards the door, but he keeps a firm grip on my arm, pulling me back. My panic kicks into high gear, my heart races, and I want to sprint out of here.

"And this way I get to meet Jasmine and spend time with her, too!" She pinches my cheek. "Did you know, he didn't even tell me your name? I've been dying to learn all about you."

"Um." What is the proper response to that?

"Mom." Cooper puts his arm around her, dwarfing her with his giant frame, and turns her towards the couch. "This is a great surprise. You being here, I mean. But can you give us a second?"

"I declare, it wouldn't have been as much of a surprise if you had answered your phone." Her tone is like she's channeling my mom when she tells me I deserve seven kids just like me. Must be something all mothers learn. Before I can protest, he pulls me down a short hallway into his bedroom. He closes the door behind us and sinks onto his bed.

I take in the small room in a quick glance. Navy bedspread, desk, dresser, hamper. A hockey team poster on one wall keeps it from being too spartan, and the lack of clutter makes it peaceful. Or it might under other circumstances.

"What the hell is going on?" I square off against him, my hands on my hips. He has some serious explaining to do.

Cooper puts his head in his hands, running his fingers through his hair. My stomach does a little flip because, damn, that's a sexy image. But I hold my ground and stay pressed against the door. Sexy or not, this guy is a train wreck.

Instead of answering, he looks up at me, eyes anguished, and sends me a verbal curveball.

"What's your relationship like with your mom?"

Where is he going with this?

I tap my toe. "Why does it matter what relationship I have with *my* mom? She's not in the other room."

"Are you close?" he says, arching a dark brow.

"Yeah, I guess." I shrug, crossing my arms over my middle. We don't really understand each other, but I know she loves me and is proud of me.

"Do you ever have moments where it's too close?" He sits on the edge of his mattress, observing me.

I grew up in Indianapolis, only an hour away from Harrison. I decided on a solid state school—couldn't afford anything else—and I don't regret my choice. But I know what he means. I'm expected to drive home at least once a month for family dinners and events. Even now, my mom will read me the riot act for letting a day go by without calling her about my summer internship. A text isn't enough. The distance only helps so much.

And his mom is considerably closer at the moment. I think I see what he's getting at.

"It's not a coincidence that 'smother' is only one letter away from 'mother'. Is that why you picked a school in Indiana?" I purse my lips.

He sighs and runs a hand over his messy hair. It shows off his bicep and I'm distracted for a second, but I force myself to focus on how not arousing this situation is.

"Don't get me wrong, I love my momma. Desperately. It's been the two of us on our own for a long time, but I chose a school a thousand miles away because I needed the space." He pauses, looking guilty, and his next words are quiet. "I felt stifled. And like a bad son. Then I... I did something horrible. I lied to get her to stop bugging me."

"You lied and told her you have a girlfriend?" It's a guess, but his stricken face confirms it. Have I been transported into a teen movie? Do people really lie about stuff like this in real life?

"Yeah. And then she shows up and sees us kissing and assumes..." Breaking off, he shakes his head. "She came to surprise me for my birthday and now I have to ruin her visit by telling her I lied."

I bite my lip, and his light brown eyes fill with sadness. My heart lurches. His love for his mom is apparent, and I don't fault him for screwing up. We've all made mistakes, and I don't want mine thrown back in my face, either. After I broke up with Chad, I drove myself crazy, asking how I could have let him control me like he did. I've always been strong and determined. How did he hold such influence over me? But what it comes down to is, I thought he loved me. I made a poor choice, but that doesn't make me a bad person. The same goes for Cooper.

But his mistake doesn't have to affect me. I can be out of here in less time than it takes Scottie to beam me up. If only he would.

He flops on his bed and studies the ceiling. He's in a tough spot, and it really sucks. I feel for him, I do. "I can't believe this is happening."

"What was your plan?" I need to blow out of here, but curiosity gets the better of me.

"Invent a fake break up by the time I'm home this summer." He sighs again, rolling to sit up. "It was a terrible idea. I don't have the sense God gave a goose."

Do geese have a lot of sense? His expressions are something else.

It doesn't matter. I know what's coming, and the answer is no. There's nothing he could say that would convince me to play along with what I'm sure he's going to ask.

"Unless..." He clasps his hands under his chin, full-on begging. His hazel eyes fill with hope and promise and I steel myself against it. "Would you be willing... I mean, it doesn't have to be forever. Just while she's here."

"Absolutely not." I shake my head, sending my waves swinging. "Remember, I gave you my 'not a relationship girl' speech before you beat me to the punch? This is your momma, your problem."

His eyes dart around the room, as if he'll find the answer to his predicament in one of the corners. Then they light up, shining with triumph.

"Your car." He bounces on the bed lightly as his words tumble out. "I'll take care of it. Everything. I'll pay to have it towed to the mechanic's and for all the repairs."

Dollar signs flash through my mind, and I narrow my eyes at him. "I..." I clear my throat. "How do you know I can't afford it? Maybe I'm rich and it's chump change to me?"

"Is it?"

"No." My shoulders sag. Why did I tell him the truth? I huff. "But it could have been."

"That's okay!" His face glows with excitement. "We can help each other out! Mutually beneficial situation."

"No way." Although... I can afford it, but it will take

months of extra shifts checking out lab equipment. Extra time with Chad. More opportunities for him to mansplain everything to me. Ugh.

Cooper brushes off my concerns, then continues talking. "You hate relationships, right?"

"I don't see what that has to do with anything."

This is not really the time to discuss my hangups. His mom is literally waiting on the other side of the door. We better hope she doesn't have her ear pressed against it. My hands get clammy at the thought.

He better hope, I mean. It's not my problem. Even if he rescued me when I needed a ride. I don't owe him anything.

"This would be totally fake." His features brighten, animated. "And it's only for a week. You do this for me, and I'll fix your car. It's a good deal for you. Please?"

I pause. Repairs on vintage cars aren't cheap. Parts are hard to come by and mechanics charge an arm and leg. There's no doubt it will be expensive. If Herbie is fixed, then I don't have to put myself through the months of torture with Chad. His condescending comments, pressuring me to go out with him again. The way he makes me feel two feet tall and does his best to take the joy out of lab work. Versus a week with Cooper, who's been a perfect gentleman. Sweet. Fun. Sexy. It might be worth it.

I bite my lip. Am I actually considering this? This is a bad idea, right? This is probably, definitely, a bad idea.

But I can pretend to be a girlfriend for a week to get my baby fixed. How bad can it be?

Against my better judgment, I hold out my hand for a shake. "Deal."

CHAPTER
Nine

COOPER

I blink. "Really?"

Jasmine scowls. "Yes, really. You just talked me into this, and now you have doubts?"

"No, no, it's great." I hold up my hands, placating her. "I guess I don't know what to do next, though. You're my first fake girlfriend."

She rolls her eyes, then points at my en suite bathroom. "I need a minute while you talk to your mom and figure this out. Just don't tell her I'm secretly pregnant or something."

"If the creek don't rise."

She stops in her path, brow furrowed. "You say the darndest things. What does that even mean?"

"It means I'll try not to."

Jasmine disappears, closing the door behind her, and I exhale. What have I done?

Pacing the length of my room, I try to get a handle on myself. My stomach is tight and a tiny tremor runs through my body. Guilt mixes with nerves as I think about what waits on the other side of the door.

But I have a plan. This isn't too bad. I can fix this.

At least Jasmine agreed to help me. I'm in deeper with this lie than I ever expected. Now I have to go sell it to my mom. Who's a wall away. After she found me about to jump into bed with my fake girlfriend. Sweat breaks out on my skin. Is there any chance I can pull this off?

God, this is embarrassing. What if Momma asks questions about my sex life? We're close, but not *that* close. Her version of *the talk* covered consent and birth control, but nothing more. She always told me to wait until I found a special person and was ready to handle it. I'm sure she's assuming Jasmine is my special person, based on my hands on her ass and the way I was trying to undress her. God.

I sigh and run a haggard hand over my face. How is this my life?

"Cooper?" Momma calls through the door. "Is everything okay?" Time to face the music. I put on a smile. Then I open the door to greet my mom.

"Pookie!" Despite everything, her gaze dances and her grin stretches wide. As she enfolds me in a hug, I'm hit with a bolt of happiness. This situation is terrible, but on the other hand, I miss her, and it's awesome she came to see me to make my birthday special.

"Well, if you were going for a surprise, you achieved it." My smile turns genuine as she pulls back to study me.

Glancing around the living room, she relocates a stack of papers and opts to perch on the brown leather couch. That's a wise move. I wasn't expecting company, and it's pretty messy. Soda cans litter the coffee table, backpacks and hockey gear clutter the entryway. I like to keep things tidy, but my room-mates don't always get the memo.

Despite the disarray, it's a nice place to live. Each one of us four guys has our own room and en suite bathroom branching off a common living room and kitchen. Hunter is filthy rich, and he's outfitted us with a seventy inch flat-screen, PS5, Xbox, and killer surround sound.

The brown leather couches arranged in front of the entertainment center are perfectly worn, plus we have a few massive bean bags for when we have people over. Jonas hung a few movie posters on the wall—vintage *Star Wars, The Godfather*, and *Rocky*—and it's comfortable.

Where are my roommates, anyway? Did Hunter go home with that redhead? Jonas is probably in the library. Are they still out for the evening? I hope so. Evan has a tendency to walk around naked and Momma doesn't need that level of trauma. It's been rough enough as it is.

I try not to look at the wall I had Jasmine pressed up against. No good can come of that.

Tucking her purse at her feet, my mom grins. "Maybe next time you'll answer your phone when I call."

Touché.

"It's a great surprise, Mom, but how did you even get inside?"

"Oh, a nice boy down the hall with a key."

That tracks. It could be any of our teammates. We all leave spare keys with each other in case we get locked out or need assistance. Evan always forgets where he's put his keys when he comes home drunk.

I clear my throat. "But I saw you last month at Christmas. Are you sure you can take off for this?"

She stares at me like my porch light's on, but no one's home. "It's your birthday this week! I just couldn't bear the thought of not seeing you. And this way I can attend your game, too!"

"But how did you get here?"

When she's flown in before, I've always picked her up from the airport. Has my mom mastered Uber? That seems unlikely.

"You'll never guess!" She bounces on the cushion, eyes bright, and I wait for her to tell me. "I bought an RV!"

My mom's family comes from money. So even though she's a single parent, between inherited wealth, a healthy prenup, and alimony, we've never had to worry about how to make ends meet. Hockey scholarships plus a college fund have left me pretty comfortable, too. An RV, though? That's plumb crazy.

"Wow." I stumble over what to say as I try to process. "I... didn't see that coming."

"It's perfect." She beams, pleased as punch with herself and everything about this situation. I wish I'd seen it coming when I invented a girlfriend and dodged all her calls. Then I wouldn't be sitting here like a moron, absolutely blindsided. "This way I can visit you and have a place to stay!"

What was wrong with a hotel?

"But Momma, all that driving by yourself?"

She waves away my concerns. "I'll see the country and not fly over it. I'm looking to travel more, anyway."

I know from experience I can't dissuade her. It would be a waste of energy to try. A thousand miles away wasn't far enough. I should have gone to Oxford. Do they play hockey in England? Or Brazil? I could learn how to play soccer. What about Australia? It's on the other side of the world. Maybe I can bring hockey to them.

"I'm camping at a park here." Folding her hands in her lap, Momma interrupts my mental escape plans. "Now, tell me more about Jasmine. She's as pretty as a peach!"

I ignore her last statement. "Camping in the winter? Can you do that?"

"I've got it all figured out. Now, about Jasmine—"

"Mom." I bite off the word, letting my exasperation bleed into my tone. "You're coming on a little strong. Don't scare her off."

"Fine, fine. I'm just excited to get to know her better. Since you've been so closed-lipped on the topic. Where is she? I can't wait to talk to her!"

"Um, Momma. It's late. I know you're on a different time zone, but I should probably get Jasmine home."

"Oh. I guess that makes sense." Her face falls. "But can we see her tomorrow? How about brunch?"

"Well, I don't—"

"Brunch sounds great." Brushing past me, Jasmine fluffs her skirt and smiles at my mom. "But I don't want to intrude on your time together. I'll just order an Uber and—"

"I think not!" my mom says at the same time I say, "Oh, no, of course I'll drive you home."

Jasmine's glance darts between the two of us. "I'm starting to see the family resemblance."

"Is Cooper not a perfect gentleman around you, Jasmine?" My mom asks, eyes narrowing. "Because no son of mine would—"

"No, everything is fine. He's great." Stepping closer to me, Jasmine gives me a peck on the cheek. It's for the briefest of seconds, but it still makes me wish we hadn't gotten interrupted. She smells good, like coconuts, and it reminds me of warm summer days. "But I hate inconveniencing him and taking him away from you. I'm happy to find my own way home."

"I insist." Lacing our fingers together, I tug her towards

the door. I did offer to see her safely home. Even if it's taken a wild detour, I'd like to keep my word.

"Oh, I'll make myself at home until he get back." Sitting on the couch, my mom makes a big production out of patting the cushions and getting comfortable. "Tomorrow?"

Her eyes shine with hope, and Jasmine nods as I hustle her out of the apartment. "Tomorrow."

I close the door behind me and halt in the hallway, leaning against the wall and taking deep breaths.

"This is unbelievable." Jasmine stares at me. "How in the world did I let you talk me into this?"

"I don't know. I really don't. I'm sorry, and thank you."

"It's only for a week, I guess." She walks towards the elevators and I follow. "I can do anything for a week."

"Yeah."

We ride to the ground floor in silence—such a contrast to our elevator ride up to my apartment when we couldn't keep our hands off each other. Not that I'd be opposed to kissing her like that again, but the mood has shifted.

I lead her out to my truck and help her up into the passenger seat. When I slide behind the wheel and start the car, I mess with the radio until I find my beloved country station again. "Fancy Like," by Walker Hayes plays and Jasmine shakes her head, smiling.

"No taste."

I smile back, and the awkward tension dissipates. "Come on. This is a great song."

"We'll have to agree to disagree on that one." She clears her throat, crossing her legs again and making me wish things were different. "Turn left here, and again on Ninth Street. So. Let's get our story straight."

"Story?" I echo. "What do you mean?"

She gestures around the truck. "How we met, how long

we've been dating, stuff like that. Geez, have you never had a girlfriend before?"

"Nope."

Her eyes go wide. "Really? Why not?"

"I don't believe in love." I shrug, staring out the windshield and waiting for her censure.

"Do you love your mom?"

"Sure. But romantic love—it's an illusion created by Hallmark to sell cards. It only creates problems."

Most girls I've said this to look at me like I'm nuts, but Jasmine shifts to face me. "That's what I keep saying! My friends think I'm crazy."

"Mine too!" I almost have a hard time believing this is happening. She's not arguing or trying to convince me I'm wrong. "It's not worth it."

"Not at all."

I glance across the console, a teasing smile playing around my mouth. "So you have no problem promising you won't fall in love with me?"

Jasmine snorts. "There's absolutely no chance."

CHAPTER
Ten

COOPER

Yawning, I take another sip of the fancy coffee I got from a drive through on the way here and park in front of Jasmine's light green, sprawling Victorian house. I didn't sleep well last night and I'm hoping the beverage helps. My dreams started out with sexy images of Jasmine, but then would switch to my mom yelling at me. It doesn't take a psychologist to decipher my subconscious, but even if the meaning is clear, I kept tossing and turning.

Grabbing my drink and the second one I picked up for her, I get out of my truck and head to Jasmine's front porch. I juggle the cups to knock, but before I can, the door swings open and she pulls me inside.

My mouth drops open. She's piled her hair into a messy bun on top of her head and she's wearing a floor-length fuzzy black bathrobe covered in bright neon-colored Star Wars quotes. It's unexpected, to say the least.

"Shhhh." She puts her finger to my lips when I go to

speak, the whites of her eyes showing and making her look wild. "I overslept and I'm freaking out."

Instead of talking, I hand her a cup and watch as she closes her eyes, takes a sip, then visibly inhales and exhales.

"Thanks for the coffee," she says, her voice quiet. "It helps."

"You okay?"

She shakes her head. "I've been up all night, overthinking everything and worrying. This is the dumbest thing I've ever agreed to."

Is she backing out on me? My stomach drops, and I gulp. "Look, Jasmine—"

"Keep your voice down!" Her words come out a hiss. "I'm not ready to explain this to my roommates. They're still sleeping. So stealth mode, okay?"

She's not kicking me out. Yet. I nod and take a swig of coffee. It's too hot and too sweet, but I drink it anyway.

"Can we talk about it?"

"Yeah." She grabs my free hand, her fingers smooth in mine. I remember all the places I wanted her to put them last night and stifle a groan. She tugs me past a riot of color in the living room. A brightly patterned rug, mismatched chairs, art prints, and vining green plants create a warm environment. It looks like a place I'd like to hang out. But I don't get to make myself comfortable because she yanks me behind her up the wooden staircase.

Are we headed up to her room? Her bed, where she—

Nope, that won't help. Not when we're supposed to meet my mom in a few minutes. I can't let my mind wander to what Jasmine may or may not have on under her bathrobe right now. I force myself to focus.

We tiptoe past a series of closed doors in the dim, narrow upstairs hallway. The only light comes in muted through a stained-glass window at the top of the stairs. Pulling me into her room, the second door on the left, she pushes me down on her bed, but not for the reason I was fantasizing about.

Muttering, she throws open her closet and flips through dresses. "I feel totally unprepared. I don't really have a 'meet the parents' outfit. I hate boring clothes."

"Wear whatever you want." I shrug. "I don't care. It's not like you have to worry about impressing my mom."

Her brow furrows. "What do you mean?"

"Well, it's only for a week. We're going to break up soon, right?"

She pales. "Oh my gosh, do you need me to be horrible on purpose? So your mom is glad when we end things?"

Before I can answer, her eyes go wide and she rushes on. "Your mom is so nice. I'm not sure I can be bitchy to her."

I'd do anything to erase the line between her eyebrows. "No, no. Be yourself. I don't want her to think I have poor taste. It's just—it's a no-pressure situation. It doesn't matter what she thinks of you because it's not permanent."

This must have been the correct thing to say because she perks up, grabbing a flouncy skirt, leggings, and a Star Wars t-shirt from her closet. I love all the girly skirts she wears, paired with random shirts and boots. Something about the combination does it for me.

Holding her clothes in front of her like a shield, she stares at me and bites her lip. "Um, I know this might sound weird, but I've been thinking about it and we probably shouldn't sleep with each other now."

I'm hit with a rush of excitement that she's been thinking about sleeping with me—and disappointment settles like a pit in my stomach that she doesn't want to anymore. It must show on my face because she rushes to explain.

"Not that I think it would be a bad experience or something. It's just—you're paying to have my car fixed. If I slept with you, wouldn't that be a little like trading sexual favors for money?"

Hmm. I see where she's coming from. I don't want her to feel weird about things.

Personally, I wouldn't mind a friends with benefits situation but, even that is too much attachment for most girls, as I learned the hard way. Chelsea, freshman year, played it like she was cool with being make-out buddies. I thought things were fine for a month until she got drunk and confessed she wanted more. When I told her no, she sobbed on my chest and sent me sad puppy dog looks in the dining hall for the rest of the semester. I'm not doing that again. I can't handle the guilt most girls pour on like chocolate syrup.

Jasmine gave me the "no strings" speech first, though, so I don't have to worry about her catching feelings. What it comes down to is, if she doesn't want to sleep with me, I won't make her uncomfortable. That's all that matters.

Although I might still flirt with her.

"I have to ask—is it because my momma is the world's biggest cockblock? You're worried I can't actually close the deal?"

She busts out laughing, easing the grip on her bundle of clothes. "She might be. I guess I should ask—does she do that every time you're about to hookup with someone?"

"You're the first."

"I should feel honored." She pauses, then stares at me, her eyes serious. "Thanks for understanding."

Linking my fingers behind my head, I lay back on her bed and make myself comfortable. "It's probably for the best."

Although I can't say it's my first choice. I'm having a hard time not thinking about how much I want to see her naked.

I clear my throat, forcing myself to recite my hockey stats in my head.

"Alright, I'm gonna shower. I'll be quick." Then she rounds on me, her voice stern as she points her finger in my face. "No snooping in my room. Stay here and be quiet."

With that, she disappears.

I don't snoop. Not really. I mean, I don't go through her drawers. But I survey her room. I don't know her all that well yet, but it fits her. It's welcoming, tidy, but not intimidating. Not fancy or upscale, but still nice. A crazy crocheted quilt covers her bed, a swirl of mismatched colors thrown together. A papasan chair is perched in the corner, with a stack of books on a side table next to it. There's a fluffy rug under my feet and *Stranger Things, Doctor Who*, and *Lord of the Rings* posters line the walls. It's not Instagram perfect, but I bet she loves everything in it. She doesn't seem like a girl who'd surround herself with stuff she's not into.

A series of framed photos on her desk catches my attention, and I peer closer. Jasmine with a group of girls, smiling wide. Squeezed in between a couple that must be her mom and dad, because she has her dad's green eyes and her mom's square jaw. Hugging a woman in a white wedding dress who has to be her sister—they share matching grins.

I don't notice the passing of time until the door creaks open behind me and I spin. Jasmine clears her throat.

"Like what you see?" She motions at the pictures on her desk, but I look her up and down instead. She wears the clothes she picked out earlier, hair pulled on top of her head in a sleek ponytail, and another pair of combat boots, this time in red. I lick my lips.

"Yeah, I do."

A blush colors her cheeks and she glances down at the

hardwood. "So, what's our story? We never did talk about it last night."

I jerk my thumb towards the door. "Can we figure it out on our way?"

Nodding, she tosses on a gray cardigan sweater and her red coat and follows me out to my truck. Huffing a laugh, she hauls herself into the passenger seat.

"What's so funny?" I slide behind the wheel and start the car, turning up the heat for her.

"Your car is about as opposite from Herbie as possible."

"Herbie? You named your car?"

"Yes, okay?" Her tone is defensive. "I think cars need names."

"Me, too." I pat the dash. "Meet Bubba. The team named him."

The smile that spreads across her face sends my pulse racing. "It's perfect."

"So." I clear my throat. "How did we meet?"

"As close to the truth as possible is probably best. At O'Bryan's, I spilled beer all over you."

"But not last week." I tap the steering wheel. "That's not enough time."

"How about... three weeks ago?" A tendril of hair escapes her bun, brushing her cheek, and god, I want to taste her again. I shift in my seat.

"Yeah, after we returned from Christmas break. That fits."

"And then you got my number, like a perfect gentleman, and asked me out to coffee, and we started dating after that."

I give her a sidelong glance. "And we definitely didn't sleep together right away."

"Nope." She fluffs her skirt over her legs. "We waited until the third date, because we're respectable."

Chewing on her nails again, she lapses into silence. Her

73

thoughts feel heavy in the small space, but I don't know what to ask.

"I'm struggling," she finally says, "with how to act around your mom."

"What do you mean? Just be yourself." I check traffic before making a left turn, then fiddle with the heat. I hope she's warm enough.

"But shouldn't you want her to dislike me because we're going to break up? Then she can bad-mouth me to feel better after I dump you."

"You dump *me*?" I fake shock. "I'm totally dumping you."

Jasmine laughs, the tension dissipating from her posture. "But then, if she likes me, she'll be mad at you for dumping me."

Her points make sense. But Jasmine is doing me a solid. It's stupid, but I don't want my mom to hate her.

"I'll figure it out when the time comes. For now, just be yourself." Reaching out, I squeeze her shoulder, then turn back to the road.

"You sure?" She hesitates, fingers hovering over the handle as I park the car.

"Yep. You're cool. It will be fine."

CHAPTER
Eleven

JASMINE

How in the world did I get myself into this? I've sworn off relationships entirely, and now I have a fake one? Am I insane?

I dated Chad for two years, but never met his parents. And the guy I dated in high school, Brady, had been a family friend for as long as I can remember. We grew up together. It felt natural to date him, almost inevitable. It was more about proximity than anything. And I had known his parents since I was a kid—there was no formal introduction moment. I'm galaxies beyond my element today.

But Cooper needed a girl, and I'm getting Herbie fixed. It's a win-win situation. Is it bad that we're lying to Cooper's mom? Totally. But I won't be around long enough for her to get attached. Plus, we only need to fool her. There's no reason for anyone else—like my friends—to hear about it. I'd never live it down.

It's no big deal. We're business partners.

After he parks his truck, he hustles around the front of

the vehicle and opens the passenger door, giving me a hand to help me out. Normally, this sort of behavior would drive me crazy—I can get out of a car on my own. But his truck is massive. It feels like I'm jumping off a cliff every time I have to exit. So I don't mind his assistance. It's kinda cute.

We're meeting his mom at Jackie's, a local place. It's a classic, and a safe bet for parents. It's also off-campus, which benefits me today. I doubt we'll run into anyone we know.

A blast of welcome, warm air hits me in the foyer. With its dark beams and wine-colored booths, Jackie's is nice without being too fancy. Framed black and white old-school Hollywood posters decorate the walls and colorful lamps create a homey feel.

Cooper's mom spots us in the entryway, waving enthusiastically from a booth. Putting his hand on the small of my back, he guides me as we weave through the tables and slide in across from her. It's a gentlemanly gesture, protective and old-fashioned, but I'm learning that's a part of who Cooper is. Instead of coming across as condescending, it feels sweet.

Her wide grin threatens to split her face in two as we sit. Three glasses of water are already waiting on the dark tabletop, along with silverware wrapped in white cloth napkins.

"Jasmine." I'm thankful she doesn't leap over the table to hug me. Her voice is brimming with delight. "I am just tickled pink to meet you!"

"Uh, hi, Mrs. Edwards. How was your trip?"

"Momma." Cooper leans across the table, whispering his words as an aside. "You're coming on a little strong."

"Oh, sorry." She covers her mouth with her hand, giggling. "And please, call me Madelyn. It's only—Cooper's never had a girlfriend before. I actually thought he was gay."

Cooper spits out the sip of water he had taken, coughing. "Mom!"

I pound him on the back as he sputters, and his mom wipes up the liquid with her napkin. "Sorry, pookie! It wouldn't be a problem if it was true—I just like knowing."

"That should be your warning label," he says under his breath. "*I just like knowing.*"

But Mrs. Edwards doesn't take offense. Instead, she beams at him. "Well, I do. So Jasmine, what's your major?"

"Chemistry. I plan to go to grad school after this so I can work for a pharmaceutical company."

Her eyes widen. "Oh, she's more than a pretty face, Cooper. This one's a catch."

I blush at her praise, and Cooper puts his head in his hands. "Could you stop? You're embarrassing Jasmine. Act like a normal person, Momma."

The waiter appears at that moment and takes our orders —omelet for Mrs. Edwards, French toast for me, and a massive farmer's breakfast for Cooper.

My face must show my surprise at the amount of food, because as the waiter retreats, Cooper says, "I need a lot of calories, what with hockey and all."

Mrs. Edwards lights up. "Oh, Jasmine, do you like hockey?"

"Um." I've seen glimpses on TV before but never actually been to a game. Like everyone in Indianapolis, my family roots for the Colts, but that's the extent of my sports knowledge. Based on her expectant stare, though, there's only one way to reply to this question. "I'm sure I'll love it."

"She, ah, hasn't seen me yet." Cooper puts his arm around me, and it feels like he's shielding me from a potential conflict. Momma must be passionate about her boy and his hockey. "Away games and schedule conflicts."

"Yeah, I have evening lab hours." I can't help it. I lean in to him. His muscular chest is so tempting. He's warm and smells fresh, like clean soap. "But I will go as soon as I can."

"How about this week?" Mrs. Edwards says, beaming. "There's a game on Cooper's birthday. You can sit with me!"

Oh god. My mouth drops open. Panic flutters in my chest and my heartbeat thuds in my ears. How long is a hockey game? If it's longer than ten minutes, how can I handle being alone with Mrs. Edwards? She's sweet, but I'll say the wrong thing for sure and blow it.

I'm saved from having to answer when our food arrives. Cooper's eggs, sausage, hash browns, toast, and fruit take up two plates, and he scoots closer to me, our knees bumping under the table. The proximity sends a charge through me. I force images of last night and what could have been out of my brain.

I drown my French toast in syrup and shove a bite into my mouth before Mrs. Edwards can ask me more about hockey. I enjoy a moment of relief as she turns to Cooper.

"What should we do to celebrate your birthday? Remember the year you turned eight and had a pirate-themed party? I could wear my mermaid costume again."

His cheeks redden. "No, thanks."

"Or what about the time I hired a clown to make balloon animals? You slept with that dog he made you until it popped!" She laughs in delight as Cooper shakes his head.

"You realize I'm turning twenty-two, right, Momma? I usually go out with my friends these days."

Patting his hand, she wipes her lips with her napkin. "I know, pookie. I just treasure those memories so much. He was so cute," she says to me. "Here, let me show you pictures."

"Mom!" An older couple at the next table glance over at

his sharp tone. "No pictures! And how about we go out for ice cream? You'd love the Silver Spoon."

Looking like the cat that ate the canary, she slides her phone back in her purse and winks at me. Wow, that was some next-level manipulation. Mrs. Edwards might seem ditzy, but she's not to be underestimated. I'll need to stay on my toes around her, even if it's only for a week.

"The Silver Spoon, it is. And Jasmine and I can go to the game together beforehand. I'll teach her all about hockey and we can have some girl time."

Cooper sends me an alarmed glance and squeezes my fingers. "Mom, that's—"

"That sounds great." I gulp. *Herbie. I can do this for Herbie.* It's only one game.

Finishing her eggs, Mrs. Edwards wraps both hands around her coffee mug and shivers. "I declare, Cooper did not prepare me for how cold Indiana is in January!"

Finally, a safe topic. "It's brutal. I grew up here and I'm never prepared for it."

"Oh, really? Where?"

"I'm from Indianapolis. It's an hour away. My mom and dad still live there, and my sister and her husband both have jobs in the city."

"That's wonderful that you stayed so close to home." After smiling at me, she turns a pointed glare on Cooper and I wince. Whoops.

"Scholarships, Momma!" He mumbles his words around a bite of toast.

"Nonsense. You had scholarships to the University of Texas, too." Then she exhales, as if she's forcing herself to let it go. "Although I'm glad you're happy here—and you wouldn't have found Jasmine if you had stayed in Texas."

Now it's my turn to choke on my water. It doesn't spray

across the table, at least, but dribbles down my chin. God, this woman is ready to plan our wedding. She's as cute as an Ewok, but I understand why Cooper lied to her. A dog with a bone is less determined.

"But anyway." She hands me a napkin, my spit-take not slowing her down. "I don't think I own enough winter clothes for this week. And I want to get a hockey sweatshirt to wear to your game. Will you two come to the bookstore with me today and help me pick one out?"

"You can borrow mine." Cooper pops the rest of his sausage in his mouth and wipes his fingers.

"Nonsense. I'd look silly, swimming in your giant clothes. Plus, I want one that says 'Harrison Mom' on it."

He rolls his eyes. "I could have gotten you that for Christmas."

"I'd like to pick it out myself. Can we go now?"

I pout outwardly, but inwardly I'm having a party. "Unfortunately, I have class and then lab hours, so I can't join you."

"Oh, I really need a woman's opinion, honey. Cooper gives terrible advice. I'll wait and go when you can come, too."

I'm not getting out of this, am I? All part of the gig, I suppose, and this woman doesn't give up. I sigh to myself. "How's tomorrow morning?"

CHAPTER
Twelve

COOPER

After exchanging numbers with her, I drop Jasmine off for class and attend mine. Afterwards, I send my mom to the grocery store, distracting her with the idea that I need a home-cooked meal. Then I get Jasmine's car towed and arrange for repairs to begin right away. She deserves it after that interrogation at breakfast.

Did Momma buy our ruse? There's nothing to indicate otherwise. Why would she suspect that her only son is lying to her?

My stomach churns. I've gotta pull it together.

A brisk knock sounds at the apartment door, and I stiffen. That was faster than I expected. I open the door and my mom breezes in, arms laden with grocery bags.

"Here, let me help."

"Nonsense." Bustling past me, she dumps them on the counter, then unloads and stocks the small pantry in the kitchen's corner. Opening the fridge, she tsks. "Beer is not on the food pyramid."

"Uh, thanks for going shopping. I've missed your spaghetti."

"Oooh, let's invite Jasmine over, and I'll teach her how to make it for you!"

"Momma." Grabbing her shoulders, I halt her progress around the kitchen and stare into her light brown eyes. "You need to stop."

"Stop what? My son finally has a girlfriend, and she's lovely. I'm happier than a pig in slop!" She shrugs out of my grip and turns back to the stove. "You have a can opener, right?"

Wordlessly, I fish it out of a drawer for her.

"I probably should have checked to see if you have the correct pots and pans first..." Her words are muffled as she throws open an oak cabinet and sticks her head inside.

"Mom, focus." Spinning to face me, her gaze flashes a warning. I hold up my hands in surrender. "I know, you brought me into this world, you can take me out. But I think you're getting a little too far down the path."

"What do you mean?" Resuming her task, she locates two pots, one big and one medium-sized, and a skillet.

"Well, Jasmine and I haven't been dating for all that long."

I can't tell her it's not serious. She found us about to jump into bed together, and she assumes I wouldn't sleep with a girl I'm not serious about. What's another lie at this point?

I tap my fingers on the counter. "And she's pretty independent—she might resent the idea that she's supposed to cook my favorite meals for me."

"Maybe you should learn to whip up spaghetti for her, then."

I latch onto the distraction. "Okay, let's do it."

My mom's face lights up. She explains how to make the sauce, demonstrating as she works. After setting up the water to boil for the noodles, I brown the hamburger. My plan was to take her focus off Jasmine, but it's sweet to get to spend time with my mom like this. I've missed the little things of home.

Stirring the sauce, she clears her throat. "I'm sorry I was a little... intense. It's just... I think I got swept away by the excitement of new love."

I stifle a gag. "It's too soon to use that word, Mom."

And it's not in the cards for me. Love isn't real. It's all meaningless emotions and brain chemicals. It doesn't last. After the illusion fades, all that's left is heartache and sorrow. No thanks. I'll never let anyone hurt me like that.

"I'll try to rein it in a little, pookie."

"Is there any chance you could stop calling me that?"

"Only a snowball's in hell."

"I figured."

She grins at me, and I grin back. We subside into silence after that. We work well in tandem, and I'm transported back to my years at home. Working twice as hard to also be the dad I needed, Momma did her best to ensure I never felt unloved or lesser. Even though her heart was broken. I'm a lucky bastard, and she deserves better than a son who lies to her.

I can't take it anymore. I have to come clean. "Mom, I—"

"Whoa, what smells so good?"

Evan and Hunter burst into the apartment, stopping short at the sight of me and my mom in the kitchen.

"Mrs. Edwards!" Evan bounds over and gives my mom a kiss on the cheek. "It's awesome to see you!"

I glare at him, reminding him to have boundaries.

"Madelyn, please, you know that." She smiles, her cheeks pinking.

"And dinner smells amazing." Hunter pops into the kitchen to hug her.

"Thank you, dear. I'm so excited to spend a little time with you boys and Cooper's girl."

Oh, shit. They stare blankly at her. Before anyone can speak, I grab my roommates' arms and drag them into my bedroom.

"Uh, y'all, I need to talk to you. Hockey stuff." I slam the door, exhaling.

"Sheesh." Evan rubs his bicep where my fingers gripped it. "Chill out."

"Evan." I stare at him. "Think about all the things you don't want your mom to know about your life. Imagine if she was here for a week."

Gulping, he pales. "Okay, maybe I can see where you're coming from. But what's going on?"

"Right." I stare at the floor. How do I explain the mess I'm in?

Hunter raises an eyebrow. "What's she talking about, man?"

"I did something stupid. My mom wouldn't get off my case about having a girlfriend, so I made one up."

Evan bursts out laughing, and I cover his mouth, shushing him and glancing at my bedroom door. "Keep your voice down! I can't let her hear this."

Once he nods, I remove my hand. "Anyway. I said I had a girlfriend—"

"Thinking she'd never meet her," Hunter cuts me off, nodding his understanding.

"Exactly. But when she got here, uh, I had brought a girl back with me. I didn't know my mom was in the living room. We were going at it pretty hot and heavy, and—"

Evan bursts into giggles again, grabbing his belly.

"I hate you." I roll my eyes.

"So wait." Hunter rubs his temples. "Your mom saw you with a girl and assumed she was your girlfriend?"

"Yes. I mean, I couldn't say I was cheating on my fake girlfriend. And I, um, bribed her to play along."

Evan's laughter stops, and he straightens. "Damn, dude. This is serious."

Chuckling dryly, Hunter shakes his head. "Don't you see the irony? Your first girlfriend, and it's fake. Do you even know how to pretend to be a boyfriend?"

"I'll be an amazing fake boyfriend."

Hunter shrugs. "If you say so. This sounds like a terrible idea to me."

"I'll tell my mom we've broken up next week when she's gone. It won't hurt anyone. But she's definitely gonna ask about this because she's obsessed. The important part is—her name is Jasmine and we've been dating for a few weeks. You haven't met her yet because, uh…"

My mind goes blank. This is the dumbest thing I've ever done.

"You were worried we'd scare her off." Hunter snaps his fingers. He doesn't approve of this, but he still won't let me fail. He's the best.

I point at him. "Right, that's good."

"Dude, it's fine." Evan claps a hand on my shoulder. "I've been lying to my mom since birth. I've got this."

Why doesn't that make me feel better?

"Y'all, supper's ready!" Momma knocks.

Hunter blocks the door. "Are you sure about this?"

"Lying to my mom? No, but I'm in deep. And it's only for a few more days."

He narrows his gaze. "No, I mean, faking this. I've seen movies, and it never ends well."

That's the one thing I am sure of. I scoff. "Please, man. It's fool-proof. I picked the perfect girl. She's sworn off relationships, and I'm never falling in love. It's not possible. There's nothing to worry about."

With that, I throw open the door and prepare to lie my ass off some more.

CHAPTER
Thirteen

JASMINE

Yesterday, before he dropped me off, Cooper programmed his number into my phone. It buzzes in my pocket now, as I slip into my lab coat and safety goggles. Pulling it out, I read his message.

Cooper: *My mom has her heart set on a trip to the bookstore with you this morning. Can I pick you up?*

It's just a few more days. I'll be fine.

Jasmine: *I'll meet you there in 30 minutes.*

It doesn't take me long to check my samples, record my findings, and reset the equipment. No graduate students or Chad interrupt the quiet of the lab this morning. I put in my earbuds and let the routine soothe me. Chemistry makes sense. The formulas, the protocols, the patterns that emerge from repetition. I lose myself in my work and when I shrug out of my lab coat, I'm ready to face this next challenge.

Time to channel fake girlfriend mode. Let's go.

It's cold today, but there's no biting wind, so instead of taking the tunnels, I walk outside. It's half a mile to the bookstore, but in my long down parka, plus the hat and gloves I crocheted, I stay warm. The trees are bare and the grass is brown, but the campus is still beautiful, with its tall brick buildings and neatly manicured lawns. There's something about the tidy order of it that reassures me.

A few minutes later, I push open the door to the bookstore, bell jangling, and Cooper hustles over to me. Mrs. Edwards waves from a rack of orange and navy sweatshirts.

"Hey, darlin'." He kisses me on the cheek, perfectly appropriate since his mom is watching, but my stomach swoops, remembering our fevered kisses the other night. "I know you don't have a car. I would have been happy to give you a ride."

I wave away his concerns. "Nah, I'm fine. It's not too bad out today."

"It's absolutely freezing!" Mrs. Edwards apparently knows me well enough now to pull me in for a hug, or it's a bid for body heat. "Come help me pick out some swag."

"Uh, Momma, you're too old to use that word."

"Nonsense, pookie!" She winks at him and loops her arm through mine, tugging me to a display of fleece pullovers. "What do you think, Jasmine? What should I get?"

I finger the soft material. "This is nice. Warm, too."

"Which one would you buy?"

I wince. "I don't have much Harrison stuff. Not really my style."

I'm not opposed to a comfy sweatshirt with leggings. But the students I see in head-to-toe Griffins gear—I can't handle that. So I've avoided the apparel section of the bookstore since freshman year.

Mrs. Edwards gasps and steers me toward a table. "I declare, you need a hockey shirt! You can wear it when we go to the game together."

"About that." Cooper appears at my side, interlocking our fingers. "Jasmine's busy. She—"

"It's okay. I want to see you play, and it's your birthday. Of course I'll be there." It's what a dutiful girlfriend would do, but I'm interested to see him in action.

His mom beams at me and starts picking out t-shirts. And probably my wedding china, too.

"Oh. My. God."

At the familiar voice behind me, I drop Cooper's palm and spin. Staci cocks a hand on her hip and gives us a once-over. Delaney stands next to her, too, gray eyes wide and mouth hanging open.

"Delaney, doesn't that look just like Jasmine?" Delaney nods at Staci's sarcastic tone, blinking. "But it clearly can't be, because she was holding hands with a boy."

Shit, shit, shit.

"Surprise." My voice is weak, and my knees get wobbly. I really didn't want them to know about this. Pointed questions from my roommates in front of Mrs. Edwards could ruin everything. Cooper laces his fingers through mine again, and I take a deep breath. His solid presence next to me keeps me grounded.

"Um, hi. I'm Cooper."

Delaney gasps. "The accent! This is the hot cowboy."

Busted. I mentioned that to them before I became his fake girlfriend. He sends me a look that absolutely smolders and then smiles at my friends. "A pleasure to make your acquaintance, ladies."

His charm is deadly. A blush colors Delaney's cheeks. It will be fun to mention that to Brian later. But Staci is unmoved. She raises a brow at our conjoined hands.

"So, how long has this been a thing?"

89

"Three weeks," Cooper says, glancing at his mom before I can say anything.

Blinking, Staci takes a step closer. "Wow. Why didn't you tell us?"

"Um." What can I say to that? We invented it two days ago? I cut my eyes to Mrs. Edwards, hoping Staci reins it in and doesn't blow this up like the Death Star.

"That's my fault," Cooper jumps in. "It was so new. I wanted to meet you in person, and I've been so busy with hockey."

"Hockey?" Staci's eyebrows practically disappear into her hairline. "You're dating a hockey player? Jasmine, could you even pick a hockey puck out of a lineup?"

"Why would a hockey puck be in a lineup? Did it mug me?" I pop a hand on my hip.

Staci rolls her eyes. "I'm just saying, you're not really sporty."

"I think it's great. Nice to meet you officially, Cooper. I'm Delaney." She elbows Staci, who says her name while he shakes both their hands.

Then Staci points at us. "This explains so much about our night at O'Bryan's."

I can't believe I'm lying to her. I'm the worst friend ever. I clutch the orange hockey shirt in my fists and think fast. "No, that's my fault. I wasn't sure what to say, how to admit I was wrong about relationships. How to tell you. But I'm happy."

With a look at Mrs. Edwards, who's watching us like this is better than a Netflix binge, I press up on my toes and plant a kiss on Cooper's cheek. I try to sell it, but I don't have to fake how much I like his hand on the small of my back. God, he smells good. I love his woodsy cologne.

"You were wrong? I love those words."

"Staci!" Delaney's tone scolds her, but she laughs, taking the sting out of it, and I have the grace to chuckle, too.

Staci points to the shirt I'm still holding. "You're buying Harrison gear? This is a day of firsts. Don't tell me this guy has already changed you."

Her voice is light, but the concern in her expression is real. And she has reason to worry after Chad. I shake my head.

"Just broadening my horizons."

Raising a brow, she looks skeptical. "It sounds like we have some catching up to do."

Delaney gasps, then grabs Staci's arm. "You know what this means?"

At our blank looks, she bounces on her toes, still gripping Staci. "We can triple date now!"

Staci's face lights up. "Yes! Finally! No more blind dates for Jasmine."

This is all it took? Interesting.

She glances at Cooper. "Can you come over for a movie tonight? We've been waiting for this day forever. We'll invite our boyfriends and we can all get to know each other better."

Cooper's eyes go wide and he blinks, stiffening beside me. "Oh, um, not tonight. My momma—"

"Nonsense!" Mrs. Edwards inserts herself into the conversation, smiling like she's won the lottery. "I don't want to keep you two apart!"

"How about tomorrow?" Delaney asks, eyes brimming with hope.

"As long as it's not on Friday!" Mrs. Edwards beams. "Jasmine's coming with me to a hockey game."

Guess I'm not getting out of that. We share a look, me silently begging and him acquiescing.

He winces, but gives my hand a reassuring squeeze. "The

hockey schedule is tough to work around. How do you feel about Sunday?"

"That would be perfect! Come over around six." Staci and Delaney look triumphant, but I feel nauseous.

"Um, great." With a smile that doesn't reach his eyes, Cooper nods to my friends. "It's a date."

This has spiraled so far out of my control, I can't imagine what's next.

CHAPTER
Fourteen

COOPER

As I step out of my lecture hall, my phone buzzes in my pocket.

Jasmine: Can you meet me at the Starbucks in the Union?

Cooper: Sure. What's up?

Jasmine: It's time to cram. See you soon.

I don't understand what that means, but I'll find out when I get there. I zip up my black parka and pull my orange Harrison stocking cap lower on my head to cover my ears. This section of campus is a freezing wind tunnel.

Jogging a little to stay warm and get inside faster, I'm out of breath as I tug open the massive door to the Student Union. Portraits of former deans and university presidents line the walls of the old building, until I round a corner and, incongruously, the Starbucks mermaid winks at me.

From a tiny circular table tucked in the back, Jasmine waves. Her wavy brown hair frames her face and she sips her drink. I point at the line, indicating I'm going to place an order, and she nods.

I study her out of the corner of my eye as I wait for the barista. She shuffles a pile of papers in front of her and organizes them into a three-ring binder. She has a cute habit of biting her lip as she reads. God, she was a good kisser. I wish my mom hadn't interrupted us, because in those few minutes in the elevator, I could tell that things would have been rockin' between us. Pour one out for the hookup that never was.

"Next!" The barista calls, and the person behind me in line pokes me between my shoulder blades. Whoops. I step up to the counter and order.

After they call my name—spelled Copper on my cup, but it could be worse—I slide into the chair across from Jasmine.

"Hey, darlin'. What's up?"

She eyes the orange beanie on my head, and I pull it off, running my fingers through my messy hair. "No cowboy hat today?"

I smirk at her. "Sorry, too cold. You think my look is hot, huh?"

Hell yeah, I heard what her friend said about Hot Cowboy. I puff up my chest with pride.

Her checks color, and she stares at her open binder on the table. But she doesn't deny it. Then she sips her drink. "It was unfortunate, running into my roommates this morning. Thanks for playing along."

"Of course." I tap my fingers on the side of my white cup, waiting.

"I've been thinking about things between us. My friends are... Well, they're going to have a lot of questions. And your mom, too, I'm sure. We have to prove we know each other." Her words come out in a rush as she points to her papers with a pen. "That's why I have these relationship questionnaires."

My mouth hangs open as I take in the color-coded sticky tabs. "How many questions are there?"

"One hundred ninety-seven. But I eliminated some that—"

"Jasmine." Leaning forward, I cut her off. "I have to confess something."

"Oh, that's question fifty-six. Tell me a secret that no one else knows." She flips through the binder, then stares at me, waiting.

"Um, it's not that sort of confession." Her face falls. "But I told my roommates you're not really my girlfriend. And you're only doing this favor for me. So if it would be easier, we can tell your friends the truth, too."

She winces. "They cornered me over lunch. I'm in pretty deep. The other thing, though..." Shifting in her seat, she twirls a piece of her hair, leaning forward. I get a whiff of her perfume, or maybe it's her shampoo? It smells like coconuts, exotic and delicious. "I get it now. Why you lied to your mom."

I raise a brow, and she continues. "My friends had been bugging me about having a boyfriend for so long, setting me up on terrible blind dates and pushing it hard. Now the pressure is off."

"Until we break up next week. Are you sure it's worth it?"

"But that can help my cause, too. When we break up, I can be so broken-hearted that I swear off men and relationships again and they give me some space."

I shake my head. "What if your friends hate me for breaking your heart and hunt me down for revenge? I don't want angry women on my tail."

"Hmm." Jasmine taps her chin with her pen. "That's a

good point. Okay, I'll get cold feet and break up with you. They'll believe that because of my relationship track record."

"Wait, how'd I come out of this looking pathetic?" I pretend to be offended.

She shrugs. "Pathetic, or harassed by my scary friends. Take your pick."

"Are you sure there's no other option? A door number three?"

"Oh, sorry." She acts like a faux-disappointed game show host, sticking out her bottom lip. "For a different option, you'd need to convince a different girl to be your fake girlfriend."

"Guess I'll stick with the one I've got." I wink at her, taking a swig of my coffee.

"So that's settled." Then she points at my cup. "What's that?"

I blink at her weird question. "Uh, a flat white?"

Flipping through her binder, she jots something into a blank on the page.

"Are you serious? You're writing down my answers?"

"Dead serious." She narrows her eyes. "We have to convince my friends we've been dating for three weeks. There are things I need to know."

"Okay." Leaning forward, I bob my brows at her. "What's your favorite sexual position? That's something I'd definitely know."

A blush creeps up her neck. Teasing her is so much fun. "Your mom won't ask that."

"No, but your friends might." I pin her in my stare, triumphant, and she squirms.

"They won't," she says, but she looks uncertain.

"Wanna guess mine?" I don't wait for her to answer, but give her a cheeky grin. "It's cowgirl, of course."

"Thanks for that extra special glimpse into your life." She rolls her eyes, and I can't help but laugh. "Now, are you ready to be helpful?"

"Never. But what's your next question?" I sit back in my chair and get comfortable. This might take a while.

"Tell me about something you did when you were drunk that no one else knows about," she reads, then smirks at me.

"We're not starting with something easier, like favorite color?"

"Okay, Cooper, what's your favorite color?"

"Blue. You?"

"Yellow. Now, tell me the drunk story. I bet you have some good ones."

"What makes you so sure?"

"Hockey parties." She stares at me like, *duh,* and she has a point. We have a reputation.

"Touché. Okay, other people know about this one, but when I was at a party my freshman year, I was trying to impress a girl, and yeah, I was a little inebriated. I walked downstairs, doing a handstand, to get her number."

Jasmine gasps. "What happened?"

I run my hand through my hair, rueful. "I fell on the dismount. Sprained my wrist and had to miss three games. Coach was pissed."

"Avoid stairs." Jasmine acts like she's making a note. "Got it."

"And what about you?"

"Oh, I don't have any drunk stories." I doubt that, but I let her change the subject. "What's your major? I know it's a boring question, but it makes sense that we'd know the basics."

"Ag Biotech."

"I've heard of that one, but I don't know much about it."

A cute little wrinkle appears between her eyebrows and I want to reach out and smooth it away. "What do Ag Biotech majors study?"

"Agriculture. Biology. Technology. Stuff like that." I wink at her, and she huffs but smiles.

"Thank you, Captain Obvious. Your sarcasm is deeply appreciated."

"Bless your heart, thank you! So often it gets overlooked as one of my many skills." I clear my throat, sipping my drink. "Basically, it's a lot of genetics and plant breeding."

"Really?" She blinks, scooting closer, and her knees bump mine under the table. It sends a jolt up my spine.

"Yeah. Genetic engineering and crop production."

"What do you want to do with it?"

"Go home to Texas. Work on a big farm, most likely."

If all else fails. I stare at the tabletop, not ready to tell her more yet. She must sense that, because she lets it go and consults her list.

"What's your go-to drink on a night out?"

"I'm not picky. Beer, mixed drinks, whatever. But I guess if I was ordering a cocktail in a restaurant, I'd get an Old Fashioned."

"Because you're an old-fashioned guy?"

"Nah, I just like whiskey."

"I support that. I'm the same—beer, wine, cocktails. I say yes. So. Are you a dog or cat person?"

"Dogs. You?"

"I don't know. We didn't have any pets growing up. Both? Neither?"

"Neither?" Shock colors my voice. "Are you for real?"

"Maybe? I know I definitely do not want any weird pets—snakes and ferrets. Those things aren't for me."

"Fish?"

"Are great for eating. But not pets."

"That's my girl."

There were too many questions to get through in one session —and nowhere near enough caffeine in all of Starbucks—so Jasmine's been texting me. The buzz of my phone makes me smile.

Jasmine: How do you spend your free time?

Cooper: Hockey, and then hanging out with my team-mates, mostly. You?

Jasmine: Reading, crocheting, baking, watching tv. Are you a morning or a night person?

Cooper: Morning, probably. But I stay out way too late with the guys a lot.

Jasmine: I tend to be more of a night owl. What is your favorite food or meal?

Cooper: Is it lame if I say pizza? It's just so good.

Jasmine: Yes ;) You're so basic.

Jasmine: But you're right, it's practically the perfect food, so I understand.

Cooper: Hey, I hate to ask but… are you free for lunch tomorrow? My mom is bugging me about seeing you again.

Jasmine: Yeah, I can be. What time and where?

Cooper: Do you like tacos?

Jasmine: Do I like to breathe air? Yes, of course I like tacos.

Cooper: Excellent. La Bamba across from the Union at noon?

Jasmine: Sure.

~

Jasmine: What is your biggest pet peeve?

Cooper: More questions? Really?

Jasmine: It would be a shame if your mom found out you lied to her.

Cooper: Good point. Do you mean, like, when my roommates leave their crap all over our apartment? Or fake girlfriends who ask 197 questions ;)

Jasmine: Yeah, or like, people who click pens in class or snap their gum. Those kinds of things.

Cooper: Want to know so you can annoy me? ;)

Jasmine: It's definitely crossed my mind.

CHAPTER

Fifteen

JASMINE

Taking refuge in the restaurant's warmth, I shrug off my red peacoat and claim a table for four by the door. It's a tall-backed booth that looks hand carved, and I pick one painted a vibrant orange. The smell of sauteed veggies and warm tortillas makes my mouth water.

While I wait, I check out the sticky plastic menu to have something to do, but I already know what I want to order. Three chorizo tacos, plus chips and salsa. I set down my menu on the tabletop, and after another five minutes of waiting, absently trace my finger over the Mexican mural of pastoral life. The murals on the wall match, and a donkey gives me the side-eye.

I shiver as the door opens and a blast of cold air blows Mrs. Edwards inside. "Oh, Jasmine, dear, there you are!"

She bustles over and throws her arms around me like we're long-lost friends. She's a hugger, for sure. After removing her puffy parka, she sits and stares at me like she's waiting for something. Where's Cooper?

Oh, shit. My body breaks out in a sweat—despite the cold —and I'm extra aware of how fast my heart is beating. Did I misunderstand Cooper's text? Is it just her and I having lunch together?

No. There's no way.

"So, how's your day?" She folds her hands on the table and gives me her full focus. But where is Cooper? I need him to take some of the attention off me. This is not what I signed up for. I glance up at the sombrero hanging from the ceiling, but it doesn't have any answers.

Our waiter arrives, setting two glasses of water, a basket of chips, and small bowls of salsa on the table. In what I hope is super-spy mode, I slide my phone out of my pocket and shoot off a quick text to Cooper under the table.

Jasmine: WHERE ARE YOU? Your mom and I are at La Bamba's. GET HERE NOW!!!!!

"Uh, I'm good. Yeah." I break off a chip and crunch on it. It's perfect—crispy, warm, and salty. The food doesn't distract Mrs. Edwards at all, and she stays staring at me.

"What classes are you taking this semester?"

"It's a lot of math and science for me right now. Physical chemistry. Calc three. Plus, I have lab hours and I work at the equipment check-in desk."

Her golden eyes, the same shade and shape as Cooper's, widen. "Heavens to Betsy, girl, you've got some gumption!"

I think that's a compliment? I'm not sure. But she offers it like it's praise, so I smile. "Thank you."

"So." She leans forward, a gleam in her gaze like we're co-conspirators sharing a secret. It makes my heartbeat speed up. "I'm so happy we have some girl time to chat without Cooper. What's your favorite thing about him? What drew you together?"

If The Doctor is real, now would be a great time for him to

show up in The TARDIS and whisk me away. Han and Chewie in the Millennium Falcon. Marty McFly and his Delorean. I'm not picky. I wait a beat, but none of them show up to rescue me. Where is Cooper???

"Um." My phone vibrates and I surreptitiously check it.

Cooper: Running late. On my way.

At least there's that. I force my breathing to slow and meet Mrs. E's gaze. When lying, stick as close to the truth as possible.

"The first thing I noticed was his cowboy hat. And then his cute accent." She laughs before I continue. How can I sanitize this part for her? *I wanted to jump into bed with him?* I think not. I swallow.

"It's kind of embarrassing, but I accidentally spilled a drink all over both of us. He noticed my Tardis dress, and we bonded over a love of sci-fi movies." I shrug. "And we've enjoyed getting to know each other better since."

"Spilled his drink! What an adorable meeting." She grins so hard I think her cheeks might split. "I thought he'd never find a girl! You're so special."

Oh, crap. We're breaking up soon. How do I let her down gently?

"I don't know about that." I shove a chip in my mouth so I have a moment to think. People like to talk about themselves, right? I chew and swallow while she sips her water. "What about you, Mrs. Edwards? Are you enjoying your visit? Cooper told me you bought an RV. What's that like?"

"Oh, it's fun. I'm excited to travel more with friends. It's different, being an empty nester. I've had to find my own interests again and decide how to spend my time. But it's been a wonderful experience."

I'm trying to come up with another appropriate topic when I'm saved by Cooper sliding into the empty chair next to me. Finally. I exhale, relaxing a little. He takes off his jacket and beanie, then shakes out still-damp hair.

"Sorry, Momma. Practice went long." He leans across the table to drop a kiss on her cheek, and then one on the top of my head. We're close enough that I get a whiff of the clean scent of soap he must have used. "What have you two been talking about?"

"Oh, just getting to know each other a little better." Mrs. Edwards smiles, then motions to Cooper. "How about you order for us? I'm sure you know what Jasmine wants."

His eyes widen and his Adam's apple bobs in a swallow as he stands. "Yeah, sure. Uh, your usual, darlin'?"

Why didn't we cover this in our cram session? Where was the section in the binder on taco orders?

"Yep." I nod, crafting a plan. "Three chorizo tacos with onions and cilantro. Just how I like them."

"Of course." His face relaxes in relief. "And chicken tacos for Momma, extra jalapeños. Coming right up."

He heads towards the counter to order, and to take my eyes off his backside, I study his mom. Does she suspect us? Was that taco thing a test to see how well we know each other? Her eyes are guileless, though. I think she just assumes we're really into each other and would know that sort of thing.

She leans towards me. "Are you excited for your first hockey game tomorrow?"

"Definitely."

"I can't believe you haven't been yet! It's going to be so much fun!"

I paste on a smile, hoping to hide my apprehension. I know next to nothing about hockey and only slightly more about her son. But I can tell they love each other. I understand why he doesn't want to disappoint her. And after spending some time with her, I also get why he made up this lie in the first place.

My gaze drifts to Cooper, leaning on the counter. His profile is visible, his nose perfectly straight and his lips curved up in a grin. It was his good looks that drew me towards him initially, but after getting to know him this week, it turns out he's more than just a pretty face.

So I square my shoulders. I've got his back, like I know he'd have mine.

"Yep. Friday night. It's a date."

CHAPTER
Sixteen

JASMINE

Tugging at the boxy, stiff, orange Harrison Hockey t-shirt that Mrs. E coerced me into wearing tonight, I head towards the arena.

Taking deep breaths, I scan the aisles for my row and will myself not to freak out.

It's just a hockey game. With my fake boyfriend's mom. No big deal.

"Jasmine! Over here!" Spinning to face me in her seat, Mrs. Edwards waves so hard I'm worried she'll fall out of her chair. As if I'd miss her in head-to-toe orange.

I shuffle sideways to slip into the narrow space and find my spot.

"Oh, Jasmine!" She pats my arm as I sit down. "I've missed you! Isn't this exciting?"

She's missed me? I saw her yesterday, and every day this week. But I dig deep and plaster a smile on my face.

"It definitely is. Thanks again for the hockey shirt." I hold it out for her to see. "It was so generous of you."

Mrs. Edwards brushes off my words but smiles wide. "Nonsense! I can't believe this is your first hockey game."

"Yeah. I'm not really into sports." I smooth my fingers over my shirt, wishing I was in clothes that were more my style. Oh well. One night. I can be a sports fan for one night, I suppose.

"I wasn't either, until I became a hockey mom." She beams at me. "Something about knowing the people I was cheering for made it meaningful to me. And it could be worse —baseball is boring and football is outside in the rain and snow."

"Huh, that's a good point." I clear my throat and gesture at the rink. "Do you think you could explain the basics? I know nothing about it."

"Of course!" Warming to her topic, she leans close and indicates various marks on the ice. "Okay, do you see the blue line? That's important for offsides. And the centerline, that's for icing, which I didn't understand at first, but it just means one team can't shoot the puck more than half of the ice without it being touched."

I nod, but it's incomprehensible.

"And that circle, there." She points to it. "Cooper is a center, so he does the face-off when they drop the puck. That's where that happens."

Talking a mile a minute, she walks me through the goals, what constitutes penalties, and how long the game lasts. I don't understand the hockey jargon, but I perk up when the guys skate out onto the ice.

"Look, there he is!" Mrs. Edwards waves at number twenty-two. Focused on the task at hand, Cooper doesn't wave back, but continues to circle the rink. If she hadn't told me which one he was, I'm not sure I would have known.

Between the orange and navy jersey, the chest pads, and the helmet, it's hard to recognize him.

On his next pass in front of us, he lifts his helmet and winks. My stomach does a little flip in response.

He's cute, even in bulky hockey gear, but he's off limits. My business partner. That wink is purely for show. I wish I could convince my body to get the memo and stop reacting to him.

The other team—the Michigan State Spartans—skate on the other end of the rink and Mrs. Edwards gives me the lowdown. From what I gather, they aren't as good as the Griffins, and we are favored to win.

The JumboTron counts down until the two lines of skaters file onto their benches. A pretty woman teeters out onto the ice, sings the National Anthem, and Cooper faces off against a Spartan in the big circle in the middle. The puck moves so fast, I can't tell who gets it until it shoots off of Cooper's stick towards one of his teammates.

I've never seen anything quite so consuming. Hockey moves like lightning and the pace doesn't let up. I can't take my eyes off the puck as it speeds across the slick surface of the ice. If I blink, I'll miss something. When the Griffins score a goal, I leap to my feet, cheering with the rest of the crowd.

"It was Hunter!" Mrs. Edwards grabs my arm as we scream together. "He scored the goal!"

The announcer confirms this and then credits Cooper with an assist. I don't know what that means, but Mrs. E cheers and I clap as loud as I can. The thing is—I'm not doing it to be a dutiful fake girlfriend. My heartbeat races, I bounce on the balls of my toes, and I can't stop smiling. I'm having a blast.

The buzzer surprises me when it blares a few minutes later. "Is it over?"

"No." Shaking her head, Cooper's mom grins at me as the players skate off the ice in different directions. "That's just the end of the first period. They have an intermission now, and another one after the second period."

"Oh." That was so intense, I can't imagine two more periods. But I also don't want it to end. And I'm not sure I can handle all the questions she'll throw at me during the break.

Standing, I jerk my thumb towards the concourse. "I'm going to run to the concession stand. Would you like anything?"

"No, dear, but thank you. There's usually fifteen to twenty minutes before the next period. Hurry back."

I grab some popcorn and a Coke and time it perfectly—I slide into my seat when the two teams re-enter the arena, and I don't have to make conversation with Cooper's mom. She means well, but she's a lot.

The second period is as exciting as the first. Michigan State scores a goal to tie it up—going five hole, Mrs. E says, whatever that means—but then Cooper gets another assist to take the lead. We're on our feet again, cheering as his name is called.

Honestly, I'm amazed at how much fun I'm having. Maybe it's like Mrs. E said, knowing the players makes it more engaging to watch. Or maybe hockey is just awesome. Either way, I can't believe I've never been to a Harrison sporting event before. I should try football or basketball, too. And I want to bring Staci and Delaney with me to a game sometime soon. They have to experience this.

The idea sobers me. After Cooper comes over for movie night on Sunday and my girlfriends agree to stop setting me up, we can break up. They'd think it was pretty weird if I still wanted to watch my "ex-boyfriend" play hockey. So I guess a game isn't in our future. I don't know why my stomach twists at the thought.

After that period ends, I excuse myself and visit the bathroom, blaming my Coke. Does Mrs. E suspect that I'm avoiding her? Being a fake girlfriend is exhausting.

I climb through the rows to return to my seat and feel a tap on my shoulder. "Jasmine! Is that you?"

Lucy Li, a friend from the chemistry program, stands in the row behind me. She stares back at me, black eyes wide. An orange beanie covers her long black curtain of hair and matches her orange Harrison Hockey hoodie. "I've never seen you at a hockey game before."

"Oh, um, yeah, this is—"

"She's dating the center!" Mrs. E spins around, beaming at Lucy. "Cooper Edwards. My son."

"Oh, hey, always nice to meet another fan. My brother, Caleb, plays on the team. He's a center, too, but a freshman. On the fourth line."

They talk hockey for a second, then Lucy's gaze slides to me. "You and Cooper, huh? That's awesome. One of those opposites attracts things? I can't wait to see it in person."

"Oh, well, it's, um, very new." I stumble over my words. Does that sound like a reasonable explanation? My palms get sweaty and my pulse trips up. It's a good thing Mrs. Edwards is leaving soon, because the anxiety of constant lying makes my stomach churn.

"I guess I'll get to see it in three weeks, though, at our department dinner."

My heart stops, then starts beating twice as fast as normal. Why did I have to run into someone I know? I should have planned for that, but I didn't think any of my friends had hockey connections.

"Department dinner?" Mrs. E raises an eyebrow. "What's that?"

I curse internally, as Lucy says, "The Chemistry Department is hosting its annual awards. It's a formal dinner in a few weeks with a special guest speaker. It's catered and in the Union ballroom. Everyone brings a date. It's always a blast."

"Cooper didn't mention it." Mrs. E blinks, as if she's trying to remember if he brought it up. Of course he didn't. Because he doesn't know about it. But I can't let on.

"Oh, um, boys." I wave at the arena, as if this is an explanation. "He's probably not as excited about dressing up as I am."

Mrs. E's face lights up and she squeals. "What does your dress look like? I'm sure you have it all picked out."

Not so much. The buzzer sends a jolt through me, saving me from having to answer. Lucy pats my shoulder as we take our seats, and the third period begins.

Unfortunately, Michigan State makes an early goal, and they tie the score 2-2. They battle hard, but the Spartans sneak in fouls (according to Mrs. E) that the refs don't call. I don't see it, but I take her word for it. With two minutes left in the game, Cooper's line rotates in. They just jump over the wall and hop on the ice. How do they know when to go? And how do they stay upright on ice skates?

The puck flies between the Griffins players. My eyes can barely keep up. How do they shoot so fast? Hunter—I recognize him by his number, thirty-four—passes to Cooper, who is suddenly at the right place at the right time. He launches the puck into the net and the red light behind the goal flashes.

He did it! Cooper took the lead! Adrenaline surges through my veins as the stadium explodes with excitement.

Mrs. E and I leap to our feet, jumping up and down and

hugging. Lucy pounds me on the back as we cheer. We stay standing as the last minute and a half winds down on the clock and the Griffins win.

"All I Do Is Win" by DJ Khaled blasts through the arena and the crowd chants along. The players pile up in a victory hug on the ice, then they wave their sticks in the air as they take a lap. Cooper takes off his helmet again, shaking out his sweaty hair, and the smile that he sends me when he skates by makes my toes curl.

We clap and yell until the guys file out, wide grins on their faces.

"I think you're his good luck charm." I barely make out Mrs. E's words in my ear, fighting to be heard over the roar of the stadium. Shooting me a Mona Lisa smile, she links her arm through mine and pulls me along. "Come on. We'll meet the team outside the locker room and take Cooper and his friends out for ice cream."

I gulp. Meeting his friends for the first time, on his birthday, while his mom watches on. No pressure there.

CHAPTER
Seventeen

COOPER

Smoothing my hand over my still-damp hair as I exit the locker room, I can't keep the silly grin off my face. What can I say? Winning feels awesome. Hearing my name announced in front of 8,000 screaming fans is a massive adrenaline rush. And having my own cheering section? Priceless.

Usually, after a game like this, I'd go bar-hopping with the guys and find a girl interested in blowing off some steam in the best way possible. But that's not happening tonight.

When I see Jasmine's beaming face, waving at me as I weave through the crowd, I can't help myself. She launches herself at me, twining her arms around my neck, and I pick her up and spin her around. Her laughing squeal rings out against the concrete. Setting her on her feet, I press my forehead to hers and stare into her green eyes. Her lips are plump and kissable, and from experience, soft and pliant. I want another taste of her.

"Hey," I say instead.

"Great game." Clearing her throat, she pulls away, and I miss the contact. "I really liked it."

I settle for lacing our fingers together. For the show we're putting on, of course. My mom is chatting with Hunter, but I still need to keep up appearances. "Yeah?"

"Yeah. Hockey is awesome." She shakes her head, smiling from ear to ear. "I had no idea."

For some reason, this makes me ridiculously happy. Like I personally invented hockey.

Usually I ignore the crowd when I play these days. My mom never missed a game when I was a kid, and my grand-parents came to a lot of them, too. I learned to stop looking for my dad in the stands years ago. But having people cheering specifically for me in the audience tonight—instead of the noise distracting me, I could focus more. Honed in, I hit a whole new level. It made the victory even sweeter, and I want it to happen every game.

"You're a fan now?"

"I think I am. I'd definitely come again."

"I'll get you tickets anytime you want." There's no way I can wipe the dumb grin off my face. Maybe she'll take me up on it.

"Pookie!" My mom interrupts our moment. "You were incredible. Birthday luck, for sure. Twenty-two is going to be an exceptional year for you. I can tell already."

She's right, it's off to a great start. No birthday text from my dad, but I know better than to expect that. I had a sweet phone call from my grandparents earlier, and that makes up for it. A goal and two assists tonight, another win in our conference. A team full of happy dudes and a pretty girl on my arm. All in all, life is good.

Well, the girl is just a friend. I need to stop imagining her naked. Friends are cool. And a friend who likes hockey is even better.

Then my mom clears her throat, like she's making an announcement, and the players, friends, and family given access to the locker room exit turn to stare.

"Today is Cooper's birthday! You're all invited out for ice cream to celebrate with us. Please, everyone, come!"

A murmur of excitement runs through the small crowd, and I get multiple pats on the back, a noogie from Evan, and lots of confirmations that people are joining us. It's not exactly how I would have chosen to spend the evening, but it's sweet and wholesome, and totally fits my mom. I don't want her to know any different. It's not beer and sex, but this is pretty great.

Silver Spoon is by far my favorite ice cream joint in Lafayette. The flavors are incredible, and it's styled like an old-fashioned soda shop, complete with a red and white striped awning out front, formica tables, sparkly red vinyl booths and spinning stools at the bar inside the brightly-lit space. The harried employees probably didn't expect forty people to show up late after the hockey game on a Friday, though, so the line is pretty long. With my fingers clasped in Jasmine's, I don't mind waiting.

Her easy excitement after we met at the locker room has disappeared. Instead, she holds herself stiff as we stand at the counter and jumps whenever anyone asks her a question. To be fair, all of my teammates want to talk to her, plus my mom keeps trying to get a word in about formal dresses—I don't ask.

Maneuvering her in front of me, I form a human barrier

between her and the world and rub her shoulders. Her tension instantly dissipates.

"God, that feels good." She lets out a little moan, and it hits me straight in the groin. I will every part of my body to stay PG while we have an audience. "I should be the one massaging your muscles, though. Aren't you sore after all those guys ran into you during the game?"

She's more than welcome to touch me everywhere. Clearing my throat, I try to rein in my libido. "I'm pretty used to the contact, actually. And we have a team masseuse if needed."

"Oh." Her head lulls on her shoulders, and she inhales. "I'll let you continue, and not feel guilty. Plus, it solidifies our cover."

Our cover. Right. I resist the urge to kiss the back of her neck and slide my hands down her arms.

The girl in front of us turns around, her long, smooth black hair swinging. "What kind of ice cream are you getting, Jasmine?"

She looks familiar, but I can't quite place her until Caleb Li, the guy with her, faces me, too. Then I see the resemblance between them. I'm pretty sure I've met her before—it's his older sister.

"Zanzibar Chocolate." Jasmine straightens, putting a respectable distance between us but still holding my hand. "It's delicious. But I don't think they have a bad one here." Then she gestures to me. "Cooper, do you know Lucy? Her brother is on the team"—Caleb nods from his place in line—"and she's in my program."

"Oh, cool. I didn't know you knew Jasmine."

"And we'll be seeing more of each other!" Lucy says, bouncing on the balls of her feet. At hockey games? Am I missing something?

Blinking into my silence, she stares at me expectantly. Like I should totally know what she's talking about.

"Uh, yeah?"

Jasmine squeezes my fingers, eyes wide. "Because of the department dinner, honey. The formal dinner in a couple weeks that you agreed to attend with me."

Stressing the words, she cuts her gaze to my mom and I clue in. "Right. How could I have forgotten? The department dinner you've told me *so much* about."

"Oh, pookie, you haven't mentioned it to me yet!" My mom can't resist inserting herself into this conversation. I smother a sigh.

"Sorry, Momma. I guess in all the excitement of your surprise visit, it slipped my mind."

"You'll have to send pictures of Jasmine in her dress! And you in your suit, too, of course."

Thanks to hockey, I own a few suits, and look damn good in them. So it won't be a problem to attend if I don't have a game that night and Jasmine actually wants me to. Either way, I'll play along for her. She's done so much for me. Even after paying for her car repairs, I still owe her.

Lucy raises her eyebrows. "I just realized—Chad will be there. Does he know about you and Cooper?"

Chad? Who the hell is Chad? Is this another thing I'm supposed to know?

Jasmine squares her shoulders, determination in every line of her posture. "I haven't told him, but I try to avoid talking to him whenever possible. It doesn't concern him. I can bring whoever I want to a department event."

Her face goes from open and relaxed to pinched and tense. I don't know who this guy is, but I don't like the way she stiffens. Whoever he is, I'll find out. And keep him away from her.

117

"Oh, for sure." Lucy takes a step away from Jasmine. "I didn't mean to offend you. Honestly, he's a jerk to everyone and I hope Cooper puts him in his place. I can't wait."

My mom elbows her way in. "Who is Chad?"

Subtle, she's not.

Jasmine tosses her hair. "No one important." Then she smiles, clearly shifting gears. "What flavor of ice cream are you getting, Birthday Boy?"

I let her get away with the subject change, although I have a lot of questions for her later. I push down my protective instincts and force myself to take some relaxing breaths. Putting my hand on her lower back, I rub circles there. Too bad I can't slip my fingers under her shirt and feel her silky skin. "Um, I want Fat Elvis today."

"Not birthday cake?"

"Nah. I don't love traditional cake. I always used to get my mom to make me a cookie cake instead."

"Oooh, cookies. Good choice." Leaning against me again, Jasmine's hair smells like coconuts, sunscreen, and swimming pools. It reminds me of childhood summers, and it's intoxicating.

Beaming at this mention, my mom launches into a reminiscence about my thirteenth birthday. While embarrassing, I let it go because it's better than whatever was bothering Jasmine earlier.

She tugs me forward in line and we order, then collect our selections. I take a bite of the creamy custard and the sweet banana flavor explodes on my tongue. Combined with salty peanut butter ripples and chocolate chunks, it's delicious.

Jasmine pops her spoon in her mouth, licking it clean, and I'm going to need to adjust my pants.

Forcing myself to think of cold showers, my hockey stats, and wrinkly grandmas, I jump at the distraction when

Hunter jerks his chin at me from a red vinyl booth. I steer us to his table. Jasmine's spine goes ramrod straight again, and I sling my free arm around her shoulders.

"Relax," I whisper in her ear. "He knows it's for show."

Her chest rises and falls in a deep breath and—I probably shouldn't stare at her chest or else my pants problem will get worse.

But she scoots into her seat across from him and smiles.

"Hey, Hunter. I'm Jasmine." Offering her hand, they shake. "Nice to meet you."

"You, too." He looks around for my mom and waves at her, clearly making sure she's observing this very natural first meeting. Then he continues the ruse. Could he be more awkward?

"God, Hunter," I say, under my breath. "You're a regular double-oh-seven. Chill, man."

"I've never met a friend's fake girlfriend before." He speaks low, his words mumbled. "How should I know what to do?"

"Try being normal."

Rolling his eyes at me, he turns to Jasmine. "So what's your major?"

Talking about chemistry, her whole face lights up. She explains what she studies and what she does in her lab, gesturing animatedly, while Lucy adds details from a neighboring booth. I know nothing about oxidation rates or deprotonation of alcohols, but I would watch her talk about it for hours.

When she asks Hunter what his major is, his features shutter closed.

"OBM." Instead of meeting her gaze, he slumps in the booth and stares at the melted ice cream in the bottom of his dish.

Organizational and Business Management. The typical "athlete" major at Harrison. It's a sore spot for him. His dad didn't think he could handle too many tough classes on top of the rigorous hockey schedule, but I know it makes him feel lesser and he resents taking his advice.

But Jasmine doesn't bat an eye. "Oh, that's great. My dad was looking to hire someone with that degree for his company just the other day. He says it's very useful."

Blinking, Hunter sits up. "Yeah?"

"Yeah." Jasmine chats with him, extolling the virtues of his chosen major, and he perks up.

It's awesome that they are getting along so well. Never having dated anyone, it hadn't occurred to me that my best friend needs to like my girlfriend.

Fake girlfriend. But Jasmine's cool. I can see us hanging out as friends after this is all over.

Except her friends don't know the truth like mine do. Pretty soon, I'm going to have to make a list of who knows what about us. Maybe things will calm down when my mom leaves and after we go to her department dinner. Oddly enough, I don't hate the thought of it. Especially if she needs someone to keep Chad away. After everything my mom has made her do these last few days, I can pretend to date her for a little longer. I don't mind. I don't mind at all.

CHAPTER
Eighteen

JASMINE

A knock sounds at the door to our house, and my wool socks skid on the hardwood as I race to answer it before Staci or Delaney get there. My stomach twists with nerves. There's no way we can pull this off. My friends are going to know we're frauds and hate me for lying.

"Hi." Stepping out onto the front porch, I close the door behind me, blocking them out of our conversation. Then I try to stop panting and take in Cooper. I swallow. In his faded jeans, boots, and a flannel shirt, he could be Mr. July on the sexy cowboy calendar. My belly flips, this time with desire. "No hat?"

Eyes darting back and forth, he shakes his head. "Miss it? Seemed like a little too much for movie night. Uh, are you going to invite me in?"

He holds out a six pack of beer and a bottle of wine as an offering, but I shake my head. "You haven't passed the test yet."

"Test?" His dark brows rise towards his tousled brown hair.

"Uh-huh. What's my favorite movie?"

"*Star Wars*?" He grimaces when I don't answer. "*Lord of the Rings*? *Star Trek*?"

I shake my head. "We're not ready for this."

"Jasmine." Setting down his gifts on the peeling wooden planks of the porch, he grabs my hands and steps closer, boring his eyes into mine. "It's going to be fine. People who've just started dating are still getting to know each other, even if it's been a month. So. What's your favorite movie?"

I stare at the tips of his boots. "You've probably never heard of it. A weird fantasy movie from the '80s called *Willow*."

Cooper squeezes my hands until I look at him. His face glows with a wide smile. "I've most definitely heard of it. Val Kilmer and Joanne Whalley? It's my favorite movie to watch when I'm sick."

"Really?" My mouth drops open. He must be teasing me, but he nods.

"Yep. My mom always used to put it on when I was a kid. I don't know why. But I love it. Makes me feel better every time. I own the special edition Blu-ray."

I picture Cooper snuggled under a plaid blanket on his couch, watching my favorite movie. The mental image makes my chest flutter, and I can't help but smile back at him. "It's a great movie, right?"

"Did you hear they are coming out with a TV show that continues it? Not sure how I feel about that."

I frown. "Me either. And *Lord of the Rings*, too. But what if they ruin it?"

"Right?"

My nerves calms, and I grin at him. He's right. We can get through this together.

Dropping his hands, I open the door behind me and wave him in as he picks up the drinks he brought. I hustle him past the foursome in the living room, watching us curiously.

"Be there in a second," I say to them as he nods hello.

Our kitchen occupies a tiny corner in the back of the old Victorian house. The stove, fridge and sink are crammed together with little counter or cabinet space, so we've learned to be minimalists. The cabinets and counters are both robin's egg blue, so it looks a bit like the baby boy section of a department store. We've wedged a rickety wooden circular table under the vintage stained glass lamp in the breakfast nook off to the left, though, and it lends a homey air to the tight space.

Cooper sets his drinks down on the table and smiles at me. "Any last-minute questions? Advice?"

My anxiety is gone. I hold out my hand, linking our fingers. "Nah. We've got this."

I lead him through the kitchen back to the living room and prepare to face the music. We halt in the doorway and I clear my throat.

"Cooper, you've met Staci and Delaney before." I indicate my two roommates. "This is Tate and Brian."

Tate and Staci have stuffed themselves into an armchair together, his tan arms wrapped around her curves. With short dark curls and deep black eyes, I can see why he caught Staci's attention. Tate waves while Staci gives Cooper the once-over. She nods an affirmation and I breathe an internal sigh of relief.

"Hey, man. Nice to meet you," Brian says from the couch. He eyes Cooper, then raises a brow. "You should do the trick with Chad."

"Zip it. No talk of him tonight. What if he's like Beetlejuice and saying his name summons him?" I give him a warning glare, and he holds his hands up in apology.

Cooper sends me a questioning look, but I shake my head. I probably need to have that conversation with him, but I'm not ready for it yet.

"Later," I whisper. "Let's focus on one thing at a time."

I breathe a sigh of relief as he drops it, then moves over to the couch to shake Brian's hand.

Brian and Delaney are spread out end-to-end on the long green velvet sofa, feet tangling in the middle. Short blond hair and a chiseled jaw lined with stubble frame his blue eyes that Delaney still raves about. They may have been dating for years and gotten comfortable, but the spark is definitely still there between them. She wiggles her stocking-clad feet against his and gives me a naughty look.

"Hey Cooper, glad you could make it. Unfortunately, Brian won rock, paper, scissors, so we're watching the latest Bond movie. Oh, and I guess you and Jasmine will have to share the other chair. Only spot left."

Ah, that's why she looks so pleased with herself. She and Brian claimed the whole couch to force Cooper and I into some PDA. My pulse trips up and I swear the temperature of the room does, too.

I take a deep breath. "Or we could stretch out on the floor."

"That chair looks mighty cozy to me." Cooper sits, then raises his brows and pats his lap in invitation.

I swallow. Holding hands is one thing, but sitting on his lap—that's a different level of closeness. But my roommates will suspect something is up if I don't sit with him. They know I'm not normally opposed to a little snuggling. So I steel myself against his enticing, clean, woodsy scent and perch on his denim-clad knee. Sitting as stiff as I can, I keep my back straight and try to touch him as little as possible, but he snakes his arm around my waist, anchoring me in place. After a moment, I let myself relax against him. It's just a little PDA. It doesn't mean anything.

"Need anything before we start the movie?" Brian asks, looking around the room. When no one protests, he grabs the remote and presses play.

The opening scene captures everyone's attention, but when the familiar Bond credits fill the screen, Cooper leans close and whispers in my ear. "Are you okay with this?"

I glance over at the other couples. Brian and Delaney have their eyes glued to the TV screen, while Tate and Staci gaze at each other. No one is looking at us.

"Yeah." I keep my voice low. "Are you?"

"Darlin', having a beautiful woman on my lap isn't a hardship."

His deep rumble in my ear sends a jolt straight through me, and I can't help but remember how he kisses. Both soft and firm, gentle yet demanding. I squeeze my legs together.

He must be able to feel it, because he shifts and says, "What was that? You trying to kill me with thoughts of your sweet ass?"

I can hear the laughter in his tone, and I wiggle a bit on top of him. "Maybe. If you're not careful."

"Oh, is that how you want to play it?" Digging his fingers into my ribs, he tickles me mercilessly until I'm gasping and howling.

Brian pauses the movie, and Cooper's hands still. Panting, I try to catch my breath.

"Are you going to do this through the whole movie?" Brian asks, his words short and staccato. He narrows his eyes at us.

"Come on, babe." Delaney launches herself into his lap

and gazes up at him. "Take a hint. Don't you remember what it was like when we just started dating? You couldn't stop trying to get in my pants."

He glances at Tate and Staci, so lost in each other that they are ignoring the rest of us, and then Cooper and I, caught mid-tickle. With a playful grin, he nuzzles her neck. "And you think that's changed? Are you saying I'm not man enough for you?"

He makes her shriek as he kisses her, but I'm distracted by how easy this is all going. How little they suspect us, and how much my friends seem to like him already. Maybe this will all be fine. And Cooper is pretty cool about the whole thing. I bet we can stay friendly after all this.

The thought erases my anxiety, and as I relax against his chest, I don't let myself analyze it any further.

CHAPTER
Nineteen

JASMINE

Jasmine: Did your mom get home okay?

Cooper: Yes, she did. She just texted me. To ask how you are.

Jasmine: What can I say? I'm a great fake girlfriend. I'm not surprised she loves me.

Cooper: You're definitely her favorite Griffin.

Cooper: So did we convince your friends?

Jasmine: Yep, they couldn't stop talking about you.

Cooper: Nice. I hope they back off the blind dates now.

~

Jasmine: Hey, have you heard anything about my car? I miss my baby.

Cooper: I guess it's hard to find a mechanic who knows a lot about classic Beetles. So they are making some calls and running diagnostics.

Jasmine: Ugh. Do you think he's okay without me? Can I go visit him?

Cooper: You're ridiculous.

Jasmine: Wouldn't you miss Bubba if something happened to him?

Cooper: Don't you dare speak of such things. My truck is precious.

Jasmine: Exactly!

～

Clad in my safety gear, I take a deep breath of the lab's unique scent and lose myself in its routine. Checking levels, recording measurements—the predictability of it all is soothing.

Life has returned to normal, for the most part. No big lies so far this week. After successfully convincing my friends that we were a couple, I haven't seen Cooper since Sunday night, four days ago. His mom went back to Texas Monday morning —thank the Lord I had class, so I didn't have to see her off in what would definitely have been a tearful farewell. I can't imagine her leaving without drama or fanfare.

I've successfully avoided questions from my friends about my relationship, mostly because I'm swamped with the first round of exams and haven't spent a lot of time at the house. We need to stage our fake breakup, but exams were all-consuming. I've barely had a moment to breathe, so I inhale again, slowly, and immerse myself in my work.

My surroundings fade away as I go about my business. Marking things off on my mental to-do list, including reviewing the list of journal articles Dr. Michelson sent me, I'm almost finished when a throat clearing returns me to reality.

Chad crosses his arms over his chest, scoffing. He tosses his sandy hair out of his blue eyes and stares at me like I'm gum on the bottom of his Sperry's. "You don't waste any time, do you?"

Don't give in to him. He doesn't deserve an answer. Don't respond.

I don't listen to myself.

"If by that you mean I'm an efficient worker, thank you. However, I asked you not to speak with me. Unless it's about something here in the lab, please be professional."

It shouldn't surprise me that Chad doesn't respect my request. When has he ever?

"That's not what I'm talking about, and you know it. I heard you're dating a jock." He rolls his eyes. "Typical."

"What's typical about it? Smart, sweet, funny, good in bed —he's pretty different from the last guy I dated." Sweat breaks out on my hairline and my blood rushes faster in my veins. Technically, I don't know that Cooper is good in bed—but Chad doesn't know that. Chad's certainly not. I can't resist the dig.

Face turning red, Chad takes a step closer, but I don't back down. Not anymore.

"Obvious rebound. Going for someone so superficial."

"Because he's hot?" I snort. "Yeah, okay."

"Because he's dumb." Chad enunciates the words slowly, like I'm a moron, too. "Must be sad for you to settle, knowing that's all you're gonna get."

I shake my head. "You don't know him at all. Besides, he's smart enough to have gotten what you wanted. *Me*."

Chad laughs sarcastically, a sound devoid of any joy. "He can have my sloppy seconds. See ya 'round, Jazzy."

I clench my fists as he saunters towards the other end of the lab. I always hated that nickname. He's right—I am an idiot. I know better than to speak to him. I should never have acknowledged him and given him ammunition to hurt me.

Fingers shaking, my eyes blur as I finish filling out my lab notebook. Then I strip off my goggles, gloves, and white coat and get the hell out of there.

I refuse to let Chad ruin my lab experience. My advisor is sympathetic and usually I can avoid him, but the scheduling was tricky this semester. Dr. Michelson didn't realize that we had history, not that it could have been helped. Chad needs to finish his senior project, and this was apparently the time that fit best into his schedule. Chad claimed he wanted more organic synthesis experience and that my advisor was the best. This surprised me, and not in a good way. He's always had more interest in analytical and electrochemistry, reflecting his future plans to work on advancing battery technology. Not drug synthesis, which is my interest.

At least he'll graduate in a few months and disappear from my life forever. That can't come too soon.

Stepping out of the Dye building, the blustery wind robs my breath from my lungs. I don't know when it started snowing, but the big swirling flakes have already accumulated three inches on the sidewalk. Why didn't I go to college in Florida or Hawaii? I should look for grad programs in warm places.

Of course, I wore my latest thrift store find today—yellow floral leather flats—instead of my customary Docs. It wasn't snowing when I left the house, and they are so cute. But it's February—I should have known better.

It's the cherry on top of the shitty day sundae. My feet are freezing and my eyes burn with unshed tears. They threaten to spill over when a honking horn interrupts my pity party.

A red pickup truck pulls to the curb in front of me, and Cooper's face appears as Bubba's window slides down.

"Jasmine!" he yells. "Get in!"

Is he a mirage? Was there a leak in the nitrous oxide and now I'm hallucinating? But the snow is real and so is his trusty ride. I don't hesitate. Rushing around the front of the truck, I clamber inside and hold my hands up to the heating vent. The interior is gloriously warm.

"What are you doing here?" I ask as I remember my seat belt. "You don't have classes on this side of campus."

Cooper shrugs, pulling away from the curb. "It's your lab hours, right? This is when you had them last week. I saw the snow and thought maybe you could use a ride."

"You… came out here just for me?"

"It's nothing. You don't have a car."

I'm speechless. My mouth drops open, but it's empty. No words. I can't believe he did something so incredibly thoughtful. I press my fingers to my lips, overwhelmed, and warmth blossoms in my chest.

"So, uh, I've been meaning to talk to you about your department dinner." He glances at me out of the corner of his eye before focusing back on the road.

"I understand if you can't make it," I say in a rush. He's probably busy, and we should break up already. His mom is gone, and my friends will back off now. I do my best to keep my rush of disappointment at bay. "It's no big deal, I don't—"

"No, I'll be there. As long as you actually want me to go." He stares ahead at the traffic and I can't read his expression. "I'm looking forward to it. I checked the schedule, and it works. It's rare to have a Friday night off, but there's a home basketball game. So they made sure not to schedule a hockey game, and we're away the night after."

I nod, like I'm familiar with the intricacies of college sports.

"Okay. If you really don't mind—"

"I don't. You're not an inconvenience, you know." He chuckles, shaking his head at me.

I blink. His attitude is the opposite of what I had gotten used to. Chad would have sighed and made a fuss about how much of a hassle I was. I swallow past a lump that pops up in my throat.

"But it's three weeks away." Does he really want to keep up the ruse that much longer? Doesn't he miss hookups and casual sex?

Cooper taps the steering wheel. "It's not a big deal."

"Um, the thing is. There's this very romantic holiday in between now and then." I bite my lip. "If we don't break up before then…"

I trail off, and Cooper winces. "I have no idea what I'd do with a date on Valentine's Day."

"Me either."

We sit in silence for a beat as he navigates traffic.

"Okay, maybe this isn't so bad." Cooper's voice is tinged with excitement and I perk up. "It's not like we need to impress each other. You can plan something you'd like, I can plan something for me, and we can tell your friends and my momma how romantic it was." He snaps his fingers. "Easy peasy."

When he says it like that, it sounds possible. He's right, there isn't any pressure. I nod.

"All right, we'll figure it out."

Cooper turns onto my street and clears his throat.

"Jasmine, I've been meaning to ask you." His expression turns serious. "Um, a few people have brought up Chad."

His name hangs heavy in the air between us and my stomach churns. I clench my hands together.

I don't owe Cooper an explanation. But he's become my friend through all this, and Chad will probably make a scene at the department dinner. Maybe we should just skip it... but no, that's giving Chad too much power over me. And I'm done with that.

I swallow. "Chad is my ex."

"I figured." Cooper cuts his eyes over to me. "Not an amicable break up?"

I huff a laugh. "No. Not really an amicable relationship by the end, either. Chad was—"

How do I explain it? Cooper reaches over and takes my hand, running his thumb along my knuckles. Is it weird that he's touching me when no one is around? He could just be a tactile guy—or maybe he still thinks about our botched hookup as much as I do. Either way, the lump in my throat lessens enough that I can speak around it.

I give him the abridged version of my saga with Chad, highlighting his recent confrontations in the lab and his progressively worse behavior. Cooper listens without inter-rupting, squeezing my fingers when my voice threatens to break.

"He knows about us—fake us, or whatever." I bite the barely there nail on my index finger. "He mentioned it. So prepare for him to be a dick at my department dinner. If you don't want to go, we can—"

"Shit, Jasmine." Cooper blows out a breath. He throws the car into park and unbuckles his seatbelt, sliding over to put his arm around me. Belatedly, I realize we're in front of my house. "He's low-key stalking you. I'm not letting you face that alone. No wonder you swore off boyfriends."

He doesn't talk me out of it or tell me it's not that bad. Leaning my head against his shoulder, my muscles go slack for a second as I relax. My heartbeat is steady, and I'd like to close my eyes and just stay here, in this warm cocoon of understanding and support. But I force myself to sit up, twisting to look at him.

"I learned my lesson, and I'll never let it happen again."

"I can't imagine ever trying to change you, darlin'. You're awesome."

He tucks a strand of hair behind my ear, and sincerity shines out of his eyes. I shiver at the gentle touch.

"Thanks, Cooper. I'm sure you're sick of having a fake girlfriend."

"Real girlfriends are not my thing, but fake ones are cool." His lopsided grin makes my stomach flutter. "And I know you can totally handle Chad on your own at this thing, but I've got your back. I mostly want to watch you eviscerate him."

"Eviscerate, huh? That's quite the vocab word. Those people who say jocks are dumb are clearly wrong."

His laughter rings out, loud in the small space. "I like to surprise 'em."

Surprising—that's a good word for Cooper Edwards.

CHAPTER
Twenty

JASMINE

Mom: Happy Valentine's Day, girls! Love you!

Maya: Love you too, Mom

Mom: Do you have romantic plans?

Maya: Joel and I are going out to dinner

Jasmine: I have a date with the guy I've been seeing

Mom: A new guy??? What's his name? What's he like?

Maya: I thought you swore off dating forever after Chad.

Jasmine: Cooper. He plays hockey, and he's a perfect gentleman. Superior in every way to Chad.

Mom: Good for you, baby!

~

Cooper: Do you know how to skate?

Jasmine: Roller skate? I think I did it in elementary school. Is it like riding a bike?

Cooper: Ice skate

Jasmine: Nope, never tried it.

Cooper: Cool, cool, cool, cool.

Jasmine: OMG why????

Cooper: No reason. Wear warm clothes you can move in for Valentine's Day.

Jasmine: Uh-oh. There's a dress code now? Should I be worried?

Cooper: Only worried about how much fun you'll have.

~

After his texts, I shouldn't be surprised to find myself staring up at the doors to the hockey arena. I wrap my red peacoat tighter around my body as my eyes dart around, taking everything in. I've been to the arena before to see Cooper play. But it looks much larger without crowds of people milling around. I swallow, and my stomach churns.

"Really?" I ask Cooper. "Are you sure about this?"

Smiling, he tugs an orange Harrison beanie over my loose waves and leads me inside. "Yep! That was our deal—we each pick one activity we like, so we know that half the evening won't suck."

"I stand by our plan. It's solid, and way easier than trying to plan Valentine's Day for someone else. But I can't play hockey."

Following him through a maze of hallways and stadium tunnels, I inhale the distinct smell of the arena—sweat, popcorn, and frozen water.

"We're not playing hockey."

"Driving the Zamboni?"

Cooper laughs, and the sound lights me up inside. We turn a corner, revealing the smooth white surface of the ice.

The sound echoes in the space, and it's weird to see all the orange seats empty without fans filling them. Navy banners hang from the ceiling, along with the American flag, massive speakers, and the JumboTron screen. The lights blaze, reflecting off the ice. I didn't realize it would be so bright down here.

"Maybe next time. Today, we're skating."

He walks through the chute, but I'm stuck in place. "I— I've never done this before."

Spinning back to face me, Cooper sends me a reassuring smile and grabs both my palms. "I know. But I'm a really good teacher."

I wince. "What if I fall down?"

"You definitely will, but it's okay. And if you're really not comfortable, we don't have to do this. You can just tell your friends we did. Make up how romantic it was as we held hands and stuff. But I have the ice time, and it's a blast. Let me teach you how to skate?"

He looks so earnest, I can't resist. Nodding, I check out the team bench with him. A clunky pair of scuffed black skates sits besides cute white ones, along with a pile of socks and gloves.

Inclining his head, he indicates the extra layers. "I wasn't sure what you'd need tonight, but the socks will help in case your skates are too big. I had to guess your size. And your outfit's perfect, by the way."

Glancing down at my black leggings under my overall shorts and fuzzy purple sweater, I warm at his compliment.

"I have this"—he points to a Harrison Hockey hoodie—"if you get cold. Now, let's get you laced up. That's one of the hardest parts."

"Really? I thought balancing all my weight on a knife blade would be the hardest part."

Cooper rolls his eyes at my sarcasm and sits me down on the bench, then kneels in front of me.

"You're hilarious." He slips off my shoes, then slides my feet into the white skates. My heart does a weird flutter in my chest. I've never had a Cinderella fantasy or a foot fetish, but in this moment, I can see the appeal.

"Hmm." Tugging on the laces, he squeezes my ankles, then fiddles with the skates again. "Nope, let's add another pair of socks."

"Okay." I do as instructed, and then he goes through the entire process a second time. Starting with the laces at my toes, he makes sure they are snug but not too tight, adjusting them all the way up the tongue of the skate. Then he secures the laces around the hooks at my ankles. After tying them in a cute bow, he tells me to stand up.

My feet are heavy and awkward. My ankles want to cave in towards each other, and I have to squeeze my abs together to keep from falling. Cooper's must be magnificent. I wobble like a toddler, throwing out my arms for balance, but he anchors me, palms on my waist.

With the added height of the skates, I'm only a few inches shorter than he is. Staring into his light brown eyes, I forget to worry about falling.

"Feel good?" I nod before I realize he means the fit of the skates and not his hands on my body. But they do, too. "You want them snug around your ankles but not pinching your toes. Give me a second to get mine on and then we'll get started."

Sitting on the bench beside him, I point at his skates. "Why do they look so different from mine?"

"These are hockey skates. See how the blade is shorter? That means I can stop and go faster. Plus, the boot is a lot stiffer." He demonstrates, showing me how the firm material doesn't bend. "This keeps us safe on the ice. Pucks and sticks bounce off, and I don't even feel it."

Lightning quick, he puts them on and ties the laces, then points at my white pair. "Those are figure skates. They're a little easier for beginners."

"You taking it easy on me?" I raise a brow, faking outrage, but he laughs it off.

"Hush your mouth. I'd never do that." Then he gives me a pair of gloves before standing and pulling me up, too. "Ready?"

Leading me out onto the ice, Cooper keeps one hand tucked in mine and the other at my waist.

"Okay, this is called the boards." He pats the top of the wall that separates the ice from the seats before putting his palm back on me. "Grab it. The first thing I want you to do is hold on to this and march in place."

"March?" I grip the wall as my balance wavers.

"Yep. Pick up your feet and take tiny little steps in place. Don't worry about going anywhere yet."

"Uh, okay." I feel like an idiot, but Cooper graces me with a wide grin. While I march, he skates away backwards, still facing me, then executes a fancy maneuver and returns to my side.

"Showoff," I say under my breath.

"Sorry." He winks, and I don't believe him. "You're doing great, though. Now we're going to try some baby steps forward."

Still holding onto the wall for dear life, I mince a few yards around the rink.

"Are you ready to let go?" Cooper asks.

No. He must read the panic on my face because he moves behind me, fingertips resting on my hips now. "You're okay.

Keep doing baby steps and stay close to the wall. Let your hand hover over it in case you need it."

Taking a deep breath, I let go of the boards. His warm presence behind me is reassuring. "How long have you been doing this?"

"Skating?"

"No, teaching girls how to do it on dates." I roll my eyes playfully. "Yes, skating."

"I started learning when I was five."

I do the math in my head, my eyes widening. "Seventeen years. No wonder you're pretty good at it. What made you want to learn?" I keep up my little march as we talk.

"My dad." His voice gets scratchy, and he clears his throat. "He's not really in my life anymore, but when I was little, I loved watching Dallas Stars games with him. I wanted to play, so I had to learn to skate first." He tightens his hands on my waist, changing the subject. "Ready to try to skate?"

"I thought I was skating."

"And doing an amazing job of it." His tone filled with pride makes warmth bubble up in my chest. "But this is still just walking on the ice. Skating—skating is like flying."

"Oh, that's not intimidating at all."

"Good."

I swallow past the lump of fear in my throat. What's the worst that could happen? I fall on my butt? I get a little cold? I can do this.

"What's the next step, hotshot?"

Keeping an arm around my hips, Cooper taps my left leg.

"Anchor this foot down, put your weight on it, and push forward," he says. "Then gradually shift your body weight from one leg to another."

Biting my lip, I make an attempt, but my feet slide apart

on the slippery surface and I lose my balance. Thankfully, Cooper grabs my arms and keeps me upright.

"I've got you. Try again."

Once I'm stable, he lets go, giving me some space, and I push and glide for one step, shifting my weight like he said. Then I take another. I glide for a few more paces, and I glance at him and grin. But once I take my focus off what I'm supposed to be doing, I wobble, losing control. Windmilling, I flail my arms before falling backwards and landing on my butt. The impact is jarring, rattling my teeth, and my tailbone aches. Cold from the ice seeps through my clothes.

Cooper looms over me and grins.

"What happened to 'I've got you'?" I glare at him.

"Now you know what it feels like to fall. Learning to get up is an important lesson."

"Don't get all philosophical on me." I hold out my palms for him to tug me up, but he shakes his head.

"No, I'm being serious. Getting up safely is a big deal." With that, he plops down on the ice beside me. "Here, I'll show you. Roll over so you're on your knees, then put one foot in front. Shift your weight so it's on that leg and then push up."

He demonstrates, and I huff. "You make it look easy. Is that what you do during a hockey game?"

"Darlin', I don't fall."

I brush off his cocky smirk and use my newfound skills to stand up. My legs are shaky and I'm about as graceful as a baby deer, but I don't care. Cooper is right. As I shift my weight from foot to foot and achieve a brief moment of gliding on the ice, I can't keep the smile off my face. I want to pump my fist in victory like the Rebels defeating the Death Star, but that would definitely throw off my balance. My heart races with adrenaline, and warmth surges through my limbs.

"Wanna keep going?" Cooper asks, eyes hopeful.

"Absolutely." I nod, determined to give this my best shot. The gleam in his gaze and his wide grin spur me on, too.

Staying by my side, he encourages me as I wobble around the rink. My feet still want to slide in two different directions and I have to grab the boards a few times to keep from biting it, but I complete another lap.

Cooper whoops and hollers, like we just won a championship. Then he picks me up around my waist and spins us, my feet flying out behind me like a train. Breathless, I clutch his neck so I don't fall and inhale his clean, woodsy cologne.

"Don't drop me," I beg when he stops spinning.

"Darlin', I wouldn't dream of it."

CHAPTER
Twenty-One

COOPER

Teaching Jasmine to skate lights me up inside like the red lamp that goes off when we score. I could tell she was nervous when we started, but she trusted me and didn't give up, even though she fell a few more times. By the end of our ice session, she managed to let go of the boards and glide around the entire rink with her palm gripped in mine. It wasn't exactly smooth, but her eyes sparkled and her cheeks were pink with color. Her determined attitude and sense of humor make her an excellent student. I hope we can do this again soon.

Hockey is my passion, and it's my greatest dream to play professionally. I love being on the team. But when was the last time I came out here just to skate and have fun? Seeing it through Jasmine's eyes sparked something new in my chest. I want to keep chasing this high.

An alarm sounds on my phone, and I frown. "Sorry, Tara Lipinski. Our ice time is up."

"It's probably for the best. I'm going to have a bruise

tomorrow." Jasmine rubs her backside, and I can't help checking her out.

"Let me know if there's anything I can do to help with that. A massage, maybe?"

Giggling, she rolls her eyes as I get her to the bench and tug off her skates. As she gets her shoes back on, I take care of our gear and leave the place as I was instructed. Three years of being kind to Maurice, the head maintenance man, have paid off today.

As we exit the arena, I sling my arm around Jasmine's shoulders and inhale. Her now-familiar coconut scent engulfs me, and the soft skin of her neck looks so tempting. I want to brush my lips over that spot right below her ear. I swallow, leaning closer—and she giggles and swipes my car keys out of my hand, running for the driver's side door of my truck.

"What are you doing?" I chase after her.

She winks, opening the door and climbing in. "I can't have you driving to your own surprise. Get in."

I shrug. "That makes sense, but Bubba is delicate. Be gentle with him."

She fiddles with the radio until she finds something that's not a country station. "Cooper, I promise I will treat Bubba like he is my own precious Herbie. Now, shut up and fasten your seat belt."

I comply, and it isn't long before we're headed past the rest of campus, out of town. It's dark and quiet as she turns down a series of country roads. "Where are we going?"

"You'll see."

"Um, it really seems like you're trying to find a place to dump my body."

"Please." She waves me off. "I'd definitely destroy your body with Drano in my bathtub and then—"

"You've thought about this entirely too much."

"I like to be prepared." She glances at me across the cab, then bursts out laughing. "Look, we're almost there."

Pointing up ahead, I make out a sign for the Harrison Observatory. "Oh! I know where we are. This shares some of the land with the Ag department."

"They probably share funding, too. Isn't that how it usually goes?" Pulling into a sparse parking lot, Jasmine tosses me the keys across the console. Hopping out, she walks towards the dome-shaped building. "Have you been out here before?" she asks as she pounds on the locked glass door.

"Not to this site, no. Um, why—"

"Hey, Jaz." A petite girl with wild curly hair opens the door and ushers us in. "The last 'Night Under the Stars' tour just finished. The place is all yours. It's locked. All you have to do is pull this door closed when you leave."

With a wave in my direction, the girl pulls her coat tighter around her and heads out to the parking lot.

"Bye, Raquel! See you in class on Wednesday!" Jasmine says to her back as she leaves. Turning to me, she rocks on the balls of her feet. "I know a guy."

"Who let you borrow the planetarium?" The entryway is dim, lit only by the security lights. It's intimate and a little spooky, like anything could happen.

"We were in the same recitation group for Calc Three. My study guides saved her GPA. She owes me a little favor."

I give her a once-over. She's so comfortable to be around, it's easy to forget that Jasmine is wicked smart. My field is more demanding than I let on, but I stopped at Calc one. And her study guides are saving the other students? She is never condescending or boastful about it, but damn. Her intelligence makes her even hotter. Pressure builds low in my groin and I fight off thoughts about how much I want to be with her.

She gestures at the building. "Wanna see the star show?"

"Definitely!" I don't have to feign enthusiasm. I've always wanted to check this place out, but it hasn't fit in my schedule. "This is awesome."

Her answering grin fills my chest with warmth. "I'm glad you think so. Come on."

Grabbing my hand, she tugs me through a few darkened hallways until we step into the observation dome.

"I don't think we'll be able to see anything through the telescope tonight. It's too cloudy. But the planetarium show is really cool."

Slowing spinning in the middle of the room, I take in the domed space. Dotted with seats along the perimeter, the ceiling has a blue tinge to it, like the sky before the sun comes up in the morning. Jasmine rustles through a cabinet along the wall, then tugs out huge floor pillows and blankets. Maneuvering them into the center of the room, she makes a nest on the floor for us.

"Ta-da! Best seats in the house." Patting the spot beside her, she settles in, then points a remote at a bank of electronics by the door. The lights dim, then wink out as I lay down next to her. The darkness is consuming. I lace my fingers behind my head, looking up, and the star show begins.

The narrator explains different constellations to us, their position in the sky, how to find them, and the stories behind them. It's fascinating, but I'm distracted by the girl only inches away.

Her coconut scent surrounds me, and her hair tickles my arm. I try to focus on the stars above us, but the curve of her mouth as she smiles up at the ceiling is too much. Maybe my mind has exaggerated it, but I don't think so. That night we were almost together, our chemistry was scorching. Would it be like that again? What would happen if I kiss her?

Shifting onto my side, I trace the outline of her cheekbone with my fingertip. She rolls to face me.

"Hey."

"Hey."

What would happen is, I would make her uncomfortable. Guilt tightens my chest and sweat breaks out along my hairline. And no matter how much I want her, I won't do that.

All because I wanted my mom off my case. Well, that backfired. She texts me more questions about Jasmine than I ever heard about getting a girlfriend. So I swallow and withdraw my hand. "This is cool."

"Isn't it? I love it." She doesn't pull away or stiffen, and her beaming grin ebbs away my anxiety.

The star show wraps up and Jasmine grabs the remote, slowly bringing up the lights so as not to blind us.

Sliding my cell phone from my pocket, I lean towards her, still in our pile of blankets on the floor.

"I have a favor to ask you." Opening my camera, I turn on selfie mode. "For my mom. You know she asks about you all the time. She'll love this romantic gesture."

"Sure." Cuddling close, Jasmine smiles as I snap a few pictures. Her dark hair spreads around her like a goddess, her green eyes shine, and the affection in her gaze seems so real. I almost believe we're a couple.

After I put away my phone, I glance over at her. "You know all about my mom, but I don't know much about your family. What are they like?"

"Hmm." She sits up, legs tucked under her, and I mimic the pose. "I'm not sure how to explain them. My dad is very corporate, very driven. I'm more like him than my mom in that regard. He travels a lot, but he always sends me texts when he sees old Beetles like Herbie on the road." She smiles, like she's reliving the memory.

"My mom—she means well. I know she loves me. She's been thrilled to be a stay at home mom for as long as I can remember, and sometimes I don't think she understands why I'd want anything other than that. I'm glad she's fulfilled—it's just not what I want for me, you know?"

I nod, encouraging her to keep talking.

"She and my sister are pretty close. Maya went to Harrison four years before me, but she's back in Indy now. She works as a nurse, just got off the night shift, so they get to see each other a lot. And they both really love her husband, Joel."

"It's been just me and my mom for so long, I can't imagine the dynamics with more people."

"Yeah, it's different. I feel out of the loop sometimes. Partly because I don't live nearby, but also because I'm not sure they really get me. But I know they love me. They'd do anything to help me if I needed it."

"I think that's the sign of a good family. They come through for you."

"No one would ever doubt that your momma would move heaven and earth for you." She laughs, then sobers. Her posture goes from easy and relaxed to nervous, twisting her fingers together. "Speaking of needing something." She bites her lip. "I have a big favor to ask of you."

"What's up?" I ask. What could be so bad to make her look this anxious?

"Um, my roommates are surprised that you've never stayed over, and I've never walk-of-shamed it home. Although I categorically object to that phrase—no one should feel ashamed the morning after."

"Walk of pride? Of satisfaction?"

She giggles. "I like that. Anyway…"

"Yeah. What should we do?"

She's not suggesting we actually sleep together, right? Blood flows south at the thought. I mean, I could make that sacrifice for the ruse, but—

"Can you spend the night at my place?" she asks in a rush. "It's totally okay if you have practice or class or something and you can't. No big deal. In fact, I shouldn't have suggested—"

"Jasmine," I cut her off, standing and offering her a hand. "I can have fake sex with you any day."

Now I'm thinking about real sex with her. I need to keep it in my pants, not complicate this further, but she's so damn delectable. Can I handle spending a platonic night with her?

CHAPTER
Twenty-Two

JASMINE

We parade past my roommates watching TV in the living room and I make sure they see me take Cooper up to my room. Once we're there, I turn on *Star Trek,* but Chris Pine doesn't distract me from the guy on my bed. I like hanging with Cooper. Things are fun and easy, and I can be myself. But there's this frisson of awareness under my skin that won't let me relax. His woodsy cologne smells so tempting. It was all I could do not to jump on top of him in the planetarium. But I made this no sex rule for a reason. He's still paying to have my car fixed, and I don't have a *Pretty Woman* fantasy. It might be fun in the moment—who am I kidding? It would definitely be fun—but I think I'd feel squicked out afterwards.

I shift, and my arm brushes his soft flannel shirt.

"Sorry," I whisper, not sure what I'm apologizing for.

In response, he nudges my toes with his own, and I giggle at the sensation. Somehow our stockinged feet end up intertwined as we watch, and I don't move away. Our heads are six inches apart—it would be so easy to kiss him.

But if I kiss him on my bed right now, all of our clothes will disappear, and we will definitely have sex. The tension is so high, I'm about to burst out of my skin. There's no way we won't hook up if we kiss.

When the movie ends, he rolls over onto his back and stares at me.

"Do we need to make a lot of moaning noises and jump up and down on the bed to convince your roommates that we're getting it on in here?"

"Um." Why is my mouth so dry? I try to swallow. He's thinking about sex, too. It's like there's an electrical current between us, liable to burn the house down.

"No, I think they can draw conclusions without that." Besides, I definitely couldn't handle hearing him moan right now. Snapping my laptop closed, I return it to my desk and rifle through the top drawer before finding a new toothbrush, still in its packaging. "Here, a little Valentine's Day present for you."

"Aw, darlin', you really went all out. Name brand instead of generic. I'm touched."

"What can I say? I'm a thoughtful gal like that. Bathroom's down the hall on the right. I'll get my pajamas on while you're in there."

But Cooper sets the toothbrush down and starts unbuttoning his shirt. His bare chest is a masterpiece that begs me to paint or sculpt it. Since I can do neither, I gulp.

"What are you doing?"

"In case I run into anyone in the hallway, it might look more natural if I was more, uh, disheveled."

"Oh, good point." All that exposed skin makes it hard to think clearly. Stepping closer, I run my hands through his hair. I want to tug his mouth to mine and never stop. He freezes and his eyes go wide.

"To add to the, you know, mussed vibe," I say, then pretend to study my handiwork. When in reality I'm trying to get myself under control. "There, you're sufficiently ravished."

Winking, he heads to the bathroom and I throw open my dresser drawers. Normally I'd sleep in a t-shirt or tank top, but do I need to put on pants? Ugh, and what about a bra? Even sleeping in a sports bra is so uncomfortable. Usually if I have a guy sleep over, he's already seen me naked, and I don't worry about such things.

My heart races and my breath comes in short pants. I force myself to inhale and exhale while I count to five. I'm spiraling, and it's dumb. There's no reason to make this situation any weirder than it is. And besides, we're just going to sleep. No funny business.

Once that's decided, I strip and throw on my comfiest, oversized gray sleep shirt and hop into bed.

The door eases open, and Cooper peers around. "Can I come in?" he whispers.

"Yes." I pat the space beside me.

He bites his lip. "Um, do you mind if I sleep in my boxers?"

"Is that how you normally sleep?"

"Yeah, but if you want—"

"Nah. Be yourself."

With a sigh, he unbuckles his belt and steps out of his jeans. I try not to stare. Laying down next to me, arms behind his head, he gazes at the ceiling. "That's what I like about you, Jasmine. Because we aren't really dating, I don't have to put on an act."

I turn on my side to face him. "It's refreshing, right?"

"Totally." He clears his throat. "Hey, I should warn you. I, uh, can get a little grabby in my sleep."

I giggle. "You're a stealth cuddler. Thanks for the warning, but I'll live." Honestly, I'm craving some physical contact. Snuggling sounds fantastic.

"Seriously." Cooper yawns, arranges the pillow to his liking, and then pulls me close to him. "You're the best."

God, he smells delectable. I inhale deeply. His chest feels like a firm, warm pillow under my cheek.

"You're not so bad, either," I say, letting myself relax and enjoy this. A few cuddles aren't hurting anyone.

CHAPTER
Twenty-Three

JASMINE

Cooper: My mom wants to know—what's your favorite flower?

Jasmine: Why does she want to know that?

Cooper: I've found it's easier to just pass along the questions than try to reason with her.

Jasmine: Tulips, I guess?

Jasmine: Hey, here's a fun one. What's your biggest irrational fear?

Cooper: Spiders. They are creepy. You?

Jasmine: Public speaking, maybe? I don't love all those people looking at me.

Cooper: It's hard not to look at you, Jasmine. You're gorgeous.

~

My cheeks heat at Cooper's flirty text. Flustered, I put my phone face-down on the wooden surface of the study room table. Sometimes I just need to eliminate all distractions and work in the library. I'd convinced Delaney to come with me, and we'd holed up in a study room for the past few hours. However, since I'm constantly checking my phone and thinking of Cooper, I haven't accomplished much. I have Calc three equations to solve, but I pick up my phone and reread the last text he sent.

It's hard not to look at you, Jasmine, You're gorgeous.

Is he just flirting with me because he's bored? Because thanks to our ruse, I'm the only girl he can direct any flirty energy towards?

Or does he really think I'm gorgeous?

My heart flutters in my chest. It's been a few days since I saw him last. After he spent the night on Valentine's Day, we woke up tangled around each other. Before I could analyze it too much—or snuggle closer—he was out of there for early morning hockey practice.

"Who are you texting?" Delaney asks, a mischievous glint in her eye.

"No one." I clear my throat and nudge my phone away.

She smiles, shaking her head. "You're lying. It's Cooper. I can tell by the lovesick look on your face."

I scoff. "I'm not lovesick."

"Sure, you're not." She rolls her eyes, then holds up her own phone. "Brian just texted. He's waiting for me outside. Are you sure you don't need a ride?"

"Nah. Thanks, though. I have more equations to finish."

Delaney closes her copy of *Democracy in America,* then packs folders, books, and pens into her backpack. She's a history major—I don't understand why. It seems useless to me. "Are you sure you're okay to get home? Still no Herbie?"

"I know, I miss him. But it's a safe campus, and not too far. I can walk home." If I'm home, I know I will get drawn into a movie or a girls' night with her and Staci. That sounds so much more appealing than the math text on my laptop in front of me, but I need to be productive on my night off.

She narrows her eyes as she slings her bag over one shoulder, and I hold up my hand, cutting her off.

"I will text you before I leave and when I get home, if I don't see you there. Acceptable?"

Relief slides across her features. "Thank you. Don't stay too late."

"I won't."

The words blur on the screen before me, so I stand and stretch. Rolling out the kinks in my shoulders, I sit down, giving myself a pep talk.

One more hour. Or two.

But when I stare at my computer again, the old-fashioned clock ticking on the wall is too loud. The buzzing of the fluorescent light grates on my nerves. And my hair is driving me crazy, tickling my neck. Throwing it up in a messy bun, I contemplate my fingernails, bitten down to the sad little numb on every one. Should I do gel nails before the department dinner? That's the only polish that works with the latex gloves I constantly wear in the lab. Will Cooper notice? Will he care? Do I care if he cares?

No, of course I don't. It doesn't matter. Although I love the way his eyes sometimes light up when he sees me. But I've got to stop letting the circumstances and his extreme hotness muddy the waters. Fake dating is too close to the real thing. Herbie will be finished soon, I hope, and then we can discuss our breakup after my dinner in a week and a half.

Sighing, I tap my fingers on the wooden table. I need to focus. Everything about this beige room is bland and boring, but I'm still distracted. I have too much energy and nowhere to put it. Being celibate is harder than I expected.

Clicking my pen repeatedly, I rest my forehead on the cool surface of the study table. I could use a quick change of scenery. A loop around the library, a stop at the drinking fountain, and then back to work.

Resolved, I throw my stuff into my rainbow bag and flip off the lights in the tiny cubicle. It's a quiet enough night that the room will probably still be available when I return, but I'm not dumb enough to leave anything in it.

I take a lap of the building, making myself inhale and exhale deeply. The dusty scent of books soothes me. When did I last read a book for pleasure? I'd love to go downtown to Main Street Books and browse. Maybe I will see if Cooper wants—

"I'm not an Animal Science major, but I'm pretty sure I learned this in one of my genetics classes."

I halt. I know that drawl. It's like I conjured him up with my thoughts of him. Cooper.

Tiptoeing forward, I peer into the open doorway of another miniscule study room. Cooper leans over the desk, powerful forearms on display, and points to something on another student's laptop.

"Here, see?"

They discuss something, but my brain zones out a bit. Brainiac Cooper is even hotter than the flannel and cowboy hat version, and that's saying something. My pulse trips up a notch.

The other guy nods. Grabbing a composition book, he jots down some notes. They chat about bovine genetics as I try not to drool. What can I say? Science talk is sexy.

I clear my throat in the doorway, and he looks up. Then his face transforms as his slow smile slides across his features. My stomach flips.

"Hey, darlin'."

"Hey, Cooper."

With a pointed glance at his classmate watching our exchange, he moves to the doorway and plants a smacking kiss on my cheek. My body can't help but react with a shiver and a rush of warmth. How does he always smell so yummy? His woodsy cologne makes butterflies swarm in my belly.

As he pulls away from me, he blinks and his eyes widen. "Did I miss a date? Were we supposed to meet here, or—"

"I was studying down the hall, just taking a break."

His lazy grin reappears.

"Good timing." Stepping aside, he motions towards the skinny guy at the table. "Jasmine, this is Andy. He and I are in Ag Business Management together."

"Hey." Adjusting the brim of his trucker hat, Andy waves.

"What are you guys working on?" I'm stalling, I know.

"Coop was helping me with an Animal Science question."

"Animal Science?" I lean against the doorframe. "Is that part of the Ag department?"

"It sure is." Cooper's Texas accent, slow as molasses, washes over me, and how can those innocent words make me flush? And yet. My insides are blushing.

"So," Andy scribbles in his notebook, then holds it up, "is this how it works?"

Returning to the table, Cooper inspects his writing. His incredible smile takes over his face. Even when it's not directed at me, I love seeing it. He and Andy fist bump and Andy stands, gathering his belongings.

"I've gotta run. Thanks again, man. I'd be failing without your help. And nice meeting you, Jasmine."

Giving me a wave, he hurries out, and I turn to Cooper. Leaning against the desk, I cock my head.

"You're a catch, Cooper Edwards. A jock and a brain all

rolled into one. You're gonna make a great farmer, you know that?"

"Thanks." His cheeks redden and he takes a step closer to me. "Can I tell you a secret?"

I nod, mirroring his posture and leaning in.

"It's dumb. I'd love a career in agriculture, helping farmers figure out how to make healthy food for people."

"What's dumb about that?"

Cooper winces. "That's the secret part. I've always dreamed of a career in the NHL. Some scouts have been sniffing around, and I'm torn about what to pursue."

I've seen him play hockey, and it's mighty impressive, but I don't really know what I'm looking for. But the NHL... you have to be the best for that. Is he serious?

"NHL scouts? How does that work?"

"If they like what they see, they can sign me and I can start in their minor league organizations. I'm not sure if I really have a shot at anything, but our team wants to make the Frozen Four, so I reckon that will garner some attention."

"Is it hard, being this fantastic?" He barks a laugh, and the mood lightens like I had intended. "You're telling me you have two amazing career prospects? That's incredible, Cooper."

"I hadn't thought of it that way." Running a hand through his hair, he looks thoughtful. "You're the first person I've mentioned it to."

"You should talk to your advisor about it, honestly, but your agriculture degree would keep, right? You could always wait and see what happens with hockey and go from there. It isn't a bad fall-back plan."

"You make it sound so easy."

I shrug. "It could be. Are you that good at hockey?"

"Maybe?"

"Do you love it?"

"More than anything else."

"You owe it to yourself to try. Keep your options open, at least."

"Thanks." He stares at me for a beat, and the moment stretches between us. What can I do to prolong it? Then he clears his throat. "You heading home?"

The thought of cloistering myself in that tiny room again makes me shiver with dread. I can't take any more. "I was supposed to study some more, but yeah, I'm mentally done. I should start walking in that direction before it gets too late."

"I'll give you a ride."

"It's out of your way," I say, waving him off.

"I don't care. What kind of boyfriend leaves his girl to walk home by herself when he has a perfectly working vehicle?"

"Uh, the fake kind?"

"Yeah, but they don't know that," he stage-whispers to the empty room. "Besides, I have to keep up appearances. And I really don't mind."

Slinging an arm across my shoulders, he walks me out of the door of the study cubicle.

"Any word on Herbie?" I ask as we make our way through the underground library to the main floor.

He winces. "Not sure if you know this, but it's tricky to find parts for classic cars."

"Yeah, I've run into that before. Did they give you a time frame?"

"Couple more weeks, if the creek don't rise." He squeezes my shoulder. "Until then, I don't mind driving you around."

I frown. "I hate being a burden."

"You're not. And we're friends—friends do things for each other."

It's nothing I expected, but he's right. We have become friends through this weird situation. So I relax and lean into him. "Okay. Thank you."

The sweet look he sends me keeps me warm all the way to his truck, despite the frigid winter air.

CHAPTER
Twenty~Four

COOPER

Momma: Oh my word, that's the cutest picture! Where are you two?

    Cooper: Valentine's date at the planetarium

    Momma: Did you plan that? I'm impressed!!

    Cooper: No, Jasmine did. I took her skating.

    Momma: I'm not surprised.

    Momma: Did she dump you?

    Cooper: No, why?

    Momma: Because she took you for a romantic date under the stars and you took her to a hockey rink

    Cooper: She liked it!

    Momma: This girl is the best thing that's ever happened to you. You should marry her.

                   ~

Cooper: How's your week going?

    Jasmine: Swamped with GRE prep. You?

Cooper: Big game this weekend against our rival.

Jasmine: Good luck!

Jasmine: Any word on Herbie?

Cooper: Ordering the part

Jasmine: What was wrong with him?

Cooper: I'll be honest. The mechanic said a bunch of words and I don't know what they mean.

Cooper: What's your favorite holiday? In case my mom asks.

Jasmine: 4th of July! I love fireworks.

Cooper: What's something new you'd like to learn?

Jasmine: Hmm. I know the basics, but I'd like to work on my cooking skills. It's not all that different from chemistry.

Cooper: I know a lady who'd like to teach you how to make spaghetti. Actually, she taught me so I could make it for you.

Jasmine: Let me guess. She lives in Texas and answers to "Momma"?

Cooper: Got it in one!

Jasmine: Also, I love spaghetti! You can make it for me anytime you want.

"Darlin', you look pretty as a peach."

Giggling, Jasmine twirls in her entryway, making her forest green retro dress spin out like a top. The dress shows off her smooth shoulders and a hint of cleavage, and I can't stop staring. My tongue is probably lolling out of my mouth like a cartoon dog drooling over a steak. Flaring out at her waist and stopping right above her knees, she looks like a 1950s bombshell. The style of it has me imagining her as a sexy pinup girl, biting her finger with ruby-red lips and giving me bedroom eyes.

Oof. Sex deprivation is a genuine concern. Shaking off my fantasy, I blink and try to tamp down my raging hormones.

At my compliment, her eyes sparkle. "You clean up pretty good yourself. Thanks for coming with me."

"Ready?" I hold out my elbow for her to take, and after she shrugs into her red peacoat, she slips her arm through mine.

She locks up, then slips her keys into a little clutch purse and lets me help her up into my truck. I've never tried walking in tiny heels like the ones she's wearing, but it looks precarious.

Bubba roars to life, and I don't even comment when Jasmine switches the radio station dial. I always make sure it's playing country music now, just so she can change it.

"So I've been to hockey banquets, but the Ag Department doesn't have any dinners. What should I expect?"

Jasmine puts her hand up to her mouth, poised to bite a fingernail, when she stops and stares at them.

"Hey." I grab her hand, inspecting her long red fingernails. The color matches her lips perfectly. "Where'd these come from?"

Her cheeks turn pink. "You noticed!"

"Of course." My sex-starved brain imagines her wrapping her hands around me and trailing these fingernails over my skin. Shivering at the thought, I bite back a groan. "It's damn sexy."

"Thanks." Clearing her throat, she fidgets in her seat, crossing her legs together. "Anyway. Tonight. Um, what to expect. Food, drinks, small talk. Then a few remarks from a visiting scientist—this is supposed to inspire us—and some departmental awards."

"Sounds good."

"Oh, there's an afterparty at one of the nicer places in town. This year it's at Blue Forty-Two. But we don't have to go if you don't want."

I shrug. "You seem to think that this is a big hardship for me, but I really don't mind, Jasmine."

She stares at her hands, clenched in her lap. "Chad—he only wanted to do things if it was his idea. He hated things with my friends. So thanks."

"Chad." I raise a brow. "Has he been bothering you lately?"

"Nope." She shakes her head, a curly tendril falling from her up-do to brush her cheek. "Whenever I've encountered him in the lab, he's been oddly silent. I wonder why?"

"Curious," I say, staring straight out the windshield. "Hopefully he won't pester you tonight, either."

"Thanks for being my buffer in case, though."

I pull into the parking garage and help her out of my truck, hustling her to the elevator so she doesn't get too cold. When we enter the Union ballroom, it's been transformed.

It's usually covered in orange and navy when I'm here for hockey banquets, but the parquet floor sparkles and the wood-paneled walls twinkle with tulle and tiny white lights. The solid oak beams overhead gleam and the bank of windows that face the campus glow with the setting sun. It's classy, beautiful, and pales in comparison to the woman next to me.

We move to gaze out the windows, but all I can picture is my hands on her body in that satiny dress. Pressed close to her, inhaling the sweet scent of her skin. Blood rushes to my groin. I gulp, coughing. Where did all the oxygen go?

"You okay?" She pats my back, a concerned line between her brows.

"Yeah, I'm great."

"I know just what you need."

I doubt that very much—we certainly can't do what I was imagining in this room full of people.

But Jasmine searches through her little purse, then emerges with two tickets and gives them to me with a flourish. "Our drink vouchers. Wanna head to the bar?"

"Sure." I straighten my tie and offer my elbow.

But before she can thread her arm through my outstretched one, Lucy comes bounding over. "Hey, Cooper! Hey, Jasmine!"

The girls hug and compliment each other's dress. Lucy's is red and strappy, very different from the usual hockey fan gear I see her in.

Lucy introduces us to her date—a tall, striking girl named Olivia from her floor, she tells us—and invites us to sit at their table. We follow them through the long room, weaving around tables and laughing students in evening dress. Jasmine is about to set her purse down when a tiny gray-haired lady in a floor-length beaded black dress appears at her side.

Jasmine's face lights up as they embrace, and seeing her so happy makes something bubble up in my chest. When they pull apart, she clears her throat and tugs me to her side.

"Dr. Michelson, this is my boyfriend, Cooper. Cooper, meet my advisor."

I shake her hand gently so I don't crush her delicate bones and her lined face wreaths in a smile. "I'm so happy for you, dear. I know there was some... unpleasantness earlier. Good to see you're moving on."

She winks at me, and I don't know why, but her approval sends a rush of pride through my body. "Before you set your things down, would you come with me?"

Jasmine looks at me, questions in her green eyes, but intertwines our fingers. "Of course."

She waves to Lucy and then hurries to catch up to Dr. Michelson, striding across the room. The professor is so diminutive, she should get swallowed up by the crowd but they part before her. When we reach a "reserved" table up front by the podium, she turns back to Jasmine with a flourish.

"Surprise!"

Jasmine stiffens against me, tightening her grip on my fingers. The four people at the table stand up, smiling wide.

Dr. Michelson continues talking. "I wanted to wait as long as possible to tell you, but congratulations! You're receiving an award tonight! I invited your family to be here to see it."

I notice the resemblance between Jasmine and the tall man in the gray suit coming around the table to greet her. They have the same eyes. And the woman at his side, wearing a navy dress, hair the same shade as Jasmine's twisted up on her head, must be her mom. I recognize her from the picture in Jasmine's room. The young woman in a purple cocktail dress, her date trailing behind her, has to be Jasmine's sister. Their faces have the same shape, the same tilt to their smiles.

Dropping my hand, she hugs them all, and a bead of sweat trickles between my shoulder blades. This night just got more complicated.

"Jasmine." Her mom glances towards me, raising her brows. "Aren't you going to introduce us to your date?"

All eyes swivel to me, and I gulp.

"Um, of course." Jasmine tugs me flush to her side. "This is Cooper Edwards, my boyfriend."

Putting on my most charming smile, I shake hands with her dad and her sister's date, who I learn is Joel, her brother-in-law.

"Boyfriend?" Mrs. Turner says, voice full of mischief. "Things are more serious than I thought!"

Jasmine blushes and stammers. I wrap my arm around her and drop a kiss to her head, inhaling her coconut scent. "What can I say? I'm a serious guy."

I'm close enough to hear her quick indrawn breath. I clear my throat. "Do you mind if I steal her for one more minute? We'll just get our drinks and come right back."

As her family nods and smiles, I steer her away towards the bar. Drinks. Drinks will help.

Jasmine stops in the middle of the crowd and I spin to face her. Her voice is shrill, her face pinched.

"What was that? You're a serious guy?" She puts air-quotes around my words. "Now what am I supposed to do when we break up next week?"

My stomach gives a lurch at the thought, but I keep my features smooth. "It's fine. You can tell them I'm too clingy, or something. I was just trying to distract them."

"Oh." Swallowing, she softens. "Thanks."

She waves her hand around, encompassing the ballroom. "I'm sorry about all this."

"A surprise visit from your family?" I grin. "I can't imagine what that's like."

She laughs, breaking the tension, and puts her hand back in mine until we get to the bar and place our orders. "What does it say about us and our families that this happened again?"

"I hope that's rhetorical." After the bartender gives me my Old Fashioned, I clink my glass against the rim of her lemon-drop martini. "Here's to getting through the night."

"I'll drink to that." Jasmine slams back her martini and drains it in one go, then motions the bartender for another. I blink as she gets her second drink.

"Are you okay?" I put my hand on her smooth, bare forearm. "A little stressed?"

A hysterical laugh escapes her lips and her eyes dart back and forth like a horse about to bolt. "A little."

"Look, I came here tonight to be your buffer. Against whatever. So what do you need?"

She takes a deep breath and I have to force myself to not stare at her chest heaving in her gorgeous dress.

"It's good. I'm excited. It's just... a lot."

"I get that." Securing my arm around her waist, I lead us back to our table. "Congratulations on your award, by the way."

"Thanks. I'd rather disappear into the wallpaper than have to go up and accept it in front of all these people."

Jasmine is so confident in her own skin that I didn't expect this. I'm pretty sure she's a genius, but she's only human, too. Everybody needs a pep talk now and then, I reckon. So I give her a little squeeze.

"You'll be fine. All you have to do is smile. Just look at me if you're nervous."

She takes another deep breath—*eyes up here, Edwards*—and leans into me as we approach our table. With a tremulous smile, we seat ourselves in with her parents and Joel and Maya.

We make small talk for a while as the cocktail hour winds down, and dinner is served. I answer all the requisite questions—where I'm from, my major, how the hockey team's faring. I learn what her dad and brother-in-law do for a living and their favorite sports teams.

This is my first "meet the parents" experience, even if it's fake, but it's not as bad as I imagined. I look Jasmine's dad and brother-in-law in the eye and aim for confident but not cocky. I'm polite to her mom and Maya, and maybe I pour on the Southern charm a little thick, but I think it works because her mom keeps beaming at me.

Jasmine seems okay. She sips her martini slowly this time, and when I put my arm around her shoulders after the plates are cleared away, she leans back against me. Her cheeks are flushed and her eyes sparkle.

When the Dean of the College of Arts and Sciences steps up to the podium, though, and the microphone squeaks, she freezes, and the color drains from her face. I grab her hand under the table, squeezing her fingers.

"Hey." Leaning close, I whisper in her ear. "You're Jasmine Turner. The smartest chemistry student in the room. You've got this."

"My knees are shaking and my stomach feels weird. I don't think I can walk up to the podium. How can you play hockey in front of so many fans and not freak out?"

I shrug. "I just tune 'em out, I guess. Having something else to focus on helps. What if you picture everyone in their underwear?"

She huffs a laugh, relaxing a little. "I've never understood why I'd want to do that. I don't want to think about my family or my professors in their underwear."

"But me." I bob my brows at her suggestively. "Think about me in my boxers."

Her startled gaze meets mine for a beat before she swallows and stares at the table. "Um, I'm not sure—"

"And we'd like to present the award for Outstanding Chemistry Student to Jasmine Turner!"

Before she can freak out, I stand with her and tug her to her feet, pressing a kiss to her cheek and propelling her towards the podium. The audience applauds, and I hear some cheers from Lucy's table. Her family claps enthusiastically and her parents' faces shine with pride.

With a mumbled thank you, Jasmine collects her plaque and rushes back to her seat, eyes downcast. Her breath comes in pants and her hands shake. Her mom and dad get up and hug her, and her sister and Joel pat her shoulders. When they are done with their congratulations, the awards move on to other students and she slumps against me.

"You did it," I whisper in her ear. "Not only did you earn the hell out of this award, but you accepted it well, too."

"Yeah." She sits a little straighter, her chin tipping up. "I did."

The smile of pure joy that lights her face makes me so happy, my chest hurts.

CHAPTER
Twenty~Five

JASMINE

The rest of the dinner passes in a blur as my adrenaline recedes. I lean against Cooper in a bit of a stupor as Dr. Sanders, the keynote speaker, one of Forbes Thirty Under Thirty who made her mark in pioneering cancer research, makes her speech. There is polite applause and then my family stands, all eyes on me.

I survived. No harassment from Chad and I didn't pass out or throw up in front of the crowd. I beam at them.

"Thanks for coming. This was a great surprise." And it was. Cooper took the attention off me and smoothed over any potential rough patches so I could sit back and enjoy it.

I hug everyone, and then they say goodbye to Cooper, too. My mom has a hard time letting go of him.

"Maybe you can come for dinner with Jasmine sometime soon? Or we could—"

"Thanks, Mom." I keep my voice firm as I untangle her grip. "We'll check our schedules."

After seeing them off, I exhale a breath, stirring a loose tendril of hair, and turn to Cooper.

"That wasn't too bad."

"Aw, darlin'." He throws an arm around my shoulders and I lean against his warmth. The scent of his woodsy cologne surrounds me and tingles zip through my body. "You're too sweet. A night with me *isn't too bad*."

Shifting, I gaze up at him and I can't help it—I want to jump in with both feet and forget about everything else. Heat floods me at the thought. I swallow, losing the train of his banter.

"Um." I lick my lips. "How do you feel about an after party?"

His hazel eyes glow, almost molten. "I'd feel good about that. Maybe I can earn higher praise than *not too bad*."

I chuckle, then take his hand. "It's good to have goals. I'll let you know how you score at the end of the night."

"Darlin', scoring is what I'm best at." He winks and I roll my eyes, but my insides flutter. Gathering our things, we say goodnight to Dr. Michelson and make our way back to Bubba.

Cooper keeps sending me smoldering looks out of the corner of his eye as he drives and heat builds in my lower belly. Is he thinking what I'm thinking? But he's off limits. Right?

He clears his throat. "I heard from my mechanic, by the way. Herbie should be finished next week."

Oh. I nod, and my throat goes dry. So that obstacle is out of the way now.

But this is our last night together. At the thought, all the butterflies in my stomach stop flying and congeal into a solid mass, settling like a rock of disappointment.

"That's great." My words come out wooden, and I stare unseeing through the passenger side window. The lights of downtown Lafayette blur before my eyes. I don't want to stop hanging out with him. Can I convince my friends it was an amicable break up? This can't be the last time I see him.

"Hey, you okay?" Cooper's voice is soft, and he reaches over and runs his thumb over my knuckles. No one is with us in the car to see, but I grab his hand anyway.

"Yeah." I swallow down the lump lodged in my throat. I still have the rest of the evening with him, and I won't let thoughts about the future ruin it. I force myself to smile and meet his gaze. "Thanks for coming with me tonight."

"Of course." His crooked grin spreads across his face and my stomach flips. "I can't pass up a date with Harrison's most outstanding chemistry student."

The note of pride in his voice warms me from the inside out. As he pulls up to the restaurant and parks the car, my skin tingles with anticipation. My hands shake as I open the door. The surprise and excitement of the night combined with knowing it's my last time with Cooper has me feeling off-balance.

Blue Forty-Two is a swanky downtown restaurant, all spartan industrial fixtures paired with luxury furnishings. It's not a typical college hangout, but it has a private room with a bar that a group of grad students rented for the afterparty tradition. The chemistry department might clean up nice, but we can party with the best of them.

With my arm in his, Cooper and I make our way into the restaurant but veer left at the hostess stand and head through a hallway off the main entrance. We utilize the coat rack they've set up for us. Once we open the door to the event space, music pours out.

Sound echoes thanks to the soaring ceilings, and the lights are dim. Normally full of tables, they've been moved aside so there's ample space to dance in front of the bar that lines the wall. The room is already full of chem students, tossing back drinks and dancing to the music.

Cooper loosens his tie with a smile, then leans in close. "Can I get you another drink?"

It's okay to let go a little tonight. I nod, and my heart gives a weird thump as I watch him walk away.

Before I can analyze it too much, Lucy bounds over, her date in tow. Her cheeks are flushed and she and Olivia both hold tumblers with dark liquid inside.

She gives me air kisses—this clearly isn't her first drink— and Olivia giggles. Slender with long legs accentuated by her black jumpsuit and long white-blonde hair, she could be an elf-extra in Lord of the Rings. She's probably a foot taller than Lucy, with her dark hair and olive skin, but they look good together.

"Congratulations on your award, Jaz!" Lucy's eyes sparkle and my chest feels light with the reminder of my hard work. It's still sinking in—my professors recognized me as an outstanding student. I start to smile, but then I see sandy hair out of the corner of my eye.

Tensing up, I wait for his attack, but then the man moves and—it's not Chad. I sigh in relief. But I'll have to keep my guard up. I scan the room so I can prepare for the conflict that's surely coming.

Lucy steps closer and raises a brow, sipping her drink. I smell something smokey mixed with the bite of alcohol in her glass.

"He's not here."

"Who?" I ask, although I shouldn't be surprised she noticed.

"Chad." Lucy sticks out her tongue and Olivia makes a tsking sound.

"Asshole," she says under her breath, and my admiration for her goes up a notch.

Lucy rolls her eyes. "He stormed out of the department dinner. Muttering about how they don't know talent, we don't deserve to see him tonight, and life is unfair." She snorts. "Yeah, we feel so bad for the poor, unappreciated white guy."

Then she links her arm through mine with a smile. "But it means he's not here."

I give her a matching grin as Cooper returns and hands me a martini glass. "What are we smiling about?"

I toss back the drink in one gulp. "We're celebrating. No Chad, chemistry awards, and Herbie's imminent return."

He clinks his beer bottle against my empty glass. "I'll drink to that."

Cooper leads me out to the dance floor, Lucy and Olivia close behind, and I let the music sweep me away. Between the alcohol flowing through my veins, the thumping bass beat, and Cooper's magnetic smile, it isn't long before I press myself closer, inhaling the woodsy, intoxicating scent of him. His muscular body gets my blood flowing and my nerves tingle.

It's more than just the fact that it's been a while. It's Cooper—I know him better than any other guy, and he's quality. I'm going to miss him.

Is this my last chance to run my hands up his arms and feel his biceps bulge under my touch? Or my last opportunity to wrap my arms around his neck and sway against him? The song turns slow, something by Ed Sheeran, and I inhale, tucking my head in the crook of his neck as he molds himself to me. His palms graze over the bare skin on my back, and I shiver.

"You okay?" he whispers in my ear, and I look up, gazing into his eyes. I nod, not sure I can speak in the face of his intense stare. It feels like he's X-raying me, looking into my heart.

My eyes drop to his lips, and all I can think about is the times I've kissed him before. Maybe he can read my mind, because he shifts closer. His mouth is inches away from mine and it would be easy, so easy, to push up on my tiptoes and make my dreams come true.

"What are you thinking about?" Cooper asks, his voice low and husky. Just the sound of it makes desire churn in my belly.

I swallow and decide to take a chance. "This."

I brush my lips across his, the softest hint of a kiss, and I feel it everywhere. How can the most chaste kiss set me on fire?

As I pull back, Cooper smiles. "Darlin', that's the best idea you've had all night."

His smile warms me, and I want to kiss him again, more, deeper, longer. All night long. But something holds me back.

I shake my head. "We're supposed to break up tomorrow." Why does my stomach sink at the thought?

"I've been pondering that."

"You have?" My head snaps up, gaze fixed on him, and he nods.

"Herbie is finished, or almost, at least. And I'm so proud of you for winning that award, Jaz. But Chad is gonna take it out on you."

I wince, because I thought the same thing earlier. "But you—aren't you tired of this?"

Cooper gives me his crooked smile and strokes my cheek. "Nah. There are a lot of perks."

"That's true." He steps closer, and I nuzzle back into his chest, taking advantage of the moment. "It's been kind of amazing to have a boyfriend as a shield from my roommate's horrible blind dates. And you're right about Chad. If we break up next week, he'd say he knew it would never last, or something, bother me about how you broke up with me or how I couldn't make it work. Make things worse than they already are. I'd never hear the end of it. At least this way I have a buffer."

"I'm happy to be your buffer anytime." He bobs his eyebrows at me, his words dripping with innuendo, and instead of laughing, it makes me shiver. I picture his body moving against mine, and tingles radiate outward from my core.

"But don't you miss, um…" What's a good euphemism for sleeping around? "The charms of your many female companions? You can't have that when everyone thinks we're dating."

Cooper cracks a laugh. "Your charms are all I need. But I'm not gonna lie and say I don't miss it. Sex is pretty fantastic."

"That it is." My heart rate trips up a notch and my blood thrums in my veins at the mere mention of the word *sex*. Clearly, it's been too long.

"And I hope I didn't imagine it, but we could be great together." He brushes the softest kiss against my neck and my knees go weak. I can't help but remember how he lifted me to wrap my legs around his waist the night we almost hooked up. My mouth waters.

I clear my throat, but my voice still comes out scratchy. "I think so, too."

"So what if we kept this up for a little longer and became friends with benefits?"

"Everyone always says that's a terrible idea." Could it be this easy? To just say yes and give in to everything I'm feeling? "That people get hurt."

He shrugs. "But we're not everyone. I promise I won't

really be your boyfriend—I won't make any demands of you, and there's no chance you'll fall in love with me."

I bite my lip, and my body throbs with desire. Cooper brushes his thumb over my mouth, and it's all I can do to stay upright on the dance floor.

"Okay, you haven't said anything, and I'm sorry if the suggestion makes you uncomfortable." He stiffens and pulls back. "I thought getting some might be better than not, but—"

"Get back here." I eliminate the space between us. It's all I can do to not climb him like a tree. "It is kind of a perfect arrangement, isn't it? And you're right. I've been walking through a long, dry desert. I could use a tall drink of water."

I try to replicate his accent and give him an exaggerated once-over, gratified when he laughs.

"So, is that a yes?"

"Yes."

I burst out in giggles, too, and we probably look like idiots, but I don't care. I want to get him into a secluded corner and have my way with him.

"How long does this shindig last?" Cooper says into my ear. Hell yes, I'm not the only one that's eager.

"I'm ready to leave if you are." I meet his gaze, full of lust and wanting, and let him lead me off the dance floor. There's too many people, too many bodies stopping me from my goal of Cooper—alone, bare skin, all mine.

CHAPTER
Twenty-Six

JASMINE

Hustling me out the door, he tugs me out into the parking lot, then presses me up against his truck. Before I can even breathe, his lips are on me. His hands are everywhere, his tongue sliding into my mouth to dance with mine. It's everything I want and simultaneously not enough, not even close. I need him right now.

I groan into his mouth. "Let's go."

"Your place or mine?" His breath comes out in pants, and I'm having a hard time getting enough oxygen to my brain, too.

"Mine. It's closer."

Somehow, I manage not to burst into flames on the car ride home. I can't stop touching Cooper, though. How does he focus on the road when I keep massaging his thigh? Thankfully, it's a quick trip.

Cooper's lips are on my neck as I unlock the front door and stumble through. I'm not sure where my roommates are tonight, and I don't bother with the lights. There's no time. I have to get him upstairs into my bed. I can't wait another minute.

But I keep getting distracted, as I have to stop and kiss him. In the entryway, on the stairs, in the middle of the hallway. Each kiss is deeper than the last—long drags on his mouth before coming up for air and continuing towards the goal.

Finally, we make it to my room and I slam the door shut behind us. Stripping off his suit coat, I throw it on my desk. The buttons on his dress shirt are roadblocks in my way. I want his bare skin under my palms.

But he must not get the memo. Slowing down, he doesn't break the kiss, but he backs off and puts some space between us.

"What's wrong?" I tear my lips away from his delicious mouth, panting.

"Nothing." Voice gravely, he traces his fingertips over my exposed shoulders and collarbone. "Everything is perfect. I don't want to rush and, uh, have things end too fast."

Oh. I can work with that.

"In that case..." Giving him a wicked smile, I turn around and look at him over my shoulder. "Will you unzip me?"

He groans. "Are you trying to kill me again? Should I worry about your homicidal tendencies?"

The sound of the zipper slowly parting fills the room. His fingers trail down my bare back and I shiver. "Maybe?"

"Darlin', what a way to go."

I turn to face him in my lacy black bra and panties, gratified by his quick indrawn breath. There are things I'd change about my body, but the spark of pure lust in Cooper's eyes as they rake over me gives me confidence. I run my hands over his chest with aching slowness. As I unhook every button on his shirt, I give him a kiss, each one longer and deeper, until he's groaning into my mouth.

"We can go slow next time." Hoisting me up with his hands under my thighs, he encourages me to wrap my legs around his waist as he carries me to the bed. It's without a doubt the sexiest thing that's ever happened to me.

For the second time, I wake with my head pillowed on Cooper's broad chest. And this time, instead of being pent up, I'm satiated. He's all mine, to enjoy as much as I want. No more denying myself and the tension between us.

I drift between sleeping and awake, that glorious land of dozing. My thoughts are full of Cooper's naked body. Am I dreaming about what could happen or reliving everything that happened last night? Either way, it's incredible, and it's not long before I want to make these fantasies into reality.

Placing kisses on his sternum, I crawl across his torso. Stirring beneath me, he pops one eye open.

"This is the best way to wake up. Ever."

He demonstrates his enthusiasm, and I lose track of time. Afterwards, my limbs are heavy with satisfaction, and my fingers and toes tingle. I never want to move again.

Note to self: buy more condoms. We're going to need them if we keep up this pace.

"Ugh, I need a shower." Cooper rolls out of bed, then throws on boxers and his undershirt. "Care to join me?"

The shower is an old-fashioned claw-foot tub with a converted shower head. I'm not sure it's safe for two. Still, the thought of company in it gets me on my feet. Throwing on my robe, I bob my eyebrows.

"Think you can wash my hard-to-reach places?"

"I aim to please."

"Let's just say you've hit the mark. Repeatedly."

With a heated look, he chases me into the bathroom and makes good on his promise.

After our shower—which we discovered is literally only conducive to getting clean and not sexy shenanigans—he puts his dress pants back on with his undershirt and sips coffee with me at the kitchen table.

"So." I cradle my mug in my hands. "What's your favorite way to spend a lazy Sunday?"

"Oooh, that's a good question." Cooper leans back in his chair. "In a perfect world, where I really have nothing to do, I'd probably sleep in, maybe go for a jog, and then watch movies all afternoon. You?"

"That sounds amazing, minus the jog. I'd sub out jogging for reading a book."

"Yeah? What's your favorite book?"

"*Lord of the Rings.*"

"Solid choice." He nods his head as if he approves and takes a sip of coffee. He takes it black, which I don't understand, but to each their own.

"Have you read them?"

"I have."

"What's your favorite book?"

"*Ender's Game.*"

"What do you think of the movie?"

"It's trash."

"You've got excellent taste, Cooper Edwards." My heart flutters in my chest at the heated look in his eyes, and I clear my throat. "We should do a marathon."

His eyebrows pop up. "Run twenty-six miles?"

"No, silly." I shove his shoulder playfully. "A sci-fi movie marathon."

His eyes light up. "Oooh, what should we start with?"

"I've been meaning to rewatch all the *Avengers* movies. In order."

"Cinematic release order or chronological?"

"Chronological."

"I'm in." He sets down his cup of coffee and stands. "Are we starting today?"

I have an exam in Calc, a homework assignment to finish for physical chem, and a practice essay to write for the analytical portion of the GRE. But his smile is so tempting. I can squeeze one movie in.

"Let's do it."

CHAPTER
Twenty-Seven

COOPER

Momma: Thanks for the pictures of you and Jasmine! She looked so beautiful. And my handsome boy!

Momma: Okay, I know I'm not supposed to say that. But it's true!!

Momma: Cooper? Don't make me call Hunter to check in. You know I will.

Rolling over as my alarm goes off on my phone, I groan. My head pounds and my body aches. What's wrong with me?

I force myself to sit up and the room spins. Not a good sign. My throat burns with every swallow and I can't breathe out of my nose. A heat wave passes through me, hotter than Texas in July, and then recedes, leaving me shivering. I grab my blanket off my bed and stumble into my bathroom. My head throbs with every step and halfway there I throw off the damn blanket. It's making me sweat again.

After taking care of things, I turn on the light and have to immediately close my eyes. It hurts too much. Sinking down, I rest on the cool gray bathroom tile. Maybe I'll just live here now. I drift away.

My rest is interrupted—hours? minutes? days?—later when Hunter bursts in.

"Dude, where have you been?"

Opening my eyes, I blink up at him and fling my arm across my head to block out the light.

"Go away," I say, but all that comes out is a hacking cough. My chest rattles with the force of it. When I open my eyes and sit up, leaning against the wall, Hunter has backed up into the doorway and gazes at me, wary.

"Are you hungover?"

I shake my head. "Sick."

Inching towards me, he pats my shoulder, then grimaces. "Ew. You're gross. Hot and sweaty."

How does he think it feels to actually be inside this body? But I'm too wiped for sarcasm, so I nod.

"Is this why you missed practice?" he asks, kneeling down to look at me.

"I did?" My voice comes out scratchy and my throat is scraped raw. "What time is it?"

"Time to get you to the trainer." Putting his arm under me, he helps me stand, bearing my weight as we shuffle back to my room. I collapse on my bed. Has it always been this soft? It's like a marshmallow. A soft, fluffy cloud of comfort that I don't want to leave. "Put on some pants, okay?"

I think I nod, but I let my eyes close again, until sweat-pants land on my face.

"Pants. Trainer. Now."

Oh yeah. I forgot.

The university's hockey trainers are primarily there for

186

injuries, but they all have medical training. Instead of bothering with the student health center, all the guys on the team usually just check in with our staff.

Sniffling, I cough again. My body throbs as I make myself sit up and slide my legs into my joggers. I'm sweating by the time I'm done.

Hunter stands in my doorway, his eyes wide. "Man, you look like shit."

Which tracks, because that's definitely how I feel.

"Come on." He hauls me up and snags my phone off my nightstand, then drags me out the door, down the elevator, and out to the parking lot. Normally we'd hoof it to the hockey rink, but after walking through the lobby, I can barely stand. Bundling me into the front seat of his car, he tosses my phone into my lap while I press my face against the cool glass of the window. Finally, a moment of relief.

My phone buzzes in my lap, jerking me out of my stupor. The words of the text swim before my eyes, though, and I'm not sure who it's from. I type something in reply before slumping against my new best friend, the window, again.

After parking, Hunter drags me inside and parks me in the trainers' office. The light is too bright, and my head throbs. There's an exam table, covered in paper. It crackles against my cheek as I lay down. Voices buzz in the background, making my ears ache.

"What do we have here?" I crack open an eye. Bob, our head of sports medicine, stands in the tiny room with Hunter. Fortyish, balding, and usually no-nonsense, his gaze is kind as he surveys me. "Can you sit up?"

I manage to swing my legs over the edge of the table and lever myself upright without falling off. A victory.

Bob sticks a thermometer in my ear, then shakes his head.

After making me open my mouth for a tongue depressor and listening to me cough with his stethoscope, he frowns.

"Sorry, son. I can't clear you to practice until the fever goes away. It looks like bronchitis. You're gonna need antibiotics. I can give you a steroid shot for faster recovery, too, but get plenty of fluids and rest."

Normally I'd be crushed to be forbidden to play, but I can't even summon disappointment over his verdict. I'm pretty sure I'd die if I tried to ice skate right now, let alone take a check into the boards. Forced rest is a gift, not a punishment.

I nod, listing to one side, and Hunter corrects me, sliding his arm under mine.

"Back to bed, then." He helps me off the table and we stumble through the hockey facility and to his car.

I don't even remember how he gets me up to our apartment. The only thing that registers is when my face hits the cool cotton fabric of my pillow. Then I sink into oblivion.

It's just flashes of images after that. Coughing and blowing my nose. Flinging the covers off my bed when I'm drenched in sweat, and then huddling back under them when I'm shivering. Hunter, forcing me to drink some Gatorade and take the pills they sent home with me.

When I wake the next time, I no longer want to die. I'm weak and tender, but when I sit up, my headache is gone. The apartment is quiet and I have no idea what time it is. It's light out behind my blinds, at least, so that's a clue. Where are my roommates? Where is my phone? What day is it?

After using the bathroom, I splash some water on my face —I need a shower in the worst way—and pad out to the living room.

I'm hit with a delicious, homey smell—chicken, garlic, and carrots, I think—and my stomach growls. How long has it been since I ate? Based on how ravenous I suddenly feel, a while. I'm about to investigate the pot simmering on the stovetop when a throat clears behind me. I spin, hit with the realization that I'm wearing my boxers—and nothing else.

"Hey." Jasmine waves at me, curled up under a Harrison Hockey blanket on our brown leather couch. It could be the fact that I've been out of it for a while, but I'm pretty sure her eyes rake up and down my bare chest and her cheeks color. Is it weird that I hope she's checking me out and enjoying the view? I can't help it—I preen a bit.

"Hey, what's up?"

But instead of answering, she gestures at my lack of clothing and won't meet my gaze.

"Aren't you cold?"

"Too much of a temptation?" I wink.

"I'm glad you're feeling more like your normal self." She rolls her eyes. "Go put on pants."

I'm hearing that a lot. "You mean this isn't a booty call?"

She shakes her head, expression one of playful exasperation. "Nope. I mean, as sexy as you are when you're sick... no."

I puff out my chest. Things last weekend definitely proved that she thinks I'm sexy, but I still enjoy that she said it. Even with a hint of sarcasm.

"And then you'll fill me in? I'm a little fuzzy on... well, everything."

She shoos me off, and I stop short when I enter my room. It's a disaster zone. I hate messes. But I've strewn clothes everywhere, left empty Gatorade bottles, and tossed a lot of tissues that didn't make it into the trash can. Just looking at it wipes me out again.

Sighing, I find my last clean pair of joggers and a soft, worn gray Henley. Definitely time to do laundry. Then I head back out to the living room.

Jasmine is on the couch, giggling at something on her phone. Wait a minute...

"Do we have the same phone case?" I recognize the Harrison Hockey grip on the back.

"Um." A stricken look crosses her face. "Don't be mad. It kept ringing and ringing. And I saw it was your mom, so I answered it."

She winces, words rushing out of her mouth. "I didn't mean to invade your privacy. I'm sorry. But she was so worried. Then we started texting."

I blink. She's been texting my mom? "How did you get the passcode?"

She shoots me an exasperated look. "Your birthday and your hockey number? James Bond, you're not."

She remembers those numbers? I swallow, my mouth dry.

"Um, okay. You can tell her I'm alive. And uh, where is everyone?"

"Hockey game." She stares at my phone, but I sit down on the couch, my knees practically giving out.

"I'm missing a game? Holy shit, how long have I been out of it?"

Tossing my phone, she crawls across the couch to put her hand on my arm. "You were in bad shape. Your coach knows, and Hunter and I took care of everything."

"Everything?" My voice comes out a croak as I try to piece things together. "What's everything? And what day is it?"

"It's Friday. What's the last thing you remember?"

Friday. Damn, I thought it was maybe Wednesday.

"Um, I didn't feel well. Hunter took me to the trainer's."

Biting her lip, she shakes her head. "That was yesterday. You sent me this." She holds out her phone, displaying a text.

Cooper: The bear has a big mouth that she has to hide behind a

"That doesn't make any sense." I reread it, confused.

"Nope. And you didn't reply. So I came over to check on you, and Hunter explained you were out of it. I thought I'd stay and make sure you were okay since everyone else was gone."

My mouth drops open. "You—you took care of me?"

"I hope it's okay that I spent the night. I stayed out here in case you needed anything." She blushes, pleating her fingers in the orange fleece blanket on her lap. "I didn't mean to be creepy, I was just—"

"No." I grab her hands. "That was really kind of you. Like, really above and beyond."

"That's what friends do." She stares at her lap.

"But you handled my mom." I gape at her. "She's probably going to try to adopt you."

"Oh, she already proposed marriage on your behalf and offered me a generous dowry to take you off her hands." Her eyes twinkle with delight and something bubbles up in my chest—happiness.

"A dowry? Isn't that a bit old-fashioned?"

"Not if you saw her offer!"

"A whole herd of goats for your village?"

"Two. Plus donkeys." She smiles at me, and I'm about to tease her back when my stomach rumbles again. Her eyes widen. "Oh my gosh, I bet you're starving. Can I get you some soup?"

Before I can answer, Jasmine hops off the couch and busies herself, ladling the golden liquid into two bowls and filling my apartment with the most amazing smell. I sniff.

Chicken and noodles, and it makes me feel warm and comfortable before I've even taken a bite.

She brings me a bowl and a spoon and settles next to me, watching as I take my first bite.

"Oh my god." The heat soothes my throat, the noodles are easy to eat, and the broth tastes rich, with hints of garlic and herbs. "This is amazing. Don't tell her, but it's way better than my mom's."

"She sent me her recipe. I just embellished a little. Cooking and chemistry have a lot in common." Her face lights up in a smile and she grabs my phone off the couch, waving it at me. "And I'm totally going to tell her."

"You wouldn't dare!" Setting down my soup, I playfully lunge for my phone, ending up draped over her lap. I could get it back from her easily, but wrestling over it is more fun. She smells good, like flowers and clean soap, and as she wriggles beneath me, giggling, I develop a new problem.

Sitting up, I fake a cough to distract her from what she may or may not have felt. It works.

"Oh, gosh, I'm so sorry! I shouldn't have—"

"I'm fine." I wave her off. "But it's not nice to steal a phone from someone who doesn't have the strength to fight back."

"Doesn't have the strength?" She raises a brow. "That's a gross exaggeration."

"You calling me gross?" I pretend to sniff my armpit, then wince. "Because you'd be right. I hope you don't pass out from the stink."

Grabbing my bowl off the floor, I take another slurp of chicken and noodles.

"I think I'll survive. But I do have an idea," Jasmine says between bites. I wait for her to swallow, then gesture for her to continue.

"I brought my laptop. I thought after you have some dinner—and a shower—we could watch a movie. One guaranteed to make you feel better." She pauses for effect. "A little tale about an aspiring magician who must protect an innocent child from an evil queen."

She grins and I gasp. "*Willow*! You remembered!"

"Of course. So hurry up."

After finishing every drop of soup (and refraining from licking the bowl, although it's difficult) I make Jasmine promise not to text anything incriminating to my mom while I'm occupied. I take a quick shower and it leaves me feeling mellow and ready to lie down.

But after throwing on athletic shorts and a t-shirt—it was all I could find—I survey my room.

I can be myself around Jasmine, but this might be too much.

I tidy the dirty laundry and put all the trash where it belongs. Then I eye my bed.

"Jasmine?" I pop my head into the hallway. "Could you give me a hand with something?"

"Sure!" She appears at my doorway as I open the linen closet. Pulling a clean set of sheets off the top shelf, I hand them to her to hold while I strip my bed. She helps me remake it, and when all the blankets are in place, I smooth my hand over the soft surface.

"There. Now it's movie-ready."

"Perfect. Be right back." Jasmine pops down the hall, then returns with her laptop and the fleece blanket from the couch.

We get her laptop situated on the middle of the bed between us. I plump my pillows and recline against the headboard, distracted by how good she smells. If I start thinking about that, I'm liable to toss the laptop on the floor and jump on top of her, and probably embarrass myself with my lack of stamina.

As the movie starts, I fight to keep my eyelids open, but it's a battle I'm losing. My body is exhausted and I'm warm in my bed with Jasmine. What could be more soothing?

She's really here. Taking care of me when I'm sick and watching over me. It's totally unexpected and amazing. I swallow down the lump that lodges in my throat.

Grabbing my pillow, I plop it down on top of her lap and lay down, getting comfortable. She runs her fingers through my hair, sending tingles down my spine. We agreed to be friends with benefits, but this feels like more than that. I don't know why she showed up for me—she certainly didn't have to—but I let myself enjoy it.

CHAPTER
Twenty-Eight

JASMINE

Cooper: Thanks again for the soup and for nursing me back to health. Come over tonight and let me make it up to you?

Jasmine: It was no big deal. You don't owe me anything.

Cooper: But what if I want to? We'd have the place to ourselves. Bring your overnight bag and stay.

Jasmine: In that case ;) What time?

⌁

I knock on the door to 3A, surprised to hear raucous laughter on the other side of the wall. Cooper opens the door, running a hand through his hair, and I'm distracted for a second by his low-slung gray sweatpants and clinging t-shirt. I haven't seen him since the night his fever broke, but he looks better. Like, awesome. The picture of health. My eyes rake up and down his body. I'm ogling, but I can't stop. He's just so nice to look at.

Another burst of laughter pulls me from my lustful haze, and I peer around him to see what might be the entire hockey team, lounging in his living room. I adjust my rainbow backpack on my shoulder and raise a brow.

"Sorry." He winces, jerking his head towards his company. "They just kinda… showed up. We can hang out in my room, if you want, or—"

"Wait a minute." I brush past him to get a look at the TV screen. "Is this *The Cutting Edge*?"

Mateo nods from the floor, a wide grin on his face, while someone from the couch—Evan, probably—pelts him with popcorn. There is a buffet of snacks lined up on their kitchen counter, and my mouth waters at the sight of Cheetos.

"Come on, guys! It's a great movie!" Mateo ticks points off on his hand. "Hockey dude. Hot chick. And think about where he gets to put his hands!"

"A figure skater fantasy, man?" Hunter asks, chuckling. "You could have gone that route instead of hockey."

But Mateo shakes his head. "Nah, I can't dance for shit. But I'd try those lifts in a heartbeat."

I giggle at their antics as Cooper comes up behind me, hands circling my waist. His voice in my ear is low and quiet. "We really don't have to stay here."

"And miss out on the Pamchenko? I think not."

He spins me to face him, question marks in his eyes. "Are you serious?"

"As a nuclear reaction! I love this movie."

"It's not sci-fi."

"It's definitely a fantasy." I snort. "And I love a good trope-fest."

"Do you have a secret hockey player fetish?"

I lean in close enough to smell his woodsy cologne and whisper, "Not until now."

Cooper's grin spreads across his face, the one that makes my insides melt. "Jasmine Turner, you're nothing if not surprising."

I don't know why, but that feels like praise. He runs his gaze over me, and I know he wants to take me into his bedroom and have his way with me. I shiver, because it's been almost two weeks since we hooked up after my department dinner, and I know what he has in mind will be good. I'm so relieved he's feeling better.

Instead, he pulls me close and drops a kiss on the top of my head. The scent of his woodsy cologne envelopes me and I have to clench my thighs together.

"If my girl wants to watch this movie, then that's what we'll do." Jerking a thumb towards the guy in the recliner, he says, "Tyler. Up," and settles me on his lap in the chair with him.

Why does my heart thump when he says I'm his girl? I don't belong to anyone. But instead of bothered, I feel cherished.

He wraps his arms around me and I cuddle into his chest, laying my head on his shoulder. I relax, watching the movie and the delicious tension between the leads, as he rubs slow, soothing circles on my back.

My eyelids get heavy and I could let myself fall asleep here, when his thumb dips lower, skimming my waistband. I'm instantly awake, my nerve endings crackling. I sit up straighter and press into him.

Like he can feel the change in my body, Cooper tenses beneath me—and then my stomach growls loud enough that Tyler on the floor turns to look at us.

"Man, Coop, be a gentleman and offer your date some

snacks. She must be starving."

I wince, rubbing my tummy. "I studied through dinner."

"Jasmine." Cooper shakes his head in disgust. "You should never be too busy to eat."

Says the guy who doesn't have the GRE looming in his future. But he helps me up, tugging me over to the buffet on the counter. The open concept design means that nothing separates the two spaces—we can still follow the movie. He hands me a paper plate and then sticks his head in the fridge. "Want a drink?"

"Yeah, I'll have whatever you're having."

Cooper emerges with two long-necked bottles of Coors, then takes a magnetic bottle opener off the refrigerator door and opens them both. I survey my snack options as my stomach rumbles again.

Cool Ranch Doritos would give me bad breath for later, so I bypass those. Cheetos are messy, but I can't resist, plus I add some pizza rolls and popcorn. Well balanced, it's not, but Cooper winks and steals a Cheeto off my plate as we sit back down.

I settle into his lap again, enjoying the movie. The hockey guys are more into it than I expected—yelling at the TV and making snarky comments. Cooper is relaxed with them, so I let myself relax, too.

I polish off my snacks but I'm still hungry, so I hop up again to grab another handful of popcorn. Hunter leans against the counter, sipping a beer and watching everyone.

"'Sup." He jerks his chin at me and runs a hand through his hair. "Sorry if we interrupted your night. Enjoying the movie?"

"Yeah, it's fun. Does the team hang out like this a lot?"

I can't help it. I'm listening to Hunter, but Cooper draws my gaze. He laughs at something ridiculous one of his teammates says, and my belly does a flip at the grin on his face.

"We do." Hunter gives me a once-over, and the scrutiny in his piercing blue eyes makes me blush. "I wasn't sure about you at first. This whole thing was weird."

He waves his hand in the air, encompassing everything between me and Cooper, I assume, and I nod. He's not wrong.

"But you're cool. It was solid, the way you showed up for him last week when he was sick. And not complaining about watching a silly movie instead of having the place to yourselves? You're okay, Jasmine."

"Thanks, Hunter." He claps me on the shoulder before walking back to the sofa and convincing Evan and Jonas to move and make room for him.

Being told that I'm *okay* wouldn't normally make me this happy, but I know it's high praise from Hunter. He watches out for his best friend, and even if he doesn't understand our arrangement—honestly, I barely understand it—he's supportive. Cooper has good friends.

As if he knows I'm thinking of him, his eyes meet mine across the room and he pats his lap. My heart races at the heat in his gaze, and I want to run and pounce on him. I force myself to walk, though, balancing my plate as I snuggle back on his lap.

"Are you sure you want to finish the movie?" Cooper's voice is low and rumbly in my ear, making my blood throb in my veins. I clear my throat.

"Don't you want to know how it ends?" I toss a piece of popcorn in my mouth and give him a flirty smile.

He tightens his arms around me. "I'm pretty sure they end up together."

"Nope." I shake my head. "Zombies attack and everyone dies."

"Spoilers!"

I can't help the laugh that bubbles out of my throat.

"What would we do instead?"

"Sneak off to my room. You can show me your sexy pajamas." His words send shivers up my spine.

"You really wanna see my t-shirt and sweatpants?" I tap my chin, like I'm pondering a mystery.

"I wanna see what's underneath them."

To demonstrate, Cooper's hand snakes up my shirt to trace my ribs and my breath catches. I wish I could think of a snappy comeback, but my mouth waters and all I can do is nod.

"They can pull off the Pamchenko without me this time." Standing, I offer him my hand and shoulder my bag, leading the way to his bedroom.

"Get some, you guys!" someone yells.

I smirk at the catcalls from his teammates. I fully intend to take their advice.

CHAPTER
Twenty~Nine

JASMINE

Cooper: You guys wanna come to a party after the game?

Jasmine: I'll ask my friends but I'm game!

Jasmine: Did you see what I did there? A little sports pun for you ;)

Cooper: Wow. There aren't even words.

Jasmine: For how funny I am?

Cooper: It's a good thing you're really good at chemistry. Because I don't think your stand-up career is gonna be enough to support you ;)

~

Leaping to my feet, I scream and cheer for the Griffins as Nick and Hunter execute a beautiful pass and score, increasing our lead by two. Cooper is back to full strength, officially cleared by the team doctor to play. So I convinced my roommates and their boyfriends to come with me tonight to see him in action.

Staci glances over at me, a tiny frown between her eyebrows. "You... actually like this. Not just rooting for your boyfriend, but you like hockey."

Taking my seat again as Cooper sets up for the puck drop, I shrug, gaze glued to him. "Yeah, I do."

"I mean, you told us you enjoyed the game—"

I interrupt her to yell when Cooper gets the puck and sends it to Nick.

"—but I couldn't fully picture it until now."

"Don't you think it's exciting?" I ask her as the ref calls a penalty on the Badgers and Cooper's line switches out.

"I guess? There's a lot to focus on. It's pretty intense."

"And you have to admit, Jaz, that you don't normally get this excited over things that aren't sci-fi and fantasy or chemistry-related," Delaney says, tossing a piece of popcorn in her mouth.

"Maybe I'm branching out."

"I like it." Brian steals a sip of her Coke. "It's nice to do something besides watch a movie."

"Yeah." Reaching over Staci, Tate gives him a fist bump. "This is way better than a chick flick."

"I think it's cute." Delaney beams at me. "But not as cute as you and Cooper."

Her voice takes on a sing-song quality and I flush. Even when he's on the bench, my eyes seek him out. I follow the long column of his throat as he swallows, taking a drink from his water bottle. Hockey gear doesn't showcase his physique, but I can't help but think about what's under the bulky pads. All those muscles straining as he skates down the ice. Yummy. I can trace my tongue along his abs tonight, if I want. The thought makes me shiver and warmth gathers in my center. I'm glad they don't play shirtless for safety reasons, but damn, if they did, they'd sell out every night.

I don't quite understand how the line changes work yet—how they know when to rotate and whose turn it is. Or how they do it so fluidly. But they must have a signal because Cooper, Hunter, and Nick hop over the wall separating them from the ice and take off, immediately in the thick of the action.

Delaney nudges me. "He keeps looking at you when he has a break. He's so smitten. It's adorable."

What is there to say to that? I don't know what's going on between us. We're playing with fire and operating in a weird in-between zone. It's best if I don't analyze it too much.

Delaney keeps talking, though. "And how do you feel about him?"

Cooper charges down the ice, the puck a blur in front of him, and I pause to watch, my thoughts racing as fast. One of the Wisconsin players gets him up against the boards, and I wince at the hit he takes. There's no fighting in college hockey, but it's still physical. He assures me he's okay, that he's used to it, but it doesn't stop my heart from lurching.

Delaney must take my silence as a sign of a problem. She puts her hand on my arm. "Jaz, is everything okay between you and Cooper?"

"Of course!" I say, trying to keep panic out of my voice.

"Have you guys said the L word yet?"

Brian rolls his eyes and moves down the row next to Tate, muttering something about girls and sports. It doesn't distract Staci or Delaney from their intense stares in my direction.

I don't know how to answer. We've been together for a while, but is it long enough that our pretend relationship has reached this milestone? Lying about dating to my friends is one thing—lying about confessions of love is different.

Swallowing, I twist my fingers together in my lap. "No."

"Are you worried he doesn't feel the same?" Staci asks.

"The same?" I echo.

"The same as you." Pointing at me, she rolls her eyes. "You clearly love him."

I must be rocking this fake girlfriend gig. But do I want my best friends to think I'm in love with someone I'm not actually dating?

"I like him," I say as the other team calls a timeout. "He's fun to hang out with. But I don't know…"

"Really?" Raising her brows, Staci shoots me a look of disbelief. "What don't you know?"

Delaney offers me popcorn, but I shake my head. "Are you worried he's not into you? Because anyone can see he's head-over-heels, too."

I didn't expect to have this conversation tonight, that's for sure. I have to tread carefully. "It's great between us. But there's probably no future here. So I'm not getting too attached."

That's the closest to the truth I've been with them. Staci shrugs, but Delaney gapes.

"No future?"

"I'm headed to grad school. He's not sure what's next for him."

Delaney squeezes my forearm, eyes wide. "Are you going to let this slip through your fingers?"

"What do you mean?"

She and Staci exchange an uneasy glance.

"Jaz." Staci frowns and speaks slowly, as if she's choosing her words with care. "It was rough for you after Chad. We know it took a lot for you to date someone again. We'd hate to see you give up on Cooper."

"I'm not giving up. I'm just admitting—this has an end-date. It's fun, and he's great, but it's not more than that."

"And you're okay with that?"

"Why wouldn't I be?"

Delaney sniffs and sends me a side-eye. "It's sad the way you're protecting your heart and lying to yourself."

Oh, I'm lying, all right. "To myself?" I ask.

"You obviously want more with this guy, and you're trying to talk yourself out of it." When I protest, she holds up her hand and ticks off points on her fingers. "One, you're watching hockey and enjoying it. Two, you get a dreamy expression on your face when you talk about him. Three, you absolutely light up when he's around. Four, you guys are surprisingly great together. Five—"

"What do you mean?" I finally cut off the flow of words. "How are we great together?"

It's Staci who answers this time. "Cooper is totally into you, Jaz. He doesn't want you to change, and he listens when you talk. He looks at you like you're the smartest person he's ever met, and he knows how lucky he is to be dating you."

Cooper's apparently awesome at the fake boyfriend thing, too.

"Well, I just, I mean, yeah." What can I say to that? "He's awesome, but—"

"Do you honestly think he's going to want to break things off with you? Have you talked to him about it?"

Does he want to break things off anymore? I assume we'll go our separate ways soon enough. Maybe at summer break, maybe before. We're friends with benefits, but the people in our lives think it's something more.

I rub my temples. This conversation is giving me a headache. It's too confusing to keep straight.

"See!" Delaney points at Cooper, skating by us and sending me a wink. "That's not a guy who's only messing around."

My heart swells at the sight of him. God, not only is he

the hottest guy on the ice, but he's also sweet and thoughtful. But it doesn't matter. Because he's acting. He doesn't believe in love. This is just something we're doing to make his mom happy and to keep Chad at bay. It's fun and we have great chemistry. That's all.

After his line hops over the boards and settles on the bench, he glances over his shoulder at me, mouthing, "Hi."

I wave back. My stomach does a flip at his crooked smile.

"See?" Delaney wraps her arm around me. "He's got it bad. It's obvious if you read the signs."

Staci leans into me. "And you're in deep, too. He makes you happier than you've been in... ever, maybe. I think you should be open to the possibility that he's perfect for you. Relax and be okay with it."

"No." I wiggle, breaking free of their embrace. "Don't get your hopes up. We're a temporary thing."

I ignore the glance they send each other. What do they know?

CHAPTER
Thirty

COOPER

The crowd roars as Hunter scores a breakaway, and even though I'm supposed to be focused, I take a minute to enjoy Jasmine leaping to her feet and cheering. Her crew is with her in the stands and they clap, but they don't match my girl's enthusiasm.

Sending a wink in her direction, I get in position for the puck drop. I win, passing to Hunter as quick as lightning, and the adrenaline rush of the game fills my veins.

Our shift goes fast, and at Coach's signal, we hop over the boards for the line change. Panting, I grab a drink of water and sit on the bench, watching the action. I can sense Jasmine's gaze on me, but I don't turn to look at her. I can't set a poor example for the rest of the guys.

Even if I don't make eye contact, my mind still drifts to her. God, it's been an awesome two weeks, and the best sex of my life. Who knew that getting it on the reg with the same girl was so great? It's easy to be with her. I don't have to put on an act, or live up to ridiculous expectations. There's no pressure. I can be me.

Speaking of me... Coach taps my shoulder and as soon as the third line clambers over the wall, I return to the ice with Hunter and Nick. Shawn and Alec will rotate out soon, but the defensive line is different. Until then, we try to get the puck away from Wisconsin.

When the buzzer sounds to end the second period, we lead by one. I smile at Jasmine as we file off the ice into the locker room, and she waves back. She's not wearing her Harrison Hockey shirt, but I don't care. She showed up for me, screaming my name and rooting for us. That's enough.

Hunter gives an impassioned speech in the locker room, but I zone out for most of it. Yeah, every game is important. Yeah, we only lead by one. I love hockey, but I've heard it all before. A talk will not change how I play. I'm not that kind of guy. I go out and give it my all, every game, no matter what. There's no point in playing otherwise.

But as we move to exit and re-enter the arena, Hunter blocks my path with his stick, staring at me like I'm a defense he can't read.

"What, dude?" I let a note of exasperation bleed into my voice. He's keeping us from the ice as the other guys file past.

"You sure you're in the zone tonight? Focused?" He narrows his ice-blue eyes under his visor.

"Of course." I frown at him.

"Because you seem distracted by a certain pretty girl in the stands."

"Nah." I shrug off his worries. "My game is rock-solid."

I try to brush past him, but he grabs my arm, spinning me to face him.

"You sure things are still fake there?" he says, his words a quiet hiss through clenched teeth.

"Don't worry about it, man," I say back. I don't know what's going on between Jasmine and me. But I don't need a label. That's part of what makes it so good. "Come on, let's go win a game."

We head down the tunnel together, and I give Jasmine a brief nod when our gazes connect. As I hit the rink, I prepare to skate my heart out for the next twenty minutes.

See, Hunter? I can acknowledge my girl and still focus on hockey. No problem at all.

We win our game, like I knew we would, and I'm ready to celebrate. I meet Jasmine and her friends outside the locker room after and convince them to come back to Hockey Hall and party with us. There's nothing like the atmosphere with the team after a win—everyone is lighter, somehow, and amped up on adrenaline.

I can hear the thumping bass music pouring out of 3B as soon as we step off the elevator. It's gonna be a hell of a rager tonight.

"Right this way, y'all." Grinning, I open the door across the hall from my apartment, ushering Jasmine's friends inside. I keep her pressed close to my side, inhaling the coconut scent of her hair. "Thanks for coming."

"Of course." Jasmine wraps her arms around my waist and plants a smacking kiss on my cheek. "You had a great game, babe."

Man, I love it when she pours on the PDA and the compliments in front of people. I'm the coolest, luckiest guy at this party when she does that. It's mostly for show, I think. But sometimes, I wonder. The look in her gaze seems so real.

I blink away my concerns. I deserve to enjoy this night without analyzing everything.

The apartment we're in, shared by Mateo, Luke, and Ryan, has the same layout as our place across the hall. I herd everyone towards the kitchen and pour tequila shots.

Holding up my glass, I wait until Jasmine and her friends lift theirs.

"To winning hockey games,"—I glance at the beautiful girl beside me and gulp—"and the best fans in the universe."

Her mouth curves up in a smile before she clinks her glass with mine and tosses back the gold liquid.

Drawn to her like a magnet, I can't help it. I pull her flush against me and capture her lips in a searing kiss. Tasting tequila and something sweet underneath, I lose myself in her.

When she finally pulls away, she's dazed. "I like you after games, all high on victory and endorphins."

"You like me after we win, you mean."

Linking her arms behind my waist, she nuzzles against my chest. "I just like you."

I like her, too. More than I ever expected. It hits me like a stick to the shins—I don't want this to end.

But that wasn't the deal. She doesn't do relationships. Neither do I. What the hell is my problem?

Saving me from my thoughts, the music changes to Taylor Swift's latest hit. I grab Jasmine's fingers.

"Let's dance."

With a smirk, she leads me into the living room and spins, landing in my embrace.

That's more like it. The tequila hits my bloodstream, loosening me up, and I take a deep breath. It's time to celebrate a win and dance with my girl. Without over analyzing anything.

Three songs and a beer later, I leave Jasmine so I can use

the bathroom. When I re-enter the living room, she's deep in conversation with Jonas. He touches her shoulder, and she throws her head back in laughter.

White-hot jealousy lances through me. Marching over to them, I snake a hand around her, planting it on her hip. Looking up at me, she leans in and grins, relaxing me a fraction.

Why am I jealous? She's only talking to Jonas. Besides, we're sleeping together, but it's nothing more than that. I can like her, think she's cool, love having her in my bed, but it's a temporary arrangement. I don't have a real claim on her.

Shouldn't that thought make me feel better?

Jonas watches this silent exchange and raises his eyebrows but doesn't say anything. He knows we're pretending, so—

Wait a minute. He knows it's fake. Is he flirting with her for real? Does he want to swoop in and ask her out once we break up?

He'd be perfect for her, actually. Smart and studious, they'd probably get married and make beautiful nerd babies.

My stomach clenches at the thought. Why do I care? There are lots of girls who like sleeping with hockey players —Evan and I have been with some of the same chicks, and it's not a big deal. We don't compare notes or anything gross, but it's never bothered me before. What's my problem?

I need a distraction. Squeezing myself between Jasmine and Jonas, I wrap my arms around her.

"Wanna dance again?" I say in her ear, inhaling the coconut scent of her shampoo. "Or we could take this party across the hall to my place."

Jasmine giggles. "Does that line work on girls?"

"Eh, it's about fifty-fifty." I rock my hand side to side and give her a little smile.

"It's a good thing you have hockey to impress them."

"Does it impress you? Because you're the only one that matters."

I say it for the benefit of anyone listening in, but the words resound in my chest and ring true. Am I in over my head? Perhaps. But between her green eyes locked on me, her hot body molded to mine, and the drinks flowing through my veins, I can't bring myself to care. I'll figure it out later. Right now, I just want her underneath me for the next twelve hours.

"I'm impressed with everything about you." She puts her palm in mine and my heart skips a beat. "Let's go."

I let her make me forget everything for the rest of the night.

CHAPTER
Thirty-One

JASMINE

Mom: How's GRE prep going?

Jasmine: Why did I think I could do this?

Maya: I know what will help! We need a girls' spa day so you can relax!

Mom: And how's Cooper? He seemed like such a great guy. I'd love to see him again soon!

Making GRE vocabulary flashcards soothes me. Color-coding them, organizing them, writing the information out in my slanted print. It helps me internalize what I'm trying to learn, and often, when I'm taking a practice test, I can see the words in my mind's eye on the little pastel notecards. If my practice test scores can be trusted, it's a successful strategy.

So why is it failing me today?

I've taken the GRE materials and made my flashcards. I've studied them for two hours already. But I still have more to go—I can't call it quits yet. I'm scheduled to take the exam in a few weeks and I'm running out of time. My mind keeps drifting and I don't know why.

The words blur together, and my frustration grows. It's like my bedroom walls are closing in on me. The house is empty and quiet... too quiet. Standing up from my desk, I pace, but there's only room for three steps in each direction. The claustrophobia adds to the anxiety pressing on my chest. This test affects so much of my future, my plans, my life goals...

My breath comes in shallow pants. I have to get out of here.

Grabbing my keys, I make it out the front door, locking it behind me, before I remember—no car. The mechanic hasn't found the right parts yet. And my roommates are out, so I can't borrow theirs.

The chill air forces me to take deep breaths, and my heart slows. Maybe a walk will help. Change of scenery, fresh air. Yeah, that's what I need.

I shove my hands into my hoodie pocket and set off. It's cold enough for the middle of March that I should have grabbed a jacket. I hustle down the sidewalk to keep warm. The late afternoon sun is weak, but at least it's not overcast. I focus on my breathing, enjoying the crisp chill. I'm ready for spring, but the weather hasn't gotten the memo. There aren't any buds on the trees yet and the grass is still winter-brown, but at least the snow has melted.

I don't have a destination in mind, but after walking for fifteen minutes, I find myself in front of Hockey Hall.

Is Cooper home from practice yet? He might help me organize my jumbled thoughts and focus on the task at hand. I search my pockets, but I must have left my cell phone at home, too. Can I just drop in?

One way to find out. Heading through the lobby, I push the elevator button and select floor three once the doors open.

Knocking on his apartment door, I'm about to give up and conclude no one's there when it finally swings open.

"Hey!" Shirtless and still glistening with water, his low-slung jeans make my mouth water. Cooper's face lights up as he towels off his hair. "This is an unexpected pleasure. How are you, darlin'?"

I stare at the delectable expanse of bare skin and bite my lip. "This is not a booty call, I promise."

"Shucks." He snaps his fingers, faux disappointed, but smiles. "You okay? Come on in."

Opening the door wider, he allows me room to enter and I brush past him, close enough to feel the warmth of his body. It would be so easy to let him distract me and take all my worries away. But later, when I go home, it will come crashing back down on me.

So I shake my head and drop my bag, plopping down on his sofa. "Ugh, I'm struggling."

Dropping his wet towel, he rushes to sit down beside me, grabbing my hand. "What's wrong?"

"I'm so stressed about the GRE, I can't even see straight." I lay down on his couch and contemplate the ceiling. "There's so much riding on this. I can't blow it."

"Hey." Cooper tugs me up to look at him. "What makes you think you're gonna blow it? You're the smartest person I know, and you've been studying forever. You're going to do great."

"But what if I don't?" I hate how my voice wobbles, and my eyes burn with unshed tears. I blink them away.

"Then you'd study more and take it again. You'd apply to other places or do a gap year. You'd revamp your plans, yeah, but it wouldn't be the end of the world."

"It would throw off my five year plan. Blow up my whole timeline. What would I do with a gap year?"

Instead of trying to answer my rhetorical question, Cooper stares at me for a beat and then puts his arm around me and I lay my head on his bare shoulder. My fingers itch to touch his smooth skin, but I resist.

"Tell me about these plans, darlin'."

He's not just shrugging me off. He really wants to hear what I have to say.

"I know pharmaceuticals might not sound like a typical dream, but Cooper, I love chemistry. And I love the idea that I could work in a lab and use my talents to make the world a better place. Cancer, Alzheimers, Parkinsons, Lou Gehrig's disease... maybe I could help develop a better treatment with fewer side effects or extend the life expectancy. Ever since I realized I was good at chemistry, that my mind is wired for it, this is what I've wanted."

He kisses the top of my head and squeezes me tight. "That's the most noble thing I've ever heard. Way better than wanting to spend your life on a stupid game."

"No." Shifting, I turn and face him. "Don't belittle yourself or your goals. Sports stars can be an incredible force for good. The platform for positive change is amazing."

Cooper stares at me, eyes full of wonder before he kisses me again, short and sweet this time. When he speaks, his voice is husky. "I know you can do this. You're Jasmine Turner. Nothing gets in your way."

I rest my forehead on his for a second, letting his affirmations sink in. Tears leak out and he swipes them away with his thumb.

"Thanks." My words are watery and I pull back, wiping my face. "I'm sorry, I don't—"

"Don't apologize. Everyone needs a pep talk now and

again." He holds his hand up to his mouth and pretends to whisper. "Sometimes I psych myself up in front of a mirror before big hockey games."

I giggle at this image, and my tension dissipates. "I'd like to see that."

"Nope, not happening." His gaze dances with mischief. "But I have an idea. There's a place I'd like to show you."

I wince, and the light in his eyes dims.

"It won't take long, I promise. And then I'll make you a deal—I'll quiz you when we get back here. It'll be fun."

"Fun?" I doubt that.

But he bobs his brows. "I'll give you a reward for every question you get right."

"What kind of reward?"

Cooper brushes a kiss across my lips, then lingers and deepens it. A shiver runs through me and it's a good thing I'm sitting down, or else my knees would give out. I run my palms over his bare chest as our tongues dance and I wish the rest of our clothes would disappear. He pulls away too soon.

"That kind. But let me take you on a little adventure first."

I'd agree to anything to get him to kiss me like that again.

"Okay. Let's go."

We don't need to take Bubba where we're going, apparently. Cooper grabs a shirt, sticks an orange and navy Harrison hockey beanie on my head and his cowboy hat on his and informs me it's close. Setting off across campus, I let my hip bump against him as we walk, and our fingers tangle together.

It's not long before we turn a corner and he stops and gestures at three low, squat buildings. "Ta-da!"

I raise a brow at the row of greenhouses. I'm sure I've passed by them before, across from a series of apartment buildings and behind a church. But I've never really noticed them or wondered what they are like inside.

"Wanna go check it out?" he asks, eyes hopeful, and I nod. He nudges me towards the middle building and unlocks the door, letting me inside. It's about as wide as my house, I'd guess, but twice as long. The sunlight filters in through the opaque glass, giving everything a soft and fuzzy filter. The muggy air is heavy against my skin and the warmth wraps around me like a soft blanket. Instead of rows of tables holding plants like a Lowe's greenhouse, this one has a dirt floor. It's divided into little plots, each with signs labeling the genus and species.

"Cooper." I glance around, taking it all in. Different shades of green glitter like jewel tones. I can't wait to explore. "This is amazing."

Hands in his pockets, he gives me a boyish grin and shrugs. "It's no big deal."

Taking a deep breath, I close my eyelids and inhale the earthy scent of dirt and growing things. My stress from the GRE prep melts away, and a weight lifts off my chest.

Opening my eyes, I study Cooper. His cowboy hat shadows his face, and his flannel shirt looks so soft. I want to run my fingertips over it, and then slide my hands under to feel his bare skin.

"You're right. This is exactly what I needed. It's so peaceful. Do you get to come here for class?"

"Yep." He takes a step closer, pressing a sweet kiss to my forehead. "This greenhouse is kinda my equivalent of a lab. I have an assigned plot for one of my classes. I'm graded on how well my plants do."

"Show me."

His eyes twinkle as I lace our fingers together. Our feet crunch on the gravel path that winds through the sections of greenery. He leads me to the far corner of the building marked with a little stake labeled "C. Edwards."

Kneeling down in the dirt, he explains what everything is, how it grows, how it's doing, and what it does. But the whole time he's talking, I can't tear my gaze off of him.

He brought me here to cheer me up. He knew what I needed. And listening to him, watching him light up inside as he discusses his passions—all my stress is gone. I lose myself in his explanation. His excitement and intelligence are a lethal combination that makes me melt. As he holds out a leaf for my inspection, the revelation is as sharp and sudden as a lightsaber to the gut—I want to see that expression on his face every day. I want to be with him, in every sense of the word. Always and forever.

These aren't the thoughts that you have towards a friend. Or even the emotions of a casual hookup.

Oh, crap.

I'm not faking it anymore. Staci and Delaney were right. I swallow. What do I do with these emotions? Falling for Cooper is the worst thing that could happen. We made it clear: this isn't permanent. We're just having fun.

But…

He brought me here to cheer me up, not because he had to or because anyone expected it. Not because we're hooking up, either. He's holding my hand and teaching me about plants not to look like an attentive boyfriend or to get some later but because he wants to. Is it possible he has deeper feelings towards me?

Crouching beside him, I'm carried away by the moment. Before I can second-guess any of it, I cup his face in my palms and kiss him. Pouring everything I have into the kiss, I practically attack him with fervor and passion.

He stays frozen for a second, clearly surprised at first, but he catches on quickly, wrapping me up in his arms and deepening the kiss. I want to lay him out on the ground and climb on top of him.

When we finally pull apart, panting, he stares at me in wonder. "What was that for?"

I shrug. "I guess plants really turn me on. I really love—this place."

Cooper gazes at me, never wavering. "I really love it, too."

CHAPTER
Thirty~Two

COOPER

"The regular season is wrapping up, Gentlemen!" Coach blows his whistle to punctuate his words. "If you want to go further, step things up. Now!"

With only one weekend left in the schedule, he's not wrong. We have an away game on Friday, and then our last home match on Saturday. After that, it's the Big Ten tournament and hopefully, the road to the Frozen Four.

The college hockey championships are like the NCAA basketball finals but on a smaller scale. Instead of sixty-four teams in the bracket, we start with sixteen. Six of those teams qualify by winning their conference tourneys. An NCAA committee selects the other ten at-large. We've made the tourney for the past few years, but it's never a guarantee. Nothing is. So the frantic edge to Coach's voice makes sense. It's crunch time.

Exchanging a determined look with Hunter, he nods at me. We both want this more than anything else. It's only a practice, but if we don't give it our all in practice, we won't be prepared to do it come game time, either.

"Come on, guys!" His voice is a low growl as we arrange ourselves on the blue line for sprints. "Leave it all out on the ice."

Coach's whistle blows, and I lose myself in the hockey zone.

It's glorious. Pushing my body to its physical and mental limits is a zen experience for me. Everything else fades away. The extreme focus is exhilarating, and a small part of me is disappointed when practice ends. But my aching muscles beg to differ and enjoy the hot water in the shower after.

Wrapping a towel around my waist, I head to my locker and retrieve my clothes.

"Well, there's Elle and Isabella. I think Reed and Charlie have girlfriends, too. Tyler's dating someone, maybe? Oh, Cooper's girl. They're pretty serious."

My ears perk up at my name and I glance over. On the other side of the room, Alec and Shawn, our two best senior defensemen, tick names off on their fingers.

"What are you guys talking about?" Throwing on boxers, I wander in their direction. Alec sits down on the wooden bench to put on his jeans and Shawn runs a hand through his dark, wet hair.

"Oh, it's something the girlfriends do for the last home game," Alec says, buttoning his pants.

"Some of the die-hards, too." Shawn applies deodorant like it's going out of style. "They get t-shirts made. It's a tradition."

"Yeah? I don't remember that from last year."

"Here." Scrolling through his phone, Shawn holds it out for me to see. It's a picture of a group of girls in the stands, all wearing matching tight, sparkly t-shirts.

"Oh. Everyone wears hockey shirts to the games. I guess I didn't know it was a big deal."

"It is to the girls." Alec shakes his head. "I don't really get it, but Elle has put a ton of time into designing them and wants to make sure every girl gets one."

Shawn's words are muffled as he pulls a gray t-shirt over his head. "They're practically a sorority."

"The... fans?" This is news to me.

"Yeah, all the girlfriends hang out together at the games and stuff. They even organize road trips when we're away."

Jasmine's never mentioned this, but she's been too busy to go to any away games. Which doesn't bother me—having her attend a few home games has been a blast.

"So what size does your girlfriend wear?" Alec asks, snapping me back to the conversation.

"What?"

"To order her a matching t-shirt." He uses a slow, extra-patient tone that implies I'm an idiot.

"Come on, man. Surely you've seen her clothes on the floor enough to know the size." Grinning, Shawn punches me in the arm. "You're practically married."

Practically married.

My mouth goes dry at his words and my heartbeat trips up. Has someone turned up the heat in here? And why does it feel like a goon is sitting on my chest, making it hard to breathe?

"Nuh-uh." I swallow as my palms get sweaty. "It's not like that.

Tying his shoes, Alec raises his eyebrows. "Dude, I saw you guys the other night. It looked like you were gonna propose. And she wants to say yes so hard and have your babies. Anyone can tell."

Shawn nods. "So much for 'never settling down', right?"

No. There's no way. I mean, I know I'm doing a believable job of faking it, but they've gotten the wrong impression from Jasmine. We're supposed to look all lovey-dovey, but something about his words cause panic to rise in my chest. Did we take this too far? Have her feelings changed? Neither of us want something serious.

"I mean, I like her, yeah, but it's not—"

"It's not a bad thing," Alec cuts off my sputter with a pat on my shoulder. "I love Elle. She's the one. I can't wait to put a ring on it so everyone knows she's off-limits."

"Isabella and I are nearly engaged, too. Does that make me whipped?"

Shawn is over six feet tall and weighs at least 220, all solid muscle. There's no way anyone is telling him he's whipped. He glares at my hesitation and takes a step towards me.

"Uh, no. It's just—Jasmine and I aren't like that."

"Okay, dude." Alec's tone is dubious. "But Elle still wants everyone to match. So I'm putting her down for a medium."

"Fine," I say under my breath, stalking to my locker.

Practically married.

The words slam into my chest again. I'm never getting married. It only leads to problems.

But what do those idiots know, anyway? I swallow, trying to refresh my dry throat. We're convincing. This is a fling. No big deal.

As if my thoughts conjured her, my phone buzzes with a text.

Jasmine: Hey! I heard from the mechanic. Herbie is finally done! Can you take me to pick him up?

Her love of that car is adorable. I gnaw on my lip to keep from grinning.

"Text from your girl?" Alec asks from across the room.

"So what?" I say back, not looking up as I type my reply.

"I can tell by the silly expression on your face."

"There's no look." I school my features into a scowl.

"Whatever you say, man."

Cooper: *Be there in ten minutes*.

I tamp down the excitement that automatically springs up in my chest at the thought of seeing her. Those guys are idiots who don't know what they're talking about. I grab my gear and hurry out to Bubba.

When I pull up out front of Jasmine's house, she jumps into my truck. Her grin makes my pulse get all fluttery, and I can't help smiling back. Her black t-shirt today has yellow Star Wars-style letters and proclaims, "The sarcasm is strong with this one," and her leggings hug her backside, making my mouth water. She buckles herself in and starts telling me about Staci and Tate and an argument they had over where to eat dinner last night. I try to listen, to focus on her words, but my reaction to her gives me pause.

I'm happy to see her. Like, really happy. Happier than I've ever been to see a girl before. It's not just because she's hot and we're sleeping together. Have I caught feelings? And she's —well, she's glowing. Her cheeks are rosy, her eyes twinkle, and her wide smile is genuine. She's happy to see me, too.

Are Shawn and Alec right? Does she have real feelings for me? Beyond friendship, beyond hooking up? She doesn't do boyfriends, so there's no chance.

I grip the steering wheel until my knuckles turn white and stare out the windshield. My posture is rigid and stiff. I just have to hold myself together until she gets out of the car so I don't do something dumb, like confess the crazy thoughts running through my head.

"So." She clears her throat, not meeting my eyes. "My car is done. That means our deal is complete. We can, uh, go our separate ways after this, if you want."

My mouth drops open. I should feel relieved that Shawn and Alec were wrong, that she doesn't care about me beyond our arrangement. So why do I feel like I just took a puck to the chest with no pads?

Her phone pings, saving me from answering, and she pulls it from her pocket and checks it. "Oh, sorry, I've been expecting an email."

She scans her screen, and her face drains of color. She closes her eyes, leaning her head back on the seat rest, and her throat bobs as she swallows.

"Jasmine? What's wrong?"

Twisting the wheel, I pull into the mechanic's parking lot and stop the car, idling it while I wait for her to answer. Eventually, she holds up her phone. Her voice is quiet and wobbly.

"Dr. Michelson just emailed me. I need some help with part of my experiment, and she doesn't have time. She wants Chad to show me."

My insides clench at the thought of him near her, his words hurting her. But I don't think that will make her feel better. So I scoff.

"Chad? He's nothing. You're the top chemistry student. Maybe you can show him a thing or two."

But she shakes her head, her eyes brimming with sadness. "My experiment used a heavy metal during synthesis. I need to make sure that it separated fully and everything is in the correct layer. So I need to do a Flame AA, but it's a senior-level skill. I haven't taken Instrumental Analysis yet. Chad's specializing in analytical chemistry, so he already knows how to do it. I need it to finish my project, and Dr. Michelson arranged for him to teach me."

"Oh." I'm not sure what to say. I hate how she's withdrawn, how the light dimmed in her gaze. No one should affect her like that. I clear my throat. "Would it help if we didn't break up officially yet? That way he'd have one less thing to harass you about? And I could even show up to the lab, be your menacing boyfriend, and remind him why he doesn't want to mess with you."

I give an exaggerated glare and bare my teeth and it works —she relaxes and smiles a little. "I'm not sure the lab is ready for that. But yeah, if you wanted to loiter around outside, it probably wouldn't hurt."

A weight lifts off my chest at her words. "So we shouldn't break up yet."

"I mean, if that's okay with you?" Jasmine's face is pinched in worry and I nod, hoping I don't look too eager.

"Yeah, of course. Chad is an asshat and I'm sorry you have to work with him. I hope this helps."

"Thanks, Cooper. And thanks for this." She gestures out the window. "I can't wait to get back behind the wheel."

"Yeah, how are you two going to celebrate? A little joyride?"

It's weird but I want her to invite me to come. I want to spend more time with her. But she shakes her head. "Not exactly. I'm heading to Indy for a spa date with my mom and Maya."

I nod, trying to hide my disappointment. "I bet it will be good to take Herbie out on the open road. Give him a chance to let loose."

"For sure." Clearing her throat, she stares at me for a beat. I can't read her expression. "Thanks again, Cooper. For everything."

And before I can say goodbye, she hops out of my truck. I turn up the music on the way home to drown out my thoughts.

CHAPTER
Thirty-Three

JASMINE

"Make sure you get her heels," my mom says to the nail tech working on my feet. "Calluses, you know."

"Mom." I roll my eyes at her in the massage chair next to me. "I think I can handle it."

I sigh. So much for a day of relaxation before the GRE. It's a nice thought, but any time away from my study prep makes me irritable. This would have been so much better after the test. And it turns out all they want to do is talk about Cooper.

"I just don't want Cooper to see your feet and get scared off." She and Maya giggle and I bite my tongue to keep from snapping at them. It's not their fault that I'm stressed. They are only trying to help, even if this isn't what I need. Between GRE prep and finding out I have to spend extra time with Chad, I'm on edge. Ignoring my mom's comment, I focus on taking deep breaths.

"So I thought all hockey players were, like, homely. Broken noses and missing teeth." Maya wiggles her toes in her foot bath. "But Cooper's hot. Hotter than your usual type."

I groan as the nail tech massages my calves. It feels so fantastic. "Don't stop." I'm ready to beg her before I turn to my sister.

"I don't care what he looks like. And what's that supposed to mean—hotter than my type?"

She shrugs. "Usually you go for the nerdy academics, not the jocks."

I blink. "He plays hockey, yeah, but his Ag major is practically plant biology. He's much more of a scientist than most people realize."

"And maybe she needed a change after Chad." My mom says his name like it's a curse word and looks like she bit into a lemon. "Cooper is clearly in an entirely different class. Why haven't you brought him home to visit yet?"

"Uh, he's pretty busy with hockey. And, um, I'm not sure that's a great idea. It's not exactly serious, so—"

"Jasmine." My mom pins me in her gaze. "What does that mean?"

"Usually it means they're just sleeping together, Mom."

"Maya!" My voice is low, almost a growl, as my mom gasps. The girl by her foot basin jumps at the sound, dropping a bottle of lotion in the water. It splashes my mom and sloshes over the side.

"I'm so sorry." The embarrassed nail tech bustles around to dry the spill.

"Maybe we can talk about this later?" I say, but my mom ignores that and narrows her eyes at me.

"Jasmine, are you just having sex with this boy?"

"Um."

I thought nothing could be worse than Cooper's mom interrupting our hookup. But I was wrong. My own mother asking me about my sex life is as bad as it gets. But if the earth didn't swallow me then, what are the odds it will rescue me now?

I wait for it—or Dr. Strange to open up a portal—but I'm still stuck here. Guess I've gotta talk my way out of it.

"No!" I shake my head so hard my hair whips me in the face. "Of course not. I like him a lot, Mom. I'm just not sure he feels the same way."

My words ring with truth, because they come straight from my heart. I do like him, and I'm absolutely tangled up in confusion.

My mom scoffs. "Oh, trust me, baby. I saw the way he was looking at you, with his heart in his eyes. He's absolutely smitten."

But I'm not sure.

When I saw Cooper last, he was distant and distracted. I don't honestly know what we're doing. Is he feeling the pressure of hockey season? Or is it me? Is he ready to end things and move on? I gave him the out, but then I found out about Chad and he probably felt obligated to stay in this weird situation we have going on. I thought for a moment in the greenhouse the other day that his feelings were deeper... but the way he acted today made me question it.

My mom doesn't sense any of my turmoil, though. She nods, satisfied with my answer that I'm more than a booty call, but Maya snickers.

"That's worse, Jaz. If you're not sure how he feels, that means he's just using *you* for sex."

I glare at her. If my nail tech wasn't holding my foot, stroking neon green polish on my big toe, I'd leap up and smack her.

"He's not," I say, my words like staccato bursts. "It's... complicated."

"It always is." Maya exhales, and I blink at her, noting her appearance for the first time today. There are dark circles under her eyes and lines bracket her mouth. How come I didn't notice that earlier?

"What's going on?" I ask, shifting towards her. "Is it Joel? Is something wrong?"

"Everything's fine." Her lips turn up in a shaky smile. "But I have news."

"You're pregnant!" My mom bounces in her chair, and Maya scowls, indignant.

"No! Do I look pregnant?"

"You look great!" I say, in a hurry to reassure her. "Just a little tired. Are you okay?"

Maya mumbles something about me calling her fat, and my mom makes soothing noises. "Of course, you look fantastic. But what's going on?"

Maya clears her throat. "Joel got a promotion. We're moving."

A riot of emotions passes over my mom's face. Happiness and pride wars with sadness and fear before she smooths her features.

"That's wonderful, Mai. Where to?"

My brother-in-law is an actuary with an insurance company. My dad has always been happy that he can "provide well" for my sister, which is a load of crap. She's a modern woman with her own college degree and a great job. She doesn't need anyone to provide for her, but my dad tells me I won't understand until I have daughters. Which is never happening, so there, Dad.

Joel and Maya are an "opposites attract" type of couple, but for all that he's staid and practical, he's been a positive, steadying force in her life. Growing up, I always wanted a brother. Joel certainly wasn't what I pictured, but I like him, and he's good for her.

"Cincinnati, Ohio."

My mom sighs—in relief, probably. "Not too far," she says under her breath. "Only two hours. Within driving distance."

"It's not that bad, Mom." Maya smiles, reaching over to pat my mom's arm. "We'll still see you, like, all the time."

My mom sniffs, getting teary. "Not once a week for dinner."

"Well, no, but…" Maya sends me a panicked glance. I can read her sister SOS—*help me distract her.*

I wrack my brain but come up empty. "What about your job?"

"Thanks," Maya mouths, glaring at me. Then she shrugs and says aloud, "It's not that big of a deal. I'll find a new one."

"What?" My voice gets shrill and my nail tech caps the polish, backing away. I need to give her an extra-large tip. I force myself to speak calmly. "But you love your job."

Four years ahead of me, Maya went to Harrison and has a job in the maternity ward of a local hospital. It's been her dream forever, and she gushes about the babies she helps deliver all the time.

"Yeah." Pain fills her gaze, but she brushes it off. "I do. But hospitals are all over the place. I'll find a new one. Or I'll go back to school. It's a good time to get my masters and my midwifery certification."

"You just earned your way onto first shift, though!" I protest. "Finally, no more graveyards!"

Again, she shrugs. "It is what it is."

"No, it's not!" My mom frowns at my raised voice, but my sister has worked so hard for this. How can she give it up so casually? I press on. "Why are you letting this happen?"

Maya grips the armrest of her chair, knuckles turning white. "We compromised, Jaz."

I shake my head. "It sounds like you did all the compromising, and Joel is getting everything."

It's so typical. Another controlling guy. Another one-sided relationship. I thought Joel and Maya were different, but I was wrong.

"It's not like he wants to move, either," she says, tossing her hair.

"He said yes, didn't he?"

"It's an excellent opportunity for him." Maya's eyes flash a warning at me, but I don't heed it. I'm willing to speak the truth here, even if no one else is.

"And his opportunities come before yours?"

"He makes more money than I do!"

"And therefore has more deciding power?"

"It's not like that." Maya speaks through gritted teeth. "We decided together. I'm sorry you don't understand it."

She's right, I don't. Because it sure sounds like the worst part of every relationship—being asked to give up yourself and your convictions, all because of love and commitment. Well, it's not worth it. Maya is selling out, letting go of her goals, giving away part of her soul for this.

But it won't happen to me. Relationships suck. I don't know what's going on between Cooper and me, but I won't let him change me and infringe upon my independence. No matter what I told my mom, it's just sex, and I won't let any messy feelings get in the way and convince me to change who I am or what I want. Not for any man.

No matter how cute he is or how many flips my belly does when he walks into the room. Nope. I'm done falling for him —I'm getting back up. I don't care how well he listens or how thoughtful he is. It's too dangerous.

Clearing my throat, I change the topic to my summer internship, and the mood lightens. After surviving mandatory girl time, I drive myself back to Lafayette, and don't let myself think of Cooper once. Not even when I hear his favorite hideous country song on the radio.

I'll focus on myself and the GRE for the upcoming weeks. That's what a smart woman would do, anyway. And I refuse to let a guy make me dumb. Never again.

CHAPTER
Thirty~Four

JASMINE

Cooper: Ready for The Winter Soldier?
   Cooper: Hey, what are you up to?
   Cooper: Jasmine? You okay?

❧

"God, not like that." Chad rolls his brown eyes and jumps in, grabbing the beaker and adjusting the position of the aspirator, which is ridiculous since the sample is uniform. But I bite my tongue and the inside of my cheek and try not to let his words affect me. The quick pain helps me focus on anything besides how close he is to me. The smell of his cologne threatens to make me gag and I force myself to breathe in through my mouth.

Just learn how to do this so you can get away from him.

He adjusts a setting on the computer and then gives me a self-satisfied smirk. "See? Have everything set just so or you'll waste your sample."

"Uh-huh." Grunts are all I can manage. I hold myself rigid and watch what he's doing while every muscle in my body wants to flee.

"You know, I'm taking time out of my schedule to teach you. You could be a little more grateful." Chad purses his mouth like he just ate Sour Patch Kids, which he would never do because he hates them. And I hate how I know that about him. I hate the way he stands too close to me, so I feel like he's towering over me. I hate that he's seen me naked. Everything about exes is the worst.

But I can't let him talk to me like that. Never again. So I scoff. "We both know you're doing this to get a good recommendation from Dr. Michelson and to say you mentored other students. And I'd appreciate it if you would not speak to me like that."

"Like what?"

I grind my molars. Explaining won't help. He's a champion gaslighter. "Never mind. Just show me the next step."

"Please." He stares at me, challenging me with his gaze to say the word. Oh my god, next he's going to tell me to smile more. I'm going to murder him and no one will ever find his body. My friends would help.

He taps his fingers on the bench, exaggerating how he's waiting on me.

"Please," I repeat through gritted teeth. If I survive this, I'm going to treat myself. I should take another GRE practice exam after this, but no. I deserve coffee. Or chocolate. Or both.

Or Cooper.

An image of him pops into my mind—his eyes dancing at a sarcastic comment, his crooked smile spreading across his face, his muscular arms around me. The way his kisses make my toes curl. A night with him would do wonders—

No. I'm not supposed to think about him. He's been mentally off-limits ever since I got Herbie back and started to worry that I was too attached, that I was giving him too much influence. I did that with Chad and look where I ended up. Regret City, population: me.

Cooper's texted me a few times about watching the next movie in our Marvel marathon, but I've put him off. I'm not lying when I tell him I'm too busy. I barely squeeze in a few hours of sleep each night.

You made time for him before, that traitorous voice in my head chimes in.

Chad narrows his muddy brown eyes. "Are you paying attention? Or are you daydreaming about your steroid junkie boyfriend? Assuming he hasn't dumped you already."

"Of course I'm paying attention." My words are short, clipped, and my fingernails dig into my palms through my gloves. I only want to do this once. "My personal life is none of your business. I think I've got it. You can leave now."

"I'll stay and supervise." He sneers down the bridge of his nose at me and I want to punch his stupid, smug face.

Crossing my hands, I pinch the inside of my wrists. Nope, not dreaming. Just a waking nightmare.

Closing my laptop, I stand up from my desk chair and stretch. I roll out my neck and wiggle my fingers, trying to get my blood flowing. I rub my eyes, scratchy from lack of sleep, and massage my temples to ward off a tension headache that's waiting below the surface. I'm just about to run downstairs for a snack when my computer dings at me.

With a sigh, I sit back down and open it up. Checking my

email, I find a message from Dr. Michelson. I scan her words, and my blood boils.

How dare he.

Apparently Chad told her I was unfocused and unappreciative of his time. He said I'd need another session with him to master Flame AA, even though I did it just fine on my own. Rat bastard.

Pushing away from my desk, I pace the small length of my room, clenching and unclenching my fists. I clench my teeth so hard my jaw aches, and I want to scream.

When my phone buzzes with a text, I cling to the distraction.

Cooper: Ready for a study break?

Jasmine: You have no idea.

Cooper: Yeah? What sounds good?

Jasmine: I need some Chris Evans asap

Cooper: Do you want to be alone with him, or...?

Jasmine: Are you suggesting a threesome?

Cooper: I'm pretty confident, but even I'm not sure I can compete with that. How about we just watch a movie with him in it?

Jasmine: I suppose that would work ;) The Winter Soldier?

Cooper: I could come to you.

Jasmine: That would be great.

I don't analyze the twinkle in my eye as I check my reflection in the mirror and swipe on a coat of lip gloss. And I ignore the pep in my step when I answer the front door and find him on the porch. His crooked smile makes my belly flutter. I throw my arms around him and take a deep breath, inhaling his woodsy scent. The smell is soothing and my stress ebbs away.

"Come on." I link my arm through his and tug him up to my bedroom.

After setting up my laptop on the foot of the bed, I pat the space next to me and Cooper settles in. Instead of lying on the pillows, we bend our heads together, close, towards the screen. It's not long before our feet tangle together and his arm snakes around my waist. His fingertips brush over the exposed skin on my back and I bite back a groan.

I forget the movie as our gazes lock. His hazel eyes draw me in like the Death Star tractor beam, and I'm powerless to resist. His mouth is a magnet for mine and I give into the inevitable. Our lips meet and I lose myself in his kiss, his arms, his body.

Before he takes my shirt off, he relocates my laptop to the floor. Then he covers me, moving with me and taking away all my concerns.

Afterwards, I lay on his chest, tracing patterns on his skin and basking in the afterglow. The movie is still playing some-where, sounding tinny and far away through my computer speakers.

We should talk about whatever the hell is going on between us, but that would ruin the beauty of the arrange-ment. I don't want to analyze it. Between extra hours in the lab to monitor results, Flame AA lessons with Chad, and the looming GRE, I can only handle things that are not compli-cated. I could lose myself in sex with him all night and not worry about anything else. The idea is as tempting as moving to Hoth on a hot day.

Clearing my throat, I prepare to proposition him again when his eyes widen.

"Oh, I almost forgot, darlin'." Shifting me, he puts his clothes on and moves across the room. I find my clothes, too, and cover up. Reaching into his backpack, he pulls out a wadded-up orange shirt. "This is for you."

Unfolding it, I can't believe what I'm seeing. First off, it's a scoop-neck, and it looks like it might reveal my belly button. Holy cow, it's low cut. But it gets worse. In sparkly rhinestones, it proclaims I'm a "puck bunny," across the front, and "property of Edwards" with Number Twenty-Two on the back.

"Wow. This is... wow."

He smiles. "I know sparkles may not be your thing, but all the girls got them made to wear to the last home game. Isn't it funny?"

"The sparkles aren't the problem." I sit up, back straight. "Girls designed this?"

"Yeah?" He raises his brows. "I think so."

"So, other females are wearing shirts like this... voluntarily?"

Cooper studies the shirt as I hold it out like it's radioactive waste. And—it might be? What if it gives me cooties? What if it steals IQ points? I shudder.

"I don't get it." He shrugs. "What's the big deal?"

Blinking, my blood boils. It thrums through my veins and my heart pounds.

"What's the big deal?" I say, voice getting higher and louder. "What's the big deal? Ignoring how revealing this is going to be on me, let's start with the term 'puck bunny,' shall we?"

"Okay, it's kinda derogatory, but it's a joke. Like when girls call themselves bitches or sluts."

"Have you ever heard me do that?"

"Well, no, but—"

"And I'm your 'property' now?" I use finger quotes around the word, and he rolls his eyes.

"You know that's just a way of saying we're dating."

"Uh, it's also a way of saying that we're totally unequal, I don't have rights as a citizen, and that you can do whatever you want with me. Like I'm a slave, basically. Is that what you think of me? Or of girls in general?"

"Of course I don't." Cooper's words are clipped, impatient. "But it's an expression."

"A totally terrible one!" I say back. "Cooper, I don't know the girls who made this shirt, but it's awful. There's no way I'd ever wear it in public. Or private, for that matter."

"Come on, Jaz. You're reading into this, I reckon."

"Reading into it? Cooper, I'm literally reading the sexist words on the shirt."

Huffing, he stands. "All the other girlfriends are wearing them."

"Oh, and I should jump off a bridge if they do, too?" Hopping up, I face him with my hands on my hips.

"Don't be like that. I just mean that it's clearly not a feminist issue if they are all okay with it."

"No, that's not how that works. All that should matter is that I'm not okay with it."

He blinks, takes a deep breath, and his tense posture softens. "You're right."

"What?" Now it's my turn to gape at him.

"Yeah." He grabs my hands, then stares at the hideous shirt I flung on my floor. "I've never liked the term 'puck bunny.' It's icky. And I'm sorry I asked you to do something that made you uncomfortable."

I gaze into his guileless hazel eyes. He's not saying this to manipulate me—he means it. I swallow around the sudden lump in my throat. "Wow. I've never had a guy apologize to me before. I'm not sure what to say."

"Forget the shirt." He steps closer, sliding his arms around my waist. "Just say you'll come."

I bite my lip. His apology makes my knees get wobbly, but I look from the orange fabric at my feet to the pile of study materials on my desk.

"I'm not sure. I took off tonight when I shouldn't have. And I'm not really in the right headspace for hockey."

Cooper's fingers slip under the hem of my tee, rubbing circles that are both soothing and sensual.

"You're so busy and stressed lately. Maybe it would be the perfect mental break for you. It could help you focus better."

He gives me his most charming smile and my resolve weakens, but my flash cards glare at me on my nightstand.

"I don't know…"

Peppering kisses along my neck, his voice is muffled against my skin. "Just come. Be yourself, because the Jasmine I know is a kick-ass person. Wear whatever you want. You could come naked, for all I care."

I huff a laugh and pull back, looking into his dancing eyes. He's earnest and eager.

"This means a lot to you, yeah?"

At his nod, I take a deep breath, then let it out. "Okay. Game's tomorrow, right?"

He sags against me, relaxing now that I've acquiesced. I run through my mental options, formulating a plan.

"Alright. I haven't started that experiment yet, but I can rearrange things and push it back a day. I'll work hard today and do extra GRE prep in the lab on Sunday. And I'll wear the matching shirt. But—"

"No!" He cuts me off, shaking his head. "You're right, it's the worst. Derogatory and totally not you. I don't want you to do that."

But I have an idea. I give him a kiss, quick and hard. "You

didn't let me finish. I'll wear it my way. With a few modifications."

Cooper's eyes widen. "You're not, like, going to stage a protest or something, right? Boycott hockey? Vancouver Stanley Cup riots?"

"I don't know what that is, but no, not a riot or a protest." I smile. "I'll be totally respectful—but I'll also be myself."

He doesn't look totally convinced, but he tucks a lock of hair behind my ear. "Can't wait to see you there."

CHAPTER
Thirty-Five

COOPER

Since the apartments in Hockey Hall have kitchens, we don't have a dining hall in the basement like most dorms on campus. But as student athletes, we have a meal plan. We eat at home a lot, but sometimes I'm too lazy. So I convince Hunter to grab burritos with me from the dining hall in Burke Commons, a few blocks away.

We make small talk about hockey as we wait in line and grab our food. After getting a drink, I find us a table in the back.

As soon as I take a bite, Hunter pins me in his gaze.

"So, what's up with you and Jasmine?"

Chewing, I swallow and sip my Coke.

"Nothing much. She's busy, I'm busy, but things are cool."

I think. She was upset over that damn shirt, but I fixed it.

"She coming to the game tonight?"

I nod, and he digs into his food.

"Good. You play better when she's there." I don't know

what to say to that, so I take a bite, and he keeps talking. "What are you going to do next year when she's not here?"

"Not here? Where's she going?"

A chunk of meat falls out of Hunter's burrito as he stares at me with it halfway to his mouth. "You will have broken up with her by then, right? This fake thing will be over."

"Oh." Why does disappointment fill my chest at that thought? "Yeah, I guess."

"Although, for a fake relationship, you guys are having a lot of real sex."

"What's that supposed to mean?"

Giving up, he sets his burrito down on his plate and uses his fork.

"All I'm saying is, I've seen her sneak out a lot of mornings."

"She's not sneaking. And I don't think that's *all* you're saying, because I've seen tons of girls leave your room. What's your point?"

I wait for him to swallow his mouthful before he asks, "Are you sleeping with anyone else?"

"No." I don't growl, but it's difficult.

"So it doesn't really matter what labels you do or don't put on it. It sure sounds like you're exclusive with Jasmine."

"Well…" I mean, I guess he's kinda right. She hates boyfriends, but she's not sleeping with anyone else. But this isn't a relationship. "It's just a little fling."

Hunter snorts.

"What?" I ask.

"I saw the way she looked at you the other night."

"How did she look at me?"

"The way I'd look at an NHL contract. Like Garfield looks at lasagna. How a girl looks at a guy she's in love with."

My bite hangs in midair on the way to my mouth, which drops open.

"No. There's no way."

"Why not, dude?" Hunter spreads his arms wide. "Why is it so impossible that she fell in love with you?"

Before I can answer, the words tumble out of his mouth. "I mean, it happens in the movies every time."

"What movies?" is what my stupid brain spits out.

"You know. That one about *All the Boys I've Loved.* Oh, don't forget *Bridgerton,* and *Easy A.*"

"No, in *Easy A*, she's faking it with the gay guy. They don't fall in love."

"Are you gay?"

"No."

"Then stop avoiding my point." He punctuates each word with a tap on the table. "Jasmine. Is. In. Love. With. You."

"Have you really seen all those movies?" I ask, trying to change the subject.

"I have a sister, man. And we're not talking about me."

Sighing, I shred my napkin into tiny pieces. "You're wrong. Jasmine is not the 'fall in love' type."

"Cooper, you should have seen her the other day."

"Uh, I did. Remember, I invited her over?"

Hunter shakes his head. "You're ignoring all the signs. She had major heart-eyes."

"She's a good actress. Besides, I saw her after that and it wasn't lovey-dovey at all."

"Yeah?"

"Yeah. We watched a movie, just as friends." I skip over the sex part since he made such a big deal about that earlier. "Trust me, there were no heart-eyes."

Leaning back in his chair, Hunter wads up his napkin and throws it on his tray.

"You should ask how she feels, dude. You need to know."

I huff. "Thanks for your concern, but I can handle it."

His raised brows indicate his doubts, but he doesn't voice them. At his show of restraint, I switch the subject—back to hockey, a safe topic.

But his words continue to echo in my mind. We do act like a couple, in every sense of the word. Watching movies, cuddling, texting.

Is Jasmine in love with me? There's no way. I think of my mom and what love did to her. I won't do that to Jasmine. If Hunter is right, I need to end this sooner rather than later.

The thought sends a pang through my chest. I can at least wait until hockey season is over. I need my good-luck charm.

CHAPTER
Thirty~Six

JASMINE

Cooper: Thanks again for coming to my game tonight.

Cooper: I'm sorry about the shirt thing. You really don't have to wear it.

Jasmine: It's okay. I probably overreacted a little. I know I don't have to wear it, but I'll make it work for me.

Taking a deep breath, I make my way down the stadium stairs, stopping to show my ticket to an usher. But he smiles and waves me through without bothering to check it.

"Enjoy the game!" he says, and I bite my lip. I wish I could relax and view it as any other hockey match, but it's become more than that in my mind. Nerves jangle in my belly and my palms are sticky with sweat.

Mumbling my thanks, I keep my gaze glued on the concrete floor, hedging my way through the crowd. The first four rows of my section, directly up from center ice, are full of chattering girls, all in their matching rhinestone-studded orange shirts. Based on the amount of cleavage spilling out of the generous scoop-neck, it's safe to say the JumboTron is going to be trained here all night.

Sighing, I scoot past them, through the row until I get to my seat at the other end. Most of them don't seem to notice, still engrossed in their conversations, but I feel a few pairs of eyes follow me. When I finally get to my spot, I take another deep breath, steeling myself, and I unzip my jacket.

The conversation around me quiets, then raises to a loud buzz. I ignore it until there's a tap on my shoulder.

"Hi, I'm Elle." The girl behind me holds out her hand to shake, smooth curtain of brown hair swinging. Her smile is perfect. Everything about her is perfect. "I don't think we've met yet."

"You're Cooper's girl, right?" The blonde next to her asks as I shake Elle's hand. "I'm Isabella, Shawn's girlfriend."

Cooper's girl? Ugh. As if that's the most important aspect of my identity. I cross my arms over my chest. "Jasmine. And yes, I'm dating Cooper."

Doesn't make me *his*, though.

Isabella's eyes widen at my frosty tone and she blinks. "We haven't seen you around at any of the hockey events yet. Our boyfriends are seniors, so…"

She trails off, but I don't know how that sentence ends. Not backing down, I meet her stare until she shifts her weight and glances away.

"What happened to your shirt?" Elle asks, and I hold the fabric out away from my body, gazing down at it.

It had taken some work, but I'd removed all the rhinestones that spelled out "puck bunny" and rearranged them to spell "puck off." I'd altered the back, too—taking off the "property of" part and only leaving "Edwards" with his number. And I put another shirt underneath it so my boobs weren't on display.

"Oh, it didn't work, so I modified it a bit."

The two girls exchange a glance.

"The size? It looks okay." Isabella tosses her blonde hair.

"You changed the words," Elle says, pursing her lips.

"Yep."

If she wants to play Captain Obvious, I can, too.

"But we're all supposed to match." Her voice stays steady but her forehead creases, a crack in her perfect façade.

"Why?"

"Well..."

Isabella steps closer. "We thought it would be cute and funny, you know?"

"Funny to call yourselves puck bunnies?" I raise my brows. "A term that's obviously derogatory?"

"Look." Elle presses her lips together and her nostrils flare as she inhales. "You're new here, you don't get it. People will call us that anyway, regardless of how long we've been with our boyfriends or how serious it is. So we figured—why not own it?"

"Say it first before they can." Isabella tucks her hair behind her ear and shrugs.

In a deranged way, that logic kind of makes sense. But it would never be how I'd handle it. Nothing will change how I feel about the term. Or the t-shirt.

"I get that." I nod, trying to extend an olive branch. "But you're right, I'm new here. So you don't know yet—I'm not okay with anyone calling me that, myself included. I'm more than my relationship status."

Isabella's mouth drops open, and Elle blinks, then stammers.

"I designed these shirts myself." She tilts her chin up, jaw firm. "If you don't want to wear the correct version, I'd prefer you take it off."

So much for my olive branch. I grind my molars together to keep from saying something I'll regret.

"Well, I designed this"—I hold it out again—"myself, and I'm rather proud of it. My boyfriend asked me to wear it, so..."

It's my turn to trail off. Spinning away from them, I drop into my seat, only to pop up again for the National Anthem and the start of the game. No one talks to me. The girl on my left makes a show of turning her back to me, giving me a literal cold shoulder.

Why did I insist on wearing this shirt I hate? I'm not sure. I could have taken it off. There is a second shirt underneath it. But once Elle told me to, I couldn't back down.

I cheer for Cooper as he takes the puck in the faceoff, but my heart's not in it. Too aware of the girls around me, their whispers and stares, I can't seem to lose myself in the game. Harrison scores, but I don't see who put the biscuit in the basket. The ice is a blur in front of me.

The girls around me pose for selfies together, making faces for the cameras and ignoring me. Every time our section is on the JumboTron, they go crazy, screaming and yelling. I slink further into my seat, arms crossed over my chest. Why did I come tonight? It was important to Cooper, but I'm clearly an outsider. He and I... no matter how I feel, this can't last. This fling has an end-date, and it's quickly approaching. Maybe already past, in fact.

But he skates by me, heading to the bench as his line changes, and winks. It bolsters me. He wants me here. That's all that matters.

I square my shoulders. I won't let anyone make me feel bad for being myself. Not anymore. Forcing myself to focus, I clap and whistle for the rest of the first period. When the buzzer sounds, I jump out of my seat and head to the concession stand. I deserve a soft pretzel, plus nacho cheese.

After getting my snack and a Coke, I stay out in the concourse until the last moment before girding my loins and returning to my seat.

As the second period starts, Elle stands up in front of our section, cupping her hands around her mouth.

"Hey, girls! Remember that cheer we made up on the bus to the Notre Dame game? Let's do that again!"

They have a bus for away games? Not like I would have had time, but it reinforces how much I don't fit in.

I sink down, my shoulders creeping up to my ears, as they all leap to their feet and start a chant, complete with hand motions and dance moves. The crowd eats it up. The image of the pretty girls fills the JumboTron and, as the only one who doesn't know the cheer, I stick out like a sore thumb. Bending down, I pretend to look for something and try to hide.

The second period gets going in earnest after that and they settle down to watch. I lose myself in the action and everything is fine, both for me and the Griffins. The surrounding girls do their own thing, and I do mine. The Buckeyes call a timeout, and the announcers must have a technical problem because instead of music or statistics over the loudspeakers, it's silent.

Silent enough that I can hear the conversation of the girls on my right. I don't know them—if they were at the hockey party I went to last weekend, I don't recognize them. One of them giggles and tries to catch Mateo's attention, so I'm guessing there's a connection. The other one gushes about Tyler and how hot he is. But then I hear them mention Cooper.

"Did I tell you about the time last season that I hooked up with Edwards?"

I stiffen. Does she know I can hear her? Is she saying this to rile me?

"You did?" Her friend's voice brims with admiration. "Does Matty know?"

I sneak a glance out of the corner of my eye. The pretty blonde shrugs, her ponytail bouncing. "Not specifics. He knows I've been with a few of his teammates, but I didn't mention names."

"Yeah, I get that." The other girl, with gorgeous black braids, gives her a wicked smile. "But just between you and me—how was it?"

The blonde pretends to be outraged, but grins. "As if I'd kiss and tell!"

Her friend snorts. "Claire, you're the biggest gossip! Of course you'd tell me!"

A smug, secretive look crosses her face and I squirm in my seat. "All I'm saying is—I'd ride that cowboy again."

The other girl's voice drops so low I can barely hear it, and I grip my armrest so hard my knuckles turn white. "Do you think he's serious about What's-Her-Name over there?"

Claire shrugs. "It's weird, right? I never thought he'd settle down, let alone with someone who's totally not his type."

Not his type.

Giggling, they speculate about my sexual preferences, and the reasons that Cooper might be with me. The blood thrums in my ears and sweat breaks out along my hairline. I can't take it anymore. Face flaming, I leap to my feet, and accidentally spill my Coke all over myself.

I gasp at the icy cold shower and mumble my excuses as I make my way down the aisle and to the bathroom. Coke drips down my torso and into my waistband. I ignore the stares and whispers and move as fast as I can.

Throwing open the bathroom door, I pat myself down with paper towels and stare at my reflection.

My green eyes look wild and two red spots dot my cheeks, but the rest of my face is pale. My hands shake and I force myself to take deep breaths.

Their words shouldn't bother me. I know I'm not Cooper's first. I don't care about that. And I guess, objectively, I'm probably not his type. I'm obviously not a good hockey girlfriend. I couldn't make myself wear the matching shirt. I don't know the cheers, and I definitely didn't know these girls planned road trips to away games. I don't have that kind of time.

It reinforces how stupid it was to entertain the idea that there might be something more between us. And I can't believe I attended this game. I should have known the minute I saw that awful shirt that it was bad news.

Goosebumps dot my skin from the cold soda, and I shiver. Cooper would understand if I went home. Do I have time to change and meet him outside the locker room? Or should I just take off and not come back?

I picture his face, winking at me from the stands, and sigh. This was so important to him. Even if we're not meant to be for much longer, I can't just leave and ghost him. He deserves better than that.

Forcing myself to exit the bathroom, I stay in the concourse for the rest of the game and watch it on the TV mounted in the concession stand.

By the time the game ends, I've dried out.

The Griffins win, 4-3, and Cooper scored one goal and had an assist on another. He'll be amped up tonight, for sure.

I stop and wash my hands in the restroom again, touching up my lip gloss on the way to the locker room. I fluff my hair and purse my lips. I look good, even if my shirt is stained and wrinkled.

Feeling less sticky, I wait on the outskirts of the crowd for the team to appear. It's not only the girlfriends this time—lots of parents, siblings, and friends are standing around, too. So while I'm ignored, it's not malicious. They all have their groups.

Too bad I don't have my flashcards in my pocket. (Although they'd probably be ruined.) Reviewing the vocab words I can recall, I distract myself. I don't realize how much I want to see a friendly face, though, until Cooper appears in front of me.

"Hi." Hair still wet, his crooked grin spreads across his face, and I leap into his arms. Laughing, he swings me around as if I weigh nothing.

"You were awesome tonight," I say into his ear, not ready to let go of him.

"'Cause you're my good luck charm," he whispers, breath warm against my skin. "Knowing you're there watching, I always play better."

My stomach twists with guilt. Maybe I wasn't watching from the stands, but I was still here. I hope he didn't notice that I was gone for the second half. Stepping out of his embrace, I tuck a strand of hair behind my ear, suddenly self-conscious as he takes in the words on my shirt.

To my immense relief, Cooper chuckles. "Oh, darlin', bless your heart. Have I told you recently that you rock? Never change."

The combination of his praise and the affection shining in

his eyes is my undoing. I box up all my doubts about this fling and launch myself at him again, this time aiming for his mouth.

Our lips meet, and I sink into it. How long has it been since I've kissed him? Twenty-four hours, maybe? But I'm like a woman in the desert, drinking him down. His tongue touches mine and desire spools in my belly. Kissing him feels right. It's maybe the only thing that does, and I don't want to stop.

But eventually, he pulls back, and stares down at me, his gaze hot.

"Do you have plans tonight?" He swallows, his Adam's apple bobbing, and I want to lick it. I want to lick every inch of him.

I bite my lip, aiming for coy.

"You'll never believe what happened to me. I accidentally spilled soda all over myself. Karmic retribution, right?" I laugh at myself, and if it sounds forced and brittle, he doesn't mention it. "I need to get out of these dirty clothes and take a shower."

If possible, Cooper's pupils go even darker when I say the word "dirty." "Is, uh, that something you need help with? Because I'd like to offer my services."

"Yes. please. Your services are exactly what I require."

With a wink over my shoulder, I weave through the crowd and he follows at my heels, hand on the small of my back. His eagerness lights me up inside. After the week I've had, studying for the GRE and then facing down hockey groupies, I deserve this. It's just sex, after all. It doesn't mean anything, and no one is going to get hurt.

Climbing in his truck, that's what I tell myself, until we get into his bedroom. Then his kisses blissfully drown out all the voices in my brain.

CHAPTER
Thirty-Seven

JASMINE

I'm relaxed and sated, floating on a fluffy cloud. I'm having the most wonderful dream. I think there's chocolate in it... but it fades away. Oooh, but that's okay, because someone is massaging my back.

When I open my eyes, a strong, bare chest fills my vision. Cooper. He smiles down at me, and I shift so he has better access to my skin.

"That feels amazing." My voice is rough with sleep, and I inhale. God, he smells good. His soap is clean and masculine, and underneath it, there's something uniquely him. It's soothing and arousing at the same time.

"You were pretty amazing last night." He kisses my temple. "I, uh, I've missed all of you, but..."

"Yeah, we're good together in that area, aren't we?"

Before I can blink, he shifts me underneath him. Wow, that's sexy. Then he nibbles on my neck, and I moan, my insides melting.

"Don't stop." I know I'm begging, but I don't care.

"Wouldn't dream of it."

After proving once again that our chemistry could set a house on fire, Cooper winks and rolls out of bed. I'm too preoccupied with trying to catch my breath to move yet. When was the last time I lazed around in bed? I'm not planning on making a habit, but it's glorious. All my stress has disappeared.

Just when I think my legs will finally support my weight, he reappears, holding out a mug of coffee. Am I still dreaming? Is he the perfect man?

No, I catch myself. The perfect man doesn't exist. But one that brings me coffee after giving me that much pleasure—he's a fine specimen, for sure.

"Thanks." Scooting up against the headboard, I reach for it. "You're the best."

Smiling, he settles next to me with his own cup. "Thanks again for coming last night."

I send him a flirty look. "Are you making a dirty joke?"

His laugh rings out. "Not intentionally. That, too. But I meant thanks for coming to the hockey game."

Staring at my cup, I blow on the surface, even though it's not too hot. I don't want him to know how badly I fit in with the other girls last night.

"You're welcome." Then I clear my throat. "So what's next, in terms of hockey? How do the play-offs work?"

That is the term, right? I have no idea.

Cooper grimaces. "Well, it's not exactly like play-offs in other sports. We have the Big Ten tournament over the next few days, and hopefully that's our way into the Finals. If not, we can still be selected, and I think our chances are good."

I nod, and he runs a hand through his tousled bed-head. "There's always a big selection party."

"What's a selection party?"

"On ESPN?" Like that explains it. I stare blankly, so he elaborates. "They show the selection live on TV and they have cameras on all the teams as they watch together, waiting to see who makes it and what our seed is. It's kind of a big deal."

I shoot him a teasing smile. "Are you just trying to impress me with how important you are?"

"Darlin'." He rolls on top of me, pinning me underneath him. "Always. Is it working?"

I'm about to show him how much when my buzzing phone interrupts. Cooper scoots away and Lucy's name flashes across the screen as I answer it.

"Hello?"

"Hey, Jasmine? I'm sorry to bother you but…"

Uh-oh. Phone calls that start that way are never good.

"Lucy, what's wrong?" I ask.

"Uh, it's the lab."

Gasping, a jolt of adrenaline shoots down my spine as I remember. Lucy keeps talking.

"I guess you were scheduled to come in today and finish an experiment? Your sample is still in the apparatus and Chad is losing his mind over it."

"Shit." I scramble off Cooper's bed. He sits up, too, watching, but I don't have time to explain.

"He tried to call you," Lucy says, "but I figured you wouldn't pick up if you saw his number."

"He's blocked." Where are my clothes? My heart races as my eyes scan the room. "I'll be there as soon as possible, Lucy. Thanks for calling me."

"Sure, anytime. I'll cover until you get here."

"You're a lifesaver." Ending the call, I toss my phone on

the bed and scoop up my clothes from the floor. Ugh, they are still gross from the Coke spill. I'm going to have to run home before the lab, plus I need to get my car, and—

"What's going on?" Cooper hops out of his bed, throwing on jeans and a t-shirt.

"Nothing. Everything sucks." Tugging on my underwear, I sigh as I slip my arms through my bra, fastening it.

"Hey, Jaz, what is it?" He stops dressing and comes to stand in front of me, stopping me in my path and tilting my chin up to meet his gaze.

"I forgot. I don't have any excuses, I just forgot. I can't believe I did that."

"What did you forget, darlin'?" In spite of everything, my stomach does a little flip at the way the endearment rolls off his tongue. I take a deep breath, forcing myself to slow down.

"I was supposed to be in the lab right now. My samples are still there, taking up space and inconveniencing everyone, especially Chad."

Cooper glares. "That asshat?"

"Yes. I'm sure he's overreacting, but at the same time, it's thoughtless of me. I'd be mad if someone else skipped out on their responsibilities like that. So I have to get changed and get there fast. He's never going to let me live this down."

Taking the bundle of soiled clothes from my arms, Cooper dumps them in his hamper. "Here's what we're gonna do. I'll wash these and return them later."

Rifling through his drawers, he tosses a pair of black sweats and a gray Harrison hockey shirt at me. "Put these on and I'll drive you there. We can pick up your car later."

Putting on the sweats and t-shirt, I shake my head. "Thanks for the clothes, but Herbie is across the street at the hockey arena. I can drive myself."

He's doing enough for me as it is. Too much. I need a little space to get out of the clouds and back to reality.

Pocketing my phone, I hustle out of his room before he can argue further. "I'll catch you later," I say, but I'm already out the door.

"Wow." Chad eyes me up and down, his lips pursed like he ate a lemon. "Thanks for bothering to show up."

"Shut. Up." I force the words past my clenched teeth, rage simmering below the surface.

His expression takes on a glint of mock-pity and he gives my clothing choice a pointed look. "I'm sure you don't want to hear this, but your boyfriend is obviously a terrible influence, Jasmine."

It stings because there's a kernel of truth in there. But I smooth my features and focus on the task before me. "You're right. I don't want to hear from you. Who I date is still none of your business."

"No, I'm serious. I think you need an intervention."

"And I think you need a kick in the balls."

Chad takes a massive step away from me, holding his hands up in surrender. "Whoa, kitty. Retract claws. And please be more professional in the lab."

Great. Now he's made me out to be the unreasonable one, when in fact, Chad is the least professional lab mate here. I roll my eyes, because I can only show so much restraint.

Lucy sends me a look from across the room, offering to step in if needed, but I shake my head. It's sweet of her, but I need to fight my battle. Hopefully not with actual kicks, but... if anyone's balls deserve it, it's Chad's. And while threatening physical violence is not a tactic I'm proud of, if it means he keeps his distance, I'll embrace it.

I clear my throat. "Yes, let's focus on appropriate behavior, shall we?"

Chad tsks at me like I'm a recalcitrant child. "I'm just saying, you're not the same girl. You've changed. And not for the better."

Ouch. That dig hurts, but I'll confront a Dalek before I let him know that. So I give him a wicked grin. "You're absolutely right. I have changed. And I feel great. This is the real me."

He sneers. "The real you is going to have a hell of a time in the future, then. You better offload your jock boyfriend before your internship at Lilly. They won't tolerate this kind of behavior. I should report you to Dr. Michelson."

My heart lurches. "Look, I was a few minutes late. You're making this into a bigger deal than it needs to be."

Chad raises a haughty brow. "I disagree. The department thinks that you're an outstanding student. They deserve to know that you're not nearly as committed as the rest of us."

I want to growl in frustration, but I bite my tongue. "I'm sorry I was late. I'll finish up here and be out of your way."

"Would have been out of here hours ago if you had shown up on time."

Glaring, he turns back to the fume hood and taps his toe, watching my every move. My hands shake with contained rage and shame.

I know he's wrong. I know his opinion is trash. He's worthless. But his words needle me. Forgetting I had a commitment in the lab? I've never done that before. I pride myself on being reliable, on time for things, and keeping my word.

But since meeting Cooper, I've literally lied to everyone I

know. His mom, my friends, my lab mates, my professors, his teammates, my family... I swallow. I mean, it's kinda true these days—we are basically dating, but it doesn't change the fact that I deceived all those people.

I like Cooper. Like, really like him. Maybe I even love him. But has he changed me? Turned me into an irresponsible girl who lies to people who are important to her?

The ice bath meant to cool the collection flask is looking a bit more like a water bath. A harried grad student bustles into my view, swiping her bangs off her forehead. I desperately want what she has—sleep deprivation and all—but what if I had slept through the GREs this morning? Has Cooper become more important than my future? My goals? My self?

There's no way that Chad is right. But if I let down my guard, Cooper could easily sway me, just like Chad. I can't let him in, not permanently. I can't let myself love him. There's too much at stake.

CHAPTER
Thirty-Eight

COOPER

Cooper: Sorry again about your alarm and lab time. How did it go with Chad?

  Jasmine: It's fine. Have a great game.

  Cooper: I know "fine" is code for "He's a massive dick." Sorry you have to deal with that.

  Jasmine: Don't worry about me! Go out and kick some Gopher butt.

When I was in high school, daydreaming about playing Division I hockey, I pictured a private jet filled with sexy stewardesses and free drinks. No waiting to board and a non-stop party. Proving once again that teenage fantasies are wack. Maybe the football team lives out that dream on the university's plane, but not us.

Flying commercial with the team is weird. We don't all sit together, everything (besides hockey gear) has to fit in a carry-on, and we have to navigate security lines and airplane mode like everyone else. My mom would say it's a good life lesson, or some crap like that.

I sigh, adjusting my neck pillow. She'd probably be right. Just think of how spoiled the football team has become. But us hockey guys—we're both tough and humble.

It's been a few days since I've talked to my mom, actually. That's unlike her. Pulling out my phone, I give a thumbs-up and snap a selfie with the airport boarding area in the background.

Cooper: Off to Minneapolis! Big Ten Tourney, here we come.

After sending it, the three little dots appear, letting me know she's replying. A bit of the weight on my chest loosens, knowing she's there on the other end of the message.

Momma: Good luck, Griffins! You know I'm cheering you on through the TV!

It's sweet that she buys a cable package solely to get the Big Ten Network and watch me.

Momma: You guys play Minnesota in the first round, right?

Cooper: Yep. Tonight.

There are over ten schools in the Big Ten conference these days, but not all of them have hockey programs. There are eight teams competing this weekend in three rounds of play. A game tonight, and hopefully tomorrow and the day after.

The airline attendants announce the first round of boarding, but we wait. It's good for the university's image if we're seen as gentlemen who let others get on the plane first. People who need assistance, business class, and families with children all get their tickets scanned and walk down the chute before the guys and I queue up.

"Remember, men: best behavior." Coach adjusts his Harrison hockey cap, his words a growl.

I try not to roll my eyes, but we've heard his "how to act in public" speech all year. Instead, I tap the brim of my hat—a baseball cap like his—and send him a reassuring smile. I learned the hard way my freshman year that my cowboy hat isn't built for travel.

Finally, it's our turn to board. Tickets scanned, we all head through the temporary tunnel to the plane and then have the joy of trying to locate empty seats and carry-on space.

As I'm walking down the aisle of the plane, I spot a dude wearing a Lord of the Rings t-shirt, advertising the Mordor Fun-Run. It says, "One does not simply walk," and I laugh out loud. Man, Jasmine would love that. I'm about to stop and ask him where he got it, when Hunter pokes me between my shoulder blades.

"Hurry up."

Sighing, I shuffle forward, feeling his glare on my back. He's been sending me looks ever since Jasmine had blown out of our apartment this morning, and I've been avoiding it.

God, I can't get her off my mind. Not just how good it was last night, but how she had to leave. Her demeanor took a 180 after her phone call and I feel terrible that I distracted her from her responsibilities.

Spotting an empty seat—the middle one, naturally—I swing my carry-on into the overhead compartment and squish myself into the space. Why are airplane seats never big enough?

Popping in my ear buds, I try to chill out and listen to music. I need to get in the zone for the game tonight, but my thoughts are still full of Jasmine.

That moment this morning, as we relaxed in my bed over

coffee, was practically perfect. Remembering Hunter's words from a few days ago, I was contemplating talking to her about our fling or whatever, but then her phone rang and she was gone.

I've texted her, but I wish we could have talked or even connected in person. I need to see her, to have her in my arms. I hate she had to deal with Chad on her own. I'm sure he was awful to her, and there's nothing I can do about it. But what choice do we have?

"Come on, Edwards!" Coach raises his voice, the veins bulging in his neck. "Get your head in the game! Sit here until you figure it out."

Squeezing his clipboard so hard his knuckles turn white, he growls and stomps off, returning to the center of the bench.

Was it something I ate? Why does everything feel so wrong tonight?

I belong on the ice, but I'm riding the bench. I'll be the first person to admit I deserve it, after the utter crap I've put out there. I've lost every faceoff, tripped over my stick, and put a biscuit in the basket for Minnesota. That was when he pulled me and put Matteo in my line instead. We're up 2-1 in the second, but it's the first round—we can't blow this. We can't screw up our shot at the Frozen Four. If we do, it's all my fault.

I scan the stands, wishing for a friendly face. It wasn't a good time for my mom to get away, and I've mostly gotten out of that little-boy habit of thinking my dad might come to one of my games. He's proven repeatedly that I'm not important enough for that. Of course, the person I really want to see is

Jasmine, and she's not here. It would be so much easier if she were. I could talk to her and—

"Dude, what's wrong?" Evan's line rotates in, and he plops down on the bench beside me.

I shake my head. "Having a rough night, I guess."

The goal light spins and the siren rips through the stadium. Matteo lifts his stick in triumph, skating a lap around the arena while the crowd cheers.

"Matty's having a good one. Must have borrowed your luck."

Is Jasmine really my good luck charm? I've played okay on the road without her this year. But I've definitely played better lately. Is she watching tonight? Did she bother to find us on YouTube? Does she think less of me because I'm sucking? My stomach twists, cramping into a tight knot.

The more I try not to think about her, about how big of a distraction she has become, the more she's on my mind. This fling is keeping me from contributing to the team, just like I kept her from her lab and study time.

As I watch Hunter skate down the ice and pass to Matteo —*it should be me out there*—I know what I have to do. It's what's best for us both.

"Yeah." My voice is raw, but Evan doesn't notice. "Must have."

We're up 3-1. It will be fine.

And it is. We beat Minnesota and advance to the Semi-finals, no thanks to me. Coach put me in a little during the third period, but I skated around like a pee-wee player. The rest of the guys give me a wide berth in the locker room after, like my bad luck is contagious.

I palm my phone, reading a consolation message from my momma. I can't call Jasmine. I want to, but that will just make it hurt more later.

"You," Hunter stalks across the locker room, pointing his finger in my face. "I don't know what is going on, but you've gotta figure it out before tomorrow."

He's right. I nod, reaching out to pat his shoulder. I've got it figured out, even if it sucks.

"It was one bad game," I say. "A good night's sleep will fix everything."

He glares, still riled up. "Was that your problem last night? Too many distractions in your bedroom?"

My temper flares at his accusation, and the blood thrums through my veins. Can't he tell how hard this is?

"What are you getting at?" I take a step closer to him, but Hunter doesn't back down.

"You're thinking with your dick instead of your head." His voice is a growl and his eyes flash a warning, but I don't heed it. "In this moment, Jasmine doesn't matter. Hockey is the only thing that matters."

"This has nothing to do with her."

I don't know why I lie to him. It's a rookie move—getting tied up in knots over my girl. But I can't have the team think I'm slipping. Besides, I know what I have to do to fix it. My heart aches with it, so I let frustration at Hunter take over.

"Yeah?" Hunter raises a mocking brow. "How many times have you checked your phone since you got in here?"

He glances pointedly at my phone, still clutched in my left hand, and I don't think, I react. My right hand closes into a fist and it shoots out, aiming for his face. God, it would feel so good to connect with flesh, to get out of my muddled thoughts and let rage take over, to be in control of something.

But as I snarl, Hunter sidesteps my punch, and my

knuckles connect with the metal locker behind him. Pain radiates up my digits and through my arm. The locker room erupts. Before I can lunge at him again, Coach has me wrapped in a backward bear hug.

"What's the first rule of my fight club?" he yells, his voice piercing my eardrum.

"No fight club!" the rest of the guys chant in unison. Coach got really, deeply into *Ted Lasso*. He even grew a mustache.

As he pulls me away, I stare at Hunter. A mix of emotions wash across his face—shock, rage, hurt—and I close my eyes against it. He's my teammate and my best friend. What in the hell am I doing?

The fight drains out of me. Coach manhandles me around the corner, into the training room, muttering about stupid asshole hockey players. I shake him off, but I can't shake off the truth of his words.

"Get your hand checked out." His face is red, his words clipped. "Better not be broken. And you're out of the lineup tomorrow, no matter what. Ride the bench, get your head on straight."

I stare at my stocking feet. It's absolutely what I deserve, but I still burn with shame. I'm letting my team down.

"And Cooper?" He takes a deep breath. "It's one poor game. Not the end of the world. Don't let it get in your head."

It's too late. I let Jasmine get in my head, and look where I'm at now. But if Hunter is right, and she's in love with me, too, I can fix this for us. I can end things before we both fall apart and lose sight of our goals.

The trainer grabs my palm, poking and prodding, and I wince.

"Nothing's broken," he says, "but you're going to have a hell of a bruise."

Nothing less than I deserve.

I should feel better after we win on Monday, but I don't. I dressed for the game but didn't move from my spot on the bench the whole time. My mom sent me a million texts after, but all I could do was respond that I was fine. Nothing from Jasmine. Which is good. I'm glad she's focusing on what's important, like the GRE. I spend the entire day and night wallowing in my hotel room.

Coach and the trainer give me the go-ahead Tuesday morning, and I'm back in the rotation for the final game against Michigan. Hunter and I don't speak as we dress in the locker room. I need to apologize, but I feel too raw for that. The rest of the team notices the tension, but no one talks about it.

I'm adjusting the pad across my chest when Jonas sidles up to me.

"Psst," he whispers, and I raise a brow. He jerks his chin towards the showers, then walks in that direction, and I follow. Why is he being so weird?

At the end of the hall, Jonas turns to face me. Shifting from foot to foot, he twists his hands together.

Finally, I can't take the suspense any longer. "Dude, what's up?"

He sighs. "You know how I like to listen to music before a game?"

I nod. Everyone knows his pre-game ritual, and not to mess with it.

"Um, I listen to the Moana soundtrack."

"What?"

"Keep your voice down!" He steps closer, eyes wide. "I

heard some athlete interviewed on ESPN, joking and saying they liked it before they had a start." He shrugs. "I gave it a try, and it's awesome."

"Are you punking me, Joe? Because I don't—"

"Why would I do that?"

He has a point. My mouth snaps shut.

"You've had a rough couple days, man. Might be time to try something new."

Pushing past me, he moves towards the changing area.

Digging my phone out of my pocket, I download the Moana soundtrack and search for my earbuds. Something new. Disney princesses can't hurt.

Jonas is right. Moana gets me in the zone and I have an amazing game, despite only communicating with Hunter through grunts.

It doesn't matter. We still lose to Michigan.

CHAPTER
Thirty-Nine

COOPER

The irony isn't lost on me that the Frozen Four selection party is in the Union. The last time I was here was for Jasmine's department dinner.

God, that night. Holding her in my arms, running my fingers across her skin. Losing myself in her.

I swallow, needing to get it under control. I wish she were here by my side, bringing me good luck and smiling at me. But I didn't invite her. She needs the time to study, and when I look back on this night, I don't want to think of her. It would hurt too much.

The selection party would make more sense if they held it in the hockey rink or a wing of the athletic facility, but the Union has the space and the equipment needed. At least we're not in the ballroom tonight—that would be salt in my wound. They've set a bunch of chairs up around a projector screen in a smaller meeting room. Buffet tables laden with snacks line the far wall and ESPN cameras face the crowd, so they can show our reactions live. I hope it's a celebration broadcast on national TV and not tears.

Shoving my hands in my pockets, I try to avoid looking over at Hunter. Things have been... fine between us. I muttered an apology to him this morning over coffee and he nodded his acceptance. It was perfunctory, at best.

What kind of guy almost punches his best friend? What's my problem? I've been a mess. I pulled it together and played well in the last game thanks to *Moana*, but damn. Those kinds of issues will not win a Frozen Four championship. Jasmine has gotten under my skin. I should have called her, should have ended things already, but I was a coward. I need to rip this Bandaid off.

Getting in line for the buffet, I snag a plate and fill it with hot wings. Hunter sits in the front with some of the other guys, his dad nowhere in sight. I should ask him about that, but it's not the right time. Heading to a spot three rows back, I sit next to Jonas.

"Hey, man. Thanks again for, uh, your playlist tip."

His brows narrow. "Did you tell anyone?"

"That a Disney princess cured my yips? No, I did not."

"Technically, she's not a princess."

"Daughter of a chief? That's kinda like a princess."

Yes, I watched the movie the other night. By myself. I wanted to see the songs in context. It was so hard not to text Jasmine about it or invite her over to see it with me. She would have loved it. But if she had said yes and missed something important, the guilt would have eaten me alive.

Before Jonas can argue about *Moana*'s proper title, Coach steps up to the front of the room and clears his throat.

"Men, you know I'm not much for speeches." That's an understatement. "But it's been a great ride, an impressive season. I hope it's not the end of the road for us, but regardless, I'm proud of you."

At that, he gives a nod and takes a seat off to the side with the rest of the staff.

The projector in front of us flickers to life. So do the ESPN cameras.

The Final Four basketball bracket starts with sixty-four teams, but hockey with only sixteen. Of those sixteen spots, six are determined by conference champs—like Michigan's bid since they won the Big Ten. That leaves ten spots for the rest of the fifty-five Division I teams to vie for.

Ten spots. Not a lot. But we've played well this season, and we were runner up in our conference. That should count for something, right?

My phone buzzes and I shift, pulling it out of my pocket. It's a text from my mom.

Momma: I'm watching! Will you be on tv?
Cooper: I hope not. I'm sitting in the back with Joe.
Momma: Is Jasmine there?

What's there to say to that? *No, Mom. I didn't invite her because I'm going to break up with her for her own good.*

Nope. Not going there. I slide my phone into my pocket and focus on the screen.

But my traitorous eyes keep darting to the doorway, wishing that Jasmine would dash in at the last minute, sweep into the seat next to me, and kiss me on the cheek. She'll explain how Lucy told her about it and—

Jonas elbows me, snapping me out of my fantasy. Blinking, I zone in on the ESPN announcers in their studios, explaining the process.

While six of the teams are already known entities, part of the selection tonight is announcing the bracket for the finals, too. With sixteen teams, it's simpler than its basketball counterpart. There are four sites for Regionals, with four teams assigned to each, ranked one to four. A top-ranked one seed plays the four seed, with two and three facing off, too. It hasn't swept the country like March Madness yet, but maybe someday.

Stewart Scott adjusts his glasses, drawing out the suspense and telling us the four teams playing in Albany, New York. My palms are sweaty. They cut to the feed of each school, guys jumping up and down as they announce their names. We're not on the list.

But that's okay. There are three Regional sites left. I glance at the empty seat next to me, wishing Jasmine were here to hold my hand.

As they reveal the four teams playing in Massachusetts, it's not only my palms that get sweaty, but my whole body. And I'm pretty sure I'm not the only one. By the time we leave, this room will stink. Michigan is in this group, thanks to their Big Ten win. Based on the way the announcers fawn over them, they are the favorite to take the trophy home at the end of the two-week championship.

I gulp and focus on my breathing as they go through the teams in the Colorado Regional. Some of our rivals are playing there, but not us. My stomach drops. Only four spots left.

Okay. The Allentown, Pennsylvania Regional. This is our chance. Our only chance. I glance down at the blank paper bracket that Jonas is filling in, and his notes scribbled in the margins. The one seed will most likely be the conference winner that's left—North Dakota. The paper shakes in his fingers, but I'm so nervous I'm ready to gnaw on my hat so I'm not going to tease him about it. In fact, the entire room goes silent.

Is it my imagination, or do the ESPN analysts slow down?

Why is this taking forever? The Number Four seed—Harvard—has to play North Dakota. Only two spots left.

Are we done? Is this it? Did my terrible games last weekend ruin our chances?

The number three seed. St. Cloud State. ESPN shows them, jumping up and celebrating, but everyone here is tense with waiting. One. Left.

My left leg bounces with nervous energy. I'm not ready for the season to be over. I want—

"The Harrison Griffins!" Stewart Scott announces us as the number two seed and the room erupts in cheers. Leaping to my feet, I wrap Jonas in a bear hug and pound him on the back. Popcorn flies through the air and someone plays our victory song. Relief floods my veins. I didn't blow it, after all.

My phone vibrates in my pocket. Jasmine? Congratulating me?

No. Trying to keep the disappointment at that out of my voice, I answer. "Hey, Mom! We're going to the Frozen Four!"

"Pookie, I'm so proud of you!"

Ugh, I don't know why. I've messed up everything this semester. I need to get my shit in order. But I swallow it down. "Thanks, Momma. I'll text you all the game details later, when I get them, okay?"

"Of course. You go celebrate and kiss your girlfriend."

She hangs up, and I stare at the empty seat next to me. Girlfriend.

My heart sinks, but it's for the best, really. It's time to eliminate distractions once and for all.

I leave the selection party soon after that. I'm excited about our berth, but I'm not feeling lighthearted enough to spend the evening celebrating with my teammates.

Instead of calling, I drive to Jasmine's house, but she's not there. Staci thinks she's studying in the Chem building and I find a spot of good luck when I run into Lucy, who lets me in. After directing me to a bank of cubicles on the third floor, I finally spot Jasmine.

At the table in the tiny study room, she's spread out books in front of her. She's piled her long hair into a mess on top of her head and dark circles alarm me under her eyes. Absorbed in her reading, she doesn't notice me until I rap on the metal doorframe.

She looks up, blinking.

"Hey." Her voice is raspy. Because she's tired? Or hasn't spoken to anyone in a while? I can't tell.

I take off my hat and spin it in my hands. "Hey."

She straightens, sitting up and stretching. Her Star Wars tee is rumpled, like maybe she slept in it. "How've you been?"

"Okay." I ache to tell her about the games in Minnesota, my emotional roller coaster, my fight with Hunter, and our Frozen Four spot. But I swallow the words. Now's not the time.

"I'm glad." She gives me a small smile that doesn't reach her eyes, but her face falls as she looks back at the table covered in books.

"Jasmine." My voice breaks as I reach for her hand. "I can't thank you enough for everything you've done for me. Especially while you've had so much going on. You're amazing, you know that?" I huff a little laugh and she stiffens, as if she knows the blow is coming. "But I've been so selfish, asking you to make time for my games and—"

"I've loved coming to your games, Cooper."

Her gaze is wary, and I swallow around the feelings lodged in my esophagus. "I know you have. And it's been so fun, hanging out with you and everything."

"But..."

"But I feel terrible, taking up all your time. You have the GRE coming up, and I don't want to distract you from your goals. I think it's best if we go back to being just friends. We're friends, right?"

She nods, pressing her lips together, and I slide into the seat across from her, dropping her hand. I miss the warmth of her touch on my fingers.

"Yeah, good friends."

"And all the other stuff." I clear my throat and try to smile. "Well, I think we can safely fake break up now. Momma will understand."

I thought she might laugh at the mention of my mom, but she doesn't. She just stares at the table in silence and I can't tell what she's thinking.

"You're the best fake girlfriend ever." I wink, trying to lighten the mood, and reach out to caress her shoulder.

Jasmine pats my hand and I let it return to the table. "Back at ya."

I stand, grabbing my hat and jamming it on my head. "And you'll let me know if there's anything you need? A study break, a ride, Chad's fingers broken?"

She follows suit, smoothing her palms down her leggings. "Of course. But don't worry. I'll be fine."

"Of course you will. You're Jasmine Turner, and you're amazing."

Her mouth twists up in what might be a smile. I wish I had known three days ago that it was my last chance to kiss her perfect lips.

"Thanks. Bye, Cooper." Her voice is a soft whisper, and it shatters my heart into tiny pieces.

I can't help it. I move close, inhaling her coconut scent, and press a kiss to her forehead before walking out of the room.

With a sigh, I head towards my truck and pull my phone out of my pocket, composing a text.

Cooper: Mom, Jasmine and I broke up. I'm not ready to talk about it.

Turning my phone off, that's more true than I want it to be. I should feel relief, right? Relief that it's over, that I'm not lying to my mom, that my priorities are in line. That I'm doing the right thing for both of us.

That relief will come soon. For sure.

CHAPTER

Forty

JASMINE

I wait until Cooper's footsteps fade down the hallway into silence before I bolt out of my chair and close the door. Then I let myself sob.

I don't know why I'm crying. It's probably stress and lack of sleep. Swiping at my eyes, I dig in my backpack for tissues but come up empty. Why am I so unprepared? Why don't I have what I need?

My tears come harder, and my shoulders shake. Why did stupid Cooper have to do this today, of all days? Honestly, I had been trying not to think about him ever since I had neglected my experiment because I was with him. A tiny, rational part of my brain recognizes that this is for the best—now I can focus on what's important. But the rest of me is stuck on being dumped and how much it sucks.

Because even if it was inevitable, it still hurts.

This room is too small, the fluorescent lights buzz too loud. I have to get out. I dab at my face with my sleeve, but I'm a mess.

Sweeping my materials off the desk and into my bag, I surreptitiously duck my head out into the hallway. Chad is literally the last thing I could handle right now. Checking that the coast is clear, I make my way to the girl's restroom down the hall.

After blowing my nose, I splash water on my red face and dab at it with a scratchy paper towel. It doesn't improve my appearance. Too bad I don't have sunglasses in my bag. Unzipping the front pocket, I dig to see if I can find anything that might help, but when my fingers brush Cooper's soft orange hockey hoodie, tears spring to my eyes again. I had borrowed it, then wrapped myself in it at night because it smelled like him.

"Pull it together, Jasmine," I say to the empty bathroom, jumping when the door swings open.

Lucy peeks in, her expression cautious. "Jasmine? You okay?"

"Yeah." Straightening, I shove the stupid sweatshirt into my bag and sniffle. "Why wouldn't I be?"

"I don't know." She speaks slowly, as if she's unsure. "Cooper seemed pretty upset when I saw him leaving, so I was worried..."

She trails off, stepping closer to me. "Bad day?"

"You could say that."

"Do you, um, need anything?"

I shake my head, wanting nothing more than my bed and a comfy blanket. Well, some chocolate, too. Maybe a bottle of wine...

"Was Cooper upset about his game?" Lucy asks, snapping me out of my pity party plans.

"What do you mean?"

"He played pretty badly over the weekend. But I thought that making the tournament bracket would have made up for it."

"The Frozen Four bracket is out?"

Lucy nods. "Yeah, I couldn't go to the selection party, but Caleb texted me. The number two seed in their regional—that's a good spot."

"So they made it?"

"Cooper didn't tell you?"

I shake my head. I might as well rip off this Bandaid. Lucy's brother is on the team; it will be common knowledge soon enough. "We broke up."

Her eyes widen, clearly taking in my tear-stained cheeks and overall terrible appearance. "Oh. Just now?"

I swallow around the sudden lump in my throat. "Yeah."

"I'm really sorry, Jasmine." Reaching out, she pats my shoulder. Even though she's not my closest friend, her sympathy is sweet, and I appreciate it.

"I thought you guys..." Trailing off, she bites her lip. "Well, this explains why he was so upset."

I'm a terrible, petty human being. "He was upset?"

"Uh-huh. Worse than after the game on Saturday, and that was about as bad as it gets." She jerks her thumb towards the hallway. "I saw him as he was leaving. He was a mess."

"Are you saying that to make me feel better?"

"No... but is it working?"

She smiles, and I can't help but huff a tiny laugh.

"A little." I square my shoulders. "I knew it was coming. I don't know why I was crying."

"Probably because he's a decent guy, and it's still sad when things end."

Huh. I didn't expect Lucy to be so wise.

"Thanks." My voice is scratchy and my eyes burn. A headache builds behind them from crying. I'm not getting anything else accomplished tonight. "Lucy, do you, by any chance, have a pair of sunglasses I could borrow?"

"No, but you could pull this down real low." Whipping a Harrison Hockey ball cap out of her bag, she winces. "Too soon?"

I frown at it. "Better than nothing, I suppose."

No matter what I do, I can't seem to escape reminders of the Harrison Hockey team.

CHAPTER
Forty-One

JASMINE

Mom: Good luck this morning, baby! You've got this!
Maya: Yeah, good luck Jaz! Show the GRE who's boss!

≈

My alarm goes off on my phone, followed by an actual ringing alarm clock that I set across the room. Rolling out of bed, I silence both. Nothing is going to trip me up today.

The GREs are just one step in my grad school process. There are still many more hurdles, but this is an important one. So I hurry to shower and curl my hair before picking out a fluffy skirt, purple tights, and my "May the Mass Times Acceleration Be With You" shirt. I bought it special for today.

Then, I go downstairs to make myself a cup of coffee and try not to freak out.

Staci leans against the kitchen counter, feet encased in T-Rex slippers, slipping from a floral mug. Raising a brow, she pops another pod in the single-cup coffee maker when I nod.

"You're doing that thing where you dress up for a test?"

I smooth my skirt before getting the cream and sugar. "Yep."

"You really think it helps?"

"I do."

"You look fantastic. Nervous?"

"No," I say, lying, scuffing my toe on the hardwood. "Maybe."

"You're gonna do great."

"Thanks."

The coffee maker sputters, and I grab my cup, doctoring it until it's basically coffee-flavored sugar milk. Yum. Just what I need this morning.

"Here." Reaching into the cabinet behind her, Staci offers me a Harrison Hockey travel mug. "You might want a little extra this morning."

I stare at the stainless steel tumbler. Cooper left it at one point, and somehow it ended up in the cupboard. My stomach swoops at the image of him drinking coffee with me in the kitchen.

Staci waves the cup at me, and I finally grab it, sitting it on the counter. I've done such a good job over the past few days, not letting my mind wander towards him or Chad or anything that's not study prep. Memories threaten to overwhelm me, and I take a deep breath, battling them away. Staci gives me a beat, then reaches out and pats my shoulder.

"I'm sorry it's been rough lately," she says, her voice soft. "I'm proud of you, you know?"

Hand shaking, I bring the cup to my lips and take a fortifying sip before meeting her gaze. It's filled with compassion and love. Pulling me into a fierce hug, she whispers, "You've got this, girl. Go kick the GRE's ass. We'll talk later."

"Thanks."

Her pep talk echoing in my ears, I leave for the testing center.

It's time to focus. Everything I've worked for is at stake. I won't let it slip through my fingers. This is all I need.

Letting myself into the house, I sink onto the couch. My fluffy skirt is creased and my new shirt is sweaty and gross. I thought I'd feel relief now that the GREs are behind me, but I don't. My brain is fried and I want to curl up under a soft blanket and take a year-long nap. But then I'd wake up and realize that while I don't have to worry about the GREs, I would have missed the deadlines for grad school. I crossed an important item off my to-do list today, but it's only the next step—there are still so many more. Why did I think I should go into pharmaceuticals again? Maybe I should switch to education and become a high school chemistry teacher.

Yeah, it could be fun. I'll sponsor the prom and... Wait. High school angst and teen cliques. Not to mention the attitudes. Nevermind, I guess I'll stick with this plan.

I've been so single-minded about the GRE for the last week that I haven't let myself think about anything else. But now without that to focus on... my thoughts crowd in.

My fingers itch to text Cooper, to tell him that I'm finally done with the GRE. But I leave my phone in my bag.

What's he doing right now? How's hockey going? I miss him more than I want to admit. But every time I'm reminded of how I missed my lab time, how utterly self-righteous Chad was, I burn with shame.

Because what if Chad was right? What if Cooper did keep me from focusing on what's most important? I totally lost track of time, of everything, when I was with him. I was a thoughtless lab mate, and everything Chad claimed had a kernel of truth to it.

Cooper's choice to break things off was the correct thing to do. No doubt about it. But I didn't expect to miss him this much. What if I called him and invited him over? Just to chill, not a booty call. We're friends; I could totally text him.

But he has hockey. He's as busy as I am. No, I don't want to be a burden. Maybe after his season is over, I'll reach out.

Staci and Delaney burst into the house and rush into the living room, interrupting my thoughts.

"Congratulations!" Staci tries to pull me up off the couch, but I don't budge. "You're done!"

Their smiles are bright, but I can't match their enthusiasm.

"Ugh, I wish. Now I get to stress over the results, and getting into grad school, and all the other things I still need to do."

Delaney frowns. "Don't think of it like that. You should—"

The doorbell cuts off her words. She and Staci exchange a secretive glance and my stomach lurches. What do they know that I don't? Is it Cooper?

"You should get the door," Staci says, smiling, and suddenly I have the energy to bound off the cushions and run to the entryway.

Throwing open the door, I school my features when it's my mom and Maya on the porch instead of Cooper. Arms laden with grocery bags, they beam at me.

"Surprise! Happy GRE day!"

I tamp down my disappointment and wrap them both in a giant hug. Unexpected tears prick my eyelids. It may not be quite who I wanted on my doorstep, but the love and support means the world to me.

They bustle past me and head down the hall. Staci and Delaney look on, eyebrows raised.

"Were you in on this?"

Staci nods. "Okay surprise?"

"Great surprise." Grabbing their arms, I pull them with me and we all squeeze into our tiny kitchen.

My mom and Maya have set out a buffet of snacks and drinks on the counter. Maya digs in our kitchen drawers and comes up with spoons and the corkscrew. She points at the spread.

"Pop quiz, Jaz. Wine or ice cream first?"

"No more quizzes today. Both."

"And that's why you're brilliant." My mom pats my cheek, her eyes glowing with pride, and dishes Moose Tracks out to everyone while Maya pours a generous amount of red into coffee mugs. I'll take practical over classy any day.

Once everyone has provisions, my mom leads the way into our living room and we follow. She settles herself in the armchair while Maya and I share the couch. Staci and Delaney arrange themselves on the floor.

After asking about the GRE, my mom gives me a sidelong glance.

"You ready to talk about it?"

"The test? I just told you." Maya shakes her head and my friends don't make eye contact with me. "Wait a minute, is this an intervention?"

Maya pats my knee. "No, but you've had a lot going on. How are you doing?"

I shake my head. Maybe if I don't talk about it, I won't think about how much I miss Cooper.

Delaney stares at me from across the room. "Your boyfriend of three months breaks up with you and there's nothing to say?"

I shrug. My emotions are too close to the surface and I will probably start crying if I open my mouth.

Delaney's eyes are still on me, waiting for a response. I gnaw on a fingernail, then swallow. "We're both busy. We don't need any distractions. So we broke up. That's it. That's all she wrote. Nothing to talk about."

"Nothing?" Staci raises a brow. "How do you feel about it?"

I shrug. "It's whatever. No big deal. I totally expected it."

"You expected it?" My mom shoots me a concerned look, brow furrowed. "Why?"

Oh right. That doesn't make sense. I wrack my poor tired brain. "Well, I just meant that it obviously had an end date. That we weren't compatible long-term."

"I don't know." Shifting, Maya tucks her feet underneath her. "I saw you guys as an opposites-attract type of thing."

I shake my head and purse my lips. "That's cute in movies, but it doesn't work in the real world."

"Joel and I are different from each other, though. It's like when strengths and weaknesses complement each other. It's not a bad thing." Maya plays with my hair and I could purr like a cat if it wasn't for this interrogation. I want to lean into it but I keep my posture stiff and straight.

"Well, Cooper and I were the bad kind of different."

"I don't know, Jaz." Staci stares at me, assessing. "It sure looked like he brought out the best in you."

"And he wasn't perfect," Delaney says, stretching. "But he was one of the good ones."

My mom folds her hands in her lap. "I didn't know Cooper all that well, but I think they're right. Honey, what happened?"

"You might feel better if you talk about it." Delaney drains her mug of wine, then heads to the kitchen, presumably for more. I play with a loose string on the cushion until she returns and tops off all our glasses.

I'm going to have to give them something or they will never let this go. I've forgotten what is fake or real at this point, but I take a deep breath.

"It's really sweet of you all to care. It was more the timing. We're just too busy right now. Neither one of us should compromise our goals."

"Did he ask you to do that?" A wrinkle appears between my mom's eyes as she studies me.

"Well, no, but I just don't have time for a relationship right now, what with the GRE. And neither does he. Hockey finals, plus a normal class load. There were too many compromises."

"Don't other hockey players have girlfriends?" Staci asks, pursing her lips.

"Well—"

"And I'm sure other girls taking the GRE have boyfriends." Maya lifts her open palms. "Why do you have to choose?"

They will never understand. I motion towards my mom. "It's like you and Dad. You gave up your career to stay home and support him." I turn to Maya. "And you're doing the same thing with Joel. Cooper and I...neither one of us has to give up anything this way."

There's a beat of silence in the room, then Maya takes a deep breath. "Yes, I am quitting my job and putting Joel first right now. But he does the same for me all the time."

"But aren't you sad about it?"

"Yes!" Putting her arm around me, she squeezes me in a half-hug. "I'm sad to move away from Mom and Dad and to be farther from you. I'm sad to leave my friends and cowork-ers. But you know what would be even sadder?"

Where's she going with this? I shake my head.

"If I hadn't married Joel." She smiles at me. "Do you remember what it was like when we were dating? I was a love-sick fool."

Despite my mood, I laugh. "Oh my god, you were. I've never heard so much sappy music in my life. Taylor Swift on repeat every night that summer you were apart!"

"He makes me so happy." Her eyes get misty. "And yes, I'm giving up my job. Because I want to. Not all compromises are bad, Jaz. But Joel and I aren't going to break up over this, either."

"Of course not." I scoff.

"So why did you and Cooper have to break up?" My mom asks. "If it's just a matter of timing, you're already done with the GRE. He only has a few more weeks of hockey. It doesn't have to be all or nothing."

I frown, trying to figure out how to explain everything.

"I missed a responsibility in the lab because I was with Cooper. I just...I really need to focus." Twisting my hands in my lap, I stare at my nails, bitten to the quick. "I worried I was changing, that I couldn't be with him and do the stuff I needed to."

Maya rubs my back in soothing circles. "That's a hard feeling."

"So is breaking up, though," Staci says from the floor. "Which is worse?"

"Breaking up." The words pop out of my mouth before I think about it. "I miss him so much."

"Then talk to him!" Delaney bounces on the carpet, licking ice cream off her spoon. "Get him back!"

I shake my head. "I don't want to distract him from hockey."

"Jaz, did you ever think you two could be better together?" My mom leans forward in her chair. "Your dad has always supported me and my goals. He lets me live my dreams, and I helped him pursue his. Compromise doesn't have to be a bad thing."

"Yeah, but..."

"Just think about it. Your problems are not insurmountable, and he's a good one."

She's right, he is. But this was a fake relationship, even if I have real feelings. It was always going to end.

CHAPTER
Forty~Two

COOPER

Momma: Congratulations, pookie! I knew you could do it!

The locker room buzzes with excitement, and even Coach cracks a smile. We did it. We beat St. Cloud State and North Dakota in our Regional. This means we're in the Frozen Four. We move on to Semi-finals next weekend—and hopefully the Championship game after that.

But we don't know who we play yet, and I don't want to jinx anything by getting too far ahead of myself.

Evan, however, doesn't have any qualms about it.

"Frozen Four, baby!" he yells, wearing only a towel and dancing around the locker room. "We made it!"

Someone plays "All I Do Is Win." Evan's towel better be tied tightly, or else no one will feel like a winner in a few seconds.

Hunter must be thinking the same thing because he

shakes his head, grimacing. He and I lock eyes, and he nods. Acknowledging my assist to his goal, our teamwork on the ice, our victory. The atmosphere is thawing between us, but I should still extend an olive branch to make up for everything.

Thankfully, Matteo throws a pair of pants at Evan. "No dancing until you're dressed. We've learned that the hard way."

"Come on, man!" Evan shimmies his hips. "Let's celebrate!"

"Clothes first," Alec says, wincing. "He's right."

Evan mutters something about us being no fun, but he's smiling. Nothing can dim the mood in here.

I wait for the pure exaltation of winning to fill my veins, but it doesn't come. There's relief that my terrible weekend in the Big Ten Tourney didn't ruin everything after all. But that lightness, that absolute joy, is muted for me. I wish Jasmine had been there to see it.

I shake it off. Maybe I need a shower or sleep. We've been gone for three days and I miss my bed and my bedroom. Sleeping in hotels is always an adjustment.

Stripping off my sweaty gear, I move towards the showers but stop when Shawn stands up on a wooden bench, arms outstretched.

"Clear your schedules when we get home, boys, because this party won't stop!"

I try to keep my face impassive as cheers break out, but I can't handle the idea of going out and dancing with anyone who's not Jasmine. I swallow and meet Hunter's gaze as he makes his way across the room.

"Hey." He gives a chin jerk of a greeting. "After you're dressed, can we talk?"

I owe him that much. Nodding, I head towards the showers.

After dressing, I find Hunter and follow him out into the hallway, then stare at him, waiting to see what he has to say. I should break the ice, but he's the one who asked to talk to me.

"Look, man." He runs a hand down his face, then shoves them in his pockets. "I'm sorry things have been weird and for what I said during the Big Ten Tourney weekend."

Something thaws inside me.

"I'm the one who should apologize to you, and for real this time. I can't believe I tried to punch you in the face. I was an ass and that crossed the line."

Hunter chuckles, rubbing his chin. "It's hilarious you thought you could get the drop on me. You'd make a terrible goon."

I shake my head. "Don't let me off so easily. I've been an awful friend to you."

"Nah." He shrugs. "You just fell head-over-heels for a girl."

My mouth drops open. "That's not what happened."

"You still gonna deny it?" I don't know what to say, so I gape at him like a trout on the line. He claps me on the shoulder. "It's okay."

"Everything with me and Jasmine was fake, remember?" I speak to the tips of my cowboy boots, my words mumbled.

"It started out that way, but I don't think that's true. It was real, and it's okay if it sucks when it's over."

I gulp. "But how do I keep it from being a distraction?"

Hunter bounces on the balls of his feet, brow furrowed.

"Okay, bear with me on this one." I jerk my chin in agreement and he continues. "If next week the game is tied and Chris lets a goal past in overtime and we lose, is it his fault?"

"Nope, of course not. The goalie is important, but maybe I should have won more face-offs. Maybe you should have gotten more break-aways or found more holes. Maybe Coach should have changed up the lines. It's a team effort, and it's not on one guy."

Blinking, Hunter stares at me until I think about the words I uttered.

"Oh. So what you're saying is—"

"I put too much pressure on you during that Big Ten game. But it wasn't your fault we were losing, no more than it was mine. One player doesn't make or break things and we both know it."

Squeezing my fingers into fists, I force myself to open and shut them a few times in a row. "I just really want to win next week."

"Me, too. So whatever you're feeling about Jasmine—hurt, anger, passion—use it."

I'm not sure what to say to that, so I just nod again.

Hunter pauses, then speaks when I don't. "For the record, I'm sorry that it ended. She's a cool girl, and she was good for you."

I clear my throat. "Thanks. For everything."

He glances over his shoulder at the locker room. "Buy me a beer tonight and it's all forgiven."

I wince. "How do you feel about a run to the liquor store instead of a night out? I'm not ready for that."

He claps me on the shoulder, blue eyes brimming with compassion. "Sure, man."

I shift my weight from foot to foot. "I should call my mom before we have to get on the bus."

"I'll save you a seat."

Knowing that things are okay between us lifts some of the weight off my chest. As he heads back into the locker room, I fish my phone out of my pocket and turn it on.

As it powers on, my heart lifts in my chest. Messages buzz through. Who are they from? Maybe....

Six of them, according to the little red number. I swipe to see, and fight off disappointment. They are from my mom and grandparents. Which is great. I wasn't expecting anything else. Or hoping for it. Nope. I'm back to my original priorities and doing better than ever. I mean, Jasmine and I are friends. She could have texted. But she's busy and so am I. It's fine.

Pressing send, I hold the phone up to my ear. "Hey, Momma," I say when she answers.

"Cooper, I'm so proud of you! You guys played great. You deserve the Frozen Four!"

"Thanks." I chuckle at her enthusiasm, and listen as she recaps the best moments of the game.

"So what's next?" she asks. "Do you have your schedule for the weekend yet?"

"No. I'm not sure who we play. The other Regionals are still going on. Once that's done, we'll find out if we're the early or late game on Friday. Then the two teams left play for the Championship on Sunday."

"Boston, right?"

"Yep." I bite my lip, not sure how to ask this next part. I don't want to be needy or pressure her. But I could use a fan. "So, um, do you think—that is, would you consider, um, coming out for it? I know it's a lot, though, so if you are busy or can't make it, that's fine, too."

"Cooper!" her tone scolds. "Of course I'm going to Boston to see my son play in the National Championship!"

Relief floods me. "Well, I didn't want to presume."

"As if you could keep me away." I can almost hear her roll her eyes at me. "I just have to decide if I'm going to fly or drive my RV."

"Oh. That might be a bit of a trek from Texas. I want you to be safe."

"Of course, pookie, I always am. I might ask a friend to share the driving with me. Speaking of friends…" She trails off meaningfully and I wince, knowing what's coming.

"I should probably go get on the bus, Momma. It was good to talk to you."

"Not so fast." Lined with steel, her voice brooks no argument, and I sigh. Better get it over with. "Are you going to tell me what happened with Jasmine?"

No? But if I say that, she'll keep pressing forever. I swallow down the lump in my throat that develops at her name. "We were too busy for a relationship right now."

"I don't understand. I mean, sure, you have a big week coming up, but it's only a week and then your season is over."

"Yeah, but Jasmine had the GRE."

"Had? As in, that's done, too?"

I pick at a loose string on my jacket. "Well, I guess, but—"

"Cooper, these aren't insurmountable problems. Please call the girl when you return and work things out."

"Not gonna happen, Momma. And like I said, I have to go get on the bus."

"Text me when you're home safely."

After ending the conversation, I slide my phone into my pocket, pacing the length of the hallway. So much for not thinking about Jasmine.

CHAPTER
Forty-Three

JASMINE

I keep busy for the next week. I don't have to study for the GRE anymore, but I still have my normal class load and I'm close to the end of my project. Dr. Michelson was so pleased by the results that she thinks I only need two more replicates. Finals are a month away, but I review for them and work on projects. Anything to avoid my roommates' questions and time alone with my own thoughts.

I'm poised to rush out of the house for the evening when an email pops up on my phone. I stop in the doorway, and Delaney comes up behind me, poking the space between my shoulder blades.

"What's up, girlie?" she asks.

Spinning around, I meet her eyes. "It's an email from ETS. I can log in and get my full, official results."

I saw my preliminary Verbal Reasoning and Quantitative Reasoning scores at the end of the test. They were good, but I didn't want to get my hopes up. The Analytical Writing essay still had to be read and graded, so there was a delay.

I gulp. My palms are slick with sweat. Am I ready for this?

"Come on!" Delaney gives my shoulder a gentle shove. "Check them, already!"

Hands shaking, I move through the entryway into the living room. Dropping my bag, I sink down on the couch. Delaney hovers beside me. I only mess up my login and password twice before it lets me into the portal.

"No way." I scan the screen, my voice barely audible. "This has to be a typo."

"What? What does it say?"

I turn my phone so Delaney can see it. "You tell me. What are my scores?"

She squints. "Uh, 169 in Quantitative Reasoning, 165 in Verbal Reasoning. Five in Analytical Writing. Only a five? Oh my gosh, I'm so sorry, Jasmine!"

"It really says that?"

She puts her hand on my arm. "It does. But don't worry, you can always—"

"Delaney, that section is scored out of six." I smile.

"So a five is… good?"

I nod.

"What are the other sections out of?"

"170." I know I'm grinning like a scary clown, but I can't stop myself.

"And you scored a…" Grabbing my phone, she peers at the screen again. "169! And a 165! Jasmine, you're a genius!"

I laugh. "I'm not sure about that, but it bodes well for my grad school applications."

"Bodes well." Delaney playfully pushes my shoulder. "Stop being so modest, Ms. Smarty Pants." Then she gasps. "Do you know what this means?"

"That I'm one step closer to being Doctor Smarty Pants?"

"No, silly!" She jumps off the couch, brown eyes twinkling. "This deserves a celebration. Call everyone. We're going out tonight!"

As she dances off, I text Staci and a couple of friends from my lab and classes, including Lucy. My heart lurches when I see Cooper's name in my string of recent texts. He'd be happy to hear about my success, but I need to let him go. It's what's best for both of us.

Staci claims a tall table by the bar for us and greets me with a fierce hug. "I'm so proud of you! All that studying paid off!"

"We'll see. I still have to get into grad school!" Catching my breath after her squeeze, I wait for the melancholy that grips me as tightly to fade, but it lingers. I look around at the girls at the table—Staci, Delaney, Lucy. Loyal friends, beaming back at me, out to celebrate my success. Why isn't this enough? What more could I want?

It's time to move past it. I'll have a drink and get out of this funk.

O'Bryan's was my pick for tonight, but now I question it. Memories of Cooper lurk in every corner. But I can't let him ruin my favorite bar, or my night out. The typical Irish music blares, the lights are dim, and paper shamrocks leftover from St. Patrick's Day dangle from the ceiling. Forcing myself to smile, I jerk my head towards the wooden bar jutting out into the middle of the dance floor. It's crowded with people tonight.

"Come on, girls! I need a shot and a dance, in that order."

Laughing, they comply as I tug them along in my wake. Shots of Jameson all around from the bartender are a start, and I feel it as it hits my bloodstream a few minutes later. My limbs are loose, and I'm finally relaxed after weeks of stress.

We dance in a circle, arms in the air, and I let out a whoop as the song ends.

I'm doing fine. Great, even. This breakup hasn't affected me at all. We were barely dating. It was mostly fake. No big deal.

Meeting Delaney's gaze across our tight group, I raise my voice as the music starts up again. "Thank you for this!"

"Of course!" She giggles and spins. "Sometimes you gotta shake it off."

Because we all know this is a GRE celebration, but also it's the first time I've let them talk me into anything post-breakup. I'm okay, though. It was sweet of them, but I don't really need it.

I glance at the bar. And swallow. My eye catches on a flannel shirt and cowboy hat at the bar and I stop in my tracks.

Am I ready to see him? Talk to him?

Regardless, we agreed we'd be friends. So I'm not going to avoid him. Making my excuses to my friends, I head over.

"Hey." My mouth goes dry as the guy at the bar turns around. It's not Cooper. His shoulders aren't as broad, he's not as tall, and his eyes are the wrong color. How could I have ever mixed them up? I stumble. "Oh, sorry. I thought you were someone else."

"I'll be whoever you want me to be."

Ew. I wince. "No, thanks. Have a good night."

Spinning on my heel, I flee back to my group of girls. My stomach sinks. As nervous as I was about seeing Cooper, not seeing him is worse.

CHAPTER
Forty~Four

COOPER

Momma: Can't wait to see you in Boston! I found a great breakfast spot right by your hotel. Can you get away Friday morning?

Cooper: Looking forward to it

"I can't believe you drove 2,000 miles for this!" Laughing, I enfold my mom in a bear hug.

"Like I would have missed it!" She pats my shoulder as I set her back on her feet in the diner. The team and I got in last night, Thursday, and we have our first game later today. If we win—and I don't want to count my chickens before they're hatched—we will play in the Final game on Sunday. There's a warm up skate this afternoon to keep us loose but nothing planned for breakfast. So it was easy to sneak away from the hotel to meet her at this little place around the corner. With vinyl benches, linoleum floors, and a counter with stools running the length of it, I'll have no problem finding the calories I need for the big game tonight.

"Well, most people would have flown."

We take an available table in the back corner, and I sit facing a glowing neon sign for the restrooms. A waitress in a blue apron brings us strong coffee and plastic menus, snapping her gum before disappearing. Is it weird that I hope she has a cliche Boston accent?

After a sip of her coffee, my mom reaches out and touches my hand.

"Pookie, I've missed you. How's it going?"

She's so sincere, so genuine in her unconditional love for me. I nod, not meeting her eye. The weight of my guilt is heavy on my chest. I've been lying to her for so long, but I won't be that guy anymore.

I take a deep breath. "Momma, there's something I need to confess. When I told you I had a girlfriend, I was lying."

Her face goes blank. She stares back at me, blinking. "What? I don't understand."

"That day on the phone. Months ago. You had been bugging me about having a girlfriend, so... I lied."

Bringing her mug up to her lips, her hand shakes. That's the only indication that she heard me. I press on.

"I thought I could make up a story to get you off my back. And tell you about the breakup before you knew any different. Then you were here...." I clear my throat. Can this get any worse? "The truth is, Jasmine was not my girlfriend. She was just a girl that I took home from a bar and was going to hook up with."

Stirring her coffee, she stares at the brown liquid in silence for a full minute before speaking. "And she agreed to this? Lying to me and pretending to be your girlfriend?"

I hang my head. The last thing I want is for her to have a poor opinion of Jasmine. "I asked her for a favor, helped her out with some things, too. But yes, she did. Although she didn't like lying to you."

"And you? How'd you feel about it?" She pins me in her death glare and I gulp.

"Terrible. But also..." I trace circles on the formica table. "But also, I really started to like Jasmine. And that was pretty great."

"So what happened? Was it one-sided?"

Blowing out a breath, I run my fingers through my hair. Images flash through my brain. Jasmine cheering for me at hockey games she didn't have to attend. Showing me the stars in the planetarium, even though no one was watching. Laughing at my jokes and holding my hand.

"No, I don't think it was."

"Then...." My mom frowns. "Why did you break up?"

"It was inevitable," I say, staring at the table. "Love isn't real."

"Cooper, that's not true. I love you!"

I laugh, but it's a harsh, cynical sound. "I know you do, Momma. But that Hallmark love stuff? I don't believe in it. Or maybe it's real, but it won't last. It's not enough."

"But—you must—how can you think that?" She sputters over her words as they tumble out of her mouth.

"Look at you!" I say back, frustration making me snap. "It didn't last for you, and it ruined your life!"

Her eyes widen. "Oh, Cooper."

Reaching out, she touches my hand again, and when she speaks, her voice is soft. "That's not what happened."

"No?" I raise a brow at her, but she doesn't rise to the bait of my sarcasm.

"No. It did not ruin my life when your father left us."

"He broke your heart, Mom. I was there." I lean forward in my seat to make my point.

"You're right, he did. It was really hard for me for a long

time. But spending a decade focusing on you doesn't mean it ruined my life."

"But you—"

"I still had plenty of love in my life." She clears her throat. "And, um, maybe this is a good time to tell you—I have a new friend."

That's a weird non sequitur. "Well, that's nice, Momma, I'm happy for you. But—"

"No, honey," she says, cutting me off. "Not that kind of friend. A boyfriend."

Oh. *Oh.*

"Mom!" I can't help the way my voice rises. "What the hell? What's going on? When were you going to tell me?"

Beaming at me, she folds her palms on the table. "When the time was right."

"Wait, is this a fake thing? To get back at me?" She glares. "Too soon?"

"Too soon."

Our waitress finally returns, and we both order. A farmer's breakfast for me, full of calories and fuel, and something with egg whites and fruit for my mom. If she thinks I'm letting food side-track me, though, she's wrong.

"So, how long have you been dating this guy? What's his name? What's he like?"

My mom laughs. "Now I know how you felt when I pestered you about Jasmine."

"Don't avoid the questions." Mimicking her posture, I fold my fingers together and stare at her until she squirms.

"His name is Matt. We've been dating for... three months." She gazes out the window, not meeting my gaze.

"Momma! And you didn't tell me?"

"Cooper, it was very casual at first. I didn't want to say

anything to you until—until there was a reason to bring it up."

I roll my eyes at her. "Can you not see the parallels here? And yet you were so pushy about Jasmine."

"I'm your mother! It's different." But she laughs, and the twinkle in her gaze makes it clear she's not upset.

"So, is it serious?" I ask as our food arrives. I dig in, forking bites of hash browns, eggs, and pancakes into my mouth.

My mom stares at her omelet, pensive. Then she nods. "Yes, I think it is. I like him a lot."

"What do you like about him?"

Her face changes, lighting up. "Oh, he's a lovely man. Great sense of humor, very kind and thoughtful. He takes me hiking and kayaking."

"Kayaking? You know that's outdoors, right? Not air-conditioned, dirty, wet?"

Shaking her head at my teasing, she continues. "It's been so fun to try new things. Matt likes to travel so the RV..." She clears her throat. "I thought we'd take some trips together. And he's a terrible cook, but I'm giving him lessons. It's been so nice to have someone to share things with."

A pang of guilt hits my belly. "I knew it would be hard for you when I went to a school so far away. I hope you haven't been too lonely."

"Cooper." Her voice turns stern. "Dating again is a choice I made for myself. It had nothing to do with you or where you live. My world does not revolve around you."

I blink. "Wow, okay. It's just... it took you a long time to feel ready for that. I wasn't sure you ever would."

She softens. "I hate that my mistakes with your father affected you this much. That's the thing—they're mine. They don't have to be yours. You get to make your own mistakes."

"Like lying to my mom about my fake girlfriend?"

"Yep, that's definitely all you. Not something I've ever done." Stirring her coffee, she pauses. "But I've found happiness again. What I have with Matt is very new, but it's worth pushing past the fear and potential pain for something good."

"I'm happy for you. And I'm excited to meet Matt." And vet him, obviously. Do my grandparents know about this? My grandpa and I need to compare notes.

She takes a bite of her breakfast, then chews and swallows. "Perhaps it started out as a pretense between you and Jasmine, but I think you had something good there, too."

I nod. I can admit it now. "Yeah, I think we did. I think maybe I loved her."

Reaching out, she squeezes my fingers. "It doesn't have to be over, pookie. It's not too late."

"I don't know." I think about the dark circles under her eyes, her obvious exhaustion. Her determination to reach her goals. I can't be the one to keep her from that. I can't let her resent me for it. It's better this way.

"What do you have to lose? You miss one hundred percent of the shots you don't take."

"Wayne Gretzky?" I raise my brows. "Really?"

"He was right, Cooper. Take the shot. Call her."

I mull it over. I've been miserable without her. I'd like to have Jasmine back in my life. I understand if she's still opposed to dating and doesn't want to be my girlfriend, but I miss her friendship, too.

Can I stand to see her and not kiss her? Be around her and not touch her? I'm not sure. But the thought of going through the last two rounds of the Frozen Four without her sounds worse.

"I…" I chicken out. I can't handle this right before a big game. "I'll think about it, Momma."

Her face falls and she sighs. "I know you have a lot on your mind. Maybe after hockey season?"

"Yeah, maybe." I lick the last drops of syrup from the tines of my fork and pat my stomach. "It's about time for me to go burn this off."

"You're gonna kick ass today."

"Momma! Language!" I pretend to be shocked, then wink at her.

"I know, you're delicate. But it's true."

"Thanks for the vote of confidence. And for meeting me for breakfast."

Sliding out of the booth, I stand, and she follows, patting me on the arm. "Thanks for being honest with me. I'm sure that wasn't easy."

"No, but I feel better."

"Excellent." Linking her arm through mine, she starts to tug me through the restaurant to the cash register, but I catch sight of a familiar face and stop.

"Hey, Lucy, Caleb." They are in the booth directly behind ours, also enjoying the pancakes.

Caleb nods hello, his mouth full, and Lucy raises her fork in a salute. "Good luck today, Cooper."

"Thanks. I love that you came to cheer us on."

I wish Jasmine would be in the stands, rooting for me, but having my mom and fans like Lucy here helps soothe the sting of it. I'm used to people I care about not being there. Besides, I need to do this for myself and not for anyone watching. Whether or not I like it, I'm on my own now, and I make my own luck.

"I'd do anything to help you guys win." Lucy shoots her brother a weird, determined look that I don't understand. Must be some kind of inside sibling thing.

"Well, cool. Thanks. And I'll do my best, too. See you in a few, Caleb."

They wave goodbye, and I let my mom propel me through the diner. Seeing Lucy makes me miss Jasmine even more.

Take the shot, Cooper. My mom's words echo in my mind.

Should I call? What would I say? Would it be weird? Or is she too busy to answer?

CHAPTER
Forty~Five

JASMINE

"Jaz, come on." Staci leans against my doorframe, clad in tight work-out gear, and I groan.

"Why in the world would I do something I hate to feel better?"

Shifting on my bed, I snap my laptop closed. She doesn't need to see I was compulsively checking the Frozen Four schedule, even though I've already memorized it. The team squeaked by on Friday night with a win over Denver, after overtime and a shootout. They had an off-day yesterday and play in the Championship game tonight. Against Michigan, their biggest rival. A repeat of the Big Ten Championship... which they lost. I tell myself I don't need to care so much about the fate of the Griffin hockey team, but my stomach is a ball of nerves.

"You know. Exercise gives you endorphins. Endorphins make you happy."

"Happy people don't shoot their roommates?" I finish the quote for her, raising a brow.

She shrugs. "Maybe? And we don't have to run. Much. We can walk."

Staci has been bugging me to go running with her for years. Why would today be different from the last hundred times she's asked me?

"I don't believe you. Besides, I'm perfectly happy." Frowning, I grab a pillow and hug it to my chest. Staci takes this as an invitation and perches on the edge of my bed.

"Um, even someone who doesn't know you as well as I do wouldn't believe that. Seriously, I promise. No running. But you should leave the house."

Flopping onto my back, I stare at the ceiling, studying the familiar brown water stain. When I squint, it kinda looks like a Care Bear. Grumpy Bear, to match my mood.

As much as I hate to admit it, Staci could be right. I've tried wine, ice cream and binge-watching. Perhaps a little physical activity wouldn't hurt. With a put-upon sigh, I sit back up.

"Okaaaaay. I guess I can go with you. I have nothing better to do."

Her eyes widen, and she rushes to my window, peering out.

"What? What's wrong?" I ask, rolling over.

She sends me a sarcastic smirk. "Checking to see if pigs are flying."

The pillow I throw wipes the smile off her face, and I get off the bed. "You deserved that."

Smoothing down her hair, she stalks out. "Probably. Hurry up and get dressed."

I do, throwing on Cooper's sweatpants—they're comfy—and my Alderan weather forecast shirt. After sunshine on Monday and Tuesday, it shows a firebomb on Wednesday and nothing the rest of the week. Dark, but it fits my mood.

Staci glances at it but doesn't comment as I move downstairs and tie my sneakers.

I slip my phone into my pocket. "Let's go."

Leading us on a loop around our downtown neighborhood, Staci doesn't push me too much, either physically or emotionally. She chats about her business classes, her final projects, and our summer plans. It's wild that we'll both be home in Indianapolis in about a month. I'll be working at Lilly in my internship program as much as possible, but knowing that Staci will be nearby when I need her makes the future feel less bleak.

My phone buzzes in my pocket, and I pull it out, surprised to see Lucy's name on the display. An update already?

"Hey, Luce. Everything okay?"

Lucy had met up with her parents in Boston so they could cheer on Caleb and the Griffins together. She had texted me score updates throughout the Semifinals game on Friday, but the Final game isn't until later tonight. So why is she calling me?

I press the phone to my ear. Silence. Did she butt-dial me? "Lucy? You there?"

"Jasmine, I don't know if I'm doing the right thing."

Stopping in the middle of the sidewalk, I meet Staci's stare. "Hold up," I mouth, before returning to my conversation with Lucy. It's clear something is wrong and my heart pounds in my chest.

"Is—is everyone okay?" My voice wavers. I don't say Cooper's name out loud, but she must know I mean him. My sweat-soaked palms make my phone slippery, and I grip it tighter. "What's going on?"

"Everyone's fine—"

"Oh, god, you had me worried there." I exhale, still a little shaky. Staci takes my arm and tugs me off the sidewalk, and we plop down on a patch of grass.

"I just…" Lucy hesitates. "I have some information. Information that may affect the game."

I wrack my brain. "Like, something about the other team?"

"No, something about ours."

Is this an ethical dilemma? She's too cryptic for me to follow. Staci can't stand being left out, so she comes to sit by me and listen in.

"Look, Lucy, can you explain what you're worried about? I'm confused."

I hear noise in the background, like a wrapper crinkling. Then, she speaks around food in her mouth. "If you could help the team win, would you?"

"Of course! But what does that have to do with—"

"I overheard something. A private conversation. But I think I should tell you about it."

"Okay?" What's the proper response to that? I look at Staci, but she shrugs.

"I sat behind Cooper and his mom at breakfast yesterday. I didn't mean to listen, but he confessed a lot of things about your relationship—it was fake?"

"Um."

Staci's eyes go wide next to me and her mouth drops open.

I choose my words, both for Lucy and Staci. "Yeah… I'm sorry about that. Things started out that way, but—"

"But that's the thing, Jasmine!" Lucy's voice vibrates with excitement. "He has feelings for you! And I think—I don't know, but—I think he'd play better tonight if you were here!"

Taking my phone away from my ear, I stare at it. "Are you insane?"

"No!" She sounds tinny through the speaker. "You didn't

hear him, Jasmine. He was all 'I think I love her, but she doesn't love me back.' Unless... you do love him, right?"

Something like hope flutters in my belly. I nod before remembering that she can't see me.

"Yes," I whisper. "I do."

"So come!" I can hear her urgency. "They have to play Michigan, and you know how that goes. I think—I think it could be the push he needs."

I tamp down whatever I was feeling. There's no way.

"Lucy, it's too silly. They won yesterday. He's fine without me." Better, probably.

"Jasmine." Staci shakes my arm. "He said you were his good luck charm. And if he's been anywhere near as miserable as you—"

"—Oh, he has," Lucy says, cutting her off. "Caleb said it's been awful. He tries to hide it, but they all know."

"—then you need to go fix it."

I gape at her. "Rush across the country to tell someone I love them?"

"Yes! Why would you wait?"

"I mean, why not a phone call?" I say. That's a reasonable idea.

"Okay, call him." Staci motions at my phone. "But don't you think it would have more of an impact if you were there? Give him the confidence he needs? Are you going to miss this big moment?"

"We've been watching way too much *Bridgerton*." I bite my lip.

"It's your fault," Staci says, shaking me a little. "Now go fix it."

"He loves you, Jasmine." Lucy's voice crackles over the line. "Come and show him you love him back."

"I can't." Staci's face falls, and Lucy goes silent. "I'm supposed to do another experiment. With Chad."

"Skip it!" Lucy's words tumble on top of one another. "Let Chad do it without you. This is more important."

"I…" Hope blooms in my chest. The thought of seeing Cooper play, wrapping him in my arms, kissing him. It's too tempting. "Lucy, can you text me Chad's number?"

Staci does a double-take and Lucy squawks. "What?"

"I need to text him and tell him I won't be there today."

They both start squealing and Staci jumps up and down, crushing me in a hug.

Lucy's voice is breathless when she finally forms words again. "Yes, I will text you that and all the other details. I'll figure out everything. Just get your butt here!"

After assuring her I will do so, Staci clears her throat and stares at me.

"So." She raises a brow and crosses her arms over her chest. "Fake dating, huh? How'd that happen?"

I wince. "Cooper apparently lied and told his mom he had a girlfriend, so she'd stop harassing him. She surprised him with a visit, saw us together, and made assumptions."

"And you went with it?" She barks an incredulous laugh.

I raise my arms in a shrug. "I did him a favor and in exchange, he fixed Herbie."

Staci stares at me, but her face is impassive. I wait for her judgment to come, but instead she throws her arm around my shoulders and starts walking.

"And you caught feelings."

"I did."

Throwing her head back, she laughs up at the sky. "Just for that, I'm making you run home."

∾

Jasmine: Chad, I won't be making it into the lab today. We'll have to reschedule.

Chad: Typical

Jasmine: You know what? I will find someone else for this. I'm done working with you.

Chad: What will Dr. Michelson think when I tell her how irresponsible you are?

Jasmine: She will probably understand when I tell her how you've been harassing me. Go screw yourself.

When we get back home, I throw some things in my backpack—jeans, leggings, a hockey t-shirt—and get ready to fly to Boston. Staci helps me book a flight. There aren't a lot of seats left, but beggars can't be choosers, so I get the middle, rear of the plane.

After lots more squealing and jumping up and down, Staci gives me a hug, and walks me to the door. I bound off the front porch, determined to see this crazy scheme through.

Jamming my key in Herbie's ignition, I'm rewarded with… nothing. Absolutely nothing. Resting my forehead on the steering wheel, I let out a groan.

"Really, Herbie? Now?"

He doesn't answer. I keep turning the key, but it doesn't make a difference. Is this a sign? Does this mean I shouldn't be flying halfway across the country to surprise Cooper? I should play it safe and text him when he returns?

Knocking on my window makes me jump in my seat.

"Come on!" Staci mouths. "I'll drive you!"

But getting out of the car, I shake my head. "This is so dumb, Stace. I can't—"

"You can." She grabs my hand and propels me into her

little tan Honda. "You are a strong, brave woman. You can do this."

Before I can argue, her car lurches forward and we're on the way. All I can do is chew my fingernails and worry.

Lafayette has a tiny airport, mostly because of Harrison. But they have a lot of direct flights to big cities, thanks to our sports program. It's only a two-hour flight to Boston, so the little Herbie setback means I have to hustle, but I can make it. Before I can stress too much, Staci pulls up into the drop-off circle and throws her arms around me again.

"Don't wimp out. You've got this."

"But…" I rip a fingernail off with my teeth.

"Take a risk, Jasmine. Put yourself out there. Show him you care." When I don't exit the car, she continues. "Is he worth it?"

Taking a deep inhale, I consider her question. Cooper— his grin, his easy-going attitude, his laugh. The way he kisses me like I'm the air he needs to breathe.

"Yeah." My voice is rusty. "He is."

"Then go."

Sending her a shaky smile, I climb out. "I'll text you!"

"You better!"

With one last nod, I slam the door and hitch my backpack up on my shoulder, jogging into the airport. I rush through security, buy an overpriced bottle of water, and check the departures board. Only five minutes until my flight boards.

Breaking into a trot, I have to halt as a toddler darts in front of me, taking slow, wobbly steps.

"Come here, Robbie, honey!" his mom calls, holding out her arms. "Yes, you can walk like a big boy." And she lets him wander drunkenly across the walkway, moving at a turtle's pace and taking up all the space so I can't maneuver around him. I manage not to growl out loud, but it's a stretch.

Following the signs to my gate, I finally turn a corner and little Robbie and his mom go straight.

"Last boarding call for Flight 116 to Boston."

No. Oh, no. Picking up my pace, I run, dodging and weaving around pedestrians and luggage in my way. But my gate is all the way at the end of the hall, and it's packed with people. Why are so many people at the airport today? I'm panting when I make it to the check-in counter.

"Flight 116. That's me."

The attendant behind the desk winces, her brown forehead creasing in a frown.

"Jasmine Turner?"

"Yes." Her gaze shifts from my face to her computer screen, and she bites her lip. Not a good sign. "Um, can I board?"

"Well... you weren't here. Unfortunately, we gave your seat away to a standby passenger."

"What? You gave it away? But I have to go to Boston."

"We can get you on the next flight." She taps on her keyboard.

"When does it leave?"

She taps some more. "Uh, in about an hour and a half. I can find you a seat. If you can fly standby."

"Standby? What does that mean?"

"It means if there's an extra spot, it's yours."

"What if there's not?" I try not to pant. Staci might be right about the exercise thing.

"Then we'll get you on the next one."

"I need to be there as soon as possible." The game doesn't start until seven p.m. but it's already noon. I have to go to the stadium and find Cooper before it's too late.

The clerk locks eyes with me, her dark ones filled with determination. "I'll do my best."

Finding an empty chair, I text Staci and Lucy to update them. Then I go buy a paperback book from a gift shop to distract myself, but nothing works.

Am I doing the right thing? Am I crazy?

Probably.

Still, I'm here. It would be silly to turn back now. Figuring I should clue them in, too, I text my mom and sister.

Jasmine: Hey Guys! I'm on my way to Boston to see Cooper!

Maya: What??? You got back together, and you didn't tell us?

Jasmine: Not yet. But I'm going to go surprise him before his big game and put it all out there.

Mom: I'm so proud of you, baby! Keep us posted!

My mom also sends a picture of a cat giving a hug. She doesn't understand memes and gifs, but she tries.

After that, my—possible—next flight is announced and people jostle for position around the check-in desk. Boarding takes forever and my stubby fingernails bite into my palms as I clench my hands into fists.

Finally, the attendant who helped me earlier jerks her chin at me and I rush over.

"Okay, Jasmine, there's a spot."

Relief floods me. I'm doing this. Taking the next step—and the next flight. I hope it's worth it.

As I board the plane and squeeze down the aisle—of course the empty seat is in the rear—I picture Cooper's face in my mind. Yeah, it's worth it.

Exhaling, I drop into the last available spot and shove my backpack at my feet. Turning my phone into airplane mode, I cross my fingers that this delayed flight is my last hurdle on my way to him.

CHAPTER
Forty-Six

COOPER

The smell of the arena hits me—a combination of popcorn, ice, and sweat—and I fill my lungs. Looking over at Hunter, I smile as we file out for our afternoon warm up.

He grins back. "We did it, dude. We're really here."

"The National Championships."

Our re-match against Michigan. Our record is even against them this season, each winning and losing a few when we've faced off. But remembering the Big Ten game, the last time we played them, makes my stomach churn. I can't repeat that.

Coach blows his whistle, and all eyes fly to him. "Okay, boys, we don't want to push it right now. Just a nice easy skate to keep us limber. We'll do a few passing drills, take some shots, but nothing too strenuous." Then he clears his throat. "In case I forget to say it later, I'm proud of you. No matter what happens tonight, there's no other team I'd rather be with."

With that, his whistle sounds again, and we arrange

ourselves on the blue line. Not even a championship berth can turn Coach into a public speaker.

I lose myself in the physical exertion, in the opportunity to burn off some steam. Not too much—I still want plenty of energy for the big game tonight, but enough to smooth away the jitters.

It's been quite a weekend. We played our hearts out against Denver on Friday. Then they booked our free time full of team events on Saturday. I reckon they kept us busy so we'd stay out of trouble and not get distracted. Today, it's been some Call of Duty with the guys, followed by a team lunch and a quick jaunt to TD Garden. I'm a little awestruck, playing in the same arena as the Celtics and the Bruins.

But it's just an ice rink. The boards are the same here as anywhere else.

Working on line drills, Hunter passes to me, I pass to Shawn, and Shawn passes to Alec. We are a well-oiled machine. It's so rote that my mind drifts to the other thing I've been thinking about—or trying not to think about—all day. Jasmine.

Is my mom right? Should I call her even today? I've been debating ever since our chat on Friday.

It would be amazing to have her voice in my ear. I thought of her as my good luck charm all season, and I'd love a hit of that before the biggest game of my life. But what if she doesn't answer? My hockey performance can't be based on her.

Hunter clears his throat and I focus in on what we're doing, my stick cutting a path to the puck. Nope, win or lose tonight, it's going to be because of me and my skills, and nothing else. I make my own luck.

Coach's shrill whistle sounds, and we huddle around him.

"Alright, men, this is it. We're staying in the arena for the rest of the day. Relax, go take a shower, enjoy the facility. They will cater in dinner for us a little later. Stay loose, stay warm. And remember—it's just a hockey game."

We file off the ice, headed to the state-of-the-art locker room reserved for us tonight.

"Just a game," Jonas snorts, removing his helmet. "Yeah, right."

Wrapping an arm around him, Shawn gives his sweaty hair a noogie. "Don't overthink it, man. Go out tonight and have fun. Play our normal brand of awesome hockey."

Don't overthink it.

After stripping off my practice gear, I sit in one of the cushy folding chairs and stare at my bag in the fancy wooden cubby that's my locker space for tonight. I can't see my phone, but I know where it is. I think about what it represents.

Take the shot.

What do I have to lose?

Not letting my brain formulate a response, I grab my phone out of the inside pocket of my backpack and unlock the screen. Moving quickly to keep my second-guesses from overtaking me, I pull up Jasmine's number before I can chicken out.

I press send.

And I listen to her voicemail.

I sigh. I'm sure she's busy. She probably can't answer if she's in the lab. Yeah, that's it. Her voice is warm and familiar across the line. Should I leave a message? What would I say?

The silence stretches as I debate. Am I going to hang up? She will have already seen my number, and listened to me breathe by this point. I might as well leave a message.

"Uh, Jasmine, hi. It's Cooper. But, um, you knew that. God, I'm an idiot." Running my fingers through my hair, regret fills me. "Um, hey, if you could call me when you get this… everything's fine but—"

Her voicemail cuts me off, putting me out of my misery. I tip my chin up and stare at the ceiling, adrenaline receding.

Okay. Okay, I did it. She didn't answer, but at least I had the guts to call her.

Gripping my phone, I stare at it until my knuckles turn white. This can't be like the Michigan match up before, when I couldn't take my mind off of her. I called her, and my reward tonight is checking to see if she's called back. No matter the outcome of the game. But until then, no distractions.

Powering down my phone, I put it into its zipper pocket. Hidden away. I'll focus on hockey for the rest of the day and get my personal life squared away after that.

CHAPTER
Forty~Seven

JASMINE

After a bumpy ride that made me question all my life choices plus the snack I ate, the wheels finally touch down on the tarmac, and I breathe a sigh of relief. We made it.

My backpack is my only luggage, so as soon as the rest of the plane empties, I'm out of there. Finding a bathroom, I freshen up. After reapplying deodorant, I change in a stall into a bright orange Harrison Hockey shirt, broadcasting Cooper's name and number on the back. Go big or go home, right?

Washing up, I check my reflection. Well, it could be worse. Smoothing my hair into a high pony, I wet it down a little to tame the flyaways and splash some water on my face so I don't feel so grimy. I wish I could take a shower, but it's not meant to be. I don't even have a hotel room for tonight—a detail I'll have to figure out later.

I touch up my lip-gloss and fix my mascara, feeling better. Then I grab my phone to text Staci and Lucy.

There's a new voicemail. And a missed call. From Cooper.

Hurrying out of the bathroom, I find the closest open seat and collapse into it. With shaking hands, I press the buttons to listen and squash the phone against my ear.

There's a long beat of silence, then Cooper clears his throat. "Uh, Jasmine, hi. It's Cooper. But, um, you knew that. God, I'm an idiot," he says under his breath, then returns to full volume. "Um, hey, if you could call me when you get this… everything's fine but—"

Then it cuts off. His voice sounds stilted and awkward, but he called. God, I wish there was more to it. Does he need something? Does he know I'm coming? Why did the stupid voicemail have to stop him before he could finish? What else was he going to say?

Biting my lip, I pace in front of the windows, oblivious to the planes beyond, taking off and landing. Only one way to get answers to my questions.

Before I can wimp out, I dial his number. He asked me to call, after all.

It goes to voicemail. I can't think of what to say, so I hang up.

Well, I'm here now. I'm not coming this far to turn around without seeing him. Once the thought takes hold—Cooper, in the flesh, in front of me, close enough to touch and taste—I can't let go of it.

I text my mom, Maya, and Staci that I arrived safely, and then I text Lucy the same and ask for an update.

Lucy: Team is already at TD Garden. We're gonna have dinner and head over soon, too. Meet me there?

That's probably the easiest. I can find the arena, talk to Cooper, and then figure out all the rest of the details later.

Following the signs, I navigate the Logan airport until I'm outside, breathing fresh air. Shifting my weight from foot to foot, I order an Uber and only have to wait a few minutes until it arrives. Checking the driver's identity, I slide into the back of his Nissan and lean my head on the seat rest. Traveling is exhausting, and I'm not at my final destination yet.

My stomach growls and I check the clock. It's already five p.m., and I skipped lunch. Pretzels on the plane do not count. Maybe I can stop somewhere first, or I'll grab a hot dog at the arena?

As I'm pondering my dinner options, the car slows and I glance outside the windows.

Not an abandoned warehouse—good. Getting murdered is not on my agenda, and I've had enough stress today. But lots and lots of orange barrels.

"Whoops!" my driver says, his voice too chipper. "Looks like we've hit a spot of construction."

"How much construction?"

He checks his GPS. "Oh, just a mile."

The airport is only three miles from TD Garden. How bad can it be? "Okay."

After inching forward a few feet in fifteen minutes, though, I bite the inside of my cheek to keep from screaming.

"Is there another way to get there?" I ask, my voice thinner than I want.

He glances at me in the mirror. "If there was, I'd be taking it."

With a sigh, I close my eyes and try not to panic.

After an hour, a trip that should have taken ten minutes ends, and the Nissan finally pulls up in front of TD Garden.

I add an extra tip for my driver in the app—it wasn't his fault—and hop out. God, it feels good to stretch my legs. Then I text Lucy.

Jasmine: I'm here! Where are you?
Lucy: Where?
Jasmine: Outside

Lucy: See you soon!

Walking around the stadium, I locate the ticket window and line up. People inch forward until it's finally my turn.

"One ticket, please." I smile at the attendant, trying to stay patient. It's not her fault I'm late.

But the woman behind the glass shakes her head. "Oh, honey, I'm sorry. But we're sold out."

Sold out? My insides deflate, like someone squeezed all the air out of a balloon. Mashing my lips in a tight line, I try to hold it together in front of her. Numbly, I nod and stumble away.

Did I come this far to fail now? I put my palm out, bracing myself on the rough brick of the stadium wall. Cooper is on the other side, but I'm stuck out here. My car wouldn't start. I missed my flight, got stuck in traffic, and still got to the arena in Boston. But it's not enough.

Tears prick my lids and I squeeze them shut. I will not break down on a public street. Find a hotel—and a bottle of wine—and sob in private. I'll text Lucy. Maybe I can meet up with them later, after the game. It's not the same, but—

"Jasmine!" A blur of orange rushes me, crushing me in a hug. Lucy's stronger than I expected, and it's so good to see a friendly face. My tears swim to the surface again. I blink them away. "You made it!"

"Yeah, but they sold out." I shrug, like my heart isn't in the Death Star trash compactor. "It's okay. I'll—"

"You'll come with me."

Mrs. Edwards steps toward us, and I gulp.

"I promised you I'd take care of it." Lucy beams at me, but I shake my head as shame floods my body.

"I can't."

Mrs. Edwards waves off my protests. "Cooper always leaves an extra ticket at will-call in case his father comes to see him play. He thinks I don't know about it." She rolls her eyes. "I know everything."

She pins me in her stare, and I swallow. "Um. About that."

"Jaz." Lucy pulls me aside. "Just because you and Cooper lied to everyone doesn't mean you have to keep doing it. Come clean and tell him how you feel."

I square my shoulders. She's right.

"Mrs. Edwards, I'm sorry I lied to you." I put my fingers on her arm, searching her face. "It was wrong. Please forgive me? You deserve better."

She pats my hand, her expression softening. "Of course, I do. It's not about deserving. It can be hard to be honest with the people we love."

"Speaking of." Lucy grabs my other palm and squeezes. "Are you ready?"

Butterflies swarm in my belly. "Nope."

"Come on." Mrs. Edwards gives me her extra ticket and we make it through security.

I don't have time to think. They propel me down the cement hallway. Lucy flashes a badge at a guard and turns a corner, navigating the stadium maze with ease. Another three turns, and we're in front of a door labeled "Visitors Locker Room."

My palms are slick with sweat and my heart pounds. I wouldn't be surprised if Lucy and Mrs. E can hear it echo in the empty concrete tunnel. Swallowing, I lick my lips.

"Are you sure this is the right move?"

"Stop stalling!" Mrs. Edwards laughs, then pulls open the door and shoves me inside.

Ohmigod ohmigod ohmigod. I'm in a men's locker room. It's full of... men. Naked men. Hockey players, in various states of dress. A squeak escapes my lips and a very large, bare-chested dude spins, looking down at me. Frozen in place for a second, he eventually blinks, then raises his voice. "Cooper! I think I found something that belongs to you."

Taking a step back, I press my palms against the wood of the door behind me. What was I thinking? This is the dumbest thing I've ever done. Have I used up all my bravery? Because it's deserted me. My throat is dry, but a bead of sweat rolls down my spine. Every head turns to see me, and Cooper leaps to his feet.

The room is incredible, brightly lit and circular, with a high ceiling. Wooden cubbies for lockers line the walls, filled with assorted hockey gear. Miraculously, it smells fresh and clean. I take in none of it once my gaze lands on Cooper.

His light brown eyes lock on mine, wide with shock.

"She doesn't belong to anyone." Then he shakes it off and rushes to me. "Jasmine! What are you doing here?"

Is he furious? Horrified? Excited? I try to read his expression, but I'm not sure.

"I—"

Before I can answer, he crushes me to him. His white undershirt is soft against my cheek and his arms hold me tight. All the breath leaves my body as I squeeze him in return.

Pulling away a hair, he stares down at me. "What? Is this real?"

"I just—I had to see you."

His Adam's apple bobs, and the room is silent, everyone still watching us.

"You came... all this way?"

Words escape me, so I nod. "I—I'm sorry. I'm sorry I missed your other games and—I missed you, too."

He huffs a small laugh. "You have no idea how much I missed you. You were all I could think about. And none of it —the games and the wins—means as much without you."

Pushing up on my tiptoes, I brush my lips across his. "I know you have a lot going on right now, and obviously we need to catch up, but I couldn't go another second without telling you—I love you, Cooper Edwards."

His mouth drops open and then transforms into a wide smile, the happiest I've ever seen him.

"I love you, too, Jasmine. I never thought it was possible, but you're the best thing that's ever happened to me."

I wind my arms around his neck, pulling his mouth to mine again, pouring everything I feel into the kiss—love, longing, desire. Dimly, it registers that the room is full of whistles and cheers as his teammates whoop and catcall us.

Setting me on my feet, he buries his face in my neck and gives a shaky inhale. I never want to let go of him, but a gruff-looking man with silver hair clears his throat. Cooper drops his arms, and I take a step back.

"You." His coach points. "You don't belong here. Edwards, see her out, please. The rest of you, get dressed."

Cooper grabs me and pulls me out into the empty hallway. I'm half surprised Lucy and Mrs. Edwards didn't stick around to spy on us, but they are probably already in their seats.

"I can't believe you're here. I can't believe you came for me."

Staring down at me, he tucks a loose strand of hair behind my ear, and I cup his cheek.

"Your mom gave me your dad's ticket. I hope it's okay."

Pressing his lips into a line, he exhales and nods, holding his emotions in check. "Yeah. It's more than okay. Thanks for showing up, Jasmine."

"I'm your good luck charm. I can't wait to cheer for you."

"I love you," he says again, and my insides turn to jelly at his words the second time, too.

"I know."

"The Han Solo move?" Face impassive, he raises a brow. "Really?"

I shrug. "I wanted to see how it felt."

"And?"

"It's okay, but this is better." I give him one more kiss, full of love and promises for later, and I pull away long before I want to. "Hey, Cooper?"

"Yeah?" His eyes glaze over, and I feel a surge of pride that I put that look on his face.

"I love you. No matter what." I smile, and I love hearing the words come out of my mouth. "But how 'bout you go win a national championship?"

"I'll do my best, darlin'. Find me after?"

"Wouldn't miss it for the world."

Because he has to go in the locker room and get his head on straight, I peck him on the cheek one last time, spin on my heel, and march off.

When I look back—I can't help myself—he gives me a tiny finger wave and mouths, "I love you, too." Then he pulls the door open and disappears.

CHAPTER
Forty-Eight

COOPER

Blinking, I touch my lips. Jasmine's coconut scent still lingers in my nose, the only proof I have that she wasn't actually a dream.

She's here. She's here, and she loves me. My dad's not, but Jasmine is. She loves me and she showed up for me. I'm the luckiest man in this stadium, if I help take a trophy home or not.

As I step into the locker room, I'm met with yelling and whistles again. Hunter bounds over and gives me a bear hug, pounding my back, and Jonas and Evan bump my fist.

Then Coach crosses his arms over his chest and raises a brow.

"Congratulations, glad you kids got that worked out, but we've got a game to play. It's time to focus."

Nodding, I wipe the goofy grin off my face and press my lips together. This is a serious moment. I can't be thinking about making out with my girlfriend.

She is my girlfriend, right? We said the love word, so I

guess we're dating for real. One of the many things I can't wait to talk to her about tonight. After stripping off her clothes and—

Coach clears his throat, and I shut down that fantasy.

"Coach, I—" I glance at Jonas. "I have an idea. A little warm-up that, uh, helped me when I needed it."

He narrows his blue eyes. "You want to be in charge of our last-minute warm-up? After that display?"

"I reckon I do." Holding out my palm to Jonas, I wiggle my fingers. "Do you have it queued up?"

"Here ya go, man." He slaps his phone into my palm, acknowledging my plan with a jerk of his chin.

"Y'all, this is a little secret weapon called 'How Far I'll Go.'" Pressing play, the sound of Moana fills the room.

At first, they chuckle and give me crazy looks. But then it happens. Alec's head bobs along to the beat. Shawn's posture tenses, his muscles taut. Evan clenches his hands into fists. They're listening, and it reaches them. One by one, I meet my teammates' eyes. They stare back, determined, focused, and fierce.

"We're ready." Hunter's voice is a low growl. "Let's do this."

Can we beat Michigan? They're good. Are we better? I don't know, but my heart is light as I skate out onto the ice. Jasmine is here somewhere, cheering for me. No matter what, I'm leaving here with everything I need.

My cheeks hurt from smiling. They've corralled us into a meeting room off the hotel lobby, and a local restaurant has brought in food and drinks. We're surrounded by friends and family, everyone radiating joy. Music pumps through the sound system and one of my teammates, this time a freshman named Brody, tackles me in a bear hug. It's probably my hundredth of the night, but it hasn't gotten old.

Slapping my back, my ears ring with his words, "Game-winning goal, man!"

Michigan was tough. Every time we'd gain ground and score, they'd match it. It was the hardest game we played all season.

But it turns out, we're tougher. Because we scored in the last fifteen seconds and won the National Championship. I can't wipe the grin off my face, and there's no reason to try.

After Brody moves on, my mom steps closer and pats my arm.

"I'm going to go grab a bite to eat. Want anything?"

"Nah. I can get something later."

"If the creek don't rise and there's anything left! I know how hungry hockey players get."

With a wink, she moves towards the food tables lining the back wall, and I check my phone again. I wasn't able to connect with Jasmine after the game—they hustled us back to the hotel so fast—but I texted her the address and she promised to meet me here. My mom said she was trying to find Lucy after the game ended. Rubbing my thumb over the last message she sent, I smile again.

Jasmine: On my way! Can't wait to see you again!

She loves me. My girl loves me and came to cheer me on. It's the best gift she could have given me.

In the periphery, Hunter stands apart from everyone else. Hands shoved in his pockets, he doesn't look like someone who just won a National Championship. Then his little sister pops out of the crowd and hugs him. He smiles, but it doesn't reach his eyes. Where's his dad? He's busy, yeah, but he couldn't make it? No wonder Hunter looks upset.

I'm about to go talk to him, when there's a flash of long brown hair and an orange hockey shirt. Jasmine launches herself at me. Finally. I catch her, inhaling her coconut scent, and I laugh as my joy bubbles over. Spinning her until her feet swing out behind her, the room blurs behind us. When I stop, her lips find mine in a searing kiss.

I want to kiss her forever and never stop. But eventually I have to breathe. Setting her back on the ground, I lean my forehead against hers.

"Hey," I say, at a loss. What words could sum up this moment?

"Hey. Pretty good game out there." Straightening, she pats my chest.

"Yeah? You liked that?"

"Yeah. The guy who scored the game-winning goal—he's way hot." She smirks, and her gaze softens. "I've never been so proud of you. I screamed my head off. Scared the people next to me."

"I guess they weren't hard-core fans like you."

I could stand here with her all night. But after a pointed throat-clearing at my shoulder, I lace my fingers through Jasmine's and spin to face the music. In the form of my mother.

We make a triangle, me between the two most important women in my life. I gulp, but Jasmine steps up and throws her arms around my mom.

"Mrs. E, thank you for everything. Without you, I wouldn't have gotten into the stadium."

"Oh, I don't know about that." My mom grins at Jasmine, her eyes shining. "You're a determined woman."

"I'm sorry again about—"

"Nonsense," my mom says, waving away her words. "We've made our peace. It's water under the bridge. I'm as happy as a June bug you came to see him tonight. It was perfect timing."

Jasmine blushes. "It felt silly and desperate. I didn't want a boyfriend—until I saw what a good one was like. Then I couldn't let him go."

My mom pats Jasmine's arm. "That makes all the difference, doesn't it?"

Then she leans in and kisses my cheek. "Pookie, it's way past my bedtime. I'm incredibly proud of you, but it won't have faded by morning. Can you excuse me?"

"Sure, Momma. Catch you in the morning before we fly out?"

"You bet." Then she jumps, pulling her phone out of her purse, and her entire face—changes. It's like she softens and lightens and sort of glows a bit. "Oh, it's Matt. I'm going to take this. Goodnight!"

She hustles off, and I shake my head.

"Who's Matt?"

"Her boyfriend."

"Your mom has a boyfriend?" Jasmine's voice raises, incredulous.

"Yeah. I just found out."

"How do you feel about that?"

I shrug. "Honestly, not sure yet."

"We have so much to catch up on."

Jasmine melts into my side, and everything else fades into the background. I take it all in—the smiling faces, the party atmosphere—but she's right. It's only been two weeks since we broke up, but what I want most is to spend time with her.

"Hey." I look down at her, still amazed she's here. "This is great and all, but... wanna find a quiet place to talk?"

She strokes my cheek. "Really talk? Or is that a euphemism for...?"

338

Her eyebrow bob fills in the blank and I shake my head, softening it with a smile. "Really talk. I've missed you. I have a room here, and that's not a come-on. Where are you staying tonight?"

She tilts her head up and all I can think about is her lips. "I checked with Lucy and I can bunk with her. But—"

"You can stay with me," I say, my words tumbling out in a rush as I give into temptation and kiss her. It's over before she can blink, but her pupils darken.

"You think you're getting lucky tonight, huh?"

Her flirty tone makes all the blood rush from my head, leaving me dizzy with desire.

"Darlin', it doesn't get much luckier than this." Capturing her fingers, I brush my lips across them.

She gestures at the party around us. "Are you sure you want to leave early? How often do you get to celebrate being a National Champion?"

"It's awesome, but I'm sure. Let's go."

Tugging her through the room, I stop in front of the food table and my stomach growls.

"On second thought, I need some fuel. How about we grab some snacks and take them to go?"

Jasmine gives me a paper plate. "Best suggestion yet."

CHAPTER
Forty~Nine

JASMINE

After filling our plates and saying goodnight to Cooper's friends and family, we head to the hotel elevators.

Butterflies swoop in my belly, and it has nothing to do with the speed of the elevator. I can't wait to get him alone. I want to rip his clothes off the moment the wooden door to his room closes behind us. The only thing stopping me is the plate of boneless chicken wings I'm holding.

"Um." I shove one in my mouth and drop my backpack on the far bed, the one that's unoccupied. Chewing and swallowing, I talk around it. "So what's new?"

"Let's see." Flopping on the bed, he props his chin on his elbow and lies facing me, ticking points off on his fingers. "I won a hockey game. My mom has a boyfriend. I miss you and was miserable without you. Will you be my girlfriend, for real?"

Sitting up, he takes a bite of pizza, and I laugh. "Not wasting any time, are you?"

Cooper shrugs. "Nope. I know what I want."

"Okay. I was pretty miserable, too. So yes, I'd like to be your girlfriend. And I promise to not freak out when we need to compromise. We can find the balance together."

"I won't let commitment and love bother me, either. I will trust you." Wiping his hands on a paper napkin, he balls it up and throws it in the trash can in the far corner. "So what's new with you, darlin'?"

Twisting my fingers together, I stare at them. "I took the GRE. Did pretty well."

"Yeah?" Sitting up straighter, pride fills his voice, then his gaze narrows. "What do you mean by 'pretty well'? Are you being modest?"

"A little. I aced it." I grin at him, unable to keep my joy a secret.

"That's my girl!" Bouncing on his bed, he moves his paper plate and pats the spot next to him. "Come here and gimme some sugar."

I do, and he plants a smacking kiss on my cheek.

"I've been dying to tell you. It wasn't nearly as exciting when I didn't get to share it with you."

He meets my stare, his eyes full of love. "I know what you mean. Let's not do that again, okay?"

"Okay."

Lying on his back, he tucks his hands behind his head. His shirt rides up, exposing a strip of skin between the hem and his waistband, and I try not to drool.

"That's so awesome, Jaz. What's your next step in world domination, then? Oh, I mean, your life plan?"

"Well." Leaning back against the pillows, I snuggle in next to him. "I have my summer internship, plus some grad schools to visit. I was thinking... what if I added The University of Texas to my list?"

His mouth drops open. "For me?"

"It's a good school!" But I laugh, negating my protest. "Not everything is all about you!"

But he's right. I started looking into it as an excuse to see him this summer, and stay close to him if he ends up there after graduation. And he sees through my excuses.

"Oh, I reckon it is!" HIs fingers slip under my tee, tickling my sides. "I think you like me!"

Breathless and giggling, I brush my lips across his. "I'll never admit it."

Rolling me underneath him, Cooper braces himself on his forearms and hovers over me. The playful atmosphere shifts into something more primal.

"That's okay. I don't need you to say it. I know."

He kisses me, long and slow and deep. Drugging kisses that make me forget everything except him and how much I want this. It's a miracle—I didn't ruin everything, and we're together. He loves me and I love him.

Somehow, I end up on top of him, straddling him, and finally I sit up.

"Here's the thing, Cooper. I packed in a hurry and... I didn't really bring any pajamas." Grabbing the hem, I ease my shirt off, gratified by his quick inhale beneath me. "These clothes have been through a lot. I'm ready to take them off. Is that going to be a problem?"

"No. No, no, no, no, no, not a problem at all." His babbling is great for my ego. "I have something you can borrow or... this could be a clothing-optional type of sleepover, if you're interested?"

"Very." I wink and proceed to show my boyfriend just how interested I am. Multiple times.

Epilogue

COOPER —THIRTEEN MONTHS LATER

Weaving through the crowd, I dodge black-robed students like they are opposing defensemen and narrowly avoid taking a mortarboard to the eye. The lawn rings with excitement as people chatter and families pose for pictures.

I scan the faces until finally—there. By the giant sycamore tree, where she likes to sit and read when the weather is nice. Jasmine's grin is wide enough to split her face, her mortarboard tilted back on her gleaming brown hair. Rushing over, I sweep her into my arms and swing her around, feet flying out behind her. Her laugh fills my ears.

"Hey there, cowboy." Tossing her hat off, she kisses me, tasting like sugar cookies. Then she pulls away and straightens the collar of my shirt. Which demonstrates how smart she is. We're surrounded—now's not the time for a make-out session, no matter how much I love her.

Mrs. Turner hovers in the background, and I make eye contact with her, giving her a smile and catching Jasmine's hand in mine as I maintain a respectful distance.

"I'm proud of you." I squeeze her fingers, and she blushes.

"Thanks. I'm proud of you, too."

"I know." I chuckle, shaking my head. "Everyone knows."

Harrison has multiple commencements for the different schools, and my graduation ceremony was yesterday. Jasmine and my momma cheered so much when the President of the University read my name, it surprised me they didn't get kicked out. Typical hockey fans, I guess.

"Well, I am. Cum laude is quite impressive."

"Not as impressive as summa cum laude."

Slinking her arm around my waist, she shrugs off my praise with a smile and turns to her mom. "Will you take a picture of us? I want to hang it in our apartment."

"Decorating already?" I ask, as Mrs. Turner holds out her iPad and snaps away.

"Of course!" Jasmine fakes outrage, her mouth dropping open. "Don't you want it to be homey and beautiful?"

"Darlin', you'll be in it. Of course it will be beautiful."

Mrs. Turner and Maya both ooh and aww at that, and Mr. Turner snickers. It's a good thing there weren't enough tickets for my mom to come. Her excitement about Jasmine hasn't waned—in fact, since we announced we are moving in together after graduation, it's intensified. She'll join us for a family dinner tonight, though, and that will be enough.

Jasmine plants a kiss on my cheek, and I hold her close. I want to freeze this moment in time forever—but also, I can't wait to take the next step with her. After we celebrate tonight, we are loading up our U-Haul and driving out to Colorado.

Hunter and I took the Griffins to the Frozen Four again this year, and multiple NHL teams scouted both of us. I have my brand-new agriculture degree, and I'd love to use it some-day, but for now, I'm going to try my hand at professional hockey. I debated between the Red Wings, the Sharks, and the Avalanche, but when the University of Colorado wanted Jasmine, that sealed the deal. Boulder has an excellent program for her, and it's close to both the Avalanche and their minor league team, the Eagles, where I'll start out.

Can I make it as a hockey player? Play in the NHL someday? I don't know. Glancing down at Jasmine pressed to my side, I gaze into her green eyes.

"I love you," she says against my skin, wrapping her arms around my neck in a hug. "I'm so glad Herbie broke down that night. Thanks for taking me home."

"You should thank my momma. Without those manners she instilled, I might have left you stranded."

Her rich laugh fills my ear. "She's quite the matchmaker. If it wasn't for her, we wouldn't have pretended to date."

"She's pretty attached to you. I wouldn't want to break her heart. I guess you're stuck with me now."

"Lucky me."

Pulling back to look at me, she smirks and gives me a kiss, but I'm the one with the good luck charm. With Jasmine cheering for me, how can I go wrong? You miss one hundred percent of the shots you don't take. I'm taking this one and not letting go.

Dear Reader

Thanks so much for reading my book! If you're so inclined, I'd love it if you wanted to leave a review on Amazon or Goodreads. I appreciate you!

STAY TUNED FOR HUNTER'S STORY, MAKING THE PLAY, COMING SOON IN 2024.

I'd love to get to know you and keep in touch. Here's where I hang out and where to sign up for my newsletter:

https://www.adlynnwrites.com/
www.instagram.com/author_adlynn/
twitter.com/authoradlynn
ADLynn's newsletter

About the Author

AD Lynn has loved reading since she first learned how, and writing books has always been her dream. Before taking the plunge with her first novel, she was a high school history teacher. She's married to a very handsome accountant, and she's the mother of two adorable girls. When she's not typing furiously on her next story, she can usually be found reading, crocheting, or watching baseball. She resides in Indiana.

You can find out more at https://www.adlynnwrites.com/
For updates, sign up at ADLynn's newsletter

twitter.com/authoradlynn
instagram.com/author_adlynn

Acknowledgments

Books are like babies. Writing one is kind of like being pregnant—there are good parts, bad parts, and it's all worth it once you hold it in your hands. It also takes a village to raise them, and this book would not exist without my village.

Katy, I owe you so much. You said, "I think you can do this," and I said, "Okay," and that's basically how this all started. And then you held my hand for every step of the way! Thank you for making this possible.

Raquel, thank you for all that you taught me about writing and friendship. I don't even want to think where I'd be without you!

Alyssa, thank you for teaching me how to ice skate for the scene in this book, and for everything else! I'm so glad I found you.

Jackie, thank you for being there for all our writing craft talks and your encouragement!

Anthony, thank you for being the best cheerleader! It doesn't matter what I need, you are always there to tell me I can do it.

Olive, thank you for being the very first person to read these words (although the end result is a little different!) and being so, so kind. You are a treasure.

Thanks to the Discord. I literally would not have ever dreamed I could do this without you.

And the Wine Girls, for being the best faithful friends.

Thanks to Leah, for letting the first words of mine she

ever read be a sex scene and not batting an eye. True friend, right there.

If it weren't for Michelle Hazen and Katie Golding, I would have given up. Thank you for going above and beyond for me!

Thank you to Katie Golding, my editor and cover designer. Creating the cover with you was my favorite part of the entire experience and I still just sit and stare at it. Thank you for making Cooper and Jasmine come alive. And for your editing—you are the best mix of encouraging and insightful and I'm forever grateful.

Lastly, thanks to Kevin. I knew when you made this a line item in the budget, you were serious and you believed in me. You inspire all my love stories, but ours is my favorite.

About the Setting

If you are familiar with Lafayette, Indiana, you probably saw some similarities (and differences) between Harrison and Purdue. In a way, the setting is a bit of a love letter to the place we called home for so long. I know my version of it is not entirely accurate, but authors are allowed to take some liberties. I also made some tweaks to the college hockey schedule—especially the Big Ten tournament schedule—to make it fit with the story. Any other errors are all mine.

Printed in the USA
CPSIA information can be obtained
at www.ICGtesting.com
LVHW040958050923
757270LV00007B/123